Moving

Jenny Eclair

sphere

SPHERE

First published in Great Britain in 2015 by Sphere

13 5 7 9 10 8 6 4 2

A CIP catalogue record for this book
is available from the British Library.

ISBN 978-0-7515-5094-8

Typeset in Goudy by M Rules
Printed and bound in Great Britain by
Clays Ltd, St Ives plc

Papers used by Sphere are from well-managed forests
and other responsible sources.

MIX
Paper from
responsible sources
FSC® C104740

Sphere
An imprint of
Little, Brown Book Group
Carmelite House
50 Victoria Embankment
London EC4Y 0DZ

An Hachette UK Company
www.hachette.co.uk

www.littlebrown.co.uk

To all the houses I have ever lived in and
all the people I have ever lived with

Acknowledgements

Huge thanks to my loyal editor Antonia Hodgson for once more taking me on, to Geof for putting up with being neglected and to Phoebe for knowing how it feels.

EDWINA

I

Edwina Makes a Decision

Edwina hauls herself out of the bath by holding on to both taps, the bath creaking as if it might escape its moorings. Roll-topped and cracked white enamel, the tub is heavily stained with tea-coloured limescale. Everything is falling to pieces, thinks Edwina, wiping the steam from the mirror and laughing at her reflection.

Who on earth is this tiny silver-haired woman with the squirrel-brown eyes? Where is the twenty-two-year-old brunette beauty with her laughing crimson lips and baby-swollen belly?

She is still inside me, Edwina decides, thinking of the Russian dolls she once owned. All the Edwinas are still in there, from lonely boarding-school girl to excitable art student, young wife, mother, widow – all her former selves are stacked one inside the other, right down to the tiniest baby-doll Edwina buried deep within her, the size of a monkey nut, she supposes.

I'm still me, she decides, sitting down to dry herself. The towel is frayed and the mirror age-spotted.

Before her cataract operation she was blissfully oblivious to all these signs of decay, but last year, when she came home from Moorfields Eye Hospital with her new plastic lenses, she suddenly noticed the filigree of cobwebs drooping from the ceilings, the mouse droppings in the kitchen drawers and the woodworm rampaging everywhere.

The house has started to turn against her. It sprouts new problems daily, worse than a sickly child. Hairline cracks run the length of the skirting boards; musty whiffs catch in the back of her throat; a fraying pull cord in the downstairs lavatory she's already had to re-knot twice.

The garden threatens to invade; the windows of the basement are bottle green, thick with ivy that makes the kitchen jungle-dark even in June.

The house is telling her to go: her allotted time is up, it's someone else's turn. This place needs a firmer hand than the freckled mitt that clings to the banister rail. Mine, she realises, my little old hand.

Georgian houses are the enemy of the elderly, concludes Edwina, and she pads back into her bedroom, where the carpet is freckled with mildew, and it takes all her strength to open the underwear drawer of her mahogany chest of drawers.

A present from Oliver's parents, all the good furniture came from them. The grandfather clock, its genial sun and moon smiling face at odds with the downturn of its hands for ever stuck at twenty past eight.

Morning or night?

Sometimes Edwina gets confused. She does her best to keep her mind and body active: a few yoga stretches before she gets dressed in the morning, some neck rotations to ease the grinding in her shoulders. As for her brain, she is well-read and cultured, her shelves groan not only with dry rot but with every type of book imaginable, from chick lit to Ladybird books on flowers of the hedgerow to heavy Booker-nominated tomes. In her purse she has membership cards for the National Portrait Gallery and the Tate, expired, but even so ...

Edwina talks quite crossly to herself: 'You are an articulate and intelligent woman. You still beat the Eggheads occasionally on

BBC 2, and if you could be bothered you could rustle up dinner for twelve.' Not that she needs to; the days of the candlelit dining room glinting with silver are long gone. These days she mostly eats down in the basement kitchen – after all, trays and stairs are a lethal combination.

More and more of the house is unused; it has been months since she ventured into some of the rooms. Maybe she should take herself on a guided tour, see her home as others would see it, or maybe the time has come to sell the thing.

She has had this thought before, and dismissed the idea as ridiculous almost immediately. But not this time: suddenly it all makes sense. She no longer wants to be a prisoner in her own past.

Of course I will have to have a big tidy, she thinks, bothering for the first time in weeks to actually make her bed. Most days there seems little point, considering she gets up late, has a lengthy afternoon nap and goes to bed early. The sheets are grimy. She used to have a home help who sorted out the laundry and the ironing, but Alicia retired a decade ago and the stress of employing someone new is more than Edwina can bear.

Everything nowadays has to be done on the internet. Fifty-odd years ago she found Alicia by accident on a park bench, and within two hours of meeting her she'd offered her a job. Ah, but that was sometime in the last century.

Dear Alicia, she still sends Edwina letters from St Lucia: envelopes thick with photographs of her great-grandchildren, Edwin, Lucinda, Cuthbert, Dibble, Grub.

Occasionally Edwina will reply with a hastily scribbled postcard. She bought a big selection of David Hockney cards when he had that show at the Royal Academy. When was that? Last year, or the year before?

She hasn't been to many exhibitions lately; silly really, when the bus into town goes right past her door, but sometimes it's easier to stay indoors and watch *Flog It!*

Edwina pulls on a pair of olive green cords. She weighs the same as she did when she was a bride the first time around, never mind the second.

She momentarily recalls her two weddings, both registry office affairs, both without honeymoons, the first in optimistic knee-length white, the second in a cautious grey.

Obviously her weight has fluctuated, but she has never been bigger than a size ten. Apart from when she had her children, of course.

These cords were bought some time back in the eighties, and were expensive at the time – she has always liked nice clothes. She is stylish even now, so it's such a shame that her woollens drawer has moth. The sweater she is pulling over her head is lacy with holes around the cuff and armpit. Oh well, it's warm. Some of the radiators aren't working, they probably need bleeding.

Edwina sits on the wicker chair that has always stood to the side of the chest of drawers. It has a faded pink velvet seat and she cannot for the life of her remember if she has ever sat on it before. It doesn't matter, nothing really matters, it's time to let it all go, the un-bled radiators, the limescale and moth. She has clung to this house for too long. Like the ivy at the back of the house, it's time she was cut free. She needs to close the door on number 137. She will take some memories with her, pack a small case of the good ones, but she doesn't need a lot of baggage. There's a lot she can leave behind.

How strange that she should be the last to go, and for a split-second she can hear them, running up and down the stairs, the tumble and laughter, followed by this silence.

Don't cry, she reminds herself.

2

Wheels in Motion

The job has been done, and Edwina is surprised at how calm she feels. She has done the sensible thing: phoned the estate agent's down the road and arranged to have someone come and value the house.

Before she does anything else, she needs to write down the appointment both in her desk diary and on the wall calendar. Her friend Joyce sends her a calendar every year, only Joyce died six weeks ago – brain embolism in the dry cleaner's – so there won't be any more pussy-cat calendars.

The estate agent is coming on Friday, which gives her two days to make the house presentable, hoover and bleach the lavatory, but breakfast first. It's very important to eat sensibly when you are in your late seventies: porridge oats and oily fish (not at the same time, obviously), plenty of green veg, lots of calcium for her bones and a cube of jelly a day for her nails. Sometimes she gets greedy over the jelly and swallows half a packet before she remembers that if she wants any more she'll have to go to the shops.

She should start at the top of the house and work her way down. Alternatively, she could start down here in the kitchen and work her way up; most of the mess is down here. This is where she spends the majority of her time: it's warm, she has a sofa and a television, the kitchen and washing machine are all down here and there's a lavatory on the half landing by the back door. She has retreated down here like a flightless bird, the basement of her house has become her nest and there have been nights when she's slept on the sofa, waking up in the morning fully dressed and whisky-breathed.

Edwina sits and thinks about what moving will really mean. She knows that under the kitchen sink there are cupboards full of pans, some of which have not been used for thirty years. There is a Kenwood mixer, an ice-cream maker and a foot spa, all shoved to the back, thick with dust, out of view. 'Unwanted, unnecessary,' she mutters. 'A fish kettle? What for?'

It's not just the kitchen that overflows with chattels collected over the last half a century. Upstairs in the dining room there is an entire green and gold Royal Doulton dinner service in a glass-fronted cabinet, and the cabinet's drawers are stuffed with linen napkins and canteens of silver cutlery, unpolished now for decades.

Of course she should start filling black plastic bags and line them up in the hallway to take to the charity shop. She could manage a bag at a time, but just for now, while she gathers her thoughts, she will boil an egg, sit down and listen to *Woman's Hour*.

Thirty minutes later, egg consumed, toast eaten and halfway through a rather distressing item on FGM, Edwina realises with a start that it's all very well selling the house, but where is she going to go? The problem with being widowed (twice, no less) and the surviving family being both estranged and far-flung, is that one ends up having to make choices alone, and if things go wrong there is no one else to blame.

Edwina grabs a biro and starts to jot down the pros and cons of selling number 137 on the back of an envelope:

It's too big. It will trip me up and kill me.

I rattle around, some nights I don't feel safe and I'm scared. On other nights, if someone broke in and murdered me in my bed I couldn't care less.

I could have fifteen years more life left in me. I don't have to stay in London.

I could go and live in Cornwall. I can afford to do what I want, I am sound of mind and independent of means.

Under these notes she writes, 'Eggs, Flash, cleaning sponges, biscuits.'

She will go out later. She tries to get out every day – it's when you stop moving that everything seizes up – but right now she will tackle the drawers in the pine dresser. She will sit on a chair, bin liner at her feet, and go through the drawers being absolutely merciless. Wherever she goes next she doesn't want clutter; she is annoyed by how far she has let this go. The trouble with having a big house is that there is always somewhere to shove stuff, there are so many hiding places, as she and her children found out many years ago.

Sometimes, if she turns her head too quickly, she fancies she can see one of them. A little dark head with a fistful of stolen biscuits. Occasionally she hears giggling from behind the sofa.

When people ask her how many children she has she never knows whether to reply one, two, three, or almost four?

The left-hand drawer is stuck but Edwina persists; she can't fall at the first hurdle. She slides a ruler into the inch-wide gap and pokes around until something is dislodged and the drawer is free.

String, and stamps from so long ago they are no longer valid, nail scissors and parking-permit applications, jars of multivitamins and rolls of Sellotape. Alicia's last letter from St Lucia, her youngest grandson has a degree now – a snap of a boy in cap and gown, self-consciously holding a scroll.

She will have to tell Alicia, in fact she might do that now: dig out some notelets and a biro that actually works, tell her old friend and housekeeper that after all these years she is moving to Cornwall.

A plan is forming in Edwina's head. She visualises herself perched high above St Ives, looking out to the sea. She is living in a wooden house with a veranda; she sits outside and drinks coffee in the cold and wine in the sun, she cooks sardines on a portable barbecue. She will paint again; she will paint the sea in oils using all the blues from cobalt to Prussian.

All this plotting is exhausting, so Edwina wraps herself up in an ancient blanket, and as she lies on the sofa, cocooned in multi-coloured knitted squares, she wonders what it would be like if the men in her life hadn't died.

Only Lucas is still alive, but then Lucas doesn't really count: they share nothing, not a shred of DNA. For many years she was a dutiful stepmother to him, remembering his birthday, wrapping his Christmas gifts, making him breakfast and washing his clothes, but she always felt like a woman in a play, pretending to care.

Lucas wasn't her child, he was Barbara's boy, and they tolerated each other on sufferance. Truthfully, if they were all to take a trip on a lake and the boat capsized, he would be the last one she would save. In fact, she has often wondered if, given the chance, she would hold his head under the water.

The trouble with being a wife and mother, Edwina decides, is you feel it is your duty to keep your family safe, but you can't. Fate has a very fickle finger, shit happens, and just because it happens once doesn't mean it won't happen again.

Of course, it all started when she met Ollie.

Ollie Treadaway, golden boy of Goldsmiths' art college, a wiry nineteen-year-old with a fashionably curly forelock, a boy for ever destined to hover on the brink of manhood.

She remembers first seeing him in the college canteen, almost sixty years ago. It is 1957, she is wearing a grey polo-neck jersey and black and white houndstooth-checked pedal pushers; he is parcelled up in a navy Guernsey.

'My mother knits them,' he explained in his buttery Kerry brogue. 'And Jaysus, they are boiling hot.' Standing in the queue, waiting for his egg and chips, he pulled the jumper over his head and instantly she fell in love with the pale slice of his oyster-coloured flesh.

Ollie Treadaway, all the way from Ireland. Like the very best leaping salmon, he was a bit of a catch.

Ollie came from a landowning dynasty, good stock with a wild streak. There was something glamorous about him, vague tales of a rapidly declining estate, of drink and fallen women.

'There's a curse,' he told her once, laughing, 'the terrible, terrible Treadaway curse,' but he was laughing so she didn't take him seriously.

Curse or no curse, when Ollie's ne'er-do-well uncle and aunt were killed in a car accident (fog, whisky and a cliff were said to be involved), his eminently sensible father managed to pull the estate back from the brink of disaster and put the fortunes of the family back on an even keel. They would never be stinking rich again, but the Treadaways nonetheless owned acres of lush Irish pasture complete with many hundreds of fat-uddered cows, yielding milk that was churned into delicious cheese.

Portraits of Ollie's dead uncle and aunt painted in oils some time back in the thirties hang in Edwina's hallway. They are possibly the two things she would attempt to save should the house catch fire.

Edwina falls asleep. She has a complicated dream in which they are all on a boat: herself, her two husbands and all three children, and one by one they draw straws to see who will be next to drown.

3

The Viewing

The doorbell wakes her up, and yet according to her watch it's only eleven o'clock in the morning. Far too early to be napping, but sometimes it's easier to sleep than face up to reality. The future is so hard to organise when you're not sure what's going to happen. At least the past is sorted: it's already over, there's nothing you can do to change events and time does heal. As long as you don't keep picking at the scabs, she reminds herself.

A boy is at the door, a caramel-coloured boy. She has no idea who he might be, Mormon or thief, and, heeding the warning she received from the Neighbourhood Watch, she demands ID.

'I'm Lee,' the boy says, offering his hand. 'Lee Clarke from Gateman and Pierce.' Of course, he's from the estate agent's. She'd written the appointment down, hadn't she? Is it Thursday already?

She hopes he doesn't think she's racist, and she wishes Alicia were here to prove otherwise.

He doesn't look old enough to be working, a child in a suit. Whatever happened to young men? There was a time when young men were a different species altogether, unburdened by adulthood but strong and tall, capable of picking up young brides, hoisting masts on sailing boats and taking apart motorbikes. This one looks barely capable of carrying his mother's shopping, never mind flying a Spitfire or playing a decent game of tennis.

Blushing, she opens the door wide and lets him into the hallway. She cannot imagine her house through other people's eyes, though she sees it herself through different lenses. There are days when she walks up the front steps and is once again a young woman faced with the impossibility of a huge pram and all those steps, always having to remember to put the brakes on at the top so that the enormous Silver Cross and its contents didn't roll into the road while her back was turned.

Fifty-five years ago she first walked through this door; or rather she was carried, carried in the arms of her darling new husband, handsome Ollie Treadaway, struggling slightly as he heaved her five-months-pregnant bulk over the threshold.

'Are you sure?' she'd asked. 'Is all of it ours?' She was used to renting rooms; they were impoverished artists. She wore slacks and little red dancing pumps, they went to cafés in Soho and danced to records played on jukeboxes. Only now they were married and she was pregnant and they had a house. She was only twenty-two.

A house with holes in the roof and fungus blooming through the cracks in the wall. 'Don't eat the mushrooms,' Ollie laughed, leading her by the hand from floor to floor, room to room, pointing out the broken cornicing that he was going to replace, caressing the curve of the banister while she tried not to smell the damp and the dust and the wet and the rot, and all the time inside her belly tiny fists drummed for attention.

He worked slavishly, always up a ladder while she sat and looked at paint charts. Her pregnancy made the colours smell strange; she inhaled deep purples and forest greens, but felt nauseous at the scent of pale blues and lavender. He encouraged her to be bold: the Georgians were colour-mad, he said, and she chose peacock green for the hall and a dark plum for the dining room.

After all, they'd been to art school, they didn't have to obey any rules. It was only many years later that 137 went through a rather beige transformation, and for a time she thought that she'd accidentally walked into the wrong house, the wrong life, but for the moment it is 1959, she is as round as a beach ball and she and her husband – Mr and Mrs Treadaway, the pretend grown-ups – are colouring in their house.

It's a race against time, after all. Edwina's due date is in March; they have just one Christmas alone together before becoming a family.

The one and only Christmas they ever spent alone together.

She recalls setting a card table up in the freshly painted blood-red kitchen where she burnt a chicken and he made enough bread sauce to feed a battalion. 'I've never had bread sauce before,' she admitted and he said, 'We usually have goose,' and they laughed at how little they knew about each other and how little it mattered because they had all the time in the world, decades to find out whether either of them had had chicken pox – Edwina yes, Ollie no – and what sort of dog they should get. Ollie instantly chose a lurcher, while Edwina opted for a rabbit because, she explained, she was scared of dogs, and for the first time since they'd clapped eyes on each other she fancied he looked a little disappointed.

No to dogs but yes to babies, that was a given: she was pregnant when they got married in the registry office in Camberwell. He was making an honest woman of her. It was the least he could do, and anyway, they were madly in love.

They sent letters, nice apologetic letters, to both sets of parents and promised to invite them all to a big party soon. His mother wrote back, tight-lipped but resigned, enclosing a cheque for five hundred pounds. She came from one of those old-fashioned Irish families, Ollie explained, absolutely loaded a couple of hundred years ago but most of it gone due to feckless sons squandering their inheritance while their sensible sisters crossed their fingers and hoped to marry well or die young.

His mother had been luckier than most: Ollie's father was an easy-going, hard-working man. Really Edwina needn't worry: neither of them was big on weddings, his mother was shy and his father too busy.

As for Edwina, her parents lived even further afield, distant and colonial. She was an only child who'd mostly lived with an aunt in Winchester. Aunt Ida was rather lovely about the whole secret wedding affair and promised to treat them to a night at the Ritz every year on their anniversary (a promise destined never to be fulfilled, not even once).

'Good luck darling,' wrote Aunt Ida, 'he seems a sweetie,' and he was.

Her blotchy reflection in the oxidised hall mirror brings her abruptly back to the present. How did a twenty-two-year-old bride turn into this?

The boy is staring at her, waiting for instruction. 'This way,' she gestures. The staircase tilts so far to the left that she had to remove the stair-rods, and then the carpet came up. She was going to have the floor sanded but she never got round to it; anyway she likes the wide scarred boards. It's like being on a boat, but the boat is capsizing.

'I suppose we should start at the top.'

She motions for him to go ahead of her and he bounds up the stairs, barely touching the banister. By contrast, she hauls and clings, her ankles feeling as if they are carved from wood, reluctant to bend. If she stays here any longer she'll have to have a stair-lift. What on earth would Ollie have thought of that?

He wouldn't recognise her if she bumped into him now, say on the bus or the Tube. He would stand up for her; imagine that, being so old that your young dead husband feels compelled to stand. But then Ollie was very chivalrous, despite it being the sixties. He always walked on the outside of the pavement, held a brolly over her head when it rained, opened doors for her, took care of her, held her hand, made her safe.

Only in the end she wasn't safe, because he left without saying goodbye and for the first time in her adult life she was left wondering what on earth to do.

The boy has reached the top of the stairs; Edwina is quite breathless. There are two doors on this attic landing; once upon a time maids would have slept here, and as the boy opens the door straight in front of him Edwina really wouldn't have been at all surprised to have seen a little scullery mite in a mob cap and white nightie. After all, there are enough ghosts here; what's another one?

4

Nursery

Of course, by the time they bought the house the days of maids were long gone. 'It used to be the nursery,' she explains, shocked by the appearance of the room. When did so much stuff end up here?

'Good proportions,' the boy replies, but Edwina can see him struggling to make sense of the space.

It looks like an auction is about to take place. A massive mahogany wardrobe squats in the middle of the room surrounded by various pieces of redundant furniture. A set of seventies bunk beds smothered in stickers. Edwina thinks she can just about make out a gummed-down football card with Kevin Keegan's face on it, all perm and wolfish grin. An upended, broken Lloyd Loom chair leans against a nasty modern bookcase, which in turn teeters on a Formica-topped table. Surely that used to be in the kitchen? A chaise longue stands on its hind legs against the far wall, its faded tapestry upholstery torn across the middle, and, buried deep beneath a pile of old curtains, she can see the corner of a school trunk. She doesn't need to read the label to know who it belongs to. My son, my only son.

Edwina feels slightly dizzy. Everything that she has not been able to deal with has been brought up here. She knows that there are companies who will clear houses for a price, but the idea of strangers touching some of these things makes her blood run cold. The boy seems to be Tasering the room. 'It's a laser,' he explains. 'It measures the area, feet and inches or metres.'

Ollie had a tape measure, a metal one that you pulled out until it buckled and made snapping noises, and then you pressed a button and it reeled back in again. He chased her round the house with it once and they laughed until they could barely breathe.

Her babies were born in this house, all of them, the ones that lived and the one that didn't, and when they were old enough they came up here to sleep and play. The toys are still here some-where, wooden building bricks, a doll's house, a million pieces of Lego.

Of course, when they were really tiny she kept them by her own bed, two babies, one at each breast.

No one had mentioned twins at her antenatal check-ups, so no one was expecting an extra guest that moonless March night when she went into labour.

A home birth by request. She was young, she was healthy and anyway, Edwina had always hated hospitals. They put down plenty of newspaper and old sheets for safety. 'Good job I was bought up on a farm,' laughed Ollie, but his eyes were terrified.

The midwife arrived on a bicycle just before lunch. She brought her own sandwiches, fish paste in tin foil, and a hard-boiled egg. 'We all have to keep our strength up,' she informed Edwina, breathing over her like a big smelly cat.

The pain had been shocking, of course it was, and there had been a moment when she thought how easy it would be to die in childbirth, to push so hard your heart burst, but she was stronger than she thought, and at five to midnight a daughter was born, scarlet-faced and grimacing, as if the experience had been as much of an ordeal for her as her mother. The midwife smacked her soundly and the baby wailed on cue. A healthy little girl was the verdict, and Edwina lay back expecting the pain to stop. 'It'll ease once the placenta comes,' assured the midwife, only it didn't, and for the first time since she arrived the midwife looked concerned.

'To be honest, I thought I'd be at home eating toast by now,' she confided. 'Let's give you a wee while longer and then we might have to think of other arrangements.'

At this point she'd looked at Ollie and mouthed the word 'complications', which he repeated out loud as if they were playing some gynaecological parlour game.

Back on the bed, in a sea of agony and bloodied sheets, Edwina thrashed and moaned until she suddenly rolled on to all fours and with one long bellow delivered another tiny human. A little boy this time, smaller, scraggier, bluer.

'Someone's not been getting their share of nutrition,' the midwife remarked, holding this baby like a conjuror with an upside-down skinned rabbit, and she gave the pinker, fatter baby a look as if to say, 'Who's a greedy girl?'

The afterbirth followed soon afterwards, liverish and hideous, and eventually at two o'clock in the morning the midwife cycled off, leaving a couple of dazed amateur parents, each holding a baby.

'Rowena,' said Ollie rather firmly. 'Charlie,' countered Edwina, and that was it: the babies were named. Even though, secretly, Edwina had always wanted Elizabeth for a girl and once, after a terrible row, Ollie admitted he'd rather Charlie had been Sebastian. 'Sounds like "spastic",' she'd snapped back. It really had been an awful row.

He was never Charles, always Charlie.

Officially, he was born a day later than his sister, so they decided to alternate the date on which they celebrated the births. 'They can take it in turns to have a party, either on the fourteenth or fifteenth of March,' she'd decreed like a queen in a fairy tale, not knowing anything of what was to come, thinking only of a future of celebration and cake.

Spring babies, crocus children that she grew in her belly, dark and warm as the earth.

Once Ollie got over the raw and bloody shock of it he was thrilled. His grandmother had given birth to twins but only one of them had survived. 'Apparently this sort of thing runs in families,' he kept saying, and his recently delivered wife shivered at the mere thought of losing one. Which one, eeny-meeny-miney-mo?

Even though she hadn't been expecting two, now she had them she couldn't imagine an only baby. They will always have each other, she decided, they never need to be lonely. They will always have a friend. Charlie and Rowena, dark heads like apple pips.

The cot is in a corner somewhere, dismantled. How silly to keep it; more than half a century has gone by.

They lay side by side, two swaddled bags of sugar, and then as they got fatter she laid them head to toe. It was only when their legs grew sturdy and Charlie kept waking Rowena by kicking her in the face that she separated them. Another cot was bought, only Charlie didn't like it. He wanted to be back in the old cot with his sister; he wanted to play the kicking game. In the end, she put them back in together and Rowena learnt to roll away from her brother.

She was a clever girl, her mother knew that from the start. She knew very early on how to distance herself from trouble.

'Bathroom through here?' asks the boy, treading gingerly around a splintered cabinet. He doesn't want to catch his trousers, Edwina realises. The cabinet looks like someone had taken an axe to it.

'Yes, a sort of en suite.'

'Could be a wet room,' the boy calls over his shoulder. 'Needs a bit of work.'

I haven't any energy left, Edwina feels like telling him. I can't even be bothered to follow you to explain and apologise. It is what it is.

Once upon a time, this little bathroom had a jungle makeover. She'd painted it herself, lions and tigers peering through lush tropical foliage, monkeys swinging from knotted vines, but of course the children had grown out of it and its next incarnation had been a slightly nautical navy and white stripe. The boys were up here by then and Rowena had moved downstairs.

'That was a disaster.' The words come out before she can stop them.

'Not a disaster,' the boy responds. 'Just a lick of paint, to be honest. And yeah, well, people like big fat shower heads these days.'

'For their big fat heads,' she ripostes.

'Mrs ... er ...' He has forgotten her name, because she is old and therefore as forgettable as she is forgetful. Two can play at this game.

For a second she cannot decide whether to tell him Treadaway or Spinner. 'Just call me Edwina,' she replies, 'it's easier. And you are?'

'Lee,' he reminds her. 'Some people really fancy a project. This is a great opportunity for the buyers to put their stamp on the place.'

'It's mine,' she is tempted to tell him. 'They can fuck off.'

But of course the decision has been made. She is selling; it's over.

The boy puts his electronic gizmo back in his pocket.

'What's next door?' he asks, and she very deliberately says 'spare room', biting her lip before the words 'Lucas's old bedroom' follow. She has not spoken his name for so long, she is unsure if her tongue can physically form the word.

She doesn't want to think of Lucas now; she doesn't want to think of her stepson ever again. Not after what he did.

5

The Nanny's Room/
Lucas's Bedroom

In the beginning, this room was where the nannies slept, then it became where Lucas stayed, and now it's just another spare room in a house that already has too many spare rooms.

The young estate agent looks around at the neatly furnished room and nods his head approvingly. It's a good size, smaller than the vast three-windowed space next door, but just about a double and comparatively empty too, which is a bonus.

In fact, there is something slightly Spartan about the place, the way the single bed is so neatly made reminds him of . . . a monk's cell, a soldier's bunk, a prisoner's cell . . . what's the word? 'Functional,' he decides.

The walls are covered with framed maps, a junk-shop scoop back in the days when South London was full of bargains. The maps are faded and pastel-coloured, whispering tales of voyages made long ago. They belong to another time, when a young man could go out and make something of himself, sail the high seas and conquer new lands, leave his mistakes behind and start afresh.

Lee went to Amsterdam on a school trip once. They tried to escape the teachers to eat hash cakes in a café, but got stuck in Anne Frank's house.

'All very straightforward, very nice,' he says for want of anything better to say, only it isn't nice, it's too empty. He doesn't want to pry, but Lee gets the distinct feeling that the wardrobe and chest of drawers are resolutely empty. Why should this feel so crushingly sad?

The old lady looks dazed. Possibly she's losing it, confused: they go like that sometimes, the old girls. Once he went to measure a little two up two down cottage down the back of the Walworth Road and the woman selling the place was completely bald. 'Chemo,' she told him, pouring him a cup of tea from a pot kept warm by a curly grey NHS wig. 'Only thing the fucker's good for,' she added.

He gets out his measuring tool again and Edwina remembers when this room was decorated for the nannies. They painted it a deep rose and encouraged the girls to personalise it. 'It's your home, make yourself comfortable. You can smoke if you like.' They put ashtrays up here, and piles of magazines, *Petticoat* and *Honey*, to make it look more welcoming. It wasn't a cold and lonely space like now; there were brightly coloured crocheted cushions lined up along the bed and she has vague memories of an orange candlewick bedspread.

Heather, she was the first, from Scotland in thick grey woollen tights and a knee-length kilt. Ollie bought her a tin of shortbread petticoat tails to make her feel less homesick, but she ran away two months after she arrived, back to Dumfries, before she'd had time to take her tights off.

The only thing she left behind was a little plastic Scottie-dog brooch; it's still in the house. Edwina might not know what day it is, but she knows as sure as eggs is eggs that the brooch is in a tobacco tin in her sewing box, mixed in with buttons fallen from summer dresses worn decades ago.

After Heather they had a girl from the Midlands, who sounded like she had a permanent cold, all adenoids and sleeves full of damp hankies. Ollie hadn't thought she was strong enough and he was right: she kept retiring to bed with her 'neuralgia', and by the time the twins were six months old they were on to their third nanny. Edwina sits on the bed; her feet are throbbing.

Lee has stepped out onto the landing to take a call. Edwina jumped when his mobile phone went off: she'd been miles away, trying to remember the third nanny's name. Rachel, that was it. These rooms are like onions, she thinks, they have layer after layer of memories. Peel away one layer and – hey presto – beneath it is another and another and another.

Oddly enough, this is probably the corner of the house she has spent least time in. It has always been earmarked for the cuckoos in her nest, the nannies and then of course Lucas.

She might not want to think about her stepson, but she can't help it, he is part of this house too, from the dandruff he shed to his fingernail clippings. In fact, the current incarnation of this room was done for his benefit. 'He might want to come back,' his father had ventured. 'Even if it's just for a night.'

She couldn't say 'no', she couldn't say, 'I don't want him here under any circumstances.' She was just very glad that when he did return to Britain he went and stayed with his mother.

Edwina shudders at the memory of Barbara, the first and original Mrs Spinner, a woman who must be approaching ninety but whose hatred of her still makes her stomach churn. Barbara, mother of Lucas. They were very close, entwined like rope. She shouldn't have tried so hard: they shared everything, from pronounced widow's peaks to their mutual loathing of Edwina.

She should have known how it would end, the very first time she set eyes on Lucas. He was covered in blood, blood on his hands, like a nightmare.

Later, when that incident had been brushed under the carpet, Lucas became a regular guest, an official, if part-time, member of the family, and like any decent stepmother-to-be, she wanted him to feel welcome. So she did her research, found out that he was very keen on the Apollo space mission, and created a mural just for him. A hand-painted tile on the door pronounced this room his.

He arrived with a small leather suitcase, a plump boy in grey flannel shorts, and barely seemed to notice the effort she'd made, blinking at the twins as they ran in and out squealing with excitement: 'Isn't it super? Isn't our mummy the cleverest mummy?'

Silently, Lucas turned his back and pushed the door shut on them all.

She mustn't take herself back there. Edwina pulls herself into the present: the walls are a pale dove grey now. The deep rose paint and Heather's Cliff Richard posters are long gone; the lumpy lunar landscape complete with an Apollo 11 rocket, astronauts and a teeny cricket-ball-sized earth in the background only exist deep in the fabric of these plaster walls, and even deeper in her own memory.

Other people will live here. They will never know what went on in this house, they won't know that an angry child scribbled all over her work, they won't know that this bed was often wet and no one was allowed to mention it. It was always his night-time glass of water that got spilt, or a hot water bottle that leaked. 'A hot water bottle?' Rowena queried. 'But it's July.'

Who'd have thought a little boy she'd tried so hard to love would have turned against them like he did.

'He was paying you back,' she mutters to herself, for stealing his father away from his mother, for smashing up his family and ruining his perfectly happy only-child status. He was ten when it happened, old enough to know what was going on and yet too young to understand.

Poor Lucas, it must have been hard on him, coming into a home where he was always going to be an interloper, where the twins already knew every nook, cranny and trick in the house, from

25

which tin in the pantry contained the best biscuits to where to sit in the kitchen so that clothes drying on the ceiling pulley didn't drip on your head.

Lee returns from his phone call. 'Lovely leafy aspect,' he says. 'Good views.' Edwina can't be bothered to contradict him. The views from this room aren't particularly great: all that is visible from the window are trees and roofs, all those grey slate lids sitting on top of other people's lives, road after road of memory boxes. If walls could talk, eh?

'Let's have a look at what's down here, shall we?'

She follows him down the stairs. She has learnt never to go first: you don't want to fall and you don't want to get pushed.

6

Master Bedroom –
Edwina and her Men

They are standing in her bedroom now; the boy is talking and Edwina isn't listening. He is using his measuring gizmo again and Edwina is suddenly aware that her nightie is visible on her pillow. It's not the sort of thing a young man needs to see.

She should have stripped the bed and put clean sheets on. The mattress droops visibly, like a car with a dodgy suspension; there is such a dip in the bed that she rolls into the middle every night. Not that it matters: she sleeps alone these days, there is no 'your' side and 'my' side any more.

That was the strangest thing about her second marriage. Not the unfamiliar surname or the shiny new gold ring (when she already had a completely serviceable wedding band), but that Dickie expected to sleep on the left side of the bed, the side she was used to occupying when she slept with Ollie.

I have fucked two husbands in this room, she silently reminds herself, and three 'gentlemen friends' – not partners, or even boyfriends. There were some times in my life that I now regard as permissive moments, she further informs herself: twice after Ollie and before Dickie, and once after Dickie when it really seemed that I had nothing to lose.

A black man, an old college friend and that man who had the wrong address and knocked on the door expecting to buy a canoe – that was the last time she did it, when she was sixty-three and had just been made a widow for the second time.

She was a virgin when she first met Ollie. It wasn't unusual back then, even at art school, for girls to remain intact at least until halfway through the second year. A lot of them were deflowered by a tutor; it seemed to be a teacher's perk back then. A sackable offence now, of course, and rightly so, thinks Edwina. Innocence is so easily abused.

She and Ollie just muddled through. She remembers a lot of poking each other in the eye and a great deal of panicking about being late with her periods (Ollie looking stricken) until the inevitable happened and she was three months pregnant before they even looked at rings.

Canoe man had been the best lover. She hadn't asked his name and he hadn't bothered with hers, it had been a purely animal experience and all the better for it.

Her husbands, now she comes to think about it, had very different styles of love-making. Ollie was all energy and enthusiasm, while Dickie was a great deal more deliberate, almost ritualistic. Basically, his technique was very good – as if he'd read a manual – but she had never enjoyed kissing him. She'd have kissed Ollie until his face was just mush against the pillow.

I loved Ollie, she reminds herself, and I was grateful to Dickie.

She often had sex with her second husband out of guilt. She had seduced him away from his first wife with her body and her brown eyes and her slow smile and little white teeth, so it wasn't really fair, once he had deserted Barbara, that she, the marriage-wrecker, should withdraw the sex. After all, it was a big part of why he'd chosen her. She was so sensual, so willing, the total opposite to Barbara. Dickie once told her that his first wife was a cold fish, all

Pond's night cream and expensive nightgowns that said 'look but don't dare touch'.

Edwina mostly slept naked, slim-hipped with dark pert nipples. Dickie liked the fact that she enjoyed cunnilingus, which was still quite a novelty in the seventies. Once they'd got married it was a hard act to keep up, the enthusiastic sex thing, but she'd tried her best. Sex, she realised, was a lot like exercise: you might not really fancy it, but once you got going you quite enjoyed it.

She's not fussed about the idea of never doing it again, though, and she no longer sleeps naked. She has become prudish in old age, possibly because the sight of her body distresses her. She used to be so comfortable in her own bare skin.

That was another thing about being a step-parent: your own children seeing you in the nude was one thing, but letting another woman's child see you in the all together was something else entirely. She knew Lucas reported back to Barbara about her behaviour, what she wore, what they ate. She didn't want to give the woman any more ammunition. Wasn't it bad enough that Barbara knew she occasionally fed her family fish fingers for Sunday lunch? She didn't need accusations of sexual perversion on top of domestic slovenliness.

Barbara was a terrible one for firing off pithy little handwritten notes. 'I noticed when Lucas came home from Kennington last week, one of his socks was missing?!!'

These missives were written in purple ink on Barbara's personalised writing paper and never directly addressed to Edwina. Never mind speak her name, Barbara couldn't even bring herself to write it.

Of course their paths inevitably crossed. They have physically come face to face with each other four times in the past forty-five years: once at a matinée of *Jesus Christ Superstar* (Edwina was too unnerved to go back in after the interval), once in Russell & Bromley, once in court and once at Dickie's funeral.

Fortunately Southwark Cathedral is quite a big place, and the two women were kept as far away from each other as possible.

The day his father was laid to rest, Lucas sat with his mother. Edwina didn't speak to him and he made no effort to seek her out. She slipped away from the wake early; it had all the elements of a works do and she'd never felt particularly involved.

Dickie was a political speechwriter for the Liberal Party, which seemed reasonable enough. Edwina wasn't by nature a political animal, but she liked the way the Liberals seemed to sit quietly on the fence just gently ticking over, not really getting anywhere but not being entirely written off either.

Of course there had been that terrible business with Jeremy Thorpe, but Dickie had survived that peculiar chapter unscathed and been kept on by David Steel, a man Edwina found rather charming, not that she socialised with these people, God forbid. This reluctance to get involved in Dickie's career was in complete contrast to his first wife. Barbara loved the trappings of political life and a great deal of her fury with Dickie wasn't just about the dereliction of his duty as a husband and father, but at his lack of political drive. Barbara was a great believer in the power behind the throne, and she would very much have enjoyed being an MP's wife like her old bridesmaid Minty Landreth.

Edwina couldn't have cared less; she was politically disinterested, and she found any talk about Dickie's work very boring. But then (fortunately), by the end of the day so did he.

She remembers brooding over whether Dickie had sacrificed too much in leaving Barbara. After all, she wasn't interested in his career and she was a rubbish cook, so apart from the (mostly faked) enthusiastic sex, she made for a rather lousy second wife.

After it all happened she often wondered if he wished he hadn't bothered. So much of all this could have been avoided if he'd stayed with Barbara, if only Ollie hadn't . . .

'I said, "Possibly a bit of damp along this wall."' The boy shouts as if she were deaf, which of course she is, a little, she is almost seventy-eight. She is deaf and ever so slightly incontinent. 'It's not just the wall that's damp,' she would like to joke, just to see his expression.

'Possibly,' she shouts back.

She is surprised to find herself sitting down on the pink chair she first sat in just the other day. It's good to get a different perspective.

This room has mostly been about sleep and sex, dressing and undressing, lying down, getting up, alarm clocks ringing, days starting and finishing. As a young mother she lay in this bed and waited for her babies' cries to pull her from her sleep. Then, later on when she couldn't sleep, when anxiety, loneliness and fear kept her awake, her own heart beating against the clock, her brain in overdrive. What am I to do? What should I do? What can I do? Oh God, oh dear, oh help.

The boy has seen enough of this room. It is not full of memories for him, it's simply a nice big double bedroom with heavy furniture and grubby sheets. It smells slightly of piss.

7

Family Bathroom

Edwina follows the boy out of her bedroom and into the bathroom next door. 'Fuck me,' he mutters, not quite under his breath.

Edwina nods; the bathroom is large and the Victorian suite enormous. Ollie came across it in a junkyard down by the river; she can't imagine how they carried it into the house and up the stairs.

The tub was big enough for all of them, Ollie, Edwina, Rowena and Charlie, the twins with shampoo foam crowns on their heads, a bright yellow rubber duck bobbing between them. 'Room for plenty more,' Ollie joked. 'You could have triplets next time.'

She had laughed too, sort of. But she hadn't ruled it out, she always suspected she might fall pregnant again. She never dreamt that a year or so later she'd be lying in this bath with her head under the water, ignoring her screaming children and wondering how long it would take to die should she run a razor across her wrists.

They'd painted the bathroom the blue of a cloudless sky, the blue of a glorious day, of forget-me-nots, the blue of the sky on a day she will never forget.

Sennen Cove, Cornwall.

Easter time, too cold to swim, but they dangled the babies' toes in the water and Charlie screamed until his face went the colour of a cherry.

A picnic hamper on a red tartan rug with friends from art school, fruit cake and cheese and pickle sandwiches. All of them young. She and Ollie were the first to have babies; Rowena and Charlie were a novelty, not just because they were twins but because they were starting to become small people. Toddlers, chubby of fist, quick to laugh and even quicker to cry, clumsy in their terry-towelling nappies and rubber pants, suddenly sitting heavily in the sand, Charlie trying to eat it. 'Waaagh!'

Life changed with the throw of a ball, a hard red round cricket ball flying through a cobalt sky. *Thwack!* She heard the bat make contact, that most traditional sound of leather against willow, and then a pause. The drone of a bee, a dog barking, a boy yelling further along the sands, flying a yellow kite, the kite nose-diving into the sand dunes as the wind changed direction, a sudden chill and Ollie lying down. Face down and not moving.

The ambulance drove across the sand and everyone stared except the boy with the yellow kite, who kept flying the thing. Up and down it swooped as the ambulance men worked on Ollie's heart, thumping and pushing at it until they shook their heads and carried him away with a red blanket pulled over his beautiful head.

She cannot recall how she got home from that holiday. She can't have driven, not by herself with the two babies in Ollie's rusty green Humber Hawk. Come to think of it, she hadn't passed her test. After Ollie died she had to learn; widows must learn to do everything.

Her mother came over from Malta, which sort of made things worse as they barely knew each other and Glenda had never met Ollie. She kept saying Edwina needed to be brave and how, just a generation ago, millions of women had lost their menfolk on the beaches. 'Yes, but not playing French cricket,' Edwina had screamed, at which point her mother had slapped her because she was 'obviously hysterical'.

Ollie's parents weren't much better, but at least they had an excuse. Yes, they were reeling with grief, their son was dead, but the farm still needed running. They came for the funeral, wept and quickly departed. In the years that followed they sent cards and gifts on the twins' birthday, but the messages in the cards grew increasingly brief and the invitations to visit gradually petered out.

It seemed unbelievable that life should carry on after Ollie's death. For weeks she was semi-catatonic, and it was only when her mother left to rejoin her father in Malta that reality hit her.

She was alone in a big old house that needed money and time spending on it, yet she had two small children and no income. There were days, too many to count, when she felt like dropping herself and the babies over Waterloo Bridge.

Years later, when life was going through a smooth phase, the bathroom underwent a transformation. She had the walls panelled to hip height in tongue-and-groove wood and painted cream, a pale pink chinoiserie wallpaper was pasted over the blue and eventually there were times when she came into the room and didn't immediately think of that Cornish sky or how the sun that day was the same colour as the twins' rubber duck. Yellow and blue, the most cheerful of colour combinations, and yet for so long reminding her of death. Irises in the church on the day of his funeral, yellow and blue.

I would have gone under, she acknowledges, if it hadn't been for Alicia. Dear Alicia, a woman with whom she had nothing in common and yet who, in the years that followed, turned out to be her closest ally.

They met in the grounds of the Imperial War Museum. Edwina was sitting on a bench with the pram some way off: she was bored with its crying contents and in two minds whether to walk home without it, bloody massive thing. She shouldn't have to bother with it any more, but she couldn't trust the twins to manage the entire walk home. One of them needing a carry was bad enough, both impossible – she wasn't a pack horse. At times she hated them. Charlie was lazy and inclined to hysterics, while Rowena was a sulker.

The woman sat down heavily to tie her shoelace and the bench see-sawed slightly in her direction. She wore black slacks and cream wing-tipped glasses, and was sporting a precarious beehive. The beehive made her nervous of the weather. Gathering her bags, she looked at the gloomy clouds above and held out her hand to test for droplets of rain. Patting the elaborated lacquered edifice, she informed Edwina, 'I hope I get home before it tips it down.'

Her accent was as deeply exotic as her looks. Edwina guessed she was from the Caribbean, Jamaican probably, and her mind filled with silver beaches and warm sunlight. Oh for a holiday, a holiday on her own.

At that moment Charlie threw his shoe out of the pram, and the woman went and retrieved it. Her face split into an impossibly wide grin when she realised there were two of them stuffed into the Silver Cross, and she immediately went into a routine of face pulling and animal noises. Some people are just better at this than me, thought Edwina, who longed for the children to be able to hold a proper conversation. Whatever the woman was doing, it was working. The pram rocked with happily gurgling babies and for a few precious moments Edwina was able to sit on the bench and breathe out.

Only, once she breathed out she found she couldn't breathe back in, not without sobbing, great gulping sobs that coincided with the sky turning a toxic yellow and large wet raindrops falling with increasing speed.

Alicia helped wheel the pram back to Kennington Road. While Edwina opened the front door the stranger bundled a baby under each arm, charged up the flight of steps and deposited them indoors before charging back for the pram, which she managed to single-handedly manoeuvre up the steps and into the house.

My mother referred to her as the negress, muses Edwina, over half a century later. 'That negress with the impossibly large behind.'

Apart from possessing an unquestionably big bottom, when Edwina met Alicia she was a part-time cleaner with two sons, who were back in Kingston being looked after by her own mother. It was the custom, she explained. She lived somewhere off the Old Kent Road with her husband and some of his cousins.

Edwina never met any of them, she never went to her house, but Alicia came to this house. Every day until the twins were too old to need a nanny, and then she stayed on to do the ironing and the cleaning.

Dear, cake-eating, hip-gyrating, mood-swinging Alicia. By the time they got indoors on that very first day they were both soaked to the skin and Alicia's beehive had fallen into a matted heap.

Down in the kitchen it was warm. The Aga was working – it was one of the things Ollie had insisted on: 'I'm a farm boy, you'll love it,' – but she didn't, she couldn't cook on it. Once he'd gone she relied on the Aga for warmth but a Baby Belling for heating up the babies' food. She didn't know how to cook so she bought tinned goods, Heinz soups and jars of baby food. She knew they weren't eating properly. Rowena had a gummy eye and Charlie coughed and coughed.

Alicia stripped the babies down, dried them off and changed them as if they were small machines: arms up, vests off, turn child, repeat process from the waist down. Once all their soggy clothes were in a pile Alicia stood on the kitchen table dragging dry clothes off the pulley. 'Could do with an iron,' she muttered, 'but them babies don't care.'

And they didn't. Dry, warm and filled to the gills with hot toast and honey, the twins were placed in the playpen where, for once, they sat and played contentedly with their toys, Rowena only lifting her head from her alphabet blocks to give her mother a look as if to say, 'There, that's how it's done.'

I couldn't wait to hand them over, Edwina admits to herself. Alicia had a lap that was big enough for two, Alicia never judged, she wasn't their mother. She might have worried about their physical wellbeing and keeping them regular was a priority bordering on an obsession (Alicia was a big fan of prunes), but she never questioned their characters. She loved the twins with a steady, unconditional love and Edwina was sometimes slightly jealous of that.

The boy is talking to her, his voice sounds distant. Edwina tunes back in to his conversation as they troop down yet another flight of stairs.

'Great road,' he enthuses. 'Fantastic location.'

It wasn't fifty years ago, she would tell him if she could be bothered, it was just bingo halls and buses and no shops. It's all artisan pizzas, noodle bars and joggers now. People never used to do that – running around the streets all sweaty. Sign of the times, everyone wanting to live for ever. I don't, thinks Edwina, I've had enough, it's exhausting.

8

Main Reception

They painted this room a deep midnight blue. 'The drawing room,' she informs the boy, and he nods. Of course it is: posh types have their own vocabulary when it comes to houses, they don't have front rooms or sun lounges, they have drawing rooms and conservatories, pantries, studies, breakfast and utility rooms, and they usually have pianos.

Bingo: in the far corner is a baby grand.

The navy paint is long gone, replaced by a colour resembling the off white of a London cloud. Dull, thinks Edwina crossly. If she were to name this paint, she'd call it 'non-committal'.

At least the books add personality, Ollie's side and Dickie's side, thinks Edwina, glancing at the shelves flanking the marble fireplace. Both my husbands were readers.

To the left are all of Ollie's art, film and architecture books, and to the right Dickie's: history, biography and political tomes.

Sometimes she looks at the pictures in Ollie's library, the catalogues from exhibitions they'd visited together, the collection of books on renaissance art inherited from his unlucky uncle. Dickie's books, on the other hand, remain untouched; the print is so small, the paper so thin, the subject matter so dry. But then Dickie was academic, he read history and politics at Oxford, he loved to read and she loved to watch him read.

Rowena was a reader too, she spent hours in here curled up on the sofa, her little dark head buried so deeply in a book that her eyelashes fluttered against the page. She was diagnosed as short-sighted when she was eight, and then began a constant round of losing, sitting on and breaking her glasses. Somehow Charlie escaped the myopic gene; he was never much of a reader, of words or even music for that matter, but he'd sit at the piano and bash out made-up pop songs, one of her silk scarves flamboyantly tied around his neck, while Lucas stood on the Chinese rug in the middle of the room, pink-cheeked with fury, his hands covering his ears and demanding that 'this awful racket cease'.

Oh Lucas, old before his time, fat-bottomed and disapproving.

She needs to light a fire, the place feels bone cold. It was one of the first things she and Ollie did when they moved in; she remembers cooking chestnuts over golden flames, their brown leathery skins splitting in a tin suspended on the end of a metal coat hanger. Ollie could make anything.

Dickie was useless with his hands. He could barely make a fire, and didn't really like doing anything that required the removal of his cufflinks, whereas Ollie didn't possess cufflinks – he was a sleeves-rolled-up kind of man. He could put up a shelf, sew on a button, change a light bulb or a nappy, rustle up an omelette. When she was pregnant he made her pancakes; he was a new man before such a thing had even been invented.

Dickie, on the other hand, was much more traditional, he literally wore an old school tie, had his shoes and shirts custom made in Piccadilly and possessed a collection of suitable hats including a trilby, a deer-stalker and a panama; he even had a top hat for weddings and Ascot. Ollie possessed precisely one hat, which was made of wool and had a bobble on the top.

Oh stop it, woman, Edwina admonishes herself. Why is she making them compete? They are both dead. So what if one could make pancakes and the other was incapable of making anything more complicated than a cup of tea and a sandwich?

She recalls sending Dickie to the supermarket just after they'd got married and him coming home with all sorts of peculiar things, including a selection of garish cakes. 'These really are super,' he said, chomping through an entire box of Mr Kipling's French Fancies.

Dickie had been brought up on a diet of proper English food – Brown Windsor soup, John Dory and seed cake – so the unexpected pleasure of artificial flavourings and brightly coloured icing was a revelation. Really, for all Dickie's education and breeding, when it came to food he was happiest at a children's tea party.

'I used to be so proud of this room,' she informs Lee, who has his back turned to her and isn't listening.

'Nice original features.' Lee nods approvingly; he knows this is what people want: the place might be falling to pieces but Gateman and Pierce have clients who would literally wet themselves over the generous dimensions, the lofty ceiling. 'This room is massive.'

Three windows wide, their panes about level with the top deck of any passing 157 bus, though each window has a set of wooden shutters to keep out prying eyes.

'I rarely use it,' Edwina replies. She looks a bit cold; this is the chilliest room in the house so far. Lee has the impression it's been a while since the radiators actually gave out any heat. The off-white paint on the walls is cracked and peeling, but the ceiling rose is intact and the cornicing around the perimeter of the ceiling is wide and elaborate, if thick with dust.

It's seen better days, thinks Edwina, sinking onto the velvet sofa and recalling the room at its loveliest, all dressed up for Christmas and scented with pine. I was so smug, I used to turn on the fairy lights on the tree and leave the shutters wide open so that the poor people on the bus could look in and envy us our good fortune.

The box of decorations is either in the top room or in her wardrobe; she hasn't bothered with that sort of thing for years now. Someone else can come and decide: Christmas tree in this corner or that, tinsel or no tinsel, star or fairy?

She liked to put the tree in front of the middle window, a ten-foot-tall Nordic fir garlanded with a mixture of expensive baubles and unidentifiable objects that the twins had made at nursery school.

No wonder Lucas never really felt at home here. All his kindergarten memories were at his mother's: Barbara was the custodian of Lucas's tiny handprints and clay pots, his cotton-wool snowmen and toilet-roll Santas.

Dickie usually went to fetch him from Chelsea on Boxing Day. One year, when he was about thirteen, he arrived in a dinner jacket complete with bow tie. He looked ridiculous and the twins, in their jeans, were hysterical. Suddenly Edwina remembers saying, 'Golly, Lucas, have you been playing snooker?' She wishes now that she hadn't; if only she'd been kinder.

Christmas apart, this used to be the most formal room in the house. Most of the remaining 'good' stuff is in here, the gold and ebony French mantel clock, a couple of Chinese vases, a walnut side table and Victorian needlepoint footstool.

Three of the 'money' paintings hang in this room: a signed etching by Ben Nicholson, whom Ollie knew back in the day; an unverified but thought to be Paul Nash; and a large multi-coloured Terry Frost.

The rest of the paintings are attractive daubs, some landscapes, a couple of still lifes, a few good prints.

The paintings serve to make the room feel more like a museum than ever. It feels abandoned, a library cum art gallery devoid of visitors. This is the room that needs a family most – and maybe a dog? Just a small one. She is not as scared as she used to be, all the worst things that can happen already have. What's a dog going to do, bite her ankles, wee on the carpet? Big deal.

'Maybe in Cornwall I shall have a dog,' she mutters, but she cannot picture what sort of dog it might be. Her mind shuffles dog pictures until it settles on a dachshund, a little black and tan dachshund. Yes, if she wants a little sausage dog then she will definitely have to move: a dachshund would never manage all these stairs, its little spine would snap.

All of a sudden she is conscious of the boy talking, his voice like a fly buzzing close to her ear.

'Pardon?' She might need to fetch a cardigan, her flesh is goosey.

'I said, should we move on?'

'Oh yes, come this way,' she instructs, feeling for a second like one of those elderly guides in a poorly run National Trust house.

9

Rowena's Old Room

'Another guest bedroom?' the boy repeats, louder this time. She's not listening, and Lee wonders if pensioners can have ADHD. Only there were kids in his old school who behaved like this, just zoning out all the time, not paying attention. The 'Ritalin kids', they called them.

This is bigger than the spare bedroom upstairs, big enough for a double bed, an eighties metal number sprayed white, with semi-circular ends. The mattress is uncovered, exposing bare ticking stripes. There have obviously been no guests for a while.

An ugly fitted wardrobe with louvred doors stretches across the far end of the room. There are tiny holes where pictures once hung, ancient traces of Blu-Tack on salmon-coloured walls, a magnifying make-up mirror on a white melamine vanity unit. The room is dated, but he guesses it once belonged to a teenage girl, grown now, probably married with teenagers of her own.

Lee is momentarily confused. Some houses give up their stories more easily than others; this room is particularly secretive.

Folded up on the bare mattress is a multi-coloured quilt – one of Edwina's phases, another hobby she took up to stop herself going mad. Long nights spent cutting up her daughter's old summer

43

dresses, the patterned fabrics reminding her of happier times, hot summer holidays, a villa in France, fishing nets and sneakers.

Just cut the fabric, Edwina, cut the shapes and sew, keep sewing, tiny invisible stitches. If only she could sew up the gaping rip in her heart. Breathe, Edwina, breathe.

The room is (according to optimistic estate-agent speak) in 'good decorative order'. A few personal items are set out on the dressing table, a silver-backed hairbrush and matching comb sit next to a glass dish containing cotton-wool balls, while a china horse rears stiffly on the window sill and a limp towelling dressing gown droops down from the back of the door, but it feels staged. This room was abandoned many years ago.

'Rowena's room,' breathes the old woman. 'She doesn't live here any more. None of them do.'

The boy is slightly creeped out but knows better than to ask who Rowena is. Showing a client any personal interest is both unprofessional and potentially time-consuming.

Old ladies get lonely: you ask about their family and the next thing you know, they've got the photo albums out and are pointing at dead cats.

Edwina feels slightly dazed. What would she tell him if he asked? Rowena is my daughter, clever, complicated Rowena, she moved down here to get away from the boys. How old had she been? Possibly just turned twelve, but wise beyond her years. It drove Dickie nuts that, out of the three children, it was Rowena who possessed the finest brain.

Education was one of the things they argued over the most. When they first met, he couldn't understand why she didn't want her children sent away to school; the fact Edwina had hated boarding school didn't matter. 'We all hated it,' was his response, 'and I went at seven so I had to hate it for even longer than you did.'

Lucas had been put down for his father's alma mater, Wyebourne College, more or less at birth. There was the formality of Common Entrance at thirteen, and off he'd go.

Until then he was happily ensconced at Witterings, a small feeder prep on the South Downs with sixty acres of playing fields and very little chance of mixing with the wrong sort.

Further down the line, it was presumed Lucas would have to decide between Oxford and Cambridge (Oxford, obviously; his father went to Brasenose) but, basically, her stepson would transfer from one establishment with an oak-panelled dining room to the next, barely noticing the difference.

After all, Dickie often said the spotted dick served in the Westminster canteen tasted almost identical to the one served at his pre-prep. 'There must be a recipe,' he mused, 'that only the kitchens of certain institutions are privy to.'

'It probably comes out of a tin,' Edwina had replied. She really didn't trust Dickie's taste buds, not since she'd caught him devouring luncheon meat out of the can and pronouncing it delicious.

Being a girl and therefore mature enough to handle Common Entrance two years earlier than her brothers, eleven-year-old Rowena aced every examination paper put in front of her. She was equally proficient in every subject, the girl was inquisitive, articulate and thorough. Even her handwriting was exquisite, unlike her brother's: poor Charlie was left-handed; he couldn't help it if his books always looked a mess, the ink never had time to dry before his sleeve made it smudge all over.

They're probably allowed to do their exams on typewriters these days, thinks Edwina, meaning laptops.

Edwina had always suspected her children were academically mismatched. It was a mother's instinct, borne out by years of watching Rowena do everything first.

For a long time no one else noticed, not even the teachers, who sat Rowena and Charlie side by side at prep school, oblivious to the fact that Rowena did all the work and Charlie diligently copied it.

Term after term he allowed his brain to slide further into neutral. What was the point in the two of them listening when Ro could listen for both? He didn't bother to learn anything, not a single spelling, historical date or times table. During break he mucked around doing *Dr Who* monster impressions and making farting noises with his hand in his armpit.

The situation came to a head at a parent-teacher evening when a more enlightened, recently qualified member of staff told Edwina that Charlie was holding Rowena back, and the twins needed to be separated because 'we can't really find out how severe Charlie's problems are until he's isolated from his sister's intelligence'.

'I think you'll find Charlie has his own talents,' Edwina snapped, and to give the woman her credit she'd agreed: 'He has a really lovely singing voice,' and he did, oh he did. Sometimes when she thinks about the waste she could scream.

'Stop it,' she rebukes herself, and to prevent herself from howling Edwina stares hard at the home-made quilt, concentrating on a hexagonal patch of red and white fabric, and she remembers her daughter sitting on a beach in Brittany wearing a little red and white polka-dot sun dress. Rowena and Charlie eating strawberry ice-creams, they must have been about four, after Ollie and before Dickie. She'd taken Alicia on holiday with them, Alicia a mountain of dimples in a lemon-coloured bathing suit, people staring, what a strange-looking family.

For a while this room next to the drawing room had been Rowena's sanctuary, a place of quiet where she could do her homework, listen to music, read books and cut out pictures of ponies.

Later on, it became symbolic of something else, a nest of lies that smelt faintly of sick, of regurgitated food wrapped in tissues and hidden under the mattress.

Edwina forces the memory away. For the moment, her diligent and biddable little girl has just moved into this bedroom. If she closes her eyes she can hear a flute playing, hesitant but melodic, Rowena practising, practising, practising, making sure that by the time she was in her second year at school she was playing in the orchestra.

'Rowena can be a little smug on occasion,' Dickie remarked after they'd schlepped out to the Blackheath Halls to hear her play yet another solo.

He was bitter, of course: Lucas had just given up the cello and the head of music at Wyebourne College refused to reimburse the rest of the term's fees. 'But he's only had one lesson,' Dickie huffed.

The truth was, that while Rowena had to slog at it and Lucas was tone deaf, Charlie had real musical ability.

Charlie was talented, he possessed the gift of a singing voice so glorious and rare that a week after the disastrous parent-teacher evening Edwina was summoned for a chat with the music master at the prep school, a funny little man with a terribly twisted spine who informed her that Charlie was pitch perfect.

'Sounds like he's going to be a professional golfer,' Edwina joked, congratulating herself on thinking up such a clever pun, but the little man with his misshapen spine ignored her joke and informed Edwina that it might be a good idea to let Charlie try for the Westminster Abbey Choir School.

It was a boarding school; it would mean he wasn't at home.

She should have stuck to her guns: she never wanted either of her children to board. Ah, but he was gifted. To this day she has never been able to decide if Charlie's 'gift' was a blessing or a curse.

Sometimes she wishes that her twins could have remained for ever babies, their pink- and blue-bootied feet fatly kicking from the same cot.

Her eyes brim instantly, and then clear with a blink.

'Are you okay?' the boy asks. What on earth is his name? Linus, Leslie?

'I am absolutely fine,' she replies. Lee looks at her again, she has eyes like a squirrel, bright but slightly distracted, as if she has hidden a nut and has no idea where she might have put it.

'Just a couple more floors,' the little woman tells him. 'Come on, this won't buy the baby a new bonnet.'

What baby? thinks Lee.

10

Dining Room

Edwina leads the boy down yet another flight of stairs, all of which, Lee notices, tilt too far to the left not to warrant extensive structural inspection.

Ahead lies the big front door. Soon, thinks Edwina, post will arrive through that letterbox and it won't be for me. Not that she receives much of any interest these days, circulars mostly and catalogues for Viking cruises, ugly orthopaedic shoes and pensioners' panic buttons.

Once upon a time everything and anything of any importance dropped through that brass-fronted plate. Before computers, before email, post was the thing: letters, bills, good news, bad news, birthday cards, Christmas cards, postcards, bank statements, school reports. Stop right there, she reminds herself. You are getting maudlin and this boy has a job to do.

The console table up against the left-hand wall is piled high with leaflets for window cleaners, takeaways, church meetings and Bikram yoga. Standing sentry next to the table is a coat and umbrella stand, and reflected in the mirror above the console table are her favourite portraits: Ollie's dead uncle, weak-chinned but handsome, a wastrel and terrible womaniser, watched for ever by the anxious eyes of his wife.

She remembers Ollie with his new hammer, hanging the pictures, standing back to see if the two of them were level. 'Poor Uncle Aiden,' mocked Ollie. 'I told you the eldest Treadaway son has a terrible habit of coming to a sticky end. Well, it's all complete codswallop: Uncle Aiden died because he was a drunken eejit and a rubbish driver to boot, and his wife died because she got into his car and together they drove off a cliff. Though to give him some credit, it was very foggy that night.'

'Silly mumbo-jumbo,' she'd agreed, nuzzling against the navy wool of his sweater, a sweater that got left behind on a Cornish beach less than a year later while the body of the eldest Treadaway son was carried away to the mortuary.

Curse, misadventure, accident, inevitability, who knew?

She leads the young estate agent into the dining room at the front of the house. Dickie insisted on wallpapering over the plum paint: 'I can't see to read the bills,' he complained. 'It's like the Black Hole of Calcutta in here.' So they went for a cream, gold and burgundy stripe paper, the burgundy stripe was flock – very formal, very Dickie. Of course, years later it looked a bit *Indian restaurant*, but by then they'd more or less stopped bothering with dinners and guests and talking and going over the same old ground.

We disappeared into books and work, she recalls, anything that filled our time and stopped us pointing fingers of blame. Back then, the television drowned out a great deal of silence.

Dickie's desk is still in the corner by the window, the only piece of furniture his ex-wife Barbara allowed him to bring south of the river.

After all, it was originally his father's, an old oak roll-topped affair that, when unlocked, revealed a maze of pigeon holes, miniature drawers and a green leather writing surface.

Dickie was much better than Ollie at handling their affairs. Thanks to Dickie, everything was neatly filed: life insurance, car tax, savings and investments, every potentially important scrap of paper was tucked into neatly labelled manila folders. Births, marriages, deaths, the deeds to the house, all the important stuff that she couldn't be trusted not to shove to the bottom of the umbrella stand and forget about.

Unlike her first husband, Dickie seemed to enjoy sitting down with his fountain pen and cheque book, sorting the bills, making sure their policies were up to date. He liked things documented, and that included family occasions. He was the one who insisted they had personalised Christmas cards, a show of posed unity snapped by a professional photographer.

The children hated them, tempers flaring over who should sit next to whom. One year Charlie had a black eye, another year Rowena had impetigo on her chin. It never crossed her mind to even think about how Lucas looked; resentful, mostly.

Edwina always thought the gruesome Christmas cards were a way of sticking two fingers up at Barbara, who was bound to catch sight of one balanced on the mantelpiece of a mutual friend. Not that there were many of those, just one, really, and for a second the awful haunted face of poor Paul Landreth flits across Edwina's subconscious. Dear God, just because of the circumstances, it didn't mean she wasn't sorry for the man, and his wife of course ... what was her name? Minty Landreth, poor bitch. Poor all of us.

Once upon a time there were a good number of photographs, properly displayed in silver frames on top of this desk, but they belong to another time, another century! They are so dated now; their presence just poses the question: and then what happened?

All of the photos are lying face down in the bottom drawer. She gets them out now and again and stares hard at once-familiar faces, the passage of time creating a gulf so wide they might as well be characters in a book. Maybe if she never looked at them again she would eventually forget who these people ever were.

In the middle of the room, a mahogany table stretches out like a wooden cat. It seats sixteen, but hasn't in years.

In fact, Edwina so seldom uses the thing she feels sorry for it. Like a toy that's never played with, it seems to be waiting for something to happen.

Pushed up against the wall and towering over the table is a huge cabinet of fancy crockery, a gift from Ollie's mother's side. Soup tureens and meat platters in green and gold porcelain with matching heavy-lidded vegetable dishes and plates of different sizes, large for roast meats and stews, small for cake, cheese and fruit.

In the drawers lie rust-spotted linen napkins and the twins' clouded silver napkin rings, each engraved with their initials, R.E.T and C.S.T.

Both Edwina and Ollie had compromised on middle names, and so the children were baptised Rowena Elizabeth and Charles Sebastian.

On the day they were christened Charlie had flung his head back so dramatically when the vicar trickled water onto his unsuspecting forehead that he'd almost dislocated his neck and knocked himself out on the font. Meanwhile Rowena looked ever so slightly bored.

Their hair, now that they had more of it, seemed to reflect their personalities. Rowena's was poker-straight and sparse while Charlie's grew wild like a bramble, tangled and prone to matting at the back. 'There is something of the gypsy about that boy,' someone commented, and Edwina had felt an overwhelming sense of both fear and pride.

There was only one christening gown, originally made for Ollie's maternal great-grandmother and embroidered all over with shamrocks. Edwina dressed Charlie in it; for some reason she felt he needed more luck than Rowena, who made do with a perfectly pleasant, if much plainer, white cotton gown from John Lewis.

'Excellent,' the boy interjects. Edwina has no idea how long he's been hovering, moving from one foot to the other, either trying to disguise his impatience or needing the lavatory.

He can wait, she thinks irritably. The table could do with a polish, it's lost its mahogany lustre, like a woman whose chestnut hair has faded to a dull brown. The tapestry seat covers are shabby; the decanters on the sideboard no longer create colourful prisms that dance on the wall.

They ate their first Christmas dinner as parents in this room, the table newly bought from an auction house in Peckham. The babies in highchairs, side by side, and Ollie in his paper hat, looking for all the world like a king. He bought a family box of twelve crackers even though only he and Edwina were capable of pulling them, which they did, one after the other, while drinking a bottle of red wine and laughing at all the jokes.

Dickie refused to wear a paper hat; he was self-conscious and thought that sort of thing rather silly. He took his bird-carving duties very seriously, though, criss-crossing the knife against the sharpener, a noise that still reminds Edwina of turkeys and Sundays and the difficult times when Lucas was here, commenting on Charlie's clumsy table manners, turning his nose up at her gravy and constantly looking at his watch, always waiting to go back to school or his mother.

If only he'd lived with us on a full-time basis, thinks Edwina, he might have grown to love us enough not to have taken the other side all the time.

On reflection, she could have tried harder. People handle divorce so much better these days – they know how traumatic it can be for children, books have been written, radio programmes have been broadcast – but back then there were no real guidelines. They just did what they thought was for the best.

So Lucas came for lunches and occasional weekends, and a percentage of the holidays, but when he left she felt nothing but relief. It became increasingly evident that he genuinely did not like anything she ever did for him: the mural on his walls, the food she cooked him, the presents she bought.

The first Christmas after she and Dickie got married, she gave her stepson a telescope – after all, astronomy was his thing – but once he'd torn a corner off the Santa Claus-emblazoned paper he pushed the semi-unwrapped gift under the sofa and looked bored until he went back to Chelsea. She remembers her hands itching to slap him.

That was the year they'd gone to see a panto, all five of them. I did try, Edwina reminds herself, there were lots of treats for everyone. Despite Barbara's demands, she and Dickie had no real money worries. The children were privately educated, Alicia was always on hand to help out, Dickie had his Bentley and she had an old Saab.

A lot of people would have been very envious of them: they ate out and visited the zoo, rode bicycles in the park and tried to glue the family together with lovely things they could all look back on.

But if I took out all the old photo albums, she silently argues, you'd still see the cracks. They look nothing like a real family. Apart from the twins, there are no family resemblances. Her children looked like their dead father, Lucas looked like his mother and Edwina and Dickie always looked slightly taken aback, as if surprised at what they had done.

'Shall we move on?' asks the young man.

Edwina nods, thinking, it was all such a gamble, and we never really knew what was at stake.

11

Study

Edwina pushes the hinged wooden door that divides the dining room at the front of the house from the room at the back.

The boy blinks; he wasn't expecting this.

'My studio,' the old woman explains, silently adding, 'my haven, my sanctuary – where even my children had to knock before they entered.'

'What, even if my head is hanging off and I am bleeding through my tummy button?' asked Charlie.

'You'd still have to knock,' replied his mother.

'Gosh,' the young estate agent stutters.

'I don't paint much any more, but I used to be rather good.'

The walls are testament to this: Edwina refused to have her work displayed anywhere but in here. A couple of Ollie's big abstract canvases dominate one wall, but the rest are all hers, a collage of finished and unfinished pictures, scribbled ideas and works in progress. Charcoal nudes vie for space with watercolour landscapes, rough pencilled portraits and intricate pen-and-ink sketches, years of work, a living CV.

'I used to be an illustrator,' she tells him, feeling sad about the state of her brushes, the tubes of dried-up acrylics, cracked cakes of watercolour, pots of inks gone solid, nibs rusted, and yet her easel is still ready, poised for action, the stool at exactly the right height.

'Then computers came in,' she nods at the Mac, 'and, well, it was never quite the same again.'

Lee marvels at the antiquity of the computer. It's shaped like a turquoise piece of Toblerone. 'I don't think I've ever seen one of those.'

'That's my latest one,' Edwina says. 'I used to have a *really* old one.'

Not that she ever used it. She never felt drawn to the computer as she did to her charcoals and paints, her fingers never itched to use a mouse like they itched for a pencil, a screen is not paper. She didn't like her work being behind glass, it meant she couldn't touch it, like a poorly baby in an incubator.

But before technology took over her career trajectory had been fairly smooth. Once she got established in the greetings-card industry other work came trickling in. Soon she was illustrating cookery books and true-life magazine stories, then came the call from the children's publishers and – bingo – Edwina had hit the jackpot.

'Have you heard of Betsy and Tom?' she asks, slightly surprised after all these years that the pilot light of her ego has not been entirely extinguished.

'No,' he answers, and she can't quite be bothered to explain how successful she used to be.

A collection of Betsy and Tom books are lined up on a shelf, all the first-edition hardbacks. She could probably get a few bob for them on eBay, if she knew how to do eBay.

Of course she didn't write the words, they were written by a husband-and-wife team who lived in Barnes. But she was the illustrator, it was her characterisation of the Love family that was instrumental to their success. The words were quite dull, it was the detail in her painting – the red button-up shoes that Betsy was always losing, Tom's freckled face and the handfuls of home-made biscuits that he shoved into the pockets of his shorts – that the children went mad for.

'I made a lot of money out of Betsy and Tom,' Edwina acknowledges, giving silent credit to Alicia for giving her the freedom to be a sixties working mother.

I had the best of both worlds really, she concludes, being able to work from home was ideal. Alicia would look after the twins in the nursery or kitchen while she drew and painted in here. Most days they'd meet for lunch, soup and things on toast mostly, her children bibbed, mouths open like hungry birds, and then she'd return here, to her turpentine-smelling kingdom.

Sometimes she cheated, dozing off on the old chaise longue.

'Thinking time,' she called it.

'Snoring time, more like,' Alicia teased.

For fifteen years she illustrated the hugely popular Betsy and Tom books and the secret to her success was in the truth of her drawings. Edwina knew exactly how a toddler brandished a spoon in their highchair, how a child squirmed in the bath, because she had all the research material she needed at home. Charlie's habit of chewing his soft toy rabbit's ear became something Betsy did; Rowena's habit of sleeping upside down in her bed – a throwback, perhaps, to how she slept in the womb – became one of Tom's trademarks.

Sometimes she felt she knew Betsy and Tom Love as well as her own children, but because they barely aged they were easier to control. She was still drawing chubby four-year-old Betsy and her bespectacled six-year-old brother when her own children had long since turned into awkward teenagers with problem skin and secrets.

Betsy and Tom had no secrets; they were uncomplicated children with a loving extended family and any number of pets.

Edwina literally drew on her own family for inspiration. The guinea pigs and pet rabbits she bought for the twins paid for their board and lodgings in royalties. Her own mother became the snooty but lonely woman next door, and she once used Lucas's face to depict a horrid boy who had thrown a stone at Betsy and Tom's three-legged dog.

She remembers feeling guilty and rubbing his face out before Dickie noticed.

To be completely honest, when things got difficult in real life it was a relief to come in here and escape into a world of fictional children who never left primary school and never did anything naughtier than bring a live frog into the house.

Of course the money was useful too, it made her financially independent, and in the years between Ollie dying and meeting Dickie she was able to slowly sort the house out and pay all the bills without needing help from anyone. As time went on she was able to send the twins to a nice little prep school in Chelsea, run a car, buy nice clothes and make sure Alicia was well looked after.

If only she'd been strong enough to remain single, but she was lonely, crushingly, heart-stoppingly lonely.

Once the children were in bed and Alicia had gone back to her own mysterious family down the Old Kent Road she didn't know what to do with herself. The house was too big and her husband too dead.

She thought about him constantly, but sometimes forgot his face, which made her panic. Some nights she was tempted to wake her children to remind her of what he'd looked like.

Each twin had inherited different components of their handsome father: Rowena had his nose, Charlie his chin. She dreamt that Ollie's face had transformed into a jigsaw puzzle and she couldn't quite get the right pieces to fit.

The loss of his face made her howl, and some nights she'd sit in her bed sorting through her tiny collection of precious family photos, a few of just him, some of the two of them, mostly taken on their wedding day, and the saddest photos of all, the handful of snaps she possessed of the four of them.

A friend of Ollie's had posted one to her after the funeral, taken on that fateful day in Cornwall. A slightly blurred colour snap of Edwina and Ollie sitting on a tartan rug, each holding a rusk-waving twin. They are laughing at the camera; if only he'd taken his sunglasses off for that photo she might have been able to see something in his eyes, a warning of what was to come.

She wonders what the young estate agent would say if she turned round right now and said, 'I lived here with a man who died very suddenly on a beach. We had two children. I married another man who had a wife before me and a son that I could never love. This house has our blood, sweat, love, laughter and betrayal seeped into its very bones. I might leave this place, but bits of me will remain here, tears soaked deep into the floorboards. You could hoover this place for ever and you'd never get rid of us completely. Our DNA is all over this place—'

'And onwards?' she suggests, taking in a last lungful of a smell that used to sum up her entire essence. I was an artist before I was a mother, she reminds herself.

12

Rear Staircase

Halfway down the stairs to the kitchen, Edwina waves her hand in the direction of a closed pine door: 'Downstairs cloakroom.'

Lee smirks. Posh types can never bring themselves to say the word toilet.

'Very useful,' he responds. 'The more bathrooms the better. Is it big enough to put a shower in?'

Edwina has no idea why anyone would want a shower down here, so she ignores him.

Even the smallest corners of this house harbour memories. She doesn't like using the downstairs loo; obviously she has to these days for convenience's sake, but for years she avoided this little tucked-away space.

Gentian violet walls, the colour of infection, cuts and miscarriages. She still cannot use that lavatory without remembering the horrible thing that happened to her in there.

'Of course it's not just me,' she admonishes herself. 'I'm not the only woman in the world to have lost a baby.'

It was a couple of years after she married Dickie. The baby was planned; she came off the pill and he made love to her with even more thoroughness than usual, pushing himself into her as far as he physically could, as if to give his sperm a racing start. On a couple of occasions, he even asked her to stand on her head for a couple of minutes post coitus.

Anyway, whatever the method, it worked. She was thirty-six when she fell pregnant for the second time, with her third child.

The doctor confirmed her condition – back in the seventies there weren't such things as over-the-counter pregnancy tests.

She'd known before he told her: the nausea, sore breasts and overwhelming sensitivity to certain smells. The craving for prawn cocktail.

The first thing she asked was whether she could be carrying another set of twins.

'Highly unlikely,' the doctor replied, 'although it's not unheard of. We shall just have to wait and see.'

She instinctively thought of the new baby as a he, while Dickie presumed it would be a girl, a girl with blonde curls, just like he'd had as a child. He was bursting with pride and excitement, but out of loyalty to his son he suggested they wait until Lucas was home from school before they broke the news.

'Let's hang on until the Easter holidays to tell the children. It wouldn't be fair on Lucas if Rowena and Charlie should find out first. We can make an occasion of it – imagine how excited they'll be when they realise they're going to have a baby sister.'

'What if it's a boy?' she felt like screaming, but Dickie had his heart set on a daughter, a pretty, companionable little creature that he could take into Knightsbridge for party shoes and ice-creams, a proper Daddy's girl.

After all, Lucas had always been a Mummy's boy. Genetically they shared everything, from colouring to black-belt sulking. While Dickie knew exactly how his son ticked, the twins remained a complete mystery to him. It didn't matter how hard he tried, they were always just beyond his reach, emotionally and physically.

Dickie was convinced a little girl would be just the thing to bring the family together, a flesh-and-blood link that would connect Lucas to his step-siblings, and the twins to both Lucas and himself.

Edwina had never seen Dickie so content. He'd always wanted a brood, but Barbara had difficulty conceiving and there had been all sorts of visits to specialists before Lucas was born.

They both knew Barbara would be horrified about the new addition to the family, but, as Dickie said, she was horrified by most things, with sex and childbirth being two of the things she found most horrifying of all. After Lucas's arrival (a particularly gruesome forceps delivery), Barbara more or less decided that was it in the bedroom department, and even the tiniest hint of affection made her flinch like she'd been stung.

Forty years on, acknowledging the little purple lavatory with a casual wave of the hand, Edwina remembers her terrible feelings of guilt.

She did nothing wrong, no one knew back then that pregnant women shouldn't smoke. After all, she'd smoked with the twins and they'd been fine. She drank too, not much: the odd glass of red wine, the occasional whisky. But while Dickie tossed potential baby names into the ring – Penelope, Jennifer, Clara – she remained silent. She couldn't think of a single baby name that she actually liked. Maybe when I see his face, she told herself.

It happened on the Friday night before Lucas came home for the Easter holidays, on the eve of breaking the news. She'd been feeling wretched all day, feverish and her back ached. She couldn't wait for the children to go to bed, but she dreaded the thought of Lucas arriving the next day.

It was around nine o'clock in the evening; she'd been washing up after supper when the pain grabbed her around the belly like a vice. Dickie was in the drawing room with a brandy.

Within ten minutes it was over. She'd lost Dickie's baby down the lavatory and flushed the clotted lumps away without thinking. Apparently she should have wrapped what she could save in newspaper for medical inspection. They might have discovered what had gone wrong.

'It wasn't meant to be' seemed reason enough to her. It just wasn't meant to be. 'A congenital abnormality,' her doctor suspected. 'Or just one of those things.'

And now she is glad, glad that nothing else came along to complicate an already complicated situation.

Poor Dickie was devastated. After picking up Lucas he spent the remainder of the weekend in bed with a brandy-induced migraine. She sympathised, but she also had to deal with his slab-faced son. She gave up just after lunchtime on Saturday, and asked Lucas for his mother's phone number.

She'd never spoken to Barbara before, but she couldn't just send Lucas back to Chelsea without checking there would be someone at home to receive him.

'Hello Barbara, this is Edwina.'

Slam, the phone went down. Silly bitch, Edwina thought, what if I needed to speak to her about something important. What if there was a real emergency?

'You ring her,' she instructed Lucas.

'Hello Mummy, may I come home please? I'm not having a very nice time.'

Barbara refused to let Edwina put him in a cab. She wanted to fetch him herself, but she refused to set foot in 'that house'.

She gave instructions via her son that Lucas should be waiting outside in precisely one hour.

Edwina stood silently with him on the steps and, bang on time, a black cab pulled up. Through the window she could see a solid cloud of ebony hair on the back seat, a flash of crimson nails.

Lucas ran down the path and the taxi swallowed him whole.

Edwina walked back into the house. She was still bleeding.

13

Breakfast Room

Edwina is tired now, and vaguely thinking of lunch. She usually has soup or a sandwich. Today is a sandwich kind of day, cheese and pickle most likely.

She walks slowly, taking care, a purple-veined hand curled around the banister. This last flight of stairs is lethally narrow. When she's finished in the basement she will take the boy outside into the garden, and then she can get rid of him.

Hopefully there's a lump of Cheshire wrapped up in tin foil in the fridge, and with any luck it won't need too much mould trimming off.

Alicia used to do most of the cooking and the laundry too, although Dickie liked his work shirts sent out. 'Because,' he explained, he needed them 'professionally done'. The day she broke this news to Alicia was a dark one. Alicia huffed and puffed and banged pans around in a fit of temper, while Edwina hid in her studio.

Alicia was as moody as any of them, she didn't like hoovering and she didn't like doing anything for Lucas. The feeling was mutual: clothes of his that needed mending were earmarked for matron. It was as if he really didn't like Alicia touching his things.

'He hasn't come into such close contact with a coloured before,' Dickie once admitted, and Edwina had almost smacked him on the nose with a serving spoon.

They were having a casual Saturday lunch down here in the basement. Alicia had made a big fish pie before she left for the weekend, and Edwina was serving peas to Dickie.

'"A coloured"? Don't you dare talk about Alicia like that, like she's some kind of negro in a film about cotton picking. Dear God, Dickie, this is the seventies – get with it.' But there was always something about Dickie that was stuck firmly in the fifties.

Edwina fumes at the memory. In some respects she blames Dickie's education: Wyebourne College was so set in its ways the only black faces Dickie or Lucas ever encountered were either pupils of exotic royal descent or staff cleaning the toilets. Stupid place.

'And this is the breakfast room,' she tells the boy, suddenly realising that clues to the room's identity are spread all over the table. The Brown Betty teapot squats under its knitted navy and white striped cosy, while a mug of congealed Earl Grey tea and a plate containing marmalade-sodden crusts complete the evidence.

Really, she is getting quite batty. She could have sworn she'd tidied away her breakfast things, but apparently not.

'How untidy,' she apologises. Lee doesn't bat an eyelid. Last week on a viewing he had almost stepped in a kid's potty full of piss.

'Lived in' would be the polite way of describing this room. Everything has seen better days: the cushions on the paint-chipped chairs are threadbare, an empty goldfish bowl on the window sill is thick with dust. The room bears the ancient battle scars of a past family life, and the tell-tale clue to its sole occupancy now is the single mouldy orange in a ceramic fruit bowl.

Edwina sits down on the sofa. It seems like she hasn't recycled her newspapers in a while as there are piles stacked up all over the place. Maybe she should have a bonfire, burn a load of stuff without even looking. Better to destroy everything than painstak-ingly sift through a lifetime of memories, deciding what to keep. Simpler to put a match to the whole lot, and maybe bake a potato on the funeral pyre of her past.

The boy is looking up at the ceiling: 'You don't see many of those.'

Edwina glances up at the clothes pulley, which once heaved with damp cot sheets and the twins' tiny newborn vests. Over the years their clothes morphed from rompers to the blue and white gingham smocks of their nursery school to their rust-coloured prep-school corduroy skirts and shorts, then later . . . Oh, then it all got complicated. Three different sets of uniform, three different schools that all played their part in the story.

If Rowena hadn't been so clever, if Charlie hadn't been so easily led, if Lucas hadn't been such a prig . . .

'You've lived here a long time?' the boy is asking.

'Yes,' she replies, glad that none of her old knickers are drying above his head. 'Longer than you've been alive, much longer. Over fifty years in the same house.'

She glances at the Welsh dresser on the opposite wall, scanning its shelves like an antiques dealer.

I shall keep the Clarice Cliff pieces, all the parrot jugs and the Susie Cooper coffee set. The rest can smash or burn for all I care. I only need keep the loveliest of my things, and that includes memories. Sod the rest of it.

'It's nice to have somewhere less formal than the dining room to eat,' she murmurs, remembering coming downstairs from her studio to see Alicia and the twins at lunchtimes, Rowena eating earnestly and precisely, quick to wield a spoon in the right direc-tion, Charlie on the other hand with his face covered in spaghetti hoop juice, his pelican bib almost overflowing with food that had missed his mouth.

She recalls Alicia nudging her big bottom around the scarred wooden table, wiping, mopping, feeding, her beehive leaning sometimes to the left and sometimes to the right.

Of course later on, in the seventies, she gave up on the rollers and the lacquer. For a while, Alicia went au naturel, an abundant afro framing her face like a massive halo.

'Can't you get that woman to cover her hair when she cooks?' asked Dickie, inspecting his dinner for any stray Alicia curls.

Honestly, Dickie could be a dick at times.

So much family life went on in this room. The biro lines where she measured the children – 'stand up straight' – are still visible behind the door, marked, named and dated. The twins more or less the same head height for years; the sudden introduction of Lucas's measurements; her stepson remaining the tallest for years, until Charlie's dramatic teenage growth spurt.

So many boiled eggs, dipped and eaten in here, the mountains of toast crumbs over the years, the packets and packets of custard creams, the special baked bean pan, Lucas hating salad cream, Rowena's love of Marmite and lettuce, Charlie chewing on crispy bacon rinds, a Mother's Day bunch of purple tulips in a spotty jug.

She opens her eyes. On the opposite wall hangs a framed picture of nursery-school-sized hands in splattery red and blue paint. Rowena and Charlie's.

For a second Edwina wonders if she could possibly just stay down here, convert this basement floor into a self-contained granny flat. She'd have to have a shower put into the downstairs loo, like the lad suggested, but surely it would be easier than actually upping sticks.

Having toured her own house, the enormity of what she has to do suddenly overwhelms her.

'Kitchen over there,' she points. She mustn't give up. She didn't when things were really bad, even when people were pointing at her on the street, she kept going. You have to really, what's the alternative? She gets up, making a small embarrassing grunting noise as she does so. If I had a gun I could always kill myself, she thinks.

14

Kitchen

There is something aquatic about the kitchen, possibly because the light filtering through the rear window is tinted a dark shadowy green by the overgrowth in the back garden.

Lee feels uncomfortable. No one wants a kitchen like this any more; there's a fine line between period features and old-fashioned tat. The whole lot will have to come out. He has a horrible feeling the Aga is dead, sitting there like an ancient relic, not breathing, a domestic dinosaur.

Middle-class women are kitchen mad. Whoever buys this place will probably get a designer in and within twelve months it'll be unrecognisable, all underfloor heating, poured concrete and a kitchen island so big it could have its own beach.

In Lee's experience, the smart London kitchen has recently morphed from farmhouse homeliness to something resembling a mortuary.

'Masses of potential,' he informs the little woman who seems to be having a kip on the knackered old sofa in the breakfast room.

Edwina is not sleeping, but she is resting her eyes and thinking how, at her grand age, she should be more at home in the kitchen.

I suppose it comes from not having much of a relationship with my mother, she reflects, who in turn never cooked because she had servants. Not servants like Alicia, but proper servants, referred to by their surnames and certainly not confided in. Alicia knew most of my secrets, and it was no secret that I couldn't really cook.

Alicia said, 'Cooking is like gardening: some folk have green fingers, others have pastry hands and you, Edwina, you have neither.'

'Mummy's got painting hands,' Rowena piped up.

Alicia could mix pancake batter in her sleep, her rice was light and fluffy, her chicken skin bronzed and crispy. She baked, she whisked, she chopped and she stirred, a kitchen dervish, fox-trotting from oven to table to sink. By contrast, Edwina was hesitant and clumsy. She remembers Ollie realising how domestically remedial she was the first time she attempted a full English breakfast.

'Oh dear,' he said as she presented him with a plate of raw sausage, burnt toast, leathery fried eggs and tinned tomatoes. But he ate it all, apart from the sausage, which he said might give him a tapeworm.

He must have been so disappointed, growing up on a farm where food was hot and plentiful, where the bread was home-made and his mother slow-cooked stews until the meat fell from the bones.

'You'll learn,' he said. 'And anyway, you have other talents,' and he slid his hand between her legs and they fucked up against the wall.

Years later Dickie bought her an 'Everyday Kitchen Cuisine' course for her birthday, and dutifully she trotted off to a cookery school in Kensington for an entire week of stuffing mushrooms, blind baking and learning how to en croute.

Like a schoolgirl she brought the spoils of the day home in a plastic-covered wicker basket. Dickie was encouraging: 'Well done, old girl, that looks delicious – can't wait.' But after a day of pounding butter and blending in carefully sifted flour, of zesting lemons and sealing joints, she had no appetite. 'I'll just have some toast and go to bed, thanks.'

She found the experience dull and exhausting, standing up all day, pretending to care, surrounded by enthusiastic newlyweds clucking and fussing over their duck à l'orange as if it were a newborn baby.

Of course Dickie's ex-wife, having spent an entire year at a Swiss finishing school, was a very accomplished cook. Her specialities included Genoese sponge, choux pastry and decorative icing. She was, apparently, a dab hand with a fondant rose.

Lucas went into rhapsodies over his mother's culinary skills, boasting about the birthday cakes she had created for him over the years. It was all Mummy this and Mummy that. He never called Edwina anything, apart from 'you'.

'Can you leave me alone?' he'd once requested. 'Not until you say please,' she'd responded.

'Please can you leave me alone?' he dutifully parroted back, pushing away another plate of untouched watery mince.

Alicia didn't work at the weekends, so unless she had time to prepare a couple of meals before she left on Friday Edwina was on her own, burning rather than caramelising onions, clumsy with garlic and indecisive over boiled eggs.

Food is so difficult, muses Edwina, it creates so many problems. And, just as firmly as Lucas, she pushes away the memory of Rowena excusing herself from the table to be sick.

Recently she has become very lazy, living off the contents of the garage over the road, with its convenient Tesco Express franchise. She eats tinned goods, buys soft, pulpy white bread and resorts to cereal for supper. If she's really hungry she will rifle through her selection of takeaway menus and order a home delivery on the telephone. Last week she had a nasi goreng from the new Indonesian place by Lambeth station: utterly delicious, and plenty left over for lunch the next day.

People make such a fuss about eating, all those ridiculous cooking programmes on the box. Once, after *Masterchef*, she had to reach for her Rennies, suffering from indigestion without having eaten a morsel.

Suddenly she remembers making Rice Krispie cakes with the twins down here when they were small, and her marrow chills even now as she remembers spooning sticky dollops of the mixture into flimsy paper cases and realising for the first time how much more coordinated Rowena was than Charlie.

From that moment on there was always a nagging doubt about her beautiful boy. She noticed how his eyes flitted restlessly from one thing to another, how he couldn't bear to be still for a moment.

Once she'd noticed it, she couldn't stop noticing it: the way Rowena would sit and study her books, staring intently at the pictures, trying to figure out a story for herself, while Charlie sat next to her, doing exactly the same but with the book upside down. Then he would suddenly get bored and toddle off to see where he could trap his fingers or bump his head.

'He's a flibbertigibbet,' Alicia told her, laughing at Charlie's antics, but sometimes she looked concerned too.

Of course there had been four glorious years when she didn't have to worry about him, four years when it seemed his future was golden and safe. 'My son, the Westminster chorister,' she had smugly told anyone who would listen.

She hadn't wanted him to board – he was only nine – but she comforted herself with the fact that the school was only down the road. She could catch a bus and wave at him through the windows, and if the worst came to the worst (for him or for her) she could break into the place and bundle him home in a blanket.

It was Dickie who encouraged her to let him go. They'd only recently embarked on their affair, he was spending more and more time at Kennington Road and Charlie was a terrible one for barging in on their love-making.

Of course, she realises now that it was very convenient for her lover to banish Charlie, but at the time she thought he had her son's best interests at heart.

'It's a once-in-a-lifetime opportunity,' he wheedled. 'Most mothers would give their eye teeth – you can't deny him this chance. Anyway, boys are natural boarders. Lucas loves it.'

So she let him take the entrance exam, and although they were worried about his academic prowess the fact that he was musically gifted, that he sang like the proverbial angel and that she, poor thing, was a widow, tipped the balance in Charlie's favour.

'I shouldn't have done it,' she mutters, knowing now that her pride, her disgusting pride, had possibly played a part in her son's downfall.

The boy in the ill-fitting suit is rattling the cutlery drawer. It's full of mouse droppings.

'Sorry,' he says cheerfully, 'I didn't mean to wake you up, but, um, I've got another measure this afternoon and I need to . . .'

'I wasn't asleep,' she assures him, 'I was thinking. Shall we finish off by looking in the garden?'

'Good idea,' he responds, and together they leave the dank green fish tank of the kitchen.

15

Garden

Edwina struggles with the back door until Lee politely manoeuvres himself in front of her and budges at it with his shoulder until it finally creaks open.

'I don't come out here much,' she admits. 'It's a bit of a jungle.'

'There's a lawn mower in the shed,' she says. Lee can't even see a shed.

Edwina is rather shocked: she hadn't realised things had got this bad, but Mother Nature can be very domineering. It's very easy to lose control of her.

The path has disappeared, but she can just about make out the skeleton of a climbing frame rising above the brambles. However, the shed has been completely obscured by a couple of enormous old fruit trees.

Alicia used to make apple chutney, heavily spiced with ginger and cardamom, thick with fat raisins.

Lee wades through the knee-height grass. 'Watch the nettles,' says Edwina. 'And the broken glass,' adds Lee, picking his way over smashed panes and splintered wooden frames.

'An experiment in growing cucumbers,' explains Edwina.

'There was a pond once,' she continues, 'but obviously, what with Charlie we had to have it filled in. The year after, a big frog came hopping by as if to say, "Where's it gone? There used to be a pond here; it seems to have disappeared." They always say elephants have good memories, but I think maybe frogs do too.'

'We buried a lot of hamsters out here,' she adds, shivering in the chill of the October wind.

The first one she bought for Rowena when Charlie went off to Westminster. Edwina thought she might be lonely without her brother, but she wasn't, it was as if she could relax for the first time in her life. Once Charlie was safely ensconced at Westminster a slightly different Rowena emerged, more sociable, less anxious. This new Rowena had friends home for tea and even attempted Brownies, before deciding that she didn't like being told how to enjoy herself.

The family dynamics shifted, and it was good for mother and daughter to spend time together on a one-on-one basis. Rowena took to coming into Edwina's bedroom first thing in the morning, quietly crawling under the covers and curling up against her mother's warmth. Maybe she missed her brother more than she let on.

The hamster was called Lulu after the pop singer – 'She has the same colour hair,' Rowena explained. Edwina didn't like to tell her that she was a he.

Rowena stopped coming into the bedroom for early-morning cuddles the day she accidentally climbed in next to Dickie.

He very rarely stayed over, but Barbara had gone to a health farm with a girlfriend and so they'd taken advantage of the situation.

Almost half a century later, Edwina still feels guilty. Why couldn't they just have waited?

She remembers telling Rowena how Dickie had been locked out of his own house, and that he was very cold so he'd got into her bed to warm up.

To which her nine-year-old daughter had replied, 'He could

have slept in the spare room. He could have made himself a hot water bottle, or worn a jumper.'

For the next six months the child more or less refused to be in the same room as her future stepfather.

Dickie tried: he bought her dolls and craft kits, which she eyed hungrily but refused to touch, preferring to use her mother's broken chalks and messy palettes rather than open Dickie's box full of pristine rows of quality wax crayons.

Edwina suddenly remembers finding those wax crayons in Rowena's wastepaper basket, unused, and all neatly snapped in two.

She has banished that memory for so many years it feels shocking again to face up to the fact it was actually true.

Of course, a truce was eventually called. Dickie found the key to Rowena's heart with books, old books, new books, rare books, picture books. Again, in hindsight, it had been to his advantage: Rowena could lose herself in a book for hours on end, and the deeper she lost herself the more time Dickie and Edwina had alone together.

At least she had the hamster for company, Edwina reminds herself, but Lulu died. It was Christmastime, and for a number of weeks they'd thought the creature was just hibernating, but Charlie, home from Westminster, had insisted on poking its sleeping box with a pencil, and soon discovered that all that lay within the sawdust and cotton wool were Lulu's tiny bones.

So they came out here and buried her, just the three of them, on a sleeting Christmas Eve. Alicia was down the Old Kent Road with her family, Dickie was in Chelsea with Barbara and Lucas, and all Edwina could think as they piled cold earth onto Lulu's lavatory-roll coffin was that she didn't want to die alone.

I still don't, she tells herself, I don't want to be one of those old ladies found dead in a chair, the air thick with bluebottles buzzing.

Her new year's resolution was to get Dickie to leave his wife and make an honest woman of her. 'Or I'll find someone else.'

She warned her lover, 'I can't wait for ever, I'm still young, I can still attract attention, if it's not going to be you, Dickie, it will be someone else.'

To teach him a lesson, she set her sights on an unmarried friend of Dickie's who dealt antiques down the King's Road. Teddy took her out for lunch a couple of times and gave her a generous discount on some nice jewellery, but he trembled when she got too close, his upper lip glistening with sweat, his palms pink and wet.

'He's queer, of course,' Dickie told her. 'Darling, there's always a few at school, and in my year there were two: Teddy and another chap called Robbins. You're barking up the wrong tree. Just be a little more patient: I'll be with you as soon as I can.'

He sounded like an assistant in a busy department store rather than her lover. She was furious. When he told her that Barbara had to have an operation 'down there' she'd snapped, 'Do you mean a hysterectomy, Dickie? Because if you do, just jolly well spit it out.'

A month later Dickie took Barbara on a cruise to recuperate, because 'Really, darling, the op was monstrous,' and he could hardly give the old girl the heave-ho when she was feeling so utterly ghastly. So rather than leaving his wife, he was taking her to the Caribbean. Doctor's orders.

Meanwhile Edwina stayed at home in Kennington, ironically illustrating *Betsy and Tom's Seaside Adventures*. Out of sheer spite, she painted a fat forty-five-year-old brunette with appalling sunburn in the background of one of the colour plates, but the publisher questioned its relevance and she had to paint her out.

Damn Barbara.

The sky has clouded over; fat drops of rain are falling just like the day Alicia arrived. It was Alicia who made her have the pond filled in: she had caught Charlie slipping out of the back door and grabbed him by the ankle as he tipped himself in. 'Heading for trouble, this one,' she'd laughed.

Edwina is jolted back to reality by the wetness on the back of her neck, on her head.

'Let's get back indoors,' Lee says. 'I should have a valuation for you, Mrs Spinner, in a few days, and someone will be round to take photos for our website.'

Ah, so she used Spinner, did she?

Back in the house, Edwina sits on the bottom step of the hall staircase and stares at the back of the front door for a long time.

Soon she will close that door for the very last time. Will the bad times stay here, she wonders, or will they cling to her like pollen and ash?

16

Culling

It is a week since Lee visited the house and Edwina is going through her wardrobe. She is making herself do at least two hours' culling a day. Today is handbags; how come she has collected so many handbags?

A great many of them are almost identical, hard-edged with a satisfying snappy clip fastening, and short hooped handles just right for tucking over the arm like the Queen.

Black patent, navy leather, crocodile, snakeskin, tan, dark tan, chocolate brown. Then there are the evening bags, metallic silver chainmail and gold satin clutches, a barely used, lavishly embroidered velvet opera bag. She hates the opera, always has done.

Of course Dickie liked her to be well dressed, despite the fact that he'd originally been attracted to her arty bohemian style. Once they got married he suggested slacks had a 'time and a place, darling: gardening, picnics, those sorts of activities'.

He bought her all these bags, for birthdays and Christmases. Even though she'd rather receive expensive paintbrushes (Siberian weasel hair, preferably), Dickie stuck to tradition and showered her with leather goods, proper Hatton Garden jewellery, and perfume.

Bottles and bottles of Joy by Jean Patou, a scent Edwina could never decide whether she liked or not.

The inside of the wardrobe still smells of it, a heady mix of jasmine and rose, combined with her own sweat and the reek of mothballs. That's one thing she won't miss: the bloody moths. Wherever she goes next, she will make sure it's moth free. Anyway, if she moves to Cornwall, she won't be wearing woollen jumpers; she will wear Breton stripes and canvas painting smocks.

She used to put Ollie's old shirts on the children when they were little and sit them down at the kitchen table with rolls of cheap lining paper and primary-coloured powder paint mixed up for them on saucers.

Charlie getting instantly in a mess, paintbrush too wet, colours running, everything ending up in a big purple blob. Rowena painstaking, waiting for background colours to dry, red apples on a green tree, competent, but with no flair whatsoever.

Lucas refused to join in with anything creative. She couldn't get him to understand that art was about freedom, about expression, about letting go. He didn't like letting go, he didn't like his hands getting dirty, he was his mother's son, he liked to be in control, and in the end they were all at his mercy.

She cleared out all of Dickie's clothes years ago when she still had a car, driving suitcases of bespoke pinstripe suits and Harris Tweed jackets to Streatham, deliberately choosing a charity shop too far away to ever walk past accidentally. Imagine how horrific it would be, catching sight of a mannequin in a charity-shop window dressed from top to toe in your dead husband's clothes.

On her lap is a navy leather bag with a crimson satin lining, an early courting gift from Dickie. The sophisticated impression is spoilt somewhat by an ancient Rimmel lipstick rolling around inside.

She always wore a poppy-coloured red, despising the apologetic coral tones of more polite women. Her lips flamed whatever the occasion, even when she was meeting the headmaster of Westminster Abbey Choir School, and she'd always found cheap lipsticks just as good as the expensive ones. According to the slightly worn label, this particular shade is 'Passion Red'.

Cautiously she removes the lid, rolls the lipstick up and paints it onto her old mouth. Checking her reflection, she sees she looks ridiculous, her teeth an ochre shade, the skin around her mouth minutely pleated. A tortoise in lipstick, what a shame.

'Yes, we are happy to take Charles on account of his exceptional voice. However, you must be aware that, academically, he is somewhat lacking. Obviously we will do all we can to rectify this situation, but Charles is coming to us late: he's nine and we like to take our boys at eight. But, due to a circumstance beyond our control we happen to have a place and I think he will fit right in.'

Edwina was shocked, she hadn't expected to hear whether he'd got in right away. Looking in the full-length mirror inside her big old smelly wardrobe, she pulls the face she imagined she pulled back then – Oh, oh, oh!

The reflection of her red, round mouth reminds her of Charlie's mouth when he sang, and she recalls how his crystal clear tones bounced off the vaulted ceiling of the Abbey, a hundred feet above his curly head.

It is a terrible pity what happens to boys, thinks Edwina. Everyone makes such a fuss about girls and their passage into womanhood, all that hoo-ha over periods.

Rowena had started hers at thirteen and been very matter of fact: 'I shall need a ready supply of Dr White's and some Anadin, please, Mum.'

But puberty hit Charlie much harder.

For starters, he grew at the speed of a sunflower, six inches in six months. By the time he came home for the summer holidays he was towering above Lucas, who looked particularly short and extremely podgy after his second year at Wyebourne.

By comparison, Charlie was like a giant Anglepoise lamp. He

unfolded and seemed to go on for ever. His height was shocking enough, but the thing Edwina couldn't get over was the sudden appearance of his Adam's apple, so sharp in his throat that the first time she noticed it she felt fearful. It looked painful; it wasn't, but the effect it had was.

Charlie's voice was changing. Sometimes it squeaked, sometimes it croaked, but mostly it just sounded a bit broken.

Occasionally she heard him in the bathroom, trying to reach the notes he'd been singing just the term before. He sounded like a wounded seagull and her heart sank.

He wouldn't sing again, not properly, not beautifully, not in Westminster Abbey, not in front of the Queen.

It was the same for all of them, Dickie reminded her: none of the choristers stayed on after thirteen. It was time to hang up his cassock and his little white ruff, and go to a normal school.

Only he didn't get into any normal schools. None of the good day schools in London wanted him. Without his voice, Charlie didn't have enough to offer. His academic record was weak; he was incapable of writing an exam paper legibly. One school said they had to turn him down because they couldn't even read his name at the top of the paper.

It was time for Dickie to pull some strings. 'I'll talk to Wyebourne,' he promised her. 'After all, what's the point in being an old boy if you don't get some perks? Let me see what I can do.'

Being in politics, Dickie could be very persuasive, but even so, Edwina was very shocked when she heard Charlie had a place.

Dickie would never tell her how he did it, but later on, when the scandal first blew up, she guessed and she was angrier than she had ever been in her life.

Looking at her red lips again in the mirror she twists her mouth into all the worst words that she spat at her husband. 'You cunt, you shitting cunt. You knew, you must have fucking known. He was in your year at that fucking school – why on earth would you entrust my child to the care of that monster?'

The worst of it was that Dickie genuinely didn't know what all the fuss was about. In his experience, all boys were interfered with by someone at boarding school. An older boy or a teacher, really, what was the big deal? They got over it. In some respects, it made you more of a man.

'It's abuse,' she screamed. 'That man was in a position of care and he abused my son.'

'Now steady on,' he'd replied. 'That's a bit strong. Don't forget I knew Robbins at school: might have been queer, but he wouldn't hurt a fly.'

'We're not talking flies, we're talking boys,' she shrieked back. 'And you wangled a place for my son at that school, knowing full well this sort of thing was going on?'

Something crossed his face at that moment, and she realised it was guilt.

The truth hit her right then. Suddenly she knew why the school had taken Charlie: because Dickie had known what this man was capable of. Dickie knew Robbins wouldn't be able to help himself, and that the school knew, so if Wyebourne didn't take Charlie, Dickie would blow the whistle.

So Wyebourne took Charlie in order to keep Dickie quiet. It still sickens her now, the enormous expense of the stupid uniform, the ludicrous trunk, all that equipment he was never going to use. And for what?

In the end it had been Charlie who blew the whistle. Two other boys then came forward and the story cracked open like a stinking egg.

Of course they did their best to hush things up. Mr Robbins was immediately put on gardening leave and a new and heterosexual to the core sports master was employed, but a court case loomed because one of the other boys' parents was determined to bring 'the pervert' down.

Obviously Charlie could no longer attend the school, not while all this was pending. It would be better if he left immediately. And so he did, with his brand-new trunk full of barely used clothing; three weeks later Robbins was found hanged in a wood near his mother's house.

The balance of his mind had been disturbed, the inquest concluded.

'And what about the balance of my son's mind?' fumed Edwina, although in truth Charlie seemed to recover rather well.

Edwina couldn't believe Dickie wanted Lucas to stay. 'In a school that colludes with paedophilia?' she blinked at him.

Again he remonstrated with her: 'Let's not go overboard, Edwina. I don't think we should bandy words like "paedophilia" around – it's not like Charlie was nine.'

Years later Dickie admitted that's how old he'd been when a prefect first came into his dorm, turned him onto his stomach and gagged him with one of his own school socks.

'What about Lucas?' she had railed. 'How would you feel if he'd had a go at Lucas?'

'Oh, I don't think you have to worry about him,' Charlie smirked. She hadn't even noticed him enter the room.

'Mr Robbins only went for us pretty ones,' and he left the room again, laughing.

Well, thinks Edwina, what a lot of handbags. What a lot of mess.

17

Tackling the Top Room

Edwina knows she needs to tackle the top room, but the sheer scale of the problem prevents her doing any more than opening the door and peering in. Is that a billiard table in the far right-hand corner?

Maybe the people who eventually buy this house would like some of this stuff. There must be treasure among the rubbish – fashion goes round in circles, so everything that was discarded thirty years ago is now covetable. G Plan furniture, for example, is all the rage again. Who'd have thought?

She occasionally buys *Elle Decoration* because it's nice to see how other people live their uncluttered lives. All those young couples smiling around their kitchen islands, with their beautiful children, photogenic dogs and carefully chosen fruit arranged artistically in a pleasingly shaped bowl. If only one could start again.

Sometimes when she can't sleep she mentally places herself in a white clapboard house on the edge of a cliff and furnishes it: a pale pink painted Lloyd Loom chair here, a bunch of peonies in a green vase there, maybe an Indian dhurry on the floor. She's sure she has one rolled up somewhere, probably here in this top room.

If only she had the strength to move some of the mess around, then 'I might be able to see the wood for the trees', she mutters, a saying she's never really understood.

Taking up a great deal of the floor space in this room is Charlie's school trunk, a huge pale blue leather box with reinforced corners, bought at great expense by the boy's stepfather.

Dickie was very fair: he bought Charlie exactly the same model as Lucas. The only difference was the colour.

'A trunk is for life,' he informed her. 'Might as well get the best.'

After Charlie left Wyebourne the luggage label on his pristine trunk had simply been removed and replaced with a new school address. In West Sussex this time, where, against Dickie's better judgement, Edwina had enrolled Charlie in a more 'artistic educational community'.

Glennings co-educational boarding school was just ten years old when Edwina drove down to inspect it. Dickie wouldn't countenance the trip; he thought the whole idea absurd. 'You simply can't have a mixed boarding school,' he told her. 'All the girls will turn into slags and the boys will be too distracted to catch a ball.'

'Charlie doesn't particularly want to catch a ball,' she'd retorted. 'He hates sport, and at Glennings it doesn't matter.'

The whole ethos of the school was to allow pupils to expand their creative horizons, and to engage only in the subjects that interested them.

'What is the point in subjecting a child to something they're not passionate about?' the deputy head pontificated as he escorted Edwina around the school's allotments. 'Here at Glennings children are encouraged to find their own path. They can also keep small pets,' he added, waving his hand in the general area of an outbuilding that housed various-sized hutches. 'Rabbits, guinea pigs, that kind of thing.'

Charlie hadn't wanted a pet; Rowena was the one interested in animals. Even back then Charlie knew pets meant commitment: they needed feeding and clean bedding, a lot of shit had to be dealt with, he didn't really have the time. Charlie was all about Charlie.

'Charlie is my darling,' Edwina sings, she often does.

Of course, Glennings was right up Charlie's street. He loved the idea of making up his own rules (none, basically) and was thrilled by the idea that sixth-formers were allowed to smoke on school premises – how cool was that? Also there was no uniform. After years of cassocks and starched white ruffs, followed by a term of slicked-down hair and earwax inspections, he was free, free to wear what he wanted. His clothes took on a slightly theatrical twist: he started buying pinstriped waistcoats and paisley cravats from charity shops; he swaggered around in a beaten-up top hat for a while; and when he was fifteen he had the ends of his black curls bleached blonde by a girl in his year. A girl he may or may not have been sleeping with.

While Charlie was swanning around wearing an original thirties mess jacket complete with a chestful of medals, Rowena and Lucas were toeing the traditional public-school line. Rowena didn't mind – her uniform was a fairly acceptable blue skirt, white shirt, blue jumper combo that no one could really take exception to – but poor Lucas's school wardrobe was a never-ending Victorian costume change. Lucas didn't have just one uniform, he had different uniforms for different occasions: everyday wear, church and formal dining, tennis, rugby, fencing. His was a bewildering array of colour-coded house kit and regulation wing-tipped collars; at thirteen, he had been expected to tie a proper bow tie and handle his own cufflinks.

Lucas was being prepared for the life of a gentleman. He even had a straw boater for summer and a bowler hat for winter. Charlie was being prepared for what? He looked like a vagabond, he looked like he came off the back of a fairground ride, he looked like his father.

Edwina sits on a pile of curtains and stares at the combination lock on Charlie's trunk. If only she had some dynamite, she'd blow the bloody lid off.

Suddenly she is reminded of the job in hand. The idea is to de-clutter, not sit and wallow in the past. She brought a bin liner up with her, and must at least fill that.

Under the curtains is a stack of *National Geographic* magazines that Dickie bought on subscription. They can all go, so she fills the plastic sack with *National Geographic*s until the seams split and they all tumble back out. She'd found one of these under Lucas's bed once, an edition filled with pictures of topless Maori girls danc-ing. Poor boy, stuck away for weeks on end without seeing any girls of his own age. No wonder he relied on magazines to fill in the blanks.

Charlie, on the other hand, had girls on tap. Not only did all Rowena's friends get silly at the sight of him, but it seemed he was a bit of a hit with the girls at Glennings too. Edwina remembers getting a phone call from the same deputy head who had shown her around the premises just a few months earlier, telling her she needed to remind Charlie of the legal minimum-age requirement for sexual relations, be they in or out of the school.

'That's what comes from having rabbits on the premises,' Dickie had huffed. 'Gives the children ideas.'

Edwina had written to Charlie, telling him in no uncertain terms that he needed to be careful, and that just because he might be ready for sexual experimentation, the girl in question might not be.

He wrote back in his barely legible scrawl, 'Don't panic, she's on the pill!' Which really wasn't the point.

Rowena lagged a long way behind Charlie in that respect. She was academically gifted and very focused on her studies; from the age of fourteen there was talk of her going to Oxford.

'Be funny if she and Lucas ended up at the same college, although in my day, of course, ladies weren't admitted,' remarked Dickie. Lucas was bound for his old college; of course there would be exam-inations and interviews, but really they were mere formalities.

Sometimes one can be very wide of the mark, thinks Edwina,

turning her back on the chaos of the attic room and setting off to make herself a nice ham sandwich. If only all things could be as simple to solve as lunch.

Walking carefully down the stairs she realises with an absolute certainty that she cannot dump Charlie's trunk without opening it. The desire to find out what lies inside that locked box is suddenly overwhelming. Surely there will be something in there to help her understand, to give her a clue. But ham first, on soft white bread with a smidge of mustard.

18

Trinkets

Unable to face the attic again, Edwina decides to spend the afternoon sorting out the contents of the tallboy in her bedroom. Once upon a time this chest sailed over the sea from Ireland, a gift from Ollie's parents along with the soup tureens and the grandfather clock whose Victorian hands froze, as if in horror, the second it left Cork.

There is something horribly pathetic about the contents of her knicker drawer, all those washed-out pants and misshapen bras. She feels like putting a firelighter among the underwear and chucking a match in.

Obviously she won't, she's not stupid. These narrow Georgian houses with their wooden joists are death traps. If a fire broke out and she was stuck on one of the upper floors she'd have two choices: jump and die or stay and die.

Choke, burn or break?

Fire is just one of the things that kept her awake at night. What if the children played with matches in their beds? What if a dry sock somersaulted off the pulley-maid and ignited on the Aga? What if she accidentally left a smouldering cigarette in a precariously balanced ashtray on the arm of a combustible sofa? What if?

Odd, how much sleep you lose over the things that never

happen. Of course, now she doesn't smoke there's even less chance of an accidental blaze. She and Dickie gave up together about twenty years ago. He was getting breathless, needing a rest halfway up the stairs, coughing for twenty minutes every morning.

As soon as he gave up the cigarettes he piled on the pounds, a sudden and surprising barrel of fat appearing around his middle, so he was still breathless on the stairs, but at least he stopped coughing.

For a few years neither of them had a clue that it was too little too late, the damage had already been done. A group of sly cancerous cells had already gathered, a mutant cluster that hid undetected for years, a tiny defect waiting in the wings.

Ollie smoked like a chimney but died before his lungs turned to charcoal. It was his heart that had let him down, a faulty valve, a blocked tube, a tragedy waiting to happen. It could have happened at any time, but it happened on a beach on a beautiful day. It happened in the blink of an eye and the bark of a dog.

Ollie smoked roll-ups, a constant supply tucked behind his ear, hidden in the tangle of his black curls. It was a habit that Charlie adopted when he was about sixteen; it shocked her, the fact that even habits can be hereditary.

Not only did Charlie have his father's bitten fingernails and long piano-playing fingers, he chose the same brand of tobacco and licked his Rizlas with an identical slow movement of his tongue across the paper, left to right, right to left, his bony wrists a heartbreaking copy of his father's.

While the teenage Charlie grew daily more like his father, Lucas continued to take after his mother. Dark and portly, with a chronic sweet tooth and a tendency to turn to cake for solace.

Edwina recalls her stepson at his heftiest, fourteen years old and already over thirteen stone. Barbara was so upset she took him to a doctor on Harley Street.

Edwina was flabbergasted. 'Why don't you just encourage him to eat less and run around more?'

'You know he's asthmatic,' Dickie replied.

Personally Edwina didn't think Lucas was asthmatic; asthma was something that Barbara had inflicted upon Lucas as soon as his father left home. It was all part of her 'poor us' scenario, and for a while Lucas would arrive bearing inhalers and special instructions that he mustn't get too 'aeriated' in case he had a funny turn. '"Aeriated", I ask you. What kind of word is that for a boy to use? It's all about control: Barbara doesn't want a child, she wants a puppet. I'm surprised he's not tied to her by strings. Inhalers my foot.'

Lucas's medical paraphernalia intrigued Rowena and Charlie, and one weekend Charlie gave his stepbrother every penny of his pocket money just to have a go on his inhaler.

Edwina was incensed. Not only was the child being instructed by his mother to have a life-threatening condition, he was profiteering from it.

Dickie just laughed it off. 'At least it shows initiative and entrepreneurial flair. He's got bankers' blood, after all.'

Lucas's future had been sealed since he was about six, his destiny to be 'something in the City' like both of his grandfathers.

Nobody ever thought to ask Charlie why he felt the need to pay for something that was prescription-only. Perhaps we should have done, thinks Edwina. Maybe Charlie's behaviour revealed as much about him as Lucas's did.

Edwina's discarded knickers form a small pile in the middle of the floor, not even fit for dusters.

Her jewellery – what is left of it – is in the top right-hand drawer, tucked under an assortment of silk scarves and tiny useless ladies' hankies, lace-edged for no good reason.

She arrived here with very few trinkets, just a silver charm bracelet given to her by her mother when she was a child. Traditionally, Lydia sent a new charm to Edwina at boarding school to commemorate a birthday, or when 'Mummy and Daddy' had a new posting. It was a way of reminding her daughter where they were.

Edwina can visualise all the charms as if they were on her wrist right now: the little rickshaw; a Leaning Tower of Pisa; a single Siamese slipper, all curled up at the toe; a Spanish bull; and a tiny cat tucked up in a rubbish bin, which for some reason was her favourite.

'But it doesn't represent a country,' Rowena had argued. 'All the others make some kind of sense.'

'Oh I don't know, darling, maybe my mother was trying to apologise for being a rubbish mother. Maybe she identified with the cat, or maybe she just liked it. I've no idea what she was thinking; I didn't know her very well.'

'Does anyone really know anyone?' her daughter had responded solemnly. Rowena could be very cryptic at times.

Of course, when her mother died Edwina inherited all Lydia's pieces, along with her jewellery box, a large suede-lined red leather box from Asprey's that concertinaed out to reveal many different compartments, pockets and drawers.

Lydia left a lot of gaudy brooches and hat-pins with ornate finials, elaborate multi-beaded necklaces and a rather disturbing rope of garnets – nothing Edwina would ever choose to wear herself; it was all a bit 'last days of the Raj'. Most of it lay unused, necklaces coiled like glittering snakes, bangles tarnishing.

Ollie hadn't been able to afford much of an engagement ring, just a tiny solitaire that she wore on top of her skinny gold wedding band until Dickie came along and persuaded her that the rings reflected badly on him. What would people think?

And so they were replaced, with bigger, shinier, more expensive rings. The originals were buried in cotton wool and hidden in a felt pouch Rowena had made at prep school.

Over the following years her collection of baubles grew, from ugly seventies pendants chosen by the children to sparkling precious gems and silky pearls courtesy of Dickie.

No doubt, had their baby survived, she'd have been presented with a multi-diamond eternity ring. But it hadn't, so she didn't. Women don't get jewels for miscarriages.

She kept other precious things in her jewellery box: the only existing photograph of the four of them on Sennen beach; a lock of Ollie's hair in a matchbox; the children's baby teeth; and some dice she thought might be lucky.

She was wrong about the dice, because one summer afternoon forty-odd years ago, when Alicia had gone home and she'd been at the dentist, the house was burgled and everything that had carefully been put away in her bright red extendable jewellery box was stolen, including the box.

The only things Edwina really cared about losing were the tiny rings from her first marriage, her children's baby teeth, the lock of never-to-go-grey hair and the precious photograph. She still misses them.

The only consolation was that Rowena, in an uncharacteristic act of slyness, had 'borrowed' the charm bracelet and 'forgotten' to put it back, so that, at least, was spared.

The break-in had been a shock to them all. 'But just think how much worse it could have been, Mum. Thank goodness you had that dental appointment,' Charlie pointed out on the phone. She was surprised he knew; she couldn't remember telling him, but she must have done. How sweet he should take any notice of her comings and goings.

After all, he was at boarding school – both boys were – on the day of the robbery. She was having a crown fixed, Dickie was in his Westminster office and Rowena was stuck in the school examination hall, sweating over her history O level. Edwina can still recall a lot about Archduke Franz Ferdinand.

Alibis were important, considering there had been no sign of a forced entry. Inevitably the police, Lucas and Dickie pointed their collective fingers at Alicia, which was so bloody stupid Edwina can still feel the same bubble of hysteria she felt at the time.

Alicia was more honest than any of them, a point Edwina made very clear to Dickie, who some months previously had suggested their housekeeper pose as his 'personal secretary' so he could claim her wages against tax.

She patiently tried to explain to her husband that Alicia truly believed in God, and not only did she believe in God, she believed that God was watching her, every minute of every day. If she borrowed so much as a bar of soap from the airing cupboard without asking, God would strike her down in flames.

It wasn't Alicia who couldn't be trusted.

Looking back, it was unbelievable how gullible they had been. The truth was already staring them in the face, and a bitter wave of sickness washes over her heart once more.

Edwina is overwhelmed with tiredness. Her bed calls and she lies down for five minutes, rolling into the cradle of the mattress's dip.

19

Drawing

Edwina is wandering aimlessly around the house. She has already established that it's a Thursday, but for the life of her she cannot decide which job needs doing next.

Right now she is in her old studio, like a retired cabaret act returned to her dressing room to smell the greasepaint of her past. She perches on her old daybed and inhales the scent of turps and oils, and casts her eye over the work that adorns the walls. Very little is actually framed; once she'd decided that she was merely an illustrator rather than a proper painter, she decided she wasn't really worthy of frames.

I was rather hard on myself in that respect, she thinks, more impressed today with the talents of her younger self than she ever was at the time.

Maybe if I hadn't needed to earn a living I could have developed as a proper artist.

Sometimes she feels mildly pissed off that she wasn't taken more seriously. She'd still like to have a painting in the National Portrait Gallery, but who would she paint, other than herself?

'What a lonely old witch I am,' she mutters, picking up a soft drawing pencil and sticking it into the jaws of the ancient sharpener still firmly clamped to the corner of her desk. The smell of the shavings is instantly comforting.

She wishes there was more of Ollie's work, apart from the two big abstracts. He did some pen-and-ink drawings of her when she was pregnant with the twins; he couldn't capture the exact contours of her face, but her expression was spot on. She looked happy, her eyes full of trust and optimism for the future. No wonder that a couple of years later, full of fury and gin, she had ripped them up.

Who knows what either of them would have become, had Ollie lived.

Maybe she wouldn't have been so commercial. Her eye strays to some Betsy and Tom roughs from the last book, the enormously successful *Betsy and Tom's Happiest Christmas Ever*.

She'd attempted a rather experimental cover, a large glass Christmas-tree bauble in which Betsy and Tom and the whole family were reflected, but the publisher thought it 'rather odd', and could she stick to the children unwrapping presents under a nice tree, please.

The preliminary sketches for that cover are buried beneath layers of other ideas and inspirations pinned to the corkboard above the desk.

'The devil's in the detail,' she says, remembering how she collected scraps of festive wrapping paper and tangerine peel for inspiration, and how she personally nibbled Rudolph's carrot into just the right shape before including it in the scene.

It was the best work she'd ever done. She recalls obsessing over a painting of a Moses basket. It had taken her hours; after all, it was the last illustration in the book, a little wicker basket containing the best Christmas gift of all: a brand-new sister for Betsy and Tom. Baby Eve, so named because she was born on Christmas Eve.

A complete load of sentimental tosh, she concludes, but the book sold in its hundreds of thousands. It's what everyone wants, she realises, her bones threatening to fossilise where she sits. 'A happy ending,' and she heaves herself up before she gets too stiff.

There could have been more books, but unfortunately the writers of the Betsy and Tom series were a pair of raging alcoholics. Felix and Yvonne Trip brought the entire Betsy and Tom empire crashing down when Felix tried to run over his wife in their brand-new Bentley. The *Daily Mail* had a field day, and ran pictures of an inebriated Yvonne, complete with black eye, screaming at Felix in the driveway of their highly desirable Victorian villa in Barnes.

'THE TRUTH ABOUT BETSY AND TOM'S PARENTS' ran the somewhat hysterical headline, and the publishing company, which was known to have strong Christian values (hence the number of harvest festivals and church visits featured in the books), severed all ties with the Trips. As a result, for the first time in over fifteen years Edwina was out of work.

Sad, really. It was inconvenient for Edwina, but for the Trips it was the end. Yvonne died of cirrhosis of the liver before she was sixty and Felix, insane with grief, ran the Bentley into a wall. The big house in Barnes became an old people's home and an era ended.

Even if the Trips hadn't idiotically hastened the demise of the 'best-loved children's fictional characters', as voted at any number of publishing awards year after year, it would probably have happened anyway.

The eighties had dawned and children were changing, they were becoming more sophisticated. Betsy with her sewing basket and Tom with his biscuits and freckles were throwbacks to a more innocent age. The Love family didn't even have a telly, but Betsy and Tom didn't mind a jot because they preferred to make up their own games or go out to play instead!

No, Betsy and Tom had to stop. They didn't have a black friend between them. In fact, at one point they'd even owned a dog named Nigger, and once, when she'd attempted to feature a few ethnic faces in the school nativity play, she'd very politely been asked not to bother, as 'it doesn't appeal to our demographic'.

For some reason, instead of stripping down her studio with the unsentimental chuck-it mentality she has promised to adopt until the house is sold, she sharpens every single blunt pencil she can find, before returning them to their Habitat holder. They all stand proudly now, with their newly sharpened noses in the air.

The temptation is too much. Her hand automatically reaches for the drawer where her smaller sketch pads are stored and she takes one out, the clean white paper as tempting as newly washed sheets, and she starts to sketch. Tentatively at first, just random objects, an old pair of glasses with unfashionable frames and pre-cataract op lenses. She refuses herself the luxury of a rubber. 'Get it right the first time,' she can hear her old art teacher's voice. 'Drawing is a science. Look, and look again. Draw what you see, not what you think you see.'

Rowena tried but was never more than competent, and decided not to do art at O level because she wanted to concentrate on more academic subjects. Edwina was disappointed, but relieved as the decision meant no longer having to warily scrutinise her daughter's painstaking efforts, resisting the temptation to criticise. 'Just loosen up, darling. Try drawing with your left hand, give in to the picture.'

Lucas was actively dismissive of Edwina's career. 'I can't really see the point of colouring in,' he'd once told her. 'I mean, it's a fairly childish thing to do for a living, and you're not a young woman.' If he hadn't been a child she'd have kicked him.

But it was Charlie whose progress she watched most keenly, from the murky splotches on coloured sugar paper that he brought home from nursery to his later efforts at the choir school, where Edwina felt his style, though a little cartoony, showed promise. If only he could be bothered to develop it.

Of course at Glennings there was no formal art teaching, no conventional study of anatomy, although sometimes the children took all their clothes off and drew one another, naked and shaking with laughter.

But what the school lacked in discipline, it more than made up for in opportunity. Glennings had space and equipment, and, most importantly, offered the right to experiment. No one was ever told not to 'waste' paper or 'go easy on the glitter'.

Consequently, Charlie's work was confident and flamboyant. She just wasn't sure if it was any good. He seemed to be getting away with an arsenal of cheap tricks, like massive canvases sprayed with metallic car paint. Ultimately, he demonstrated very little skill but a great deal of show.

He got an A for his O level, and Edwina was delighted but slightly shocked. It was the only A he did get, and it gave him a direction. From then on, Charlie decided he was going to go to art school. After all, loads of pop stars went to art school: it was how you got to be in a band. Yes, he was going to be an artist, or a pop star. Probably both.

Edwina looks down at what she has drawn. It's a competent, if slightly tremulous, coloured-pencil sketch of the spectacles and surrounding flotsam and jetsam on her desk: an unidentified skull, possibly monkey, and the old-fashioned snow globe she always used as a paper weight for her receipts.

The snow globe is old, possibly from the thirties, a heavy glass orb on a ceramic base. Inside is a tiny Eiffel Tower. She shakes the globe and snow obliterates the Tower; a few seconds later all is still again. Like life, she supposes: just when things are all calm and settled and the future seems clear, along comes the blizzard that blinds you and knocks you off your feet.

'I never saw any of it coming.'

20

Dickie's Desk

Edwina wanders from the chaos of her studio into the relative order of the dining room. She closes the folding doors between the two rooms. How do you pack away an entire career?

I need to pare it down to the necessities, she decides, an easel, obviously, and a little stool, but she can't deal with it right now. She will hide in here for a while and gather her thoughts.

There will be paperwork to be done, she supposes, bored already by the thought of having to find the deeds to the house, proof this place actually belongs to her. Which it does: there are documents somewhere.

The first thing she needs to do is find the key to Dickie's desk.

Why are men so keen on keeping things locked, she wonders, her mind flitting back to the trunk in the attic. Maybe men are more secretive than women – but then she corrects herself. Everyone is secretive when they have something to hide; Rowena certainly was. When was it that she first suspected something was wrong? Possibly when her daughter was about fifteen, sitting at this very table. It suddenly dawned on her that her child no longer ate food normally. She smeared her plate and cut everything into minuscule squares and chewed and chewed and chewed. In reality, she was cheating: she might look like she was eating, but there was precious little swallowing going on.

That was the start of it. Then came the excuses not to join them at meal times, the lies about huge portions of school dinners eaten earlier, invented tales of post-school toast binges.

At first she'd tried to ignore it, hoping it was just a phase. Or perhaps Rowena genuinely wasn't very hungry. After all, she was studying very hard – it was her O-level year. The boys were away at school and maybe she was bored of eating alone with two adults. Maybe the formality of the dining room put her off. Maybe if they ate more casually downstairs in the kitchen. Maybe if Dickie didn't expect meals all the time, proper meals with plates warmed in the oven and the table set properly.

Dickie loved his food. He was always slightly disappointed by a kitchen supper: for Dickie, an omelette simply didn't constitute a proper evening meal. He liked the ritual of the dining room, an aperitif beforehand and Edwina wearing something other than her painting smock, asking him about his day.

There were times when she wondered if he would like her to actually dress up, like Penelope Keith's character in *The Good Life*.

Barbara used to. Barbara made an effort, but then Barbara had sod all else to do apart from think about food and clothes. No wonder the poor cow was so utterly barmy. Apparently she used to diet too. 'Most women do,' Dickie told her. 'I shouldn't worry about Rowena, it's entirely normal.'

But her uniform was hanging off her; she was obviously losing a great deal of weight. Edwina recalls a nagging sense of fear, but Dickie kept reassuring her. He said a lot of girls went through funny eating phases. In fact, Barbara's goddaughter Elise had been sent home from boarding school because she stopped eating and had developed something called 'anorexia nervosa', but she was fine now, as far as he knew. He often had a chat with her father in the House. Terribly nice fellow, Paul Landreth.

She'd stopped listening then. Everything always came back to the House. 'What about *this* house?' she felt like screaming. 'What about the things that are going on under this very roof? I don't care about Elise bloody Landreth. What about the fact that your son loathes me and my daughter no longer eats like a human being, she squirrels food away in her room and regurgitates her meals into the lavatory. What about that?

I heard her, Edwina admits, I heard her throwing up and Alicia found napkins full of putrefying food tucked behind the radiators in Rowena's bedroom, evidence of chocolate binges, empty laxative packets.

Alicia had immediately alerted Edwina to these upsetting finds and Edwina had rung Rowena's school, which resulted in distressing meetings with therapists and doctors, Rowena looking ashen-faced and caught out. 'It seemed to be the only thing I could control,' she told her mother and Edwina held her daughter and they both cried. Her back was like a xylophone and they all congratulated themselves on nipping the problem in the bud.

Only she never really fully recovered. She never cleaned her plate or had seconds, she never ate pudding unless she was drunk, and the look of guilt on her face when she was caught eating cheese was desperate. Rowena rejected food whenever she was upset or stressed, unlike Lucas, who turned immediately to the biscuit tin for comfort.

How lovely it would be, thinks Edwina, to have one last meal here. If I could make everything perfect for everyone, if I could set the table with all these glorious old pieces of china and light lots of candles and dress the table with ivy and roses and we could all be together, like other families do. I could paint place names like I did when the children were small, and once again she is struck by how much this house needs a family. This room deserves to smell a big bowl of buttered Jersey Royals again, it needs chocolate cake crumbs on the floor and the after-dinner reek of old port and Stilton, candle wax dripping onto the tablecloth.

Of course, the key to the desk is in the candlestick to the left of the mantelpiece, it always has been. How could she possibly have forgotten? If she finds some of the paperwork she needs, then she will have achieved something today.

Everything creaks as she stands, the table and herself groaning in unison as if sympathising with each other. 'I know, awful isn't it?' she tells the table. Jesus, I'm talking to furniture now. What stage of madness is this?

The key is small and deeply tarnished. Probably brass, it hangs on a frayed piece of red ribbon and turns stiffly in the keyhole, allowing the lid of the desk to fall open. Fortunately the same key opens all three drawers, but she will start here, where Dickie refilled his fountain pen from a bottle of tar-black ink, solemnly drew a cheque book from the requisite compartment and paid the household bills, the biggest expenses being Barbara and the school fees.

Not that he paid for Rowena or Charlie: she paid for her own children's education, thank you very much. But, oddly enough, Dickie didn't like the schools to know that this was the case.

It wasn't the done thing. Wives and mothers didn't pay school fees, they sat on committees, helped out at charity drives and raised funds for poor children in Africa. They donated money and cakes and prizes for the Christmas tombola, but they didn't actually pay the fees.

They argued a great deal over it, but she was insistent, transferring funds from her bank account across into his every term.

The reason had been quite simple: she never wanted Rowena or Charlie to feel beholden to their stepfather. She hoped they'd be glad he stepped into their dead father's shoes and provided their mother with some much-needed company and a social life again (no one likes widows), but she didn't want them to be grateful to him for their schooling.

Whether they passed exams or not had to be up to them. She didn't ever want to hear Dickie say, 'After all that money, what a waste.' Not about her children: if they squandered their education it had to be her money they wasted.

Dickie had very high academic expectations, especially for his son. He genuinely thought Lucas was a chip off the old block. After all, they were both Wyeburnians, with the same ingrained sense of entitlement, taught by men in black gowns and mortar boards. They were used to coming out on top; failure wasn't really an option. You don't pay good money to fail.

It's hard to see our children for what they are, Edwina thinks. We treat them like precious baubles, to us they shine brighter than any other bauble and so we handle them with care, terrified they might break.

Dickie had a lot of guilt when it came to Lucas. He knew the divorce had affected him badly, then there was his weight issue, the fictional asthma, the stutter (mercifully fleeting), and so he made up for his guilt by being Lucas's number-two fan, after his mother.

It seemed to Edwina that Lucas's parents competed to see who could inflate their son's ego the most. 'One day that lad will burst,' she thought privately.

There had been times, often during Sunday lunches in this very room when Lucas had been pompously holding forth with some half-baked theory about immigration or the unions, when Edwina had been tempted to interrupt. 'Oh shut up, you spoilt brat. You know nothing about anything, so pipe down and eat your carrots.'

But maybe they all were all spoilt; she certainly indulged Charlie. It was only Rowena who was somehow immune to praise, who rolled her eyes when her mother said she looked gorgeous, who was unflinching in facing up to her own shortcomings. Unlike Lucas, whose ego constantly needed stroking.

'He's less confident than you might imagine,' explained his father, and Edwina hoped it was true. Perhaps the insufferable conceitedness was just an act, and behind the self-important façade was just another young man unsure of how to wear his own skin.

Edwina closes the desk lid and opens the top drawer. The first thing she sees is a buff-coloured folder entitled 'Lucas: school reports'.

Academically the boy struggled even to be average, and his father couldn't understand why his efforts didn't rate more highly with the school. According to Lucas, there was always an excuse: favouritism prevented him from getting into any sporting A team; bad luck in tests affected his marks; undiagnosed glandular fever resulted in disappointing O-level results.

'How do you know he's had glandular fever?' she asked Dickie.

'Because these results show every indication of something not being right. A C for history? He can't have been well,' replied Dickie, puzzling once again over his son's disappointing grades.

She could have been honest, she could have simply said, 'Maybe he didn't work hard enough.'

But she didn't. Dickie and Lucas were both big sulkers.

After the O-level debacle Dickie decided not to take any chances and paid for Lucas to have extra tuition in the holidays. After all, it was vital that his grades improved enough for Wye-bourne to enter him for the Oxford examination.

So Dickie sat at this desk and wrote out more cheques in his lovely black-ink handwriting, cheques to pay for a nervy young man with a double first from Balliol to cram Lucas's head with information during every holiday.

Unfortunately for Dickie, Lucas connived to spend most of his holidays in Chelsea, where Barbara was always cutting his study time short in order to take her 'handsome prince' to lunch.

The rejection letter Lucas eventually received from Oxford is buried away in one of these drawers, unless his father ritualistically burnt it.

She recalls Dickie demanding to see physical proof of the news, because for a moment after Lucas told him he thought his son was joking. He'd played a similar trick some months earlier, when he'd pretended he'd failed his driving test.

But it wasn't a joke. After all the effort and expense Lucas had failed to get in to his father's old college, and Dickie retired to bed for the weekend with yet another migraine.

He got another bad head a year later, when his stepdaughter was offered a place at Hertford. How could Rowena triumph and Lucas fail?

'Oh Rowena,' and suddenly the desire to stroke her daughter's head and bury her face in her neck is almost too much to bear.

I have been wrong, Edwina concludes. I have been so very wrong and I am running out of time to put things right. Before she can change her mind, her hand reaches for a stash of blue airmail letters addressed to both her and Dickie, letters she has never replied to. She just hopes she's not too late.

21

The Valuation

It might be the following Monday; Edwina is not sure. Ever since she decided to sell the house the days of the week and the hours of the clock have lost all consistency. She spends so much time thinking about the past it's sometimes a shock to find herself in the present.

She is down in the basement drinking coffee in which the milk may or may not be off. It's on the cusp, concludes Edwina, drinking it anyway.

The boy has come round to show her the photographs of the house that they intend to put on the estate agent's website.

Lee (yes, that's his name, though she may have called him Lenny on the doorstep) is pulling a face at the cup of tea she gives him. The milk floats on top of the brown liquid in cheesy lumps. It's definitely off.

'I thought you might want to have a look,' he says, proffering an iPad. 'You just swipe with your finger.'

Oh does she, indeed? Sometimes she swipes too hard and the picture disappears, and he has to start her up again. She can feel his patience wearing thinner than filo pastry, but he remains encouraging.

'You should get one of these,' he tells her and she fights off a yawn so vast she can hear the back of her head creaking under the strain of it.

What's really impressive is how grand they have made her house look. Of course it's all clever camera angles and close-ups of the Georgian period detail. You can't see that the stairs are all skewed and the plasterwork is cracked; they have played with light and shadows, concentrated on the subtle colours of the marble fireplaces, the intricate cornicing and the original oak shutters.

Edwina scans the blurb that accompanies the photos and is slightly taken aback to see her house described as 'This grand old lady of Kennington, sitting elegantly on one of Southwark's premier Georgian terraces, is ideal for the West End and transport links to the City. Don't miss a rare opportunity to purchase a faded four-bedroomed beauty in need of some TLC.'

Aren't we all, muses Edwina, drinking her funny-tasting coffee, but it is the price that knocks the breath from her chest. Two million pounds; her falling-down old South London house is worth two million pounds?

She asks him if there has been some sort of mistake, and at first he thinks she is insulted by the estimate. 'You haven't got a garage or off-street parking,' he stammers.

'I haven't got a helicopter launch pad on the roof either. Two million pounds! It beggars belief.'

How ridiculous to be so wealthy when one is too old to care.

She decides not to think about the money. The other day she found the name of a solicitor in Dickie's desk upstairs, a grown-up who can help with this sort of thing. She forgets for a second that she herself is very much a grown-up. Yes, but not that kind of grown-up, she argues back.

The boy looks uncomfortable; she must have been moving her lips. That's the trouble with being slightly deaf: you can't always hear when you're talking to yourself.

She signs the papers that he pushes across the kitchen table, with a pen he has already removed the lid from.

He seems pleased. 'We'll be booking viewings from next week – I'll keep you posted. Don't get up, I'll see myself out.'

She is slightly dizzy; all this is quite overwhelming. I could buy a boat, she thinks. Ollie always wanted a boat.

'Goodbye, dear.' She's forgotten his name again. Really he should wear a badge like they do in the Tesco Express over the road, which reminds her . . .

Milk, she needs milk. She should write a list. She is still holding the pen that the boy lent her, a biro, she should write a shopping list. Edwina finds a piece of paper and begins to write.

My dear Alicia,

I hope this finds you well and your corns are neatly cut and your bunions are not giving you too much trouble. As for the diet, there's no point. The last thing you want to lose is that splendid bottom of yours. I remember how it used to take up half a Tube carriage.

Anyway, the point is, I'm selling the house. She has to go to a good new owner, someone who can keep her under control. She's like a big dog, Alicia, I can't cope with her any more. I wish you were here to help me, I am finding it difficult to throw anything away. I counted eleven plastic things that you use to fill the iron up with water the other day, I couldn't decide which one to keep so I've kept them all.

I think I might go and live in Cornwall. I'd like to die with a paintbrush in my hand, painting the sea on a blue-sky day. I find little bits of you all over the place, Alicia. I'm writing this in the kitchen and I can see your hands covered in flour, I see you bibbing up the babies, I hear you singing and I can smell the sweet potato that you went all the way to Brixton to fetch, and I remember the babies' faces when they first tasted mango. This house wouldn't be mine if it hadn't been for you.

I will write again soon.

Milk, jelly, jam.

But then she remembers Alicia is dead, she died last year. She was going to go to the funeral, but by the time she managed to get a new passport it was too late. She mustn't keep doing that, she mustn't keep leaving things until it's too late. There is someone else she needs to write to, someone she needs to beg for forgiveness, and she will, she will say sorry. But not now. She is so tired.

Edwina falls asleep on the sofa and dreams of making cakes for the twins' birthday party. They are three years old and Ollie is there. Even in her dream she knows he is dead, but she thinks that if she keeps quiet he might be able to stay. Together they help the children open their presents, a plastic container to fill a steam iron with water, some biros and a mango.

The children are laughing but Rowena won't eat the birthday cake. She lifts up her T-shirt and she is all bone, white and brittle as a cuttlefish. Ollie looks at her, horrified, and she knows she has lost him. Ollie has gone for good again.

Edwina wakes up with tears running down her face. Even dreaming of the twins' birthdays makes her emotional; she could never sing 'Happy birthday dear Rowena and Charlie' without getting choked up. She can see their faces shining in the glow of birthday candles, cheeks puffed out, ready to blow. Alicia in the background mixing jugs of orange squash, piles of sandwiches, the games they organised. One year she made a treasure map with clues that led the party guests all around the house and garden. Everyone came dressed as pirates and Alicia made a cake in the shape of a treasure chest.

Seven, they would have been seven, big crooked adult teeth breaking into their sweet baby faces. All their school friends, girls with silk-ribboned bunches, tow-headed boys running and shouting, wrestling each other, showing off, girls screaming.

The twins' birthday parties were always big news because they were on such a grand scale. Edwina and Alicia were determined to make up for the fact they didn't have a dad. She recalls the life-size cardboard donkey she made for pin the tail on the donkey, the elaborately wrapped pass the parcel; she can see her hand hovering over the record player, ready to lift the needle – quick, quick, up, count to ten and then down it went again – 'We all live in a yellow submarine', that was their favourite. The going-home presents, a slice of cake in a paper napkin, a pencil with a rubber troll on the end, a balloon.

The relief when it was all over.

'Goodbye, thank you for having me.' The mothers and sometimes fathers arriving to take their children away, the looks of curiosity as they hovered in her hallway. Who is this woman with the dead husband and dark-haired twins? Look at the black housekeeper. Some say she's an artist.

Between them she and Alicia did everything. If only Alicia had been better with a camera, but she was hopeless, and so Edwina had to take over Leica duties. Consequently, in all the birthday-party snaps the twins appear to be both fatherless and motherless.

There were a couple of years when they insisted on separate parties; after all, they weren't born on the same day. Edwina remembers a tense weekend spent hosting Rowena's girls-only pottery-painting party, followed the next day by Charlie's swimming and fish and chips bash.

By the time Dickie officially came on the scene the parties were calming down. Rowena had become a great deal more selective, preferring to take a small group of friends out for a sophisticated treat – tea at the Ritz, a matinée, dinner in the revolving restaurant at the top of the Post Office Tower – while Charlie opted for cinema trips and pizza.

As for Lucas, Barbara insisted on hosting his birthday celebrations, and the twins were never once invited to River Walk.

His twenty-first was particularly fraught. Obviously she, Edwina, wasn't asked, but Dickie had to show his face; he was the boy's father, after all. There was protocol to observe, a silver and black invitation had been RSVP'd.

Dinner at Claridge's, followed by dancing in a West End discothèque.

Rowena and Charlie weren't invited either, not that they would have gone. Rowena was too busy with university and Charlie wouldn't have wasted the coach fare down from art school in Manchester. Anyway, it was a black tie do and Charlie didn't own a black tie, unless you counted his narrow leather one.

She decided to rise above it. She painted her stepson an innocuous landscape and reminded the twins to send cards. Typically, Rowena did and Charlie didn't.

Dickie eventually arrived home from the party at three in the morning. He came upstairs with a whisky and a cigar, very much the worse for wear and slurring incoherently about the party.

Apparently all the old gang were there, all his ex-wife's chums from her finishing school and her old bridesmaids, Minty and June. 'Old and a bit fat,' chortled Dickie, 'but still just about recognisable. Of course, Minty married Paul Landreth.' He hiccupped, balancing on the edge of the bed. 'My chum at the House. He was there, and the daughter, Elise. Quite a looker, if you like them wild.'

He was struggling to take his socks off, but he kept gabbling on about how slim Lucas looked in his dinner jacket, and how many people from Warwick University had turned up and what a fun crowd they all were. Meanwhile Edwina lay in bed soberly biting her lip and thinking, if he tries to have sex with me I might kill him.

Eventually Dickie fell snoring into a pyjama-top-less slumber. She ensured his cigar was properly extinguished by dropping it into the remnants of his whisky.

Edwina's memory of that night is vivid; she can almost smell the cigar in the Glenfiddich. It was the calm before the storm.

They were approaching a good time in their lives. The children were nearly grown: they just had to get the twins to twenty-one and then she and Dickie could really think about the future.

Their plan was that Dickie would retire early with a decent-enough pension for frequent trips to France and Italy. She would take commissions for portraits, and possibly have sittings in the house. Middle age would suit them; they would go to the theatre, visit art galleries and museums. She saw them clearly in her mind's eye, wearing straw hats in the sun. Their future was all creamy Brie, carafes of wine and dips in the Mediterranean.

How wrong she was, how wrong. Fate tripped them up. Just when she thought they were all home and dry, suddenly the world tipped upside-down and they all got lost in the snow.

22

Edwina Remembers

It happened less than a year later. Nothing could have prepared them, the run up to the disaster was so smooth, a gentle take-off before the turbulence hit.

March 1981. She is allowed to remember the nice bit; this is the scene she plays in her head when insomnia and anxiety dance around her bedroom.

Mid-March and the twins are turning twenty-one, twenty-one years on the planet and they are coming home for the weekend. A Sunday-lunch feast is being prepared and even Lucas is coming, a proper slap-up family celebration.

Alicia made a chocolate cake and Edwina got out all the best china. The air was scented with a pot of blue and white hyacinths. 'My favourite smell on earth,' mutters Edwina.

The photographs from that day are in the cupboard of the Welsh dresser, stripped of their frames, demoted from the tops of desks and mantelpieces. They ask too many questions. 'The boy on the right, he doesn't look like the other two. Gosh, the girl is thin, and who is the other boy? Who is the boy with the dark gypsy eyes, and why is he wearing a woman's necklace?'

Dickie's voice: 'Charlie, are you experimenting with queerness?'

A snigger from Lucas, a sigh of irritation from Rowena.

As for Charlie, he simply touches the necklace and grins, and in that moment Edwina's heart feels easy. He is happy, he is in love.

Rowena came home first. After all, it was her actual birthday on the Saturday. She took the coach from Oxford and arrived in time for lunch. She was much better, but she still had rules about food: she ate painfully slowly, shredding a butterless ham sandwich into tiny crumbs before swallowing them between endless sips of water. Her eating was oddly ritualistic and Edwina knew from experience not to watch, so she busied herself with other things, wiping surfaces, silver-polishing the candlesticks, popping in and out of the garden, anything rather than watch her daughter swallow.

She arranged forsythia in the newly gleaming candlesticks. Dickie was in Twickenham for the rugby; it was glorious to spend time alone with her daughter and so much easier to talk about Oxford in Dickie's absence.

Rowena had found her niche at university. For the first time she wasn't the only freak in the class, finally there were other young women who cared more about reading than shoes, and while it was a relief that Rowena was happy, Edwina still wished she'd make more of herself. She'd arrived home wearing a hideous jumper that looked like knitted porridge, and did nothing for her sallow skin.

Rowena was a very quiet beauty, her mother decided. If only she would cut her hair: a nice jaw-length bob would make all the difference, bring out her features, but instead she insisted on hiding her face behind two lank curtains of rattish-coloured hair. Charlie had obviously stolen all the genetic curl, but a few inches off would give it so much more bounce. It was all Edwina could do not to start snipping at it with the kitchen scissors.

She knew better than to pry about men. Rowena was very private about her friendships, and when Edwina vaguely broached the subject she batted her off, laughing that the only man she was interested in was Chaucer.

She talked vaguely about friends who lived on her staircase, the plays she'd seen and the Thursday evening art class she attended, 'Just to keep my hand in.' Edwina allowed herself a small flicker of both pride and relief: here was her clever grown-up daughter, more or less recovered from her eating disorder, with hobbies and everything. Now, if she'd just put a bit of lipstick on . . .

Charlie arrived home around five, smelling like he'd swallowed a distillery, laughing and hugging his 'girls'. As skinny as his twin, he dived straight for the biscuit tin. Custard cream in one hand, roll-up in the other, handsome Charlie holding court, patting his mother on the head, teasing his sister, taking his shirt off so his mother could wash it, fading bruises on his ribs.

He disappeared later, had a bath and slipped out, a casual wave and off. 'Where are you going?' But the front door had already banged shut.

That evening she and Rowena iced the cake that Alicia had made and Edwina tried not to mind that Rowena took not a single lick of the sticky chocolate icing. Not from the knife, the bowl or even from her finger.

Dickie came home, pink-cheeked from the March wind, and there was a stilted conversation about how it could be possible for Rowena not to know anyone who rowed at Oxford.

'But everyone I knew rowed,' spluttered Dickie.

'Well, my friends don't,' his stepdaughter replied and they congregated around the television for a light scrambled-egg supper on their knees. 'We're having a big lunch tomorrow,' said Edwina, excusing herself for not being able to face two shifts of domesticity over the weekend.

Dickie looked over his paper to inform Edwina that Lucas had been in touch, to say he would be there by twelve-thirty.

'I hope Charlie's back by then,' Rowena muttered darkly.

Edwina slept fitfully. Eventually, at two, she heard Charlie slowly mounting the stairs, struggling with every step as if he were climbing Everest. At last her children were all safely home, and with relief she was able to surrender herself to the darkness.

In the morning there was a flurry of card-opening and gift-unwrapping. In typical unselfish fashion, Rowena had insisted on waiting so they could celebrate both birthdays together.

Edwina noticed that Charlie drank the entire contents of a carton of orange juice without bothering to use a glass, but he didn't seem too much the worse for wear and she was grateful for that.

The twins seemed genuinely delighted with their gifts. Dickie had bought them new-fangled cameras and Edwina had commissioned a jeweller friend to make silver cufflinks for Charlie and matching earrings for Edwina. One cufflink and one earring were inscribed with Rowena's birthdate, the other with Charlie's. Put together, they each had a set of their mismatched birth dates: 14.03.60 and 15.03.60.

Lucas arrived promptly at half past twelve, with neither card nor gift but bearing a good bottle of vintage champagne, freshly chilled from his mother's fridge. Edwina was surprised Barbara hadn't somehow managed to smash the bottle, but she kept her trap shut. We're all adults now, she reminded herself.

In the absence of Alicia, who had a nephew's christening that weekend, Edwina was left to her own devices in the kitchen. But, with the help of handwritten instructions from Alicia and Rowena on vegetable duty (making sure no butter went anywhere near them), she eventually delivered a feast to her beautifully set dining-room table, daffodils bursting with hope from a blue glass vase in the middle.

Spring lamb, Charlie's favourite, with mint sauce, gravy, new potatoes, peas, cauliflower and carrots, and plenty of butter in a dish on the side. The twins' freshly starched napkins were carefully rolled in their freshly shone silver christening rings, and the moment they noticed was the moment her heart silently screamed out for their father.

It was lovely. Rowena made a Herculean effort to eat normally, Charlie kept his ashtray off the table until cake time and Lucas was only moderately prickish. He'd grown a beard, which really did nothing for him, and seemed full of plans to take over the Bank of England.

Charlie didn't give much away, but he wolfed his food down and praised every mouthful, saying it was even better than his flatmate Rob's roast. He told them that Rob had learnt to cook because it was the only way he could get women to sleep with him.

They all laughed a great deal that day.

After lunch, Dickie insisted that commemorative photographs were taken, and directed the three children into various poses. Edwina wanted to ask why Lucas was in the pictures when it was the twins' birthday, but she played nicely and even took some Polaroids with one of the new cameras.

She was secretly rather miffed that Dickie's gift idea had gone down such a storm. Charlie in particular was over the moon with his magical instant camera, beaming as he watched image after image materialise in front of him.

'Of course Polaroid film is very expensive for a student,' remarked Lucas, who was revelling in the fact that, at the age of twenty-two, he had both a job and a car. No girlfriend, though, thought Edwina sourly.

And then all of a sudden it was over. Charlie made a dash for the train station and Rowena followed not long after, she had an essay to finish. Dickie and Lucas disappeared upstairs to talk about the boring things they talked about and Edwina was left sitting amongst the debris of the dining-room table, holding a Polaroid of her two children.

Edwina pulls herself sharply back into reality. The Polaroid has long since faded, the colours muted to limp pastel shades, the outlines blurred, but in her head she can still see the freckles on their faces. Rowena and Charlie, spying at her through the silver hoops of their christening rings. Charlie is wearing his cufflinks and Rowena has her earrings on.

14.03.60 and 15.03.60.

Of course: why hadn't she ever thought of it before? It's like staring at a crossword clue for days before the answer suddenly hits you in the face.

Edwina climbs to the top of the house. She is going on an adventure, she is going to explore Charlie's trunk. She has realised what the combination will be: the only other set of numbers that Charlie would ever commit to memory, apart from the date, month and year of his own birth, are those of his sister's. After all these years, it's suddenly so obvious.

Edwina upturns an old laundry basket and sits eyeing the battered leather trunk in front of her. There will be secrets in that box, and possibly things she doesn't want to know, but there might also be treasure, or at least clues to why things ended up like they did.

She is reminded of the treasure-chest birthday cake Alicia made all those years ago, how no one had wanted to cut into it, but in the end they had to.

The combination lock is rusty. In her cardigan pocket is a stick of lip salve; she rubs the stick over the lock and works the grease into the mechanics. There are four numbers to crack. She tries 1-4-0-3 but it doesn't budge, so then she tries 1-4-6-0 and as she rotates the last cog into its final position there is an instant feeling of release. The shackle springs away from the body of the lock. She's done it.

But after so many years the trunk is still resistant to being opened. Fleetingly she thinks of Tutankhamun's tomb: could prising the trunk open bring her even more bad luck? Dismissing her silly, old-lady-ish superstition she pulls at the lid, easing each corner up millimetre by millimetre, feebly tugging and pulling and pulling and tugging until the top of the trunk surrenders. Edwina pulls the lid wide open and finally the contents of the trunk are revealed.

For a moment she fears everything may have turned to dust, but as she blows away what looks like a thick layer of grey fur the first thing she is reunited with is Charlie's art school portfolio, an over-sized vinyl zip envelope. She tugs at the zip and it glides around the case with peculiar ease. Edwina holds her breath, he wouldn't let her see his work, he was secretive about it and she backed away gratefully, worried she might think it dreadful.

The case falls open to reveal a picture of a girl, red chalk on grey paper. This drawing must be over thirty years old. Whoever it is will be well into her fifties by now. The pose is a classic life-drawing exercise; she is naked, she is beautiful, there is something about her, something she recognises. Who is she, and where has Edwina seen her before?

FERN

1

October 1980

Eighteen-year-old Fern Woolbright – red-haired, alabaster-skinned – shivers in a bra and knicker set purchased some months ago, at great expense, from the Janet Reger lingerie boutique in Guildford.

Oyster satin with a shell-pink lace trim, 34B bra and matching size ten cami-knickers. Up until this evening, the only male who has ever seen her in this get-up is her boyfriend, but now she is preparing to expose herself to a mixed class of twenty grubby-looking art students. She is entirely covered in goose-bumps.

They have put a screen up for her, a battered wooden affair behind which is a plastic chair and a feeble two-bar electric heater. 'Come on then, let's be having you.' The art teacher is a woman in her fifties with cropped grey hair, like a Schnauzer recently returned from the dog groomer's.

Fern covers herself up with her dressing gown. It's quilted and slightly childish, but warm and all-encompassing. She ties the belt, breathes in and steps out.

'Okay, Fern, is it?' barks the dog woman.

Fern nods, head down. 'Let's get you into position.' Ms Schnauzer points to the middle of the room where a lonely wooden stool is entirely surrounded by a battalion of paint-splattered easels. Fern weaves her way through. This is it. Oh God, what would Daddy say?

She drops her dressing gown as nonchalantly as possible and holds her stomach in. She has spent the last week drinking only low-calorie Cup-a-Soups and eating oranges in preparation for this moment.

'Very pretty I'm sure, dear, but our models don't wear bras and knickers. This isn't some sort of soft-porn shoot for a kinky magazine, this is bone and muscle, this is knickers off and tits out.'

Rather than walk back behind the screen, Fern switches into actress mode, divorcing herself from the reality of a tittering audience. She elegantly but casually peels off her deluxe underwear, stuffs both bra and knickers into the pocket of her dressing gown and stands awaiting further instruction.

She is eighteen, naked and beautiful. Her fiery ginger bush proves that not a hair on her head has been chemically treated.

If only her stomach wasn't churning like one of the ancient washing machines in the coin-operated launderette that she uses every Sunday. But, unfortunately, her soup and citrus diet has caused havoc with her digestive system, and in between the deep breathing of the students and the strokes of charcoal sweeping across paper, the entire room can hear the irate grumblings of a ravenous belly.

Halfway through the session she has a break, at which point a cup of tea is placed behind the screen with a plain digestive biscuit balanced in the saucer. She eats the biscuit in an attempt to calm her stomach, and fifteen minutes later she is repositioned like a marionette, this time on a filthy red velvet chaise longue.

'Very Lizzie Siddal,' growls the dog woman, who then proceeds to reel off a number of pertinent facts about the Titian-haired Victorian muse. 'Born 1829, modelled for Millais and Rossetti, died young, of course. A combination of pneumonia brought on by lying in a cold bath while Millais created his famous *Ophelia*; anorexia, because girls have been stupid about food from the year dot; and an addiction both to laudanum and to Fowler's Solution, a nineteenth-century acne cure made from dilute arsenic. Siddal went from muse to painter and poet herself, although ill health and lack of confidence curtailed her promise.'

I haven't got acne, fumes Fern silently, furious that she should be likened to some spotty, ginger Victorian nutcase.

However, she composes her face into an expression of tragic curtailed potential, which she feels is in keeping with the suffering of this Siddal woman.

'Looks a bit constipated,' comments the tutor as she passes by one of the front-row easels. The entire class hoots and Fern feels herself blush. She is an extraordinary blusher: as soon as she feels it creeping around her hairline she tries her utmost to stop it from spreading, but to no avail – she is as powerless as a chameleon sitting on a cerise-coloured cushion. The dreaded pink stain travels down her face, across her chest and further still, until she feels the very tips of her toes flush crimson.

She is sure she hears someone mutter 'blimey', as if she's just pulled off an impressive magic trick. Fuck, she no longer feels lovely or tragic, she feels uncomfortable and crampy and cold. She also feels like she might be building up for a fart. Imagine if that happened, if she actually let off in front of all these people. Forget arsenic, she would quite simply die of shame.

Fortunately the rest of the session passes without major incident, and when it is finally over, despite having pins and needles in both feet, she manages to retreat behind the screen without falling over.

The dog woman thrusts a couple of grubby fivers at her. 'You'd be quite good if you could loosen up a bit. Maybe come back when you've lived a little – you're a lovely girl, but a bit marble, if you get my drift?'

'Not really,' she responds.

'Cold, stiff, a bit dead, if you like. We like our models rather more lived-in, droopy tits, bellies, hammer toes, that sort of thing. Perfection is all very well, dear, but it's a teensy bit boring.'

Fern begins to blush again, this time with temper. She'd like to screw up the limp five-pound notes and throw them into the bitch woman's hairy face, but she quite fancies buying herself a nice bottle of wine on the way home.

So she adopts an expression of blank disinterest. 'I didn't really enjoy it that much. I was a bit bored, and the quality of the work, as far as I could see, was rather poor.'

The dog woman barks a laugh into Fern's face. 'Go on then, hop it.'

Burning with fury and embarrassment, Fern marches out of the art faculty building and on to the main road. It is raining, it is always raining in this fucking city. It really is the most awful shit hole.

Fern has been living in Manchester for a fortnight. She is meant to be ecstatically happy. After all, the first part of her dream has come true: she has a place at drama school.

Sometimes at night, when she can't sleep for loneliness and homesickness, she still goes through her audition speeches. Lady M from the Scottish play, the bit about killing the baby: 'I would, while it was smiling in my face, Have pluck'd my nipple from its boneless gums'. She'd been a bit embarrassed about saying the word 'nipple', but in the end had decided to really attack it, so much so that she kind of shouted it and the rest of the speech lost some of its rhythm. She blushes at the memory.

Her song had been from *Sweet Charity*. She has a good voice and she'd performed it well, even risked a few moves – nothing full-on, just enough to make the men on the panel sit up a bit. It was her character piece that had let her down; she just wasn't very funny, and the Northern accent she'd decided to do came across as ridiculous up here in Manchester.

As soon as she'd begun one of the other girls auditioning had rolled her eyes and laughed at her behind her hand. Nasty fat cow. They'd been made to perform in front of one another; she hadn't expected that, maybe none of them had. It was nerve-shredding, a day of wet palms and dry mouths.

Oddly enough, from that hideous day of auditions the only person Fern recognises among her fellow first years is the sniggering fat girl. The adjudicating panel must have seen beyond her thunder thighs and utter butchering of 'Send in the Clowns'. Apparently she's a 'Geordie', whatever that means, and her name is Jill Miller.

The letter of acceptance came after the rejection from RADA, which still smarts because that's where she'd really wanted to go.

In fact, given the chance, she'd swap schools in a heartbeat. Manchester is so frightfully wet and cold and full of people who look like they've walked out of a Lowry painting, all skinny dogs and bent old men smoking. Fern has never seen so many people smoking, apart from that time she went on a school trip to Barcelona, of course.

Finally a bus rounds the corner with a number Fern recognises as stopping near where she lives, and she jumps aboard, taking a seat on the top deck behind two women with rollered hair tucked under cheap chiffon scarves.

My mother would rather shoot herself than go out looking like that, thinks Fern. Rosemarie Woolbright gets her hair done once a week in a salon in Godalming unless she's visiting her sister Minty in London, in which case she goes to Vidal Sassoon.

Mummy had been a little bit disappointed. 'Manchester's so far away, darling, and it's only got one shop. What if I wrote a letter to RADA, explaining that you want to be in London so that you can live with Elise?'

Her cousin is studying fashion at St Martin's; she is a bit older and wears all sorts of strange things. 'Gone a bit punky,' as Fern's mother would say.

Fern's own wardrobe strays more towards Laura Ashley and

Princess Diana than black bin-liners, although since becoming a student she has become more experimental. Last week she bought a pair of Doc Marten boots and a denim jacket. Her mother would be horrified.

The bus rumbles south of the city; it's impossible to tell precisely where they are due to the heavy condensation on the windows and the thick yellow fug of tobacco.

It's probably warmer on this bus than it will be at home.

Fern slightly dreads getting back to the flat. At the moment she is sharing the attic of a crumbling red-brick corner house in the heart of Didsbury.

Her flatmates are Felicity, a large furry-chinned ginger lesbian, and Felicity's minute girlfriend Dee, a woman who could pass for eight at a distance, but at close quarters turns out to be pushing thirty.

Both Felicity and Fern are at drama school; Felicity is in the third year. Fern has no idea what Dee does, apart from stay at home, henna her hair and read tarot cards. Fern has a feeling Dee shouldn't be there, it's a two-bedroom flat and the tiny one pays no rent (nor does she buy milk or lavatory paper). Fern suspects Felicity hides her when the landlord makes one of his surprise visits, quickly tucking her up in a drawer or shoving her under a pile of coats.

Fern isn't meant to be in the flat either. She was meant to have a room in a nice hall of residence on the well-lit campus some miles away, but due to an administrative error she has ended up in a woefully dilapidated Victorian dump with no central heating.

Rosemarie isn't at all happy with the change of address. 'Top floor, darling. Is there a fire escape?' There isn't, but there is plenty of damp.

Quite often Dee is poorly and stays in bed. Fern has noticed that Felicity likes it when Dee is ill; it means she can look after her. Really, thinks Fern, she should just get a dog.

But dogs aren't allowed, or cats for that matter either, and the middle-floor bathroom shared with the old couple downstairs is full of unmentionable stains and other people's pubic hair. No one cleans it properly. If only Mummy's little treasure Mrs Bibby could pop up once a week and leave the place smelling of Ajax and lily of the valley.

Fern misses her pony Bruno and the dogs, Pippin and Smudge. Sometimes she is so lonely and cold and uncomfortable that she cries herself to sleep. The other night, to take her mind off how lonely she felt, she tried masturbating, really tried, but it didn't work. She just ended up feeling frustrated, with a rather sore vagina.

2

Back at the Flat

Fern is slightly lost. She eventually gets off the bus two stops after the one nearest the flat and walks back via the off-licence. Sod it, she's going to get some chips too. Fern has never really bothered with chips before; Mummy doesn't really approve of them – 'They're terribly greasy, darling, and we don't want spots' – but up here the takeaway chips have been a delicious revelation, although she cannot for the life of her understand Felicity's penchant for curry sauce.

Felicity and Dee are culinary savages. They are also terrible thieves: if Fern buys anything nice, like Brie or pâté, Dee and Felicity will maul at it with their filthy fingers, and Fern has a horrible feeling that neither are particularly conscientious about washing their hands after going to the lavatory. Her flatmates' standards of hygiene are generally suspect. Just the other night she caught Dee pissing in the kitchen sink because the bathroom was occupied.

Mrs Bibby would pass out at the very thought.

Holding a portion of newspaper-wrapped chips in one hand, and with the bottle of red wine tucked under her arm, Fern turns the key into the blistered front door of number 2, Old Lansdowne Road. This is the first time I've lived in a house which is just a number and not a name, she realises, adding, I'd call it the shit pit – if I had to name it anything at all.

The carpet on the stairs smells and there is always a tide of circulars and official-looking letters behind the door. Light bulbs dangle bare of shades, and the wall next to the payphone is scribbled all over with random names and numbers.

Up in the attic flat, Fern is relieved to find that Felicity and Dee are out. She grabs a corkscrew, rescues the remains of her pâté from the fridge and retires to her bedroom.

Five minutes later, with her rain-soaked jeans drying over a chair in front of a kerosene heater, Fern is in bed, contentedly swigging from a bottle of Fitou and smearing flabby white chips with pâté while a cigarette burns in the ashtray on her bedside table.

She's still at a loss as to what to put on the walls of this oddly shaped room. Who is she anyway, what does she like? That's what you're here to find out, she tells herself, dismissing the temptation to adorn the walls with photographs of Bruno. After all, she's not a boarder at Tillinghurst Girls' now.

It's all so dingy, a mix of grubby magnolia paint and mismatched dark-brown post-war furniture. The only splash of colour in her bedroom is the lovely paisley duvet cover she brought from home. Maybe if she bought some flowers and arranged them nicely in a vase it would brighten the place up. But then Felicity and Dee would probably say something snide and she'd feel uncomfortable and embarrassed, like she does most of the time anyway.

Fern is finding it hard to let go. She has been called 'uptight' by one teacher and 'as stiff as a broom handle' by the dance tutor, a vile unshaven man in stained tracksuit bottoms and a stinking vest with massive dark sweat patches under the arms.

That's why she signed up to do the life modelling, to prove to herself as much as to anyone else that she's not just some Home Counties ninny. Only most of the time that is exactly how she feels. There have been so many moments over the last couple of weeks when she's been tempted to pack it all in and go home to Three Paddocks, admit to her parents that she's got it wrong, and could she please swap her drama course for the Robert Carrier cookery course at Hintlesham Hall in Suffolk, where she can learn to make meringues and not worry about trying to be someone she clearly can't be.

There is a lot of humiliation in learning to be an actress, Fern has discovered, and she spends a great deal of time trying not to cry. Sometimes she hides in one of the horrible smelly old wood-wormy cubicles in the girls' lavatories, locks the door and just sits there inhaling the scarf that she sprays every morning with Anaïs Anaïs, a scent she loves so passionately that if she finds Felicity so much as looking at it she will kill her.

But it's the accusation of not being able to dance that stings Fern the most. The bloody cheek of it: she has a collection of ballet, jazz and tap medals at home. The teacher is obviously a con-genital idiot, despite the consensus among her peers that he is the most exciting and innovative of all the tutors.

At the beginning of term he told her she moved 'like a virgin', and demonstrated what he meant by doing a stupid, tight-bottomed walk across the studio. Everyone fell about laughing, so obviously she'd pretended to laugh too, but she was so upset that instead of eating any lunch she smoked five Dunhills and drank a pint of cider in the pub across the road. That afternoon she'd almost thrown up into her fencing mask.

Anyway, she isn't a virgin. She has had intercourse – or, as everyone else says, 'fucked'. In fact, she has fucked two men already and she won't be nineteen until next August.

Her first lover was the brother of her French exchange student Véronique, a sallow, dull girl whose sibling turned out to have stolen all the family personality. Henri was delightful and she learnt a great deal more colloquial French in his tiny single bed than she ever did either at school or with the monosyllabic Véronique.

Sadly, despite this vital extra tuition she still only scraped a D at A level.

Then there was James, her sort of official boyfriend who, presuming she was a virgin, had been as gentle as he possibly could be in a small Alfa Romeo.

Afterwards he kept saying, 'I hope I didn't hurt you.' And she was glad it was dark so he couldn't see the disappointment on her face. She had no idea that men came in different sizes; Henri was like some kind of elephant compared to James, whose penis matched his tiny rodent-like kisses.

James is in the army; he's an officer, which is completely different from being a soldier because it means you don't hang about train stations in fatigues reeking to high heaven and drinking cans of beer.

James is all mess jackets and polished shoes. Last month he had to escort Princess Margaret at a function; apparently she kept needing her cigarettes lighting. James has a solid gold Cartier lighter, a twenty-first birthday gift from his grandparents.

James has got everything: breeding, looks, money. 'What more could a girl want?' her mother asks.

When James comes to pick up Fern from Three Paddocks her mother goes really pink and laughs at every single thing he says, while her father gets up and rocks backwards and forwards on his heels, and offers him 'a snifter'.

James tells her she is special and beautiful, and quite possibly highly talented, but he also warns her that he doesn't like going to the theatre as he's more of a rugby man, so he'll only come and see her on stage if she has a really good juicy part and not just a walk-on. He also says he wouldn't like her to do any kind of work that involved 'revealing herself'.

James is tall and handsome and brave and strong, even if he

does kiss like a hamster. Not that I've ever kissed a hamster, thinks Fern before she dozes off and dreams of Jill, the fat Northern girl, revealing her massive double-F charms to James, who lights a cigarette with his Cartier lighter and accidentally ignites his face. Behind the leaping flames his right eyeball melts like chocolate down his cheek.

3

Pâté Stains

Fern feels a bit rough; she isn't used to drinking entire bottles of wine all by herself. It was a slightly piggy thing to do and there are only four cigarettes left in her crimson Dunhill packet. The brimming ashtray on her bedside table is testament to last night's fag binge. What's even more disgusting are the dubious-looking pâté stains on her bed sheets. It looks like she might have pooed the bed in the night – what would Mrs Bibby think? She'd have a conniption.

Oh well, she rapidly seems to be acquiring all the skills a drama student requires. In just a few short weeks she has ticked off stripping, drinking, smoking and toying with an eating disorder. With any luck, first-hand knowledge of such experiences will give her the necessary tools for her chosen profession.

For a moment she feels reckless and punkish. She is also late and will have to leave the house without breakfast. Her mother would be aghast: 'There's always time, darling, even if it's just half a grapefruit and a boiled egg.'

Fern's stomach churns at the mere thought of an egg. She pulls on a black V-neck sweater and a pair of sixties black stretch ski pants complete with elasticated stirrups that she found just the other day in a second-hand shop.

'But you've got perfectly good salopettes.' Her mother's voice again. 'Why would you bother with those silly things?'

Quickly she sprays her armpits with Anaïs Anaïs, pushes her feet into her Docs and makes her way down the stairs with her laces trailing.

'I didn't recognise you with your clothes on.'

A man in the hall, a man in a donkey jacket, an unshaven man slouching in the door-frame of the ground-floor front room.

Fern jumps, just like she did that time she was walking through the woods behind school with Effie Hunter, the diplomat's daughter, and a man appeared from behind a tree with his willy out. Effie had started running and screaming before Fern had actually seen the thing. Typical Effie.

'Charlie,' the man says, taking a crumpled roll-up from behind his ear. He isn't a man, he is a boy: a tall, black-haired boy, a boy wearing eyeliner, 'a Jessie', her father would say. Pencil-thin legs in skin-tight black jeans, pointed black shoes all scuffed at the toe, red laces, a tartan shirt. He looks half-asleep; he smells slightly sour, unwashed.

'I was in the class last night. I've got a picture of you, and I'm going to put it in my attic and you will never get old.'

Fern did A Picture of Dorian Gray for English A level, so she understands the reference. How thrilling.

A girl appears from the bedroom behind him, ducking under his arm. A dark-skinned girl with matted, back-combed hair dyed jet black and bruised-looking lips. Pausing only long enough to throw Fern a filthy look, she marches to the front door, opens it and slams it behind her.

'Uh-oh,' says Charlie, 'that'll be the Spanish blood boiling over. I tell you, it's like going out with a coffee percolator. Mad bitch.' And, untangling a bike from the collection in the hall, he asks, 'I don't suppose you know whose this is, do you?' indicating the bike.

'Obviously not yours.' She means the retort to be spiky and

funny but she sounds like a fifty-year-old magistrate – she knows she does, because she sounds like her mother's friend Brenda, who is exactly that, a fifty-year-old magistrate.

'So hang me,' he laughs, and wheels the borrowed bike down the steps and cycles off after his bad-tempered girlfriend. He doesn't even bother to shut the door.

'What a cunt!' bellows another voice from the back of the hallway. 'I swear Charlie Treadaway is the most selfish arsehole I have ever had the misfortune to meet. He really is a complete prick. I'm Rob, by the way. Whatever you do, don't sleep with him.'

This boy Rob is Charlie's polar opposite: fair-haired, thickset, a rugby type, hairy of arm, bearded.

'I won't,' laughs Fern. 'I've got a boyfriend anyway.'

A boyfriend who still goes to the barber's for a short back and sides, a boyfriend who wouldn't dream of stealing another fellow's bike, a boyfriend who doesn't pull bedraggled rollies from behind his ear like some kind of shambolic conjuror. I've got a perfectly nice, perfectly dull boyfriend.

Insists the voice in her head.

'Oh, and I'm Fern,' she adds out loud. It's nice to be able to attach names to these neighbours at last. In Godalming, they'd have knocked on her door and asked her over for a sherry.

Fern walks to college; she has a horrible feeling that if she gets on a bus she might possibly vomit. As it is, she feels weak and has to concentrate hard just to put one foot in front of the other.

At the Barlow Moor Road traffic lights another set of Doc Marten boots falls into step with hers. It's that dreadful Jill girl, sniggering fat Jill.

'What-ho, Fern?' the girl trills in a ridiculously posh accent.

Fern was going to snap back with an equally snide Geordie 'Alooo djull', but as soon as she opens her mouth sick sprays out. 'Ergh,' Jill bleats, jumping back, but it's too late, there is puke on her Doc Martens. There is puke everywhere. Once Fern starts she can't stop: she pukes onto her own boots, into a litter bin and then, shamed by the disgust of a nearby bus queue, she staggers into a convenient front garden and throws up onto a rockery.

'Blimey,' breathes Jill, 'that's one 'eck of a lot of sick.'

'Urgh,' spews Fern.

Eventually the sick stops and Fern gets up off her grass-stained knees and splutters, 'I wonder if you would mind most awfully telling college that I won't be coming in today. I seem to have contracted some kind of bug, or possibly food poisoning.'

'Better than being up the duff,' remarks Jill cheerfully. 'Yeah, I'll tell them.'

Fern emits one last dribble of pâté and red wine vomit onto the driveway of a stranger's house, then begins to drag herself weakly back in the direction she has come from. For a good hundred yards she has a horrible feeling that she can hear Jill laughing.

Twenty minutes later she is back in bed shivering, nauseous but simultaneously oddly ravenous. Staggering into the kitchen she realises that her own food supplies are dangerously low. There is a packet of smoked mackerel – 'So lovely with horseradish, darling, for a nice healthy supper' – a head of celery and a green pepper. Hanging out of its waxy wrapper on the draining board is a loaf of thick white sliced bread, and on further inspection of the fridge there is a packet of butter and a jar of raspberry jam, not home-made, just the cheap pink stuff that Dee likes. Fern can't help it, she slathers four slices of bread with a thick layer of yellow grease and piles jam on top, squishing the slices together. She takes her doorstop jam sandwiches back to bed.

'Darling, it would look so much daintier if you cut the crusts off,' instructs her mother all the way from Godalming.

'Oh fuck off, Mummy!' snaps Fern.

Well, this is a turn-up for the books: she only left home a fortnight ago and already she is telling her mother to fuck off (albeit from the comparatively safe distance of two hundred miles), taking all her clothes off in public, getting so pissed she throws up and misses college and now, to top it all, she has stolen her flatmates' food.

Good – they are most welcome to her mackerel, celery and pepper in return. And, feeling a great deal more human, just enormously tired, Fern curls further down under her duvet and falls soundly asleep.

Waking up two hours later desperate for a pee, she peeks over the banisters on her way to the bathroom, wondering if there is anyone down there. The yellow bike that Charlie rode off on hasn't returned, but the postman has been. Mail is scattered on the filthy lino behind the front door. Hanging over the rail on the top floor, she recognises the creamy rectangle of her mother's personalised stationery. Inside the envelope will be a page of writing paper with a specially commissioned pen-and-ink drawing of Three Paddocks in the top right-hand corner, beneath which, in perfect copperplate, their address and phone number is printed.

A wave of homesickness engulfs her and she runs down in her bra and pants to fetch the letter. Halfway down the stairs the front door opens and Charlie wheels the yellow bike through the door.

'Don't you ever wear any clothes?'

Behind him the terrifying Spanish girl scowls and jabbers in her mother tongue. Fern turns tail and runs back up to the attic.

'This is ridiculous,' she mutters, reaching for her dressing gown and hovering on her own landing until the coast is clear. She gives it ten minutes, ten minutes of dithering before she darts down to the ground floor, snatches up the letter and flies back to the safety of her top-floor eyrie.

Her mother's familiar handwriting tugs at her throat. Every week when she was at boarding school her mother would write and every Sunday night she'd write back. Her mother has kept all her letters; they're in a special box. She is so loved, she is so lucky, she has the perfect home life. Her mother even makes her own jam, proper strawberry jam with strawberries she picks from the garden.

Fern rips open the envelope. Her mother's violet-blue handwriting is smudged and blotched across the page.

Darling Fern,

I am crying as I write this, but I thought you should know: darling Smudge had to be put down yesterday. Our dear little doggie friend was so brave, but in the end there was nothing else we could do. We shall bury him with Tinker and Bun under the weeping willow. I'm so sorry, darling, I know you loved him very much.

At six the payphone on the middle landing starts ringing and Rugby Rob, who must share the ground-floor flat with Charlie, answers it on the third trill. 'A Captain James Frobisher for a Miss Fern Woolbright,' he yells, and Fern, pink-eyed in her dressing gown, takes the receiver from his meaty fist and collapses onto the mangy carpet to cry some more.

James is direct and to the point:

'Darling, your father phoned and told me the bad news. I'm so terribly sorry: he was a super little dog. Anyway, I thought I'd give you a call and make sure you're okay. Listen, if you can make it I'm going to be back in Surrey in a couple of weeks. What do you think about making it back south? We could pay our respects to old Smudge. Now, no more tears: we don't want your lovely face getting all swollen and blotchy.'

James doesn't like her crying. They once went to the cinema and she cried so much at *Kramer vs. Kramer* he refused to take her for a drink afterwards because she looked so unattractive.

Fern is reminded of this when she eventually hangs up the phone and checks her reflection in the mirror on the landing. She looks like she has been hit in the face by a football while suffering from measles.

As she collapses back into bed her last thought before she goes back to sleep is that at least Charlie didn't see her looking like this.

4

The Dead-Doggie Card

Dear Mummy and Daddy,

I hope you and the doggies are well. I still can't get over the idea that I won't see my darling Smudge again, but having his collar here in Manchester is a great comfort and I sleep with it under my pillow.

Actually, a couple of times she has worn it around her neck. That sort of thing is terribly fashionable these days.

Things are getting better for Fern. She is toughening up, her eyeliner is becoming noticeably thicker and she is now able to apply a Debbie Harry smoky eye in under two minutes. Sometimes she back-combs and sprays her hair into a great big orange cloud.

She is a striking girl; even the tutor who said she moved 'like a virgin' has noticed the difference. 'Someone's been at the forbidden fruit,' he whispered into her ear as she was leaving his class, and just for a moment his hand seemed to cup her buttock, the left one! How very peculiar. She didn't think teachers were allowed to do that.

Some years ago there was a male teacher at her friend Victoria's brother's school who used to 'help' boys over the wooden horse in gym, until one of the first years blew the whistle and all hell broke loose. The teacher's body was found hanging in a wood some months later. 'Bloody pervert,' Fern's father had blustered. 'I'd have had his guts for garters.'

She has been home for the weekend, which was lovely because she ate such yummy food, with lots of scrummy veg from the garden. Mummy made her favourite bread and butter pudding, but wouldn't let her have seconds because 'We don't want to get fat.'

And of course it was really super to see James, who was home on leave and staying with his parents because it was their pearl wedding anniversary, which thrilled Mummy because, as she said, 'it's very reassuring when people come from a stable background'. Daddy had mumbled 'bodes well for the future' from behind the *Telegraph*.

It was just a bit strange being at James's parents' wedding anniversary party, which turned out to be an oddly subdued affair in a country house hotel with a golf course attached. The pheasant was delicious, but Fern was horribly aware that she was under intense scrutiny.

James's grandmother in particular stared at her so hard she could have bored a hole through Fern's frock. No doubt the old lady was inspecting Fern's womb with her ancient X-ray eyes, checking to see if her ovaries were healthy and plump with eggs.

She was careful not to guzzle her wine, because, as James said, too much wine made her cheeks go purple. 'I like my English rose creamy not vermilion,' he told her, and made sure her water glass was full at all times.

James's older brother, a weaker-chinned version of James with thinning hair, was there with his wife Amanda, who was only twenty-three, and pregnant, so she couldn't drink anything.

'Apparently,' Amanda told Fern, 'recent medical studies suggest that alcohol can lead to foetal abnormalities', and she didn't want to risk the baby being ugly or stupid.

Fern got rather stuck with Amanda, and by nine o'clock she was bored out of her head, which was a shame, considering that Elise had invited her to a party at her flat in London.

Typical: rather than raving it up in Pimlico she was stuck in a hotel miles from anywhere, surrounded by cranberry-faced men talking about golf, and fat women in hideous taffeta dresses that resembled giant Quality Street wrappers.

James gave her a lift home, but they only had time for a quick snog because he needed to get back to ferry his grandmother home.

He still kissed like a rabbit; at one point, when he poked his tongue tentatively into her mouth, she was tempted to bite it, feeling at that precise moment an overwhelming desire to taste blood.

When she got indoors Fern went straight to her parents' walnut and brass filigree drinks cabinet and took a big swig from every single bottle of alcohol that she could lay her hands on, from cherry brandy to amaretto via whisky and gin, swig after swig. It was only after a rather too large gulp of amontillado sherry that she felt drunk enough to go to bed.

She didn't go to church in the morning, which meant Mummy and Daddy were a little frosty at lunch, but even so they had delicious roast beef, but no Yorkshire pudding 'because the extra calories aren't necessary, darling', and then suddenly it was all over.

She had to catch three trains back north, but at least Daddy gave her enough money for a cab from Piccadilly station back to Didsbury. Even so, she didn't get in until almost midnight!

Manchester really is a million miles from Godalming, but oddly enough, even though the inky-skied north-west was, typically, teeming with icy rain, it was a relief to be back.

Fern has decided that, apart from the bore of using a coin-operated launderette and not having a daily little treasure to tidy up after her, she rather likes living away from home. She likes doing what she wants, when she likes, smoking in bed and eating a packet of biscuits instead of a nice balanced meal. She likes the way that people at drama school have rumbled that she is posh, but really know nothing whatsoever about her. She is a stranger here; she is free.

But the best thing about returning from the weekend in Godalming was finding the picture. A picture, painted on a torn piece of brown cardboard and shoved under her door while she was away visiting her parents.

On the front is a hand-drawn picture of dogs, lots of dogs, all in dog heaven. The dogs have angel wings and halos, and they are all shapes and sizes. None looks particularly like Smudge; even so, it made her cry, but only in a controlled, single tear sliding down the nose kind of way, which looked great in the mirror.

Whoever made the card didn't sign it, they just scrawled 'all the dead doggies having a laugh' on the back in really bad handwriting.

She can't imagine either of her flatmates made it. Anyway, she's seen various notes they've left for each other and the writing doesn't match. Could it be from Rob? He'd handed her the phone when James called about Smudge, so he knows how upset she was, but she seems to recall he is studying engineering, and in any case his hands are too pudgy to have created this. It is beautiful, her best thing ever.

The truth is, she wants more than anything for Charlie to have made it, for the smelly, curly-haired, black-eyed boy to be the one who cares enough to draw her a lovely picture of all kinds of different dead dogs.

She keeps the card in her underwear drawer, under her best bra and knickers and the plastic box containing a diaphragm, which she recently had fitted at a women's health centre here in Manchester. Just in case.

After all, it was impossible to fix up any contraception back in Surrey. The family GP plays squash with her father and some of her mother's friends volunteer at the family-planning clinic in Godalming, so far safer to attend a clinic up here.

The nurse who helped fit her with the diaphragm told her to practise inserting it now and then, so she didn't 'lose the knack', but she can't bring herself to even look at it. It is here for emergencies, should James ever visit, which he has promised he will. 'Before Christmas.'

Until then, it nestles in the top drawer among her underwear, the blue velvet case containing a string of pearls left to her by her dead maternal grandmother and her new most treasured possession, prettier than the diaphragm and more precious than the pearls: the dead-doggie card.

5

Learning

Fern is feeling quite pleased with herself. She has finally had it out with Felicity and Dee about touching her things, an argument that escalated so quickly Dee started hyperventilating and had to breathe deeply into a brown paper bag.

'You're a selfish, spoilt psychobitch,' yelled Felicity, her freckles radiating fury.

'And you're a light-fingered, fat, ugly cow,' Fern retaliated. The row ended in tears and whisky, followed by apologies and hugs.

In some respects it has cleared the air, and the three girls are getting on a great deal better. In fact, twice recently they have shared meals: Dee and Felicity made a communal dish of brown rice, tinned tomatoes and broccoli with grated cheese on top, which was disgusting but nonetheless well-meaning, and in return Fern conjured up a goulash with possibly a bit too much paprika. Dee sneezed a great deal and her eyes streamed throughout the entire the meal, which she ate with a roll of toilet paper standing on snot sentry by her plate.

For pudding she presented her flatmates with an apple Charlotte accompanied by proper home-made custard. The only thing

Felicity complained about was the custard; she much preferred it out of a tin.

Things are improving at college too. She's been cast as the piano-playing Masha in Chekhov's *Three Sisters*, an accolade marred only by the director's decision to base the play in Brontë country, thus requiring the sisters to speak in a broad Yorkshire accent.

'Dammit and buggeration,' fumed Fern.

Typical: for once in her life she gets a nice juicy part that will showcase her Grade 4 piano skills, not to mention how brilliant her hair looks in a bun, and it's all spoilt by setting it in the stupid North. Oh well, the production is still two weeks away. She can't worry about it all the time.

Socially, now that she is on better terms with Felicity and Dee the three of them occasionally venture to The Railway round the corner, a minute Victorian jewellery box of a pub with red velvet banquettes and shiny brass fittings. A massive specimen jar of pickled eggs takes pride of place by the till. 'I didn't think pickled eggs were actually a real thing – I thought they were like unicorns,' blinks Fern.

Quite frequently meaty Rob from downstairs joins them, and now and then Charlie will turn up, which makes Fern's heart beat faster than a basket of kittens. Sometimes he is with Fabiana, sometimes he's alone, a roll-up hanging off his lip, his thin, tremulous hands raking through his curls. Now and then he walks in, has a look around to see if there's anyone worth staying for and walks straight out again. If he stays he drinks red wine, and Fern immediately wishes she wasn't drinking lager and lime; she'd like to be drinking red wine with Charlie.

'He's in a band, you know? Charlie and some of his art school mates,' Rob informs them, rolling his eyes. 'A sort of punk choir. Sounds awful: they sing hymns but punk them up. Some of them are sung in Latin, I believe.'

Rob is comforting and bearish. He wears rugby shirts and buys bags of crisps, which he tears open for everyone to share. 'He fancies you something rotten,' whispers tiny Dee one Sunday night as Rob went dutifully off to the bar to get a round in.

'Don't be silly,' laughs Fern, but inside she is thinking, of course he does.

'I'd love to see you in this play,' says Rob, sloshing lager onto the table. 'Can you put me down for a couple of tickets?'

James has mentioned he may come too. Sometimes, when Fern thinks about the production, she feels like she has a massive pickled egg stuck in her neck and can barely swallow. Her mother is definitely coming; she phoned Fern to inform her of her plans: 'I was going to bring Minty or June, but June is having a gallstone removed and Minty has a Tory Party function to attend. Poor Minty, she's worried sick about Elise: apparently she's burning the candle at both ends and rumour has it she ended up in hospital the other week, having her stomach pumped, but keep it under your hat. Anyway, darling, poor Daddy can't come because he's got a do on at the club. I was thinking of staying in a hotel after the show, unless you've got a spare room?'

'No, I haven't got a spare room,' says Fern, relieved that her mother needn't see the squalor of number 2 Old Lansdowne Road. She really wouldn't understand the bikes in the hall: 'Why can't they go in a garage or an outhouse, darling, and by the way, where have all the lampshades gone?' Rosemarie's voice is still very loud in Fern's head.

Northern Jill is playing one of the other sisters. She's very happy to be doing it in a Yorkshire accent, although she is constantly being reminded to make her performance smaller. 'It's not a cartoon,' their choreographer and director repeats, absent-mindedly stroking Fern's waist.

He is worried about her accent. Jill offers to coach her, but, 'I think you should work on learning your lines,' the director snaps waspishly. Jill has a horrible propensity to ad lib when she forgets her words. The other day, instead of 'Moscow' she said, 'We must go back to Macclesfield.'

The director asks Fern to stay behind after rehearsal; he needs 'a word'. Fern blushes before the others have even left the room.

Left alone, he criticises her and she cries. He cajoles and she cries some more, then he takes her into his arms and strokes her back, his hand slides under her shirt, he undoes her bra with such ease it's as if it were his own, and he caresses her breasts. 'She is a beautiful girl, the most beautiful girl in the school.' He walks over to the rehearsal room door and locks it, he turns off some of the lights and, as he strolls back to her, his penis is poking at his flies as if it is a small animal making a bid for escape.

She is shocked but strangely passive. He pulls her down on to a rubber exercise mat that smells of feet and they kneel facing each other. He kisses her rigorously, his tongue soft but firm. He's better than James and it all feels quite harmless until he places something clammy in her hand.

It's like that game Mummy used to organise at her birthday parties, the one where everyone was blindfolded and Mummy told a ghost story with chicken bones for dead men's fingers and, right at the end of the story, you put your finger in a cup of jelly and screamed and screamed because it felt like you were poking a dead man's eye.

Only this isn't an eye full of jelly, or a chicken finger bone, it is her tutor's penis, or his cock, as people call them these days. He is pushing her head down: 'Suck it,' he instructs, and so she does. I might as well learn, she tells herself. Funny how blowjobs require absolutely no blowing whatsoever.

She is wearing darling Smudge's dog collar, and he loops his fingers under it to guide the motion of her head. Up and down she bobs while he thrusts himself further and further into her throat. When the liquid comes it is thicker and warmer than she expects and she swallows it because she doesn't know what else to do with it, and anyway, spitting is one of Mummy's pet hates.

'Good girl,' he coos, and he licks away the residue of his semen from around her mouth like a dog. 'Very good girl. Now, let's keep this between you and me – we don't want the other girls getting jealous and accusing you of flirting with me just to get better parts. We don't want anyone thinking I've got favourites, you promise? Because you must remember, Fern, it's very important that I'm fair to all my students.'

And, true to his word, he's been off-hand and cold with her ever since. Yesterday he threw down his script when she forgot a cue line, but then at the end of the rehearsal he gathered them all around him, all Chekhov's sisters, and told them he'd decided the Yorkshire thing wasn't really working, and that he'd decided to revert to RP.

Fern went quite pink with pleasure; she knew he'd done it in exchange for the blowjob. Sex, she is realising, can be a very powerful thing, and she wonders whether the next time she sees James he would like her to suck him off.

Anyway, today it is Jill's turn to be kept back after rehearsal; she is struggling with her Received Pronunciation. 'I could help her,' offers Fern.

'I think you should keep your big posh nose out of it,' the tutor snaps.

Fern blushes violently, her face instantly the colour of the cheap jam that Dee likes, and she leaves the rehearsal room with Olya (a mousy little thing called Sandra) and Natasha (Louise, a pleasant Scottish girl).

Five minutes later, realising she's forgotten her script, she returns, only to discover that the door to the rehearsal room is locked and yet some of the lights are still on.

Oh well, she's offered to make a lasagne for the girls tonight. 'What, from scratch?' Dee marvelled. 'Not a Findus one?'

It is only as she is paying for half a pound of mince in the Co-op that it dawns on her that Jill might be getting the same sort of personal tuition she'd been on the receiving end of just three days ago.

The trouble with men, Fern decides, is that just when you think you might be in control, just when you think you might have the upper hand, you find you don't. It's 1980 and they still hold all the power. Fern flushes, but this time with fury, and she stomps home from the supermarket mentally making a pact that she will never do anything so stupid ever again.

6

First Night

Fern is genuinely contemplating running away. The dress rehearsal was frightful, two torturous hours of petticoats trapped in doors and peeling false beards. The handle fell off the samovar, the Baron tripped over his cane and the piano is so out of tune Fern's supposedly atmospheric introduction to the play sounded like a comedy sketch. It was a mess, a skin-crawling, scalp-itching mess.

'That's a sign of good luck, of course,' rallies Jill. 'Crappy dress rehearsal means tonight will be ace.'

Ever since Fern found the rehearsal door locked last week, she has been desperate to find out whether Jill went down on Mr Tate, or Dave Tate, as their director prefers to be known: 'I'm like your mate, not just a tutor. Call me Dave, Dave Tate.'

She has given no outward sign of it, and as for Dave, well, Mr Tate has been equally dismissive of them both, so who knows. Maybe he *was* just helping her with her received pronunciation.

If so, it really hasn't worked. Jill still sounds like she is serving chips on a Northern seafront, which is apparently what she used to do.

'That's why a'hve to werk me arse off,' she confided in Fern. 'I don't want t'go back t' fish scraps 'n' pissin' vinegar.'

Given the choice, thinks Fern, apart from serving chips in Redcar, which sounds like some extreme circle of hell ('Maggots in t'fish like yerve never seen'), I'd rather be doing anything else than sitting here preparing to go on stage.

I hate it, I hate this place, Fern is fuming now. I hate Dave Tate. I'd like to go home and train to be a florist. I'd like my own flower shop, that's what I'd like, and every day would smell beautiful.

Real life, by contrast, reeks of stale sweat. All the female leads are sharing a dressing room and mousy Sandra, who plays the oldest Prozorova sister, doesn't believe in using deodorant or shaving her underarms.

It's a good job her dress has sleeves, thinks Fern. My mother might pass out at the sight of a lady exposing her underarm hair! She wouldn't believe it; she'd think she was keeping a gerbil under each armpit.

Fern's hands are shaking so much she can barely pin her hair into a bun, a bun which she has been practising putting into place on a much more regular basis than her diaphragm.

Frantically she stabs at it with pins, there, it's almost done. A few stray tendrils frame her face, it's a good look. Now, if only her hands could stop shaking enough to get her make-up right.

They are all going for matching pale faces with Aunt-Sallyish pink-spotted cheeks and purple lipstick. The idea is to create an illusion of uniformity, as if they really could be sisters – a highly unlikely scenario considering their accents are still careering up and down the M4.

She left her mother's tickets and a couple for Rob at the box office, which consists of a canteen table in the narrow hallway outside the studio theatre. Fern is momentarily embarrassed. If only this place was a bit smarter, if only it didn't smell so badly of meat pie. Her mother will find the lavatories traumatic: it's only been in the last couple of weeks that Fern has given up hovering three inches above the woodworm-riddled seats. Sometimes a girl's just got to sit down.

A musical third year student has been called on to deal with the piano, but there's been no time to sound check it before the show. If it hasn't been sorted the whole night will turn into a Les Dawson farce.

Fern feels like an alien has taken over her body. The real Fern is safely rolled up in a foetal position in her bedroom at home, counting all the plastic ponies she collected when she was at boarding school and missing her real live pony.

There are forty-seven of them, all individually named – Star, Blaize, Monty, Suki, Moon, Goldie, Prancer, Joe ... – and as she mentally recalls her little plastic friends a complete stranger with a big white face is simultaneously painting her lips a dark plum colour in the mirror.

Velvet, Chestnut, Whitey, Galaxy.

A yell from the floor below interrupts her lip-line. 'This is your fifteen-minute call, Company, you have fifteen minutes.' The rest of the year, those who haven't been cast in the production, are acting as stage management. There are varying degrees of resentment about this situation, and even more varying degrees of competence.

Fern sighs. Jill is pulling her costume over her head; her bra is grey and utilitarian but her breasts aren't, they are extraordinary. 'Bill and Ben, I call 'em,' Jill sniggers, arranging her cleavage in the mirror.

It's on the tip of her tongue. Should she ask her, should she just come out with it? 'Jill, did you suck off Dave Tate?'

But there's no time. There's a sudden commotion on the stairs and one of the canteen ladies, the one with the missing thumb, barges into the dressing room carrying an enormous bunch of flowers.

'I'm on refreshment duty downstairs, but your mother twisted my arm and asked if I wouldn't mind bringing these up – she was worried about getting lost in the rabbit warren back here – and she said to tell you she's in the pub over the road with James, whoever he might be.'

'Blimey, it's like a real bookay,' breathes Jill. Fern buries her nose in twelve yellow roses. The scent takes the edge off Olya's BO.

She is dazed. James, James is here, he must have driven her mother up to Manchester. Where is he staying? Oh God, she hasn't changed her sheets since the pâté incident. This is really the last thing she needs just before she goes on stage, bloody James turning up. Shit and fuck. 'But darling, it's so sweet and supportive of him.' Her mother's voice reminds her that she should be grateful, and of course he won't come back to hers – Rosemarie would go bananas. Fern tries to pull herself together. She can't think about it now, she is Masha, disappointed, headstrong Russian Masha, but for a terrifying number of seconds she cannot remember any of her lines and her mouth is ash-dry.

'This is your beginners' call, your beginners' call. To the stage please Miss Woolbright, Miss Jackson . . .'

Two and a half hours later it is all over. The sisters are back in their dressing room but Fern is still feeling like she is having an out-of-body experience.

She'd noticed her mother within seconds of being on stage; she was the only one to clap after Fern's very short and mercifully melodic introductory piano piece. Rosemarie sat three rows back; James was to the right of her and, Dear Fucking Christ, Charlie to the left. Her mother's girdled thigh was touching Charlie's denim-clad leg! Holy mother of fuck, how was she meant to concentrate on wanting to go back to Moscow when all she wanted to do was suck Charlie Treadaway's cock?

From then on she became hyper-aware of everything. There was no point on that stage when she could fully relax, no moment when she wasn't conscious of the gaffer tape around the samovar handle, the zip on Jill's dress gradually creeping down, of the number of cues before she next had to speak.

And suddenly it was over and she was bowing with Olya's damp hand in hers. Everything had been fine, even the piano, but she hadn't been able to let go, she was always Fern pretending to be Masha, an impostor.

Back in the dressing room, Jill is buzzing. Scrubbed free of her make-up she is rosy-cheeked; even her cleavage is glowing. 'Told you,' she screeches into Fern's face. 'We were fookin' amazing, right? Pub, pub, pub, pub . . . ' The others take up the chant and Fern joins in – 'Pub, pub, pub' – trying desperately hard not to sound hollow.

By the time the cast make their way over the road and into the Grapes, her mother is already ensconced in a corner with a lurid-coloured drink in front of her. 'Gin and lime, darling. James is at the bar, he'll get you whatever you fancy. He drove me all this way and he's driving all the way back so I don't have to stay in some dreadful hotel. Isn't he the best?' James is waving a ten-pound note at her. 'Pint of lager!' she yells. His face clouds over and he mouths back, 'Why don't you have what your mother's having?'

Rosemarie embraces Fern, a familiar rustle of silk and the over-powering scent of Rive Gauche. 'Well done, darling, you were by far the prettiest. There are some very odd-shaped girls in your class.'

Fern feels a sudden and unexpected wave of annoyance. Her mother never can see beyond the purely physical: women are either lovely or like the back of a bus, fat girls are a particular no-no. 'The brunette could be stunning in a rather obvious way,' her mother continues. 'If she would just lose a stone or two—'

'What about the play?' Fern interrupts, eyes scanning the pub. Where is Charlie? Did he hate it so much that he had to leave straight away? 'Oh you know,' her mother responds, 'it's all very wordy. I mean, they do go on a bit, don't they? At one point I thought, if you really want to go back to Moscow, why don't you just go?'

Fortunately for Rosemarie, at this precise moment James arrives with the drinks. 'Well done, darling, I don't know how you managed to remember all those words. Chin-chin,' and he hands her a gin and lime to match her mother's before adding, 'So this is what a real Northern pub is like? I should have treated you ladies to some pork scratchings!' Fern's mother laughs until she almost chokes. 'Can you imagine?' she heaves, wiping a tear away with a lace-trimmed hanky.

'I wanted a lager because I'm so thirsty,' grumbles Fern, and to spite both James and her mother she knocks back the weirdly fluorescent drink in one and marches to the bar to fetch her own fucking lager.

Where is he? Where is Charlie?

Transporting her Heineken back through the post-show throng, she notices Rob in the opposite corner of the pub. She makes the universal sign for 'two minutes' to her mother and James, and nips over to where he is squashed next to Jill. 'Well done,' says Rob. 'I thought you were all great, truly.'

Suddenly she is aware of a presence behind her, a hand on her neck. She senses one of the long metal pins being taken from her hair, and another and another. She feels the weight of the bun drop as her hair unfurls to her shoulders, a whisper in her ear, 'I'm keeping these, I want your DNA.'

She turns, but he is already leaving. He salutes her at the door, how dare he? He is mocking her soldier boyfriend, but despite this she wants to scream at him to stay. She wants him to know James won't be sleeping at Old Lansdowne Road. She wants him to know her bed is his.

'Who is that young man?' her mother asks. 'He's devilishly handsome, but ever so slightly unwashed.'

Before she can reply James interrupts. 'Sweetheart, maybe you should go to the ladies, give your hair a brush. You're a little bit, how can I put this ... hedge backwards?'

7

Advent

Suddenly it's almost the end of term and Fern can't wait to get back to Three Paddocks, where the Woolbrights celebrate a proper traditional Christmas. She can't imagine ever not waking up in her childhood single bed under the eaves, with her stocking, all lumpy with surprises, at the foot of the bed.

'What, you mean you still get a stocking?' gasped Felicity. 'That's just freaky at your age. It's like your parents want you to be their little baby girl for ever.'

'And who wouldn't want to be Mummy and Daddy's little baby girl for ever?' asks Fern, but not out loud.

But maybe it is a bit weird, and to be honest most of the presents in the stocking are a bit crap. Maybe she should tell her mother not to bother with all the cheap little rubbishy bits and instead she could have one extra, decent present, like an LP.

Rosemarie Woolbright loves Christmas. She adores spraying twigs silver with the metallic spray paint that makes her a bit giddy, and creating an arrangement on the telephone table in the hall. Rosemarie can be quite imaginative when she chooses; she likes to scent the house with cinnamon sticks and make her own punch.

There are certain Woolbright Christmas rules that everyone

must abide by: church on Christmas Eve, a smoked salmon and scrambled egg Christmas Day breakfast, followed by presents around the tree, then a lovely crisp walk with the doggies to the stables and lunch at around five. Just the three of them and Gordon's mother Nanny P, who, as Mummy says, is 'really quite marvellous for her age, even if she is a teeny bit difficult'.

There are always silver sixpences and an ancient threepenny bit to be found in the pudding. Gordon is always in charge of setting the pudding alight and bringing it through from the kitchen into the dining room, all wreathed in purple dancing flames, and at this point everyone must cheer.

On Boxing Day they go visiting, spreading cheer and charm around the neighbourhood, and with any luck this is when she will see her cousin Elise. She can't wait to catch up with her naughty cousin, because Elise has all the best gossip.

Felicity and Dee don't seem that bothered about going home for the Christmas break. Felicity doesn't like her parents because they don't approve of her sexuality: indeed, her father chokes on the very word 'lesbian', while her mother freely admits that Felicity's lifestyle makes her 'sick to her stomach'.

As for Dee, she is very vague about her family and won't be going anywhere. However, they both join in when Fern decides to make a surrogate Christmas tree out of the yucca plant in the kitchen. The three of them festoon it with clip-on earrings, a few strings of plastic popper beads and some random shapes made from the silver foil found in fag packets.

Fern's radio, which has somehow migrated from her bedroom to the kitchen for communal use, is tuned to a station playing carols. The atmosphere in the ugly little kitchen is oddly festive and Fern feels really excited for the first time in weeks.

Things have been rather flat since the play. Mummy had rung the day after to rave on about how brilliant James was and how he'd got them back south in record time, and wasn't he the knight in shining armour?

'Yes,' agreed Fern weakly.

She has barely seen Charlie. It's as if Fabiana has sensed that the two of them can't be trusted and is constantly vigilant.

According to Rob, she has Charlie's name tattooed onto her thigh. She did it herself with the point of a compass and a bottle of Charlie's drawing ink; apparently her leg became infected and Charlie stayed with her for a week to make sure she took the antibiotics given to her by the hospital.

Fern dreams Fabiana's leg is so infected that it has to be amputated, and her dancing ability is reduced to hopping about on her one remaining leg. She is disappointed, on waking, to realise that the scenario is not real. Bloody Fabiana.

Everyone is winding down. On the Friday night before the mass student exodus to far-flung families, the tiny pub around the corner is packed to the gills. Fern is squeezed on a banquette at the rear of the pub next to Rob, who has Jill on his knee. Everyone is drinking, apart from Rob and Jill, who keep pausing to snog. They are pretty well matched, thinks Fern. Jill is wearing one of Rob's rugby shirts; the broad burgundy stripes emphasise the generosity of her bosom, and Rob is transfixed.

Charlie is at the bar with Fabiana, her dark head tucked under his armpit, like a plague boil. A bubo, recalls Fern suddenly back in a third-year history class, surrounded by Tillinghurst girls in purple tunics.

Desperate for his attention, Fern laughs wildly at anything remotely funny. When will he notice her? When will he see sense, dump Fabiana and fuck her instead?

Charlie and the boil disappear. He's got a gig and then he's going back to London to see his folks, Rob informs her, removing his tongue from Jill's throat for just a second before poking it back down again like a piece of Dyno-Rod apparatus.

Ah, so he comes from London. Of course he does. She wishes for a moment that she did too. Three Paddocks is all very well, if you want to stand around the Aga making mulled wine in

Mummy's special copper pan, but it isn't exactly swinging. It's a bit dull really. Christ, for the first time in her eighteen years Fern suddenly feels bored at the prospect of Christmas at home with her bloody parents.

The pub chucks them all out at eleven and Fern wanders home with Jill and Rob and Felicity and Dee. She feels like a gooseberry, this is awful.

Don't forget you have James, she reminds herself. Dear James, who has all the sex appeal of a gerbil. I wonder what he'll buy me for Christmas; it had better be good.

'Merry Christmas Jill, Merry Christmas Rob. Don't do anything I wouldn't do!'

Ha-ha, fat chance.

Someone has pushed another card under her door, another drawing, a pen-and-ink Christmas card featuring a naked angel at the top of a fir tree. The angel has long red hair. It's Fern; he has got her, right down to her pale pink nipples.

Oh Charlie, gorgeous, sexy, London boy Charlie, and alone in her bed Fern finds her hand wandering down to her private parts, where, after a bit of digging around, she finds what she has been looking for. Once she chances upon her clitoris she knows she will never have to search for it again, it will always be there, waiting for her whenever she should need it. Rhythmically she fondles and teases this nub of a million nerve endings, losing herself and her fingers into her own aching wetness, and suddenly something happens that she has never experienced before.

Hahahaha.

Once the mission has been completed, and she is still struggling to get her breath back, she mentally congratulates herself – well done, Fern, you have successfully wanked yourself off, good work – and she falls asleep oblivious to the grunting noises from both next door and downstairs. Everyone is at it tonight.

8

Christmas Day

It's lovely to be home, of course it is – Fern finds herself constantly opening the fridge just to marvel at its festive contents – but Mummy is being a bit of a nightmare.

Rosemarie is obviously going through *the change*. The day after Fern got home from college she became suddenly weepy and accused everyone of 'not pulling their weight' and leaving her to do all the 'shitty work', which at that precise moment happened to be painting walnuts with gold enamel.

'You never lift a finger, either of you,' she ranted, paintbrush trembling in her manicured hand.

Of course, the more hysterical Mummy got, the more Daddy retreated behind his paper or disappeared off to the pub to 'see a man about a dog', which made Mummy spit the word 'bastard' three times while making puff pastry for some 'sodding' home-made mince pies.

Fern had really tried. She'd even attempted a woman-to-woman chat with Rosemarie, confiding how she too was held hostage by her hormones, suffering the most awful PMT, not to mention excruciating period pains, but Rosemarie just said she didn't want to listen to such vulgar nonsense and that these kind of things were best kept between a woman and her doctor.

'Well go and see the doctor then,' Fern had snapped, at which point Rosemarie had thrown all her golden walnuts in the 'fucking bin'.

So that had been tricky.

But apart from a few minor skirmishes and the fact that Mummy insists on treating her like a nine-year-old, it really is lovely to be home, even if it is a bit boring and Mummy has banned ashtrays from the bedroom.

'Really, darling, smoking in bed is a filthy habit,' which is ridiculous, because as anyone who smokes knows, the best cigarette of the day is the last one at night, inhaled deeply while naked under the duvet, preferably with a glass of something dark and red to accompany it. Fern has smuggled a bottle of sloe gin up to her bedroom and hidden it in one of her old riding boots.

But apart from a few silly rules, who would want to be anywhere else?

Fern stretches in her childhood bed and realises that her mother has crept in with a stocking in the middle of the night. She hopes Rosemarie didn't notice the eggcup full of cigarette butts on her bedside table and goes back to sleep. The stocking can wait; it'll be full of rubbish anyway.

Two hours later, having gutted and discarded most of her stocking, Fern is sitting by the Christmas tree, opening her proper presents. Her mother has just given her a pair of sheepskin mittens, which Rosemarie thinks are just the ticket for 'horrid damp Manchester', and Fern, feeling an instant pang of affection for her Northern home, has to swallow hard and pretend to like the fucking hideous mittens. Have her parents always got it so wrong? Gift after gift seems to have been bought with another Fern in mind, a fictional daughter who likes scented drawer liners, the kind of girl who might actually open the *Good Housekeeping Step-by-Step Cookbook*. A pair of lacy woollen tights would be great if they weren't beige; the brown leather handbag is expensive but dull; and a tartan tam-o'-shanter could almost work if it didn't make her head itch.

After the traditional walk to the stables, where her old pony Bruno barely recognises her, his ancient blue eyes clouded with cataracts, Fern finds herself back in her childhood bedroom, slugging sloe gin and devouring segment after segment of Chocolate Orange. She feels sleepy and bored, and in desperate need of someone her own age to talk to.

She dresses more carefully than she would like, anxious not to upset her mother, whose mood has been teetering on a knife-edge ever since she opened a cashmere sweater from Gordon that is a funny mauve colour rather than the deep blackcurrant that she had specifically pointed out.

'Stupid fucking idiot,' Fern heard her mother mutter as she threw all the wrapping paper on the fire. At this moment Gordon observed that Rosemarie had also thrown the socks Fern had bought him onto the blaze, and she'd tried to retrieve them with the poker. There is now a charred patch on the golden carpet where the smouldering socks had landed.

Fern decides against the Alice band her mother likes her to wear. A headache is already pounding at her temples and she still has Christmas lunch with her grandmother to get through.

She is wearing a cream silk ruffle-fronted shirt tucked into a green velvet skirt. She dons the boring beige tights and slips her long, slim feet into a pair of Russell & Bromley black suede loafers that have been in the bottom of her wardrobe since she left for Manchester, because, as Mummy said, 'suede and the north don't really go, darling'.

Nanny P is getting very old and Fern doesn't like watching her eat. She is as blind as poor Bruno and mistakes the white pepper for the salt, sneezing over her meal for a good ten minutes as a result. Rosemarie's 'Bless you's get more threatening with every explosion.

Pulling a cracker with her grandmother, Fern is shocked by the old woman's frailty. If she's not careful, she'll wrench Nanny P's ancient arm out of its socket, and yet her grip remains vicelike. Eventually the octogenarian is victorious, winning a little yellow plastic whistle and almost falling off her chair in the process.

The carved-up bird on the table reminds Fern of her grandmother: grey flesh, sinew and bone. It's not quite cooked through, and thin trails of blood ooze from its splintered joints.

Gordon is very kind to his mother, but Rosemarie is snappy and it's a relief when Nanny P asks to be driven back to her nursing home, where she loves her carers more than her daughter-in-law. 'We're having Christmas carols in the day room,' says Nanny P, kissing Fern with her chewed-up turkey-breath mouth.

Fern feels a bit sick. She doesn't want to get old. She helps her mother clear the table and knocks back the champagne that her grandmother didn't drink.

The evening passes in a blur of over-indulgence. James phones and Fern sits in the draughty hallway where her mother has festooned the banisters with ivy and arranged a festive bowl of Quality Street on the telephone table. Fern puts a golden Toffee Penny in her mouth and realises as she chews that she can't speak for dribbling. In the mirror she pulls faces at herself, toffee dribble running out of the sides of her mouth, while James drones on.

He will take her out for dinner tomorrow night. 'That's something to look forward to,' says her mother, who has left the mauve jumper partially unwrapped under the tree all day. 'Don't forget we've got the Harrisons' wine and nibbles first.'

They all go to bed rather early. There's always next Christmas, thinks Fern, and her spine shudders involuntarily.

9

Boxing Day

Ten minutes after arriving at the Harrisons' Boxing Day wine and nibbles party, Fern is realising quite how posh her parents are and quite how posh and annoying their friends are, and quite how posh, annoying and fucking hideous their friends' children are. Even the ones her age, the ones she used to play with when she was little, the Pony Club girls with their country complexions, bouncy hair and discreet pearl earrings.

All the older men are physically repulsive, with hairy nostrils and appalling breath, while their immaculately groomed wives look like they don't know whether to laugh or cry.

Depending on their sex, her parents' friends either shriek or bray into Fern's face, and without exception think her chosen career is a matter for extreme hilarity. 'Here she is, Godalming's answer to Glenda Jackson,' snorts a fat man from behind a haze of cigar smoke. 'Hahahahaha,' convulses his stick-like wife.

Thank God for Elise. As soon as the girls spot each other across the circulating plates of mushroom vol-au-vents, they sneak off through the conservatory and into the Harrisons' boot room, where they take refuge, sitting on the floor among dog bowls and outdoor footwear.

Elise has a brand-new cockney accent, a huge amount of gossip and a bottle of Cinzano swiped from the Harrisons' drinks table.

Basically, she tells Fern, she's been having the most God-awful time since she had to have an abortion. Just a silly accident really, but the father-not-to-be was a Nigerian semi-pro boxer from Stepney Green who did a runner as soon as she mentioned she was a couple of weeks late. So then after the op, which was loads easier than having her wisdom teeth out, Mummy arranged for her to see this shrink, but he's in bloody Chiswick and there's no way she's going to flog out to West London from Pimlico! Anyway, Daddy's paid for her to go skiing for a fortnight in the new year, and she thinks Val d'Isère will do her a lot more good than being stared at by a doleful Jungian therapist for two hours on a Friday morning.

Fern wishes Elise had managed to swipe some lemonade to go with the sickly Cinzano, but she continues to take turns swigging the stuff neat from the bottle.

Elise has some faded yellow bruises around her neck; they peek above the piecrust collar of her Sloane Ranger shirt. 'I'm trying to be good,' she insists, pulling hard on a menthol cigarette. 'But good is so boring.' She giggles, and for some reason once she starts giggling she can't stop; Elise laughs until she starts to choke and a bit of Cinzano comes out of her nose.

'Fucking hell, I feel like crap,' she admits once the choking subsides. 'I don't suppose you've got a bit of a pick-me-up on you?'

Fern doesn't know what Elise is talking about. The only pick-me-up she is aware of is a tonic that their GP occasionally prescribes for her mother. 'Have you tried yeast tablets?' she suggests, which sets Elise off again. The odd thing is, the more Elise laughs, the more it looks like she is actually crying.

She has only just recovering her composure when a furious-looking Aunty Minty stumbles across them. 'I've been looking for you everywhere. What are you doing, hiding like a couple of six-year-olds? Honestly, Elise, after everything we've been through you might at least try and make a bloody effort. We'll be in the car.'

And with that Aunty Araminta kicks the nearest dog bowl, sending it scudding across the York flagstones, and slams out of the room.

'Daddy has to do a lot of festive palm-pressing,' confides Elise, unsteadily getting to her feet and shrugging her shoulders into a brand-new Miss Selfridge plum-coloured leather jacket. 'Lots of constituents to visit.' She yawns without putting her hand over her mouth and in that fleeting moment Fern gets a glimpse of how awfully stained her cousin's teeth are.

The cousins hug each other; Elise is very thin. She cheerfully tucks the Cinzano bottle into her bag, winks at Fern and follows her mother's furious march across the back lawn. Before she forgets, Fern yells, 'Thank you for the bubble bath!' at the departing figures and Aunty Minty raises a black leather glove in acknowledgement. Hopefully they'll catch up again at Easter.

Fern sits alone in the boot room for a while and thinks about Charlie. What kind of Christmas is he having, and where does he live? She wonders for a moment if he comes from one of those estates that are always in the news. Gosh, maybe he lives in a council flat. Rob mentioned he had a stepfather, which means he must come from a broken home. Poor Charlie, only she can truly save him. Suddenly remembering that cold floors cause piles, Fern drags herself up and braves a re-entry into the party. It's reached the parakeets screeching in a cage level, but at least the vol-au-vents look good.

On the way home, a gin-scented Rosemarie mentions how exhausted she thought her sister looked, and Gordon replies, 'Well, Elise has always been a bit of a handful. I think they've both been too busy to keep an eye on her.'

'Yes, well apparently Mrs Thatcher just adores Paul,' Rosemarie continues somewhat pointedly, knowing full well it will irritate Gordon.

Sitting on the back seat of the car, Fern watches the colour of her father's neck darken to a deep shade of magenta, but in the split-second that follows an argument is averted by the appearance of a young roe deer, standing as if paralysed on the road in front of them. Its eyes are huge and petrified in the headlights, 'Christ, and almighty fuck,' swears Gordon, swerving to avoid the animal, and in the drama of the moment they forget all about Minty, Paul and Elise.

'We could have been killed,' gasps Rosemarie, clutching at her throat, and Fern can tell by her voice that the mauve jumper is forgiven. After all what's the point in making a song and dance about a funny-coloured sweater when they could be dead in a ditch?

James picks her up on Boxing Day evening and whisks her off for dinner at the same hotel where his parents celebrated their wedding anniversary. They are the youngest couple in the restaurant by about fifty years, but James doesn't seem to mind. In fact, he seems to revel in the subdued yet sophisticated, heavily draped, thickly carpeted atmosphere. He appreciates the man gently 'tickling the ivories' at the baby grand; he likes the way the wine waiter stands by respectfully while 'Sir' tries the wine; and he is positively smug that sitting opposite him, glowing in the candlelight, is 'the loveliest girl in all of Godalming'.

Fern is still full from the Harrisons' canapés but tries to show willing. James has the liver, which Fern thinks is a strange choice at Christmas, while she has ordered venison but is struggling to eat it. The animal's flesh on her fork reminds her of the deer they'd narrowly missed that afternoon, a deer with exactly the same liquid brown eyes as Elise.

How can she possibly eat anything with exactly the same eyes as her cousin?

James doesn't mention coming to see the play. In fact, he doesn't seem at all interested in her drama course, which she feels a bit miffed about, but she is even more miffed when he very firmly states that he can't stand the sight of women drinking pints.

'But that's all my flatmates ever drink,' Fern responds, to which James very calmly pulls a face and replies, 'Yes, well, they are from the Island of Lesbos, aren't they?'

It takes her a while to work out that he means they are lesbians. Dear God!

Between pudding and coffee he presents her with a Christmas gift. As soon as she puts her tiramisu spoon down he clears his throat several times and reaches inside his jacket pocket for a small square parcel that has obviously been professionally wrapped. Fern vaguely recognises the gold and silver striped paper and elaborately curled scarlet ribbon from the jeweller's on the High Street.

Tearing at the wrapping paper she discovers a dark blue velvet box and she fumbles with the fastening until it eventually opens to reveal a delicate silver fern-shaped necklace lying in a crimson satin nest.

It is lovely. She really likes it, it is very her, she knows she will wear it every day, she is an incredibly lucky girl, but as his hands do up the clasp at the back of her neck she again has that strange urge to turn around and bite him.

Maybe she should write to the agony aunt at *Woman's Own*:

Dear Mary,
I have the best boyfriend in the world, he is handsome and kind, but for some reason I would like to inflict physical pain on him. Basically, I often feel like sinking my teeth into his flesh. What should I do?
Worried Blue Eyes of Godalming

Once the necklace is successfully fastened around her throat the man at the piano starts plinking out 'If You were the Only Girl in the World' and a few very old people with napkins under their chins start clapping while Fern tries not to die of embarrassment.

He is going back to his barracks tomorrow; she won't see him for a while. 'I'm so sorry,' he tells her as he parks the car outside Three Paddocks and treats her to an extra-long lettuce-eating rabbit kiss. I feel like I'm in a hutch, thinks Fern, trying to push her tongue further into James's mouth and encouraging him to do the same, but just as he starts squirming and feeling for her breast a light appears in the kitchen window and he rears away from her as if she were suddenly contaminated. 'Don't want to upset the parents,' he chuckles and Fern gets out of the car.

10

The Magic Trick

Fern is on her way back north three days earlier than necessary. Another night under the same roof as her mother and she'd have set fire to the thatch.

Bones of contention between mother and daughter revolve mostly around Fern's ability to loll about in bed all day – big deal. Her old school friends bore her, her favourite doggie is dead, her beloved Bruno is lame as well as blind, and if all that wasn't enough, Mrs Bibby the cleaner complained about the cigarette butts in her bedroom and returned the bottle of sloe gin from the riding boot back to its rightful place. Bitch.

Daddy could at least have paid for me to go skiing, she sulks as the train finally pulls into a decidedly snow-free, rain-sodden Piccadilly station. If only she could have joined Elise in Val d'Isère, but the offer was not forthcoming. It was almost as if her father didn't want her spending time with her cousin.

So, having endured the dullest New Year's Eve of her life, playing charades with Evelyn and Glen, her parents' next-door neighbours, she has returned to Manchester, and as she waits in the taxi queue, desperately trying to keep her hands warm, she is happier than she ever thought she would be to be back. If only she'd bothered to bring those bloody sheepskin mittens with her.

Number 2 Old Lansdowne Road feels even more neglected than usual. A blizzard of brown paper envelopes has fallen through the letterbox and no one has bothered to pick them up. Well it's not my job, decides Fern, dragging her bags up the stairs.

Once safely out of view, she stops on the first-floor landing and leans over the banister to check for any sign of human habitation on the ground floor. As usual, there is a clutch of random push-bikes leaning against the wall, but considering Charlie just takes whichever he fancies, she's no idea if any of them is his.

Oh well, at least Felicity and Dee should be home. In fact, she can smell Dee's joss sticks from here, or maybe it's not joss sticks. The smell is sweet and sickly, and emanating from Charlie's room at the front of the house. Suddenly she hears a crash and a shriek of wild laughter; scabby Fabiana is obviously in residence, and she wonders whether Charlie bought her anything for Christmas. She looks like she needs a nit comb, thinks Fern.

Up in the top-floor flat, Felicity and Dee have left a note saying they've gone into town to see the Specials, and Happy New Year. The yucca plant is still bejewelled, but quite dead, like a wealthy elderly resident left to rot in a run-down nursing home.

Suddenly Fern is swamped by a feeling of utter desolation. She has grown out of her old life at home, it feels small and tight, like an old jumper that has shrunk in the wash and is too uncomfortable to wear any more, but she hasn't found a new life that really fits.

This Northern student life is cold and uncomfortable, and just when she is thinking of giving up and going to bed with a hot water bottle and one of Mummy's mince pies (not quite as good as usual) there is a knock on the door.

Jill's face, round and very pink of cheek, peers in. 'Hi, um Rob and me are cooking a chilli con carne. Fabiana and Charlie might be joining us but there's plenty and we've got wine. Anyway, ready in ten minutes if you fancy it.'

'I do, thank you,' says Fern, blinking back sudden unexpected tears of gratitude. Who'd have thought she'd be so pleased to see Jill?

Ten minutes later, having given her eyelids the full-on siren treatment, Fern takes the tin of mince pies downstairs. 'Pudding,' she announces. Fabiana isn't there. Fern checks Rob and Charlie's kitchen again; she wouldn't put it past the mad Spaniard not to be crouching in the corner or hiding under the table.

Rob is wearing a big wipe-down PVC apron with a picture of a bottle of Lea & Perrins on it. A Christmas present from Jill!

Gosh that was quick, they've reached the gift-buying stage already, and because she can't think of anything better to do she shows Jill the necklace James gave her.

'Very nice, and how was Captain Frobisher?'

But she doesn't reply because at that moment Charlie makes his entrance. He is wearing a slightly battered paper chain around his neck like a mayoral chain.

'One less for dinner, Rob, mate. The señorita's got her castanets in a twist and pissed off back to her place. Time of the month or something. Oh hello, it's Lizzie Siddal,' and he turns to Fern, who is still holding her mother's biscuit tin, the one with the Queen Mother on the lid, and a scarlet blush rises from her throat like a fever.

She doesn't know how Jill does it. She's obviously besotted with Rob but she can still eat, whereas Fern can barely choke down three grains of rice at a time. Under the table, her vagina beats as if she has a spare heart tucked away down there.

This is my first adult dinner party without my parents, she thinks, and momentarily she pictures the dinner parties her mother hosts back in Surrey: the days of preparations, the ritual polishing of the silver, the flower arranging. 'I'm actually very good at this, darling – I once won an award for a mounted spring display with forsythia when I was at finishing school.'

Here in Rob and Charlie's garlic-infused kitchen they are squeezed around a small red Formica table, with a brimming ashtray as a centrepiece. Fern drinks red wine from a brown earthenware mug with no handle and finally starts to relax.

They banter easily among themselves, telling tales of their family Christmases. Fern is the only only child.

'Is that why you're so spoilt?' asks Jill.

'Probably,' replies Fern. 'And possibly because my parents are quite rich.'

This makes Charlie laugh, a strange yelping noise through the cloud of his roll-up. His little yellow teeth are pointed like a fox's; he shouldn't be attractive, thinks Fern, he's actually got horrible teeth.

'Charlie's a twin,' says Rob.

'Golly,' says Fern before she can stop herself. 'So there are actually two of you?'

Then Fabiana can have the other one, she decides internally.

'What's his name?'

'Rowena,' Charlie replies.

'Are you identical?'

Jill hoots. 'How can they be identical, you noggin? Rowena's a girl and Charlie's a boy. There's a difference in genitalia for starters.'

Fern blushes again. Sex education at Tillinghurst Girls' had been rather limited to the reproduction of flowers, stamens and anthers mostly.

Jill is a great deal more scientifically informed – her mother is a biology teacher in North Shields – and on the back of a piece of paper she and Charlie demonstrate how some twins are identical, 'One egg which splits in two,' instructs Jill, and Charlie draws matching screaming babies falling out of one egg, and how some are fraternal: 'Two eggs fertilised at the same time by different sperm,' explains Jill as Charlie draws two eggs with non-identical babies waving out of them. 'I'm a boy,' says one in a speech bubble.

'I'm a girl,' says the other. Ha, it was definitely him that made the doggie card, thinks Fern gleefully. The evidence of his drawing style is right in front of her.

'Of course, even weirder than that,' Jill goes on, 'is the situation where a woman can get pregnant twice in one month and have babies who aren't actually twins.'

'Does that mean that, technically, they can have different dads?' asks Rob.

Jill laughs. 'If the woman's a bit of a slag and shags two blokes when she's in a super-fertile state then yes, technically it's possible. And I'll give you one last freak twin fact: there's this thing called vanishing twin syndrome, where basically a woman can be pregnant with twins, one can die and the remaining twin will absorb it, just soak up the dead twin into its own blood and cells!'

Charlie tries to draw this medical phenomenon, but he gives up.

'That's a bit weird. So do you think the twin which survives has some of the other twin's soul and some of its brain?' asks Rob, puncturing a tin of Carnation milk to go with Rosemarie's mince pies.

'I wish I had some of my sister's brain,' responds Charlie. 'She's dead clever – she's at Oxford.'

Fern feels a pang of jealousy over Charlie's clever sister, which is silly considering they are twins, but she is envious of the way he talks about her, how he obviously loves her. She wants to keep the pictures Charlie drew; she wants to sleep with the pencil he used under her pillow. She is spell-bound.

Halfway through the mice pies, which are pronounced good, but apparently not as good as Charlie's nanny's. 'Not that she's a nanny now,' he corrects. 'She's more of a home-help these days. Alicia, she's Jamaican, she loads 'em up with rum.' And both Fern and Jill sit round-mouthed. Who is Charlie Treadaway, and how come he has a black nanny and a twin? He's full of surprises.

Suddenly the record player slows down, and as Brian Ferry slurs to a halt, the lights go out.

'Bloody hell, has anyone got any fifty pees?' yelps Jill, but as Fern reaches for her purse she feels a hand take hers, and in the pitch black she is led away from the kitchen and into Charlie Treadaway's lair. By the time the lights come back on she is completely naked. It's the best magic trick she's experienced since she went to Elise's tenth birthday party

11

Falling

Felicity and Dee are quite cross with Fern. 'He's got a girlfriend, it's unsisterly,' Felicity admonishes her. 'But I'm an only child, how can it be unsisterly?' Fern retorts, to which Felicity huffs, 'You can be really fucking thick sometimes, Fern,' while Dee tuts and chews the skin around her fingernails.

They don't do it all the time, they do it when Fabiana is out of the way and the coast is clear. They sometimes do it in his room, cave-like and dingy, jeans all over the floor. His bedroom is a pirate's den reeking of red wine, cigarettes and dope.

She won't let him smoke 'that stuff' in her bedroom; she really doesn't like the smell and it makes him lazy, too lazy to clean his little yellow teeth. She buys him a spare toothbrush to keep by her kitchen sink, and tells him that oral hygiene is important.

He laughs at her and calls her his beautiful mermaid. He writes in biro on her body, 'Funny little naughty Fern, good girl gone bad, my sexy siren Fern.' And she panics that the ink will never come off and James will see it, and what will he say.

He laughs at her then, and writes 'Mrs Frobisher, the Major's wife' across the creamy curve of her belly.

She prefers it when they sleep in her bed: her sheets are cleaner, the duvet cover is fresher. He asks the names of her pets, and in turn he tells her stories of his childhood.

Bit by bit she pieces together the jigsaw of his family. There is his clever sister, his talented mum, the family treasure that is Alicia, his dead dad, his stuffy but okay stepdad and the step-brother whom he thinks is a bit of a prick. He barely mentions him by name – it might be Luke – he's a stuck-up ponce, a wanker, and then he tells her about being a choirboy and sings a gravelly 'Pie Jesu' into her ear.

They are an open secret in the house, but not outside it. He doesn't want her as a girlfriend, he wants her as a delicious treat, and explains that if they were a proper couple she would get bored with his lousy timekeeping, his dope-smoking, the way he sometimes just wants to stay up till five a.m. unwashed, listening to music and scribbling. Fabiana is his girlfriend, her role is to nag and wheedle. Fern is his courtesan, his pale-fleshed, ripe-melon beauty.

Jill is sympathetic but feels the relationship is doomed. 'He's slippery,' she says, secure in the knowledge that Rob isn't.

Rob has rapidly become her faithful Labrador and, chronic ath-lete's foot or not, she loves him as much as he loves her. Theirs is a steady 'your turn to buy toilet roll' love. Charlie never buys toilet roll; Rob tells Fern that he wipes his arse on Rizla papers, but that still doesn't put her off.

And when she is not fucking Charlie or hoping that she might see him, smell him, taste him, everyday life goes on. She is doing better at college because she is more relaxed and confident, and makes for a decorative and accomplished Titania at the end of January, which her parents sadly miss as they are in Paris cele-brating their twenty-fifth wedding anniversary.

But James manages a flying visit, and because Rosemarie isn't there to disapprove he stays at Old Lansdowne Road, where his polished shoes look out of place, and he insists on sleeping with the window open, because 'Darling, it's a very stuffy flat.'

All night, somewhere out in the Manchester dark, a vixen screams, and while James makes his usual tentative love to her she silently makes the same noise as the fox.

Charlie stayed at Fabiana's in Fallowfield that weekend.

She hates him spending time at Fabiana's flat. He always comes back in a terrible state. Their relationship isn't healthy: sometimes they cut each other, thin razor slices, crusted purple with dried blood.

Rob tries to reassure her, he says they're just showing off, that it's a faux punk thing, and what she has to remember about Charlie is that actually, deep down, he is a well-brought-up middle-class boy.

'His mum is a really successful illustrator,' Rob tells her. 'She does those Betsy and Tom books. You know, with the biscuits and the red shoes?'

Of course she knows Betsy and Tom; the books were the bedtime stories of her childhood. Secretly she buys the latest edition, the chart-busting *Betsy and Tom's Happiest Christmas Ever*, and searches for Charlie-clues on every page.

Inside the book, on the title page, is an illustration of a narrow Georgian house with a small front garden hemmed in by railings. Every window in the house is covered by cardboard shutters, which open like a nativity calendar, revealing the scene behind each window. Behind the middle window on the second floor a Christmas tree sparkles. Instinctively, she knows this is Charlie's house in London.

But she doesn't tell him what she's done. She doesn't want to start acting like Fabiana, spying and being suspicious.

She hides the book in her drawer with all her other Charlie things, the cards he's made her and a lock of his hair that she snipped off with a pair of nail scissors while he slept off a Sunday morning hangover in her bed. In the cold grey January light his lips were stained with damson-coloured wine and he left dribble stains on her pillowcases. He is a dirty boy really.

While Charlie is too clumsy to be sexually competent, he is both adventurous and oddly romantic. One night he knocks on her door at one o'clock, blindfolds her and leads her to the bathroom, where he has lit candles of every shape and size on every surface, including tiny birthday-cake candles pushed into a bar of soap, and run her a bath with real rose petals floating in it.

The petals are withered and brown and the bathwater too tepid to stay in for long, but no one has ever done anything like that for her before.

If only he'd bothered to clean the petals out of the bath, but in typical Charlie style he 'forgot', and so the romantic gesture slightly backfired, with the rest of the house utterly pissed off about the state of the bathroom.

James might lack imagination, but is consistent and reliable. He telephones every Sunday evening without fail. The payphone hangs on the wall of the first landing and Charlie takes great pleasure in answering his calls before Fern can make it down from the attic flat. It isn't fair, Charlie refuses to give her any privacy while she attempts to talk to James. He rolls around the filthy stair carpet pretending to be a cat, licking her ankles, and once he gently finger-fucked her through an entire twenty-minute conversation with her military beau. He is impossible.

She loves him.

But she knows better than to tell him so. She tries to act hard to get, she tries not to be so available. One night she refuses to play with him because she is hennaing Dee's hair. He wants his hair hennaed; she won't do it, she likes his black curls.

'Did I ever tell you I come from Irish gypsy stock?' he says in a terrible accent, dancing a jig. 'Shame about the curse, of course. Ah the terrible fate of the first-born male Treadaway. Some drown, others crash and burn, but do we make old bones? No we don't. Right, I'm going to get some fags.'

When he doesn't come back for five hours she get hysterical, thinking that the curse is true, and he laughs and laughs, then kisses her blotchy, tear-stained face.

'I went to meet a man about a pig,' he explains, and his dark eyes shine bigger than ever.

12

Hearts, Flowers and Pickled Red Cabbage

Valentine's Day is approaching. Rob corners Fern and asks her what he should do for Jill, and together they hatch a plan which involves Rob making Jill's favourite meat and potato pie with red cabbage, a Northern side dish that Rob, who is from Kettering, really doesn't understand. 'It will show her you really care,' insists Fern. 'Oh and flowers too, obviously.'

Rob looks stricken. 'What kind of flowers?'

'Roses, of course,' she snaps. Honestly, she can't do all the work for him, and he wanders off muttering 'roses and red cabbage'.

She is on tenterhooks as to whether Charlie will choose her or Fabiana to be his valentine. 'Are you sure he knows what day it's on?' asks Jill, who is planning on buying Rob a Dinky Porsche and herself a new fancy bra and knicker set. 'Let's face it,' she sighs contentedly, 'he can't get enough of these big old tits of mine, and he likes them gift-wrapped.'

Fern wonders if either Charlie or James are underwear men. James might think anything that involved stockings and suspenders was a bit whorish, whereas she doesn't think Charlie really cares. He likes her skin most, her sweet pale skin, so different from Fabiana's olive muscle.

She can't understand how he can like both. 'Lobster and steak,' he says and grins at her. 'You're my delicate lobster, she's a lot more chewy.'

'Like a rancid kebab,' she sneers, and he laughs and says, 'Ooh, maybe you're more crab than lobster. Put your claws away.'

Fabiana is training to be a dancer, which is another thing Fern cannot bear about her. Apparently, back in Spain she was training to be a ballerina but her breasts got too big, so she is studying contemporary dance over here. Oh, and apart from the home-made Charlie inscription on her thigh she has a tattoo of a scorpion on her left shoulder blade.

In Fern's head all she can hear is her mother saying 'Only navvies, tinkers and Chinese drug barons have tattoos, darling.' But for the first time in her life she imagines choosing a design for herself, a heart pierced by a dagger maybe? 'Don't you dare,' shrieks Jill. 'You're an actress. Imagine if you're doing Shakespeare or some Restoration: you can't have a bloody great tattoo on show.'

'I hadn't thought,' Fern admits. He is driving her insane.

Charlie vanishes on the evening of Friday the thirteenth of February. Fern happens to be looking out of her bedroom window at the precise moment he disappears, quicker than a cat's tail, round the corner of the road and her heart sinks. Downstairs, Rob is making pastry for Jill's pie.

Why does her love life have to be so complicated? Why can't she fall for someone like Rob? On second thoughts, she knows why: she has seen Rob's feet and they belong on a yeti.

At least my men are good looking, she consoles herself. James is almost classically handsome, he is tall and broad-shouldered, his waist is neat because he exercises so much. Charlie is painfully thin with a slight wine gut and rounded shoulders, his posture is dreadful, but he has no inhibitions and he has the face of a modern-day Lord Byron, albeit with yellow teeth.

'That'll be the speed,' Jill tells her. 'Dreadful for your teeth is speed.' Fern isn't actually sure what speed is, but if it turns your teeth yellow then it's not for her. She must have looked blank, because Jill continues, 'That's why sometimes he stays up all night, that's why he sounds like he's got a permanent cold, that's why he buggers off to really dodgy places and meets highly insalubrious characters and never has any money. Speed,' she explains, 'is an illegal powder which you snort through a rolled-up ten-pound note.'

'Don't be silly,' replied Fern, 'Charlie never has any ten-pound notes.'

Jill shakes her head. 'You won't listen. Anyway, don't take it, it's addictive. Personally I wouldn't go near it. I've got enough of a problem with pickled red cabbage.'

On Valentine's Day itself Fern finds a large red envelope behind the front door, postmarked Aldershot. The card has a teddy bear on the front, holding a padded red heart. It's one of the most hideous things she has ever seen in her entire life. Twelve long-stemmed red roses follow a couple of hours later; she can't even be bothered to put them in a vase. She leaves them in the kitchen and wanders back to bed. It's a Saturday, no college today. Across the hallway Dee and Felicity are having noisy sex, and judging by the shrieks and weird buzzing emanating from behind closed doors, their Valentine's gift to each other is a large and noisy vibrator.

Fern spends the day sulking under the duvet. She sleeps fitfully and dreams about Dee and Felicity leaving the vibrator in the kitchen sink, along with all the other utensils they can never be bothered to wash.

In the evening her post-coital flatmates get all dolled up for a Valentine's gay and lesbian fancy-dress disco in town. Felicity is dressed as Al Capone, Dee is her tiny moll. 'We were thinking of dressing her up as a mole,' snorts Felicity. 'Moll, mole – do you get it?'

'Have a great time,' waves Fern from the top of the stairs. She can smell Rob's romantic meat and potato pie for two wafting up from the ground-floor kitchen, and for some reason the smell makes her cry. Later that night Jill creeps upstairs and leaves a dish of hot pot and a glass of red wine outside her bedroom door, and even though she thought she was too depressed to eat Fern wolfs it down. Fuck him. Fuck Charlie Treadaway.

He comes knocking late on Sunday night. She opens her door, just a crack. He is shame-faced, with purple shadows under blood-shot eyes. She tells him to go away. He stinks of Fabiana, of musk, sweat and marijuana, and off he slinks, an alley cat in disgrace.

On the Monday night, when she gets home from college, a picture has been slipped under her bedroom door. It's another pen-and-ink sketch; this time it depicts Fern holding Charlie's broken heart. She feels fury and elation in equal measure, and just to punish him for another night she makes a noisy exit from the house to meet Jill at the Scala cinema to see *Xanadu*, starring Olivia Newton-John, which they both agree is dreadful.

'I want to do comedy and character work,' confides Jill as they walk home via the chicken grill on Burton Road. 'And I wouldn't mind doing some Theatre in Education when I leave college. You know, form a company, buy an old van, tour schools and try and do stuff that's got some kind of message.'

Fern nods in agreement, although deep down she can't think of anything worse than touring schools in a smelly old van for a load of disgusting children. Yuck.

'What about you?' asks Jill, and Fern is rather stumped. Obviously she'd like to be in the West End, because that's where all the nice shops and decent restaurants are, but beyond picturing herself taking curtain calls with large bouquets of flowers in her arms, she really can't think.

'Two chicken burgers, please.'

'And chips,' adds Jill, who is getting increasingly fat due to Rob's insistence that he likes something to grab hold of.

Charlie is waiting for her behind the front door. He sits blinking on the stairs, looking thin.

Tactfully Jill disappears into Rob's bedroom, and immediately there are hoots of laughter.

We don't laugh anything like as much as those two, thinks Fern as she rips what is left of her chicken burger in two and gives the bigger piece to Charlie. He follows her up the stairs.

At least he has washed. There are scratches fading down his back and what look like small bite marks around his hips – seriously, what is wrong with Fabiana? Charlie eats the burger in her bed. He wipes his greasy hands on her pretty paisley duvet cover and grins at her; bits of burger bun clog his teeth, but instead of getting up to brush them he lies back on Fern's pillows and burps three times.

By the time Fern has finished in the bathroom – i.e. chased, caught and inserted her diaphragm, which for some reason seems extra bouncy tonight, brushed her teeth and lightly dusted her bits with Kiku talc – Charlie is asleep, and gently snoring. His face is cherubic; the relief at having been forgiven makes him smile in his sleep. Naked, she slides in next to him. She needs to cover him in her scent, show Fabiana who's boss.

13

Love and Lady Di

A truce has been called. He brings her tea in the morning: she likes Earl Grey with lemon; he makes it with milk, but she is pathetically grateful. Squashed into her single bed, they drink their tea and he says, 'This is nice,' and she says, 'It certainly is,' and she feels his cock twitch against her thigh, and even though it's going to have to be quick because she has to get to college, at least her diaphragm is still in from last night, so they fuck and he moans 'I'm sorry, I'm sorry, I'm sorry' into her hair as he comes, and she feels like she is the winner and it's all she can do not to yell, 'Fuck you, Fabiana, he is mine, all mine!'

Of course, as soon as the fucking is done he goes all weird and distant again. He hops up and down trying to get into his jeans, knocking stuff off her dressing table, almost bringing down the curtain rail. He is so clumsy, for a second she thinks he's an idiot, but when she attempts to get out of bed herself he pushes her back down and somehow rolls her up in the duvet like a human sausage roll and says, 'Stay in this cocoon until I come back, because you are my most beautiful butterfly,' and he kisses her on the nose. The next thing she hears is the slam of the front door and Rob shouting 'He's done it again! That arsehole has swiped my fucking bike,' and inside her duvet cocoon Fern giggles.

And so the relationship takes a deeper root. Charlie still won't choose between Fabiana and Fern; sometimes Fern pretends not to mind and sometimes she cries herself to sleep.

Fabiana rarely comes over to Didsbury any more, but when she does, Fern's semi-resident ground-floor spy reports back to her.

According to Jill, Fabiana speaks very little English and barely eats. 'All she does is smoke and drink,' whispers Jill. 'However, she can do the splits without a warm-up, and the other day she walked down an entire flight of stairs on her hands.'

I hope she falls and breaks her neck, thinks Fern, wondering what her mother would say if she knew what was going on under the Peter Jones duvet that she bought for her only daughter. Rosemarie would be horrified; she would use words like 'defiled' and 'besmirched'. Her father simply wouldn't believe it, he will presume that Fern is a virgin until her wedding day, or at least until she has a ring on her finger.

Life was so much simpler before promiscuity, she concludes. Sexual freedom is so confusing. If she conducted herself properly, i.e. in the way her father thinks she does, she wouldn't have second thoughts about James because she wouldn't know he was a lousy shag. She'd only discover this fact on her wedding night, and even then, if she really *had* saved herself, she wouldn't know there were bigger-cocked men (Henri, for starters) and men who made her heart tremble when she kissed them (Charlie).

'You're stuck between the devil and the deep blue sea,' says Jill, who has a habit of reeling off colloquialisms that don't quite make sense.

'What on earth does that mean?' Fern queries.

'Oh, I dunno. I think it means you're going to burn in hell or drown. Do you think athlete's foot is catching?'

James still calls every Sunday night, and sometimes he writes letters. The most recent informs her of some leave he is due next month, and that he would very much like to come and stay on the third Saturday in March, before leaving early on the Sunday morning for a charity rugby match in Birmingham.

She can't get enthusiastic about the idea, because it means two weekends on the trot when she won't see Charlie: the weekend before James is due to visit, Charlie is heading back to London for his shared twenty-first-birthday lunch.

'My mum doesn't put her foot down often,' he said, 'but she insists. She's even sent me the train fare. I can't not go.'

Ha, at least she now knows when his birthday is. He is a Pisces, which makes perfect sense: that's why he swims in two different directions, that's why he thinks he needs both her and that bendy Spanish witch.

'Fuck me!' says Jill. They are drinking a swift lunchtime half of lager and lime in the pub across the road from college, and the slightly fuzzy television in the corner has just broken the news that Prince Charles is to marry Lady Diana Spencer, the doe-eyed nineteen-year-old nursery nurse from Kensington, the one with the fringe.

'Blimey, she's my age,' responds Fern. 'How can she possibly know she's doing the right thing?'

'Fucking mental Royals,' spits Jill. 'Come the revolution, we'll have all their heads on a stick.'

For a second Fern thinks her friend is joking. She has never, in her entire life, heard anyone speak a word against the Royal Family.

But Jill's eyes are blazing. 'Silly fucking idiot girl, they just want a baby machine. Poor bitch, I feel sorry for her. It'll end in tears, just mark my words – this has got disaster written all over it.'

Fern isn't sure that she agrees. Surely there is something rather lovely about a big sapphire and diamond engagement ring from a prince (even if he is a bit past it) who has chosen you from all the virgins in the land to be his bride.

Her mother had always entertained high hopes for Fern and

Prince Andrew. 'I'm sure if you just happened to meet . . . imagine a red-haired princess walking down the aisle at Westminster Abbey.'

She doesn't mention this to Jill, who would be horrified.

'I can't see why women are still getting married,' seethes her friend. 'It's utterly barbaric, being paraded down the aisle like a sacrificial lamb, being given away by your father as if you were some kind of a chattel. For fuck's sake, this is the twentieth century.'

'Don't you ever want to settle down and have children?' ventures Fern.

'You don't need to get married to have children, Fern. To be honest, yes, I think I do want children, but not with someone who wants to put a ring on me like I'm a cow at a cattle fair.'

'I hadn't really thought of it like that,' admits Fern meekly, mentally recounting the hours she spent with her cousin when they were little, drawing wedding dresses. Which reminds her: she must try to contact Elise. She might even know this Diana girl!

After all, she moves in all sorts of different London circles, from punks to the very posh.

But even more pressing than buying the *Daily Mail* and poring over pictures of the ring and wondering if she should have a Lady Di cut and break her mother's heart – 'Your hair is your crowning glory, darling,' – is the fact that Charlie is about to turn twenty-one. What on earth should she buy him for his birthday?

She's never really bought a boy or man a gift before. Apart from her father, of course, in whose case it's always ties, socks, soap on a rope and hankies.

She needs to get Charlie something really lovely and personal, something that he will for ever associate with her.

Fern's search for something meaningful for Charlie has her ferreting around the second-hand shops of Didsbury. He is, after all, a bit of a dandy. For a while she toys with buying him a snuff box, but considering he already spends an inordinate amount of time sneezing, she decides against it.

There's a silver tiepin in the shape of a fox, with glinting ruby eyes, but the rubies are real and she can't afford it. Ditto a gold fob watch and an ivory-topped cane.

'An ivory-topped cane?' Jill laughed. 'He's not a tap dancer. He'd be happy with a bottle of red wine and half an ounce of Old Holborn.'

Poor Fern, she dithers and faffs and talks about it until Dee and Felicity tell her straight to her face that she's becoming very boring, and what about that bitch Thatcher and the demise of two million manufacturing jobs?

Once again Fern keeps her trap shut. It seems that the only person who isn't entitled to freedom of speech is her. It's all very well for Jill and Felicity and Dee to get on their high horses about the Royals, Thatcher and feminism (you'd think they'd be pleased a woman was leading the country), but in all honesty the only thing Fern disagrees with the Royals over is their choice of dog. Out of all the dogs in all the world, no one in their right mind would choose a corgi. I'd have Afghan hounds, she decides.

As for the decimation of manufacturing jobs, she keeps very quiet because she doesn't actually know what a manufacturing job is. Jill does: her dad used to have one, but he doesn't any more.

Life, Fern is fast finding out, isn't always fair.

Eventually she buys Charlie a pewter hip flask, which she takes to a funny little place off Lapwing Lane to have engraved. His birthday is on the Sunday, but he is going up to London on the Saturday, 'Please stay with me on Friday night,' she begs. 'I want to give you your present,' and he agrees, making her promise to wake him early on Saturday morning so he doesn't miss his train to London.

On the Friday afternoon before Charlie Treadaway's twenty-first birthday, Fern is stuck in a 'Using Your Diaphragm Properly' workshop, the name of which makes her laugh uncontrollably because, as she points out to Jill, 'a diaphragm, as in a contraceptive device, and a diaphragm, as in the muscle behind your ribs, are two very different things!'

'Shall we all calm down?' snipes the visiting lecturer.

After the class, Fern makes a dash for the engraver's. She can't decide whether to run or catch the bus. Eventually she does both, catching a bus and then jumping off and running when it gets stuck in traffic, but to no avail: the shop is shut by the time she gets there, and Fern feels like slapping herself in the face. This is a dreadful start to Charlie's birthday celebrations.

He, of course, couldn't care less. 'I don't need presents,' he tells her, squeezing her bum with one hand and holding a roll-up in the other. He quite fancies going to the pub.

So they go to the pub, where Fern feels conspicuous, because in an effort to impress Charlie she has overdressed and stands out like a silly frilly idiot compared to all the other girls, most of whom seem to be wearing lumberjack shirts.

She loses him for a while in the Gents' and sits miserably nursing a Bacardi and Coke until he reappears, all smiles but seemingly coming down with a cold. She asks if he wants to go home, especially if he's not feeling great. He says he is 'feeling great', and they join a crowd of people she doesn't really know very well. He keeps forgetting to introduce her and she feels tired and a bit hungry. She thought at least he'd want to eat.

By the time they get home it's almost midnight. Felicity and Dee have devoured every last crumb of bread, so Fern has to resort to stale Sugar Puffs with reconstituted powdered milk. The evening is not what she had imagined.

Charlie is so drunk he is barely able to stand. 'It's my birthday,' he hiccups, looking at his watch, and then corrects himself. 'Well, not till tomorrow, but it's my twin sister's birthday today.'

How can that be possible, thinks Fern.

Jill explained all the different kinds of twins to her ages ago, but she never mentioned twins who aren't even born on the same day. Charlie sees her puzzled face and slurs the explanation: 'Ten minutes apart, but she was before midnight on the fourteenth and I was a few minutes after on the fifteenth, and I will never, ever catch up.'

Charlie proceeds to fall face-down onto Fern's bed. It's all she can do to get his coat and shoes off. Furious, she lies down under a blanket on the floor. She's fed up with him, but halfway through the night she climbs next to his fully clothed body and breathes in his smelly hair and BO.

He is hung over but loving in the morning. He nuzzles up to her and tells her he'd like to take her breasts in his rucksack to play with on the train when the journey gets dull; every man on that train would be jealous.

And although the sudden image of her breasts being pulled from a rucksack makes her feel sick, she removes her fern necklace and puts it around his neck. 'Take this – it'll remind you of me. Every time you touch it, you will be touching me,' she gushes, a touch theatrically.

She is fairly convinced that he hasn't a clue James bought it for her. If he did, he would probably break it or throw it out of the window. She has to give him something; she can't give him her grandmother's pearls – he would look ridiculous – but the fern pendant suits him. It's girlie but not too girlie. He loves it. He smothers her in sour-breath kisses and apologises for leaving her like this, and then, without so much as a wash, he leaves for London to share his non-matching-twin birthday with his clever sister, his talented mother, his stuffy but okay stepfather and his prick of a stepbrother.

As soon as he's gone Fern removes the Betsy and Tom book from her special secrets drawer and stares yet again at the tall narrow house that she is convinced is Charlie's childhood home. What does he do behind that door? How does he behave? Who is the Charlie that his family knows?

14

On Polaroid

Without him, she is bored. Everyone else, including the invisible old couple on the middle floor that no one ever sees or speaks to, has a partner. Felicity has Dee, Rob has Jill, and Fern has no one to play with. She tries to ring her cousin, briefly hoping that Elise might invite her up to London for a party and fantasising that she'd end up coming back to Manchester on the same train as Charlie. They'd bump into each other on the concourse at Euston; he'd be with his mother and his sister and they would all instantly get along like a house on fire, and then she and Charlie could drink miniatures and kiss all the way home.

Elise isn't in. The person she speaks to on the number Elise gave her on Boxing Day has a very thick Colombian accent and hasn't heard of anyone called Eleeeese. Another voice shouts something in the background and the foreign voice informs Fern that 'Eleeeese no longer resides at this address, and good riddance.'

She thinks about ringing Mummy, but she doesn't have much change left and anyway, if she tells Rosemarie that Elise has gone AWOL then Mummy will call Aunty Minty and the whole thing will get blown out of all proportion. She'll call Elise's parents' flat later. Her cousin is probably staying there: she doesn't call it 'the bolt hole' for nothing.

Fern sits halfway up the stairs. On the ground floor Rob and Jill are cooking what smells like a giant fry-up; upstairs Felicity and Dee have filled the kitchen sink and are soaking their growing number of sex toys in a mild antiseptic solution. 'Dee has been getting a lot of thrush lately,' Felicity explained.

Fern decides to take all her bedding to the launderette and finish reading *The Thorn Birds*. She's a slow reader and prefers fashion magazines, which she smuggles back into the flat and hides under her bed because they make Felicity froth at the mouth.

Even Jill disapproves, though Fern really can't understand why. What's the big deal about looking at pictures of eye shadow and leg warmers? Sod *The Thorn Birds* – she accidentally on purpose leaves her book at home, carries her bedding round the corner to the launderette and enjoys a couple of hours watching the world go round (literally) while reading *Cosmopolitan*.

A couple of times, people try to engage her in conversation. A hirsute boy flirts across a basket of filthy rugby shorts but she sends back chilly vibes. She already has two men complicating her life, she doesn't need a third.

One of the articles in *Cosmo* is entitled 'Could You Be Mrs Right to a Royal?'

Fern actually thinks she could. She is polite and decorative, suits all manner of special-occasion hats, and can curtsey (thanks to Miss Collette's dance classes for infants and juniors, which she attended from the age of three). Then there's her life-modelling experience, which proves she has the ability to remain completely still for hours on end, and, most vitally, her current acting studies, which have taught her to look like she is listening even when she's not. So yes, actually, she very much does have what it takes to be a convincing Mrs Royal. What a shame Charlie isn't a prince.

With her bed linen smelling less like the contents of a dog

basket she returns to number 2 Old Lansdowne Road, manages to track Elise down at her parents' flat for twenty pence-worth of feverish gossip and then settles down to watch a black and white film on the ancient TV set that Felicity has rigged up with a coathanger aerial in the kitchen.

While Bette Davis goes tragically blind in *Dark Victory*, Fern weeps and her flatmates simultaneously sniff and pat their sex toys dry.

The evening falls in typically abrupt Manchester style. By half-past four it's dark and wet so she wraps herself up in the men's plaid shirt that she bought from the same second-hand shop that she ... Shit, she has forgotten to pick up Charlie's hip flask. She runs hell-for-leather in needle-sharp rain, catching the shop just before closing time.

On close inspection she's not sure the engraving has been done particularly well. In fact, it looks as if a slightly pissed dentist has cack-handedly drilled the letters onto the flask. The C is noticeably smaller than the T. Oh well, back at home she mashes up some of Dee's millet and nut roast with ketchup and a dollop of cottage cheese to loosen it up a bit, and rather spend the evening listening to her flatmates try out their freshly swabbed sex aids she troops off to the pub with Jill and Rob.

Some of the rest of her drama-school year turn up and the evening passes in a pleasant fug of bitching, booze and cigarettes. It's just a weekend, she reminds herself. He will be on his way home now; he might already be back at the flat. But he isn't, and she spends what feels like hours alternately hanging over the banister and peering out of her bedroom window, checking out fuzzy shapes in the yellow streetlight, before she hears the clang of the garden gate.

He is back, he is back, the boy is back, the train journey was awful, he is starving, good job Jill has make some flapjack. He looks like he has slept and washed and changed his clothes. Is that a new shirt?

'Yes, it was a present from my sister, she has really good taste. It was really nice of her, considering I didn't buy her anything. I wanted to get her a hamster but my mum wouldn't let me.

'Yes, yes, it was nice. So many questions! Why are you so interested? Just a meal really, a big family meal.' He laughs and fingers the silver shape at his throat. 'Oh yeah, and my stepdad asked why I was wearing a woman's necklace.' And he laughs and kisses her on the nose.

'But the best thing is this,' he says, and reaches into his rucksack and brings out a camera. 'It's a Polaroid: my stepdad gave us one each, me and Rowena, obviously. It was my mum's idea – he'd never have come up with the idea himself. I got some cufflinks too, but my mum wouldn't let me bring them back with me in case I lost them, and I got some cash, some lovely cash for lovely treats.'

She wants him to suggest taking her out for dinner some time this week, to make up for Valentine's Day. She wouldn't mind if there was an old man playing shit music on a baby grand in the corner and fake flowers on the table, she wants to sit across a white tablecloth from him and stare into his eyes and hold hands and be seen, and she allows herself a small fantasy that involves Fabiana walking past the restaurant and trying to smash in the plate-glass window by kicking it.

Ten minutes later, once Charlie has eaten all Jill's flapjack and pretended that it has given him an erection, which is sort of funny but not when he starts pushing the pretend erection up against Jill's backside, they are in his bedroom.

She would rather they go up to hers, the sheets are clean on her bed. Charlie has no sheets, just a mattress with a coverless, stained duvet. 'The Charlie nest,' he calls it, and swept up by his enthusiasm for his new birthday gift he loads a new cartridge of film. 'Just ten shots,' he tells her. 'Come on, take those clothes off.'

In the morning she makes him promise not to show anyone. He doesn't understand why she is making a fuss: after all, she did the life modelling. 'There's just something more permanent about a photograph,' she says. 'And anyway, some of these are quite rude.'

He laughs and tells her that Polaroids fade. In time, no one will really be able to see what she was doing with her wide-apart, lily-white legs.

'If only my pubes weren't so red,' frets Fern. 'They really stand out in some of the photos.'

'Ah, the burning bush,' laughs Charlie, delighted with his new toy.

15

Gone Boy

Fern has to make a dash for college. They are working on the physical aspects of Restoration comedy, including fan work, the etiquette of bowing and curtseying, and learning Baroque dance.

In the make-up session after lunch, as Fern finishes painting her face with white panstick, she realises her teeth look almost as yellow as her lover's. 'My lover Charlie,' she whispers to herself and paints a black heart below her left eye, a clown's teardrop.

When she gets home he is gone. Rob avoids her, scuttling like a cockroach into the kitchen, and instinctively she knows he has gone to see Fabiana.

She hasn't even given him his birthday present yet. He was too excited by the stupid camera and she let him get carried away with taking all those filthy pictures. What the hell is wrong with her?

Why is she mooning over this stupid boy and wasting her money buying him ridiculous presents when all he does is fuck her around and play her off against that stinking double-jointed maniac?

What's even worse is that he will be fucking her with Fern's necklace around his neck. Her necklace might be touching Fabiana's oily yellow skin. Yuck.

She is so angry she wants the Polaroids back, right now, but

Charlie's room is locked and it takes a lot of time and energy to persuade Rob to tell her where Charlie hides his key. She knows he won't take it out with him, he'd only lose it. Eventually she wears Rob down and he opens the cupboard under the stairs where a brass key lies on top of the fuse box. Hanging off the key-ring is a miniature wooden Pinocchio – fucking typical.

Rob hovers by Charlie's bedroom door while she hunts for the pictures. This morning he splayed them out on his pillow in order of preference, but now they are nowhere to be found. She starts pulling at random drawers until Rob intervenes. 'No Fern, it's not on. You can't start rifling through his personal things, stop it.' An ashen-faced Jill agrees with him, even though, later on, she admits to being firmly on Fern's side.

The bedroom standoff is interrupted by a phone call. It's James, 'just calling' to remind her that he's driving up this coming week-end and that he should arrive at around midday on Saturday. He tells her not to worry about food because he'll take her out for lunch, and dinner too, obviously. All she need think about is where to go and what to wear: after all, he doesn't get to see his gorgeous Godalming girl very often, so it's time to push the boat out.

She is almost weepy with relief at the sound of his voice. How in control of everything he seems. He'll be driving up because he is a man, she reminds herself. He is a man who can jump out of planes, command tanks, polish his shoes, stand up straight and put his shoulders back. All of a sudden she sees Charlie in a new and cruel light. He is a snivelling, spineless, yellow-toothed idiot and she hates his fucking guts.

Good, that feels better. Tomorrow she is going to bunk off college and nip into town to buy something special to wear on Saturday night. Maybe something vintage, but then she remembers that James doesn't really like vintage because he says second-hand clothes smell like old people's homes, and that he prefers her in something fresh and pretty.

*

The following day, Fern goes a bit mad in Miss Selfridge. She buys a black pencil skirt that clings to her hips and has a massive slit up the side, a black and white polka-dot silk shirt with a piecrust collar, and a four-inch-wide scarlet patent-leather belt.

The whole outfit is slightly vampish, so she buys a crimson lipstick, a set of red and black satin underwear complete with a suspender belt and a pair of fishnet stockings just in case. She almost takes the stockings and suspenders back. James isn't very adventurous in bed; they're more the kind of thing Charlie would want to take photographs of her in, and once again she is inflamed by the cheek of him, the things he has made her do. Not just the Polaroids: he makes her touch herself in front of him and he likes her to beg him to fuck her in her poshest Tillinghurst Girls' School voice because it makes him laugh.

She refuses to think about that creep for a second longer and nips into a wine bar for lunch. It feels incredibly grown-up to be ordering a glass of Frascati and a slice of quiche with salad in the middle of the day, and she feels momentarily like her own mother, who is very fond of shopping sprees and lunches in town with her sister.

Sitting in a window seat, Fern relishes not being in the mince and chips fug of the college canteen. She hopes Jill isn't too worried about her, it's true that she's upset about Charlie, distraught even, but she's not about to throw herself into the Manchester Ship Canal and . . . well, talk of the devil. Fern puts down her fork and tries to work out whether the figure ricocheting out of the snooker hall opposite actually is Charlie Treadaway.

Black curls – tick; oversized greatcoat from a charity shop – tick; shoulders rounded – tick; smoking against the wind – tick. Why on earth isn't he at college?

At least she's got a reason to be AWOL – she has to look nice for her handsome soldier boyfriend who is coming to see her this weekend – and by the time she has pushed aside what remains of

203

her salad and quiche she has decided that not only is Charlie completely dead to her, but she is going back to Dolcis to look at those black patent-leather spike-heeled shoes.

After all, if she is going to impress James with her elegance and sophistication this weekend, then the Doc Martens are going to have to go. Fuelled by self-righteous indignation, Fern stomps back to the Arndale Centre and purchases shiny black stilettoes that are more in keeping with her new-found 'I am woman, I am strong, I am not taking any fucking nonsense' attitude.

Striding back to the bus stop, she finds herself singing the lyrics to an old Helen Reddy song that her mother used to play on repeat until her father banned the record from the house.

'I am woman, hear me roar,' she mouths, hearing the song quite clearly in her head, seeing the black vinyl rotate. 'I am strong, I am invincible, I am woman,' and the song swells in her head until she is settled on the back seat of the top deck of the bus, at which point she starts crying, and she cries and cries all the way back to Didsbury.

Felicity, Dee and Jill are worried about her. Jill brings tinned tomato soup up to the top floor and the three of them sit on the end of her bed like concerned Shakespearian witches. 'He's no good for you . . . He's unreliable . . . He'll never change . . . I think he's a bit mental . . . You can do better than him.'

As the platitudes circle she chews tiny buttered triangles of toast and pretends to be listening to her friends, when in reality her ears are straining to hear the front door. Where is he?

'Rob's told him to stay away,' Jill eventually informs her. 'Just for another couple of nights, give you some breathing space. You've got James coming on Saturday – just concentrate on him.'

'Yes, me and Felicity are going to be really good this weekend,' Dee chips in.

'We're going to be really polite and non-threatening,' adds Felicity, 'and we're not going to mind if he cooks bacon, as long as he uses your pan. We just want you to have a nice time.'

'Come back to college tomorrow,' urges Jill. 'Bring some knickers and a toothbrush and stay at mine for the night, just for a change, and then it'll be the weekend and you'll feel better. It's a horrible lesson to learn, but we all fall in love with the wrong person at least once in our lives.'

'Dee used to have a girlfriend called Mavis,' sniggers Felicity.

'And Felicity once shagged a bus driver called Alan,' Dee snipes back.

She sleeps a deep, dead dreamless sleep, and in the morning she shoves her toothbrush and some pants into her college rucksack. She is a robot: she will do as she is told.

At college, she is braver than normal in an improvisation class because she simply doesn't care about anything any more. It's hard to feel embarrassment when you are emotionally numb. At the end of the college day she and Jill drink a pint each at the pub opposite and Jill tries to persuade her that life doesn't begin and end at Old Lansdowne Road. There are other places to be, other people to hang out with.

Jill shares a tiny flat with a girl who is studying fashion and textiles at the part of the Poly everyone refers to as the Toast Rack. Belinda is currently making a purple boiler suit with outsized shoulder pads. She is very excited at the sight of Fern: 'You could model for me at the end of term,' she whoops. 'You might be able to make even quite shit things look good.' Fern looks doubtfully at the lumpy seams of the plum-coloured all-in-one, but pretends it's a really great idea.

Jill cooks chicken cacciatore but without the red wine, which all three decide would be a waste of good booze, so they drink it instead and Belinda sews while the chicken stews. There is an atmosphere of calm, and because Belinda is studying fashion she is allowed to bring women's magazines into the flat, so when the room-mates retire to bed Fern makes herself as comfortable as possible on the two-seater sofa and reads *Vogue* until she drops off.

Her dreams involve Charlie in a pair of ridiculous striped leg warmers and nothing else. His body is covered in bruises; Fabiana has bitten every inch of him. In the morning, the previous night's chicken bones are still on the kitchen table and the sight of them makes her feel anxious.

She doesn't want to see him again, but she would like to know he's okay.

Jill says she can stay at hers until the weekend, but she wants to go home. She needs to sort the flat out for James, she needs to shave her legs and pluck her eyebrows. Anyway, Jill and Belinda's flat is minute and oddly characterless. The landlord has coated every surface with a bland cream-coloured woodchip paper and banned the use of posters or Blu-Tack.

It's strange, Fern utterly despised the top-floor flat at number 2 when she first arrived six months ago, but she has grown fond of its Steptoe's-yard ramshackle charm, the sloping eaves and raspberry-coloured kitchen walls, the golden birdcage stuffed with plastic flowers hanging in the hallway, and Felicity and Dee's framed postcard collection of female Music Hall turns.

It's dark by the time she gets back and there is no tell-tale light coming from Charlie's room. She creeps up the stairs; even if he was in, she wouldn't want to see him.

Thursday night is Felicity and Dee's conversational Spanish class at the local institute – Felicity's Plan B, should the acting career not work out, is to bugger off to Spain and open a gay and lesbian bar. 'With vegetarian snacks,' Dee added, 'like nuts and crisps, and maybe olives.'

She is glad to have the place to herself. What's more, the bathroom is free and the hot water plentiful for a change. She bathes and shaves and oils herself, she plucks her eyebrows and conditions her hair, she applies an Anne French face mask and pushes down her cuticles. She knows James doesn't really like painted nails, but the lure of scarlet talons to match her new red belt is too much, and in the end she paints her toenails too for good measure. After all, I am a scarlet woman, she secretly admits to herself.

Opting for an increasingly rare alcohol-free night, she sits at the kitchen table and writes a list of things to buy from the super-market. Butter (James hates margarine), croissants for a sophisticated Sunday-morning breakfast, but also eggs, bacon and bread should he prefer a fry-up. A quick check of the kitchen condiment shelf shows they are low on ketchup and brown sauce. She adds both to the list, along with Earl Grey tea.

The list reads competently enough, but her handwriting makes it look like a little girl is playing house. She tears the list up and scrawls gin and tonic on the back of her hand in biro, then goes to bed with the remnants of a bottle of cloudy-looking red wine.

The front door slams an hour later. Every muscle tenses – could it be? But Felicity's heavy tread and Dee's high-pitched Spanish practice phrases give them away. 'Good to have you back, amigo,' bellows Felicity through the kitchen wall. '¡Arriba, Arriba!' Fern yells back in the style of the cartoon mouse Speedy Gonzales, and she drifts off to the delicious aroma of toast being grilled. It reminds her of her childhood, the most comforting smell in the world. Unless, of course, they forget to turn the flame off and the grill pan catches fire and they perish in a blazing inferno because her mother was right, without a bloody fire escape this flat is a death trap.

Sod it. If she burns in her bed then Charlie will be really sorry and he will spend the rest of his life mourning her loss, and with this reassuring thought drifting around her brain she sleeps.

It's been four days now.

16

The Return

On the fifth day she wakes up feeling like she's lost something, but can't remember what it might be.

At least the flat didn't burn down in the night. They are all alive, although Felicity has finished Fern's Marmite, which momentarily makes Fern want to kill her. She breathes deeply and slathers peanut butter on her toast instead. 'It's okay, everything's going to be fine,' she repeats under her breath. Even the weather is trying hard to make things easier. Watery sunshine leaks through hairline cracks in the usual leaden skies, tiny streaks of optimistic pale blue amongst the sulky grey.

'Spring,' Fern announces to herself.

At Three Paddocks, there will be huge swathes of yellow daffodils. The sap is rising, and soon there will be blossom and lambs. She needs to go home; it's not long until the Easter holidays. Her mother still buys her a giant chocolate egg.

Homesickness engulfs her for a moment and she decides to set off early and walk to college. She's done enough moping, she's sick of waking up with an overflowing ashtray on her bedside table and the dregs of a glass of red wine. She's tired of having a tight chest and a slight hangover. She's glad she's given up Charlie Treadaway, he is just another bad habit, a health hazard, and she strides purposefully out into a deceptively biting March wind.

By the time she gets to college her eyes are streaming, but for once she can blame it on the weather.

College serves as a great distraction. She receives extra praise for her unusually aggressive fencing tactics, and when people ask about her weekend plans she tells them 'My boyfriend is coming to stay – I'm really excited. He's an army officer.'

There is, Fern realises, an odd attitude among some of her fellow drama students regarding James being in the army. People look surprised, disapproving even.

Jill explains why in the girls' loos: 'Well it's a peculiar job, really, going round the world killing people.'

'I don't think James has killed anyone,' laughs Fern, but then she really has no idea. He's been to Northern Ireland and awful things happen over there all the time.

Suddenly she recalls the bombing of Lord Mountbatten's boat and how the death toll included one of his grandsons, a boy of fourteen, a twin like Charlie. She remembers her father furiously drinking whisky and calling the IRA 'filthy scum', while her mother watched the news and kept repeating, 'That poor boy, how awful to lose your twin.'

Everyone is poised for Friday night: there is a party in Rusholme and at least half her year are going. Even Fern is tempted. She's been crap at going out recently; it's been ages since she's had a really good dance. All of a sudden she doesn't want James to come, she wants to go dancing in town. She wants to let her hair down at the Old Conti Club and snog a nameless boy in a beer-sodden corner. Instead she goes home after college and cleans the flat, suddenly horribly aware of the stained lavatory and the fact that this is the first time in her life she has ever thought to pick up a lavatory brush.

The brush is almost bristle-free and useless, the bath needs re-enamelling and the sink is thick with other people's toothpaste spit. Lightning suddenly ignites the sky outside and thunder growls in the distance. Manchester, it seems, has rejected spring, and rain pelts against the window.

Back in the kitchen she tackles the fridge and removes a number of objects from the salad tray that no longer bear any resemblance to any known fruit or vegetable. There is a lot of slime involved and a couple of times she gags. How can Mrs Bibby bear to do this on a daily basis? Fern suddenly remembers that Mrs Bibby wears rubber gloves, of course she does. Oh Christ, she has forgotten the first rule of housework. God knows what hellish germs she may have picked up in that stinking bathroom. Fern boils the kettle and plunges her hands into scalding water to be on the safe side, but cannot stop thinking about other people's piss and shit.

Settling her stomach with just one gin and tonic from the supply she has bought for James, she makes herself a lonely little cheese on toast. Jill and Rob have gone to the party in Rusholme and Dee has taken Felicity into town for a curry, which means that, by morning, her carefully cleaned lavatory will be disgusting again. As Felicity says, 'I love a curry, but curry doesn't love me.' Mortified by the prospect of James encountering her flatmate's bodily functions, she pours herself another gin and tonic and scans the draining board for forgotten dildos.

She is on her third gin and tonic when the front door slams and she hears someone running up the stairs. There is a knock on her kitchen door and in comes Charlie, rain-soaked and shivering. 'I'm sorry,' he says, 'I know I've been a shit, but I want you to know that it's over, I won't be seeing Fabiana again. It's taken a while to untangle myself because the woman's got tentacles like a giant squid. It wasn't very nice: I think I've had to be quite horrible and I'm a bit worried she might do something silly.'

Fern knows instinctively that Fabiana won't, and even if she does, she will survive – the woman is half cat. She silently pours Charlie a gin and tonic and then another when he immediately knocks the first one back. 'Let's get you dry,' she says, like a mother would to a child, and she warms up the kitchen by lighting all the rings on the gas stove and fetches him a towel from her bedroom.

She still hasn't touched him, she still isn't sure. He lights a cigarette off one of the gas rings and instantly there is a crackle and the stench of burnt hair. He is a danger to himself. She turns off the gas and tells him she is going to bed. 'Can I come too?' he asks. She nods her head and he follows her into the bedroom with the gin bottle under one arm, the tonic under the other, glasses in one hand, a squashed little roll-up in the other and a pouch of tobacco and Rizlas clenched between his little mustard-coloured teeth.

They fuck and drink and drink and fuck, and at five, when Charlie nips naked to the loo, he suddenly remembers that he needs to pack a bag as soon as it gets light because he is going to his sister's joint twenty-first pre-exam-season party in Oxford.

He invites her to go with him, he says it will be a laugh. He's going via London to see some mates in the afternoon, and then making his way to Oxford for the party. He tells her Oxford is quite mental and that his sister lives in this really ancient place that looks like it should be a convent or something. He burbles on about Rowena knowing some quite strange people – German counts, Persian princesses and even a Welsh giant – and of course they're all really clever, but sometimes you'd never guess.

He tells her about the bowler-hatted porters who guard the college's massive wooden entrance: 'Like a portcullis – I'm surprised there isn't a moat.' He says Rowena would like to meet her. 'Does she know about me?' interrupts Fern and Charlie looks puzzled for a minute. 'I think I mentioned you last weekend,' he hazards, but is not entirely convincing.

'Where would I sleep?'

'You wouldn't sleep, silly, it's a party. We'd be up all night and then we'd get the coach back.'

'I'm not going to Oxford and back on a coach,' she laughs, but then it hits her: the real reason she can't run off with Charlie is because James is coming. James is coming to sleep in this bed that reeks of spilt gin and cheap tobacco and, worst of all, another man's semen. Horrified and shocked by her actions she lies wide awake with Charlie sprawled on top of her snoring his head off, her silver fern necklace still safely fastened around his neck.

He leaves her bed at eight; the coach is leaving Piccadilly at nine. 'You'll never make it,' she despairs, wondering if he will always live by the seat of his pants, by the skin of his teeth.

'I will, I'm lucky,' he throws back over his shoulder. 'It's the Irish in me.'

He pelts down the stairs, and a few minutes later the front door slams. He really is very selfish: it doesn't occur to him that some people might want a lie-in this morning. From the window she watches him leg it down the road, his worldly goods in a Co-op plastic bag.

In an attempt to air her bedroom between lovers she heaves her sash window open. The morning air is an immediate, cool-handed slap of reality. What the hell was she thinking?

Several hours later, as she waits nervously for James to arrive, she realises that Charlie has swiped her gin and she's not sure whether to laugh or cry.

17

Entertaining James

James arrives bearing champagne – two bottles, both chilled – a whole side of smoked salmon and some pumpernickel bread. Of course, he has recently been in Berlin. How very continental and grown-up.

'I thought we could go out, or have a picnic,' he says as they skirt around each other, suddenly shy.

Fern is panicking. The post-gin blues are hovering, the weekend stretches interminably and she hasn't planned anything. Maybe she should take him to an art gallery or the cinema. What is he expecting? It's raining again.

'Let's go to bed,' she suggests. 'Let's have a picnic in bed,' and she tries to sound a bit husky and sensual but her nerves get the better of her and she sounds high-pitched and unhinged.

She decides against dressing up in her stockings and suspenders. Maybe she'll do that tonight – sex and salmon should be enough entertainment for a while.

In the bedroom he congratulates her on the open window. 'I told you last time, it's much healthier,' and he kisses her like a maiden aunt nibbling at a cucumber sandwich.

By mid-afternoon, Fern is sore from all the fucking. For some reason, when she and James make love her bed turns into a sand pit, everything is dry and uncomfortable. Her vagina is like an oyster with grit in it; maybe one day she will find a pearl up there. Oh God, he takes for ever to come.

James finally climaxes and as he snoozes off the first bottle of champagne Fern creeps off to the bathroom to root in her wash-bag for some paracetamol. Her head is pounding.

As soon as she locks the bathroom door behind her she realises that Felicity has obviously had a recent and terribly explosive shit, and almost gags at the stench.

'Honestly, that woman has the bowels of a truck driver,' she mutters, digging deep into the pretty quilted wash-bag that Mummy gave her for her birthday last year. She's in luck: there's a packet of painkillers under the tube of gunky stuff, the gloop she's meant to cover her diaphragm with ... what's it called? Spermicide, the sperm-killer, the stuff that kills the sperm, the gel that turns her vagina into a killing field of dead sperm, thousands of them exterminated by this sperm poison, and she wonders if it's the smell that kills them, if they are gassed on entry and whether dying sperm scream.

A split-second later it hits her, the realisation that she hasn't put her cap in. Oh Christ, she can feel the flush of guilt and shame flood her entire body. Fuck, oh fuck, oh fuck.

Right ... A bath, she can at least sluice some of the sperm out with water. Surely if they can be gassed, they can be drowned. She fills the bath to selfish levels and ignores anyone who knocks on the door. She has a lot of sperm to kill: there are two lots up there, Charlie's and James's.

Fifteen minutes later, thoroughly rinsed, she squeezes a large amount of spermicide onto her fingers and physically rubs the stuff around the walls of her vagina – just in case there are any tiny tad-poles clinging to the sides. Then, feeling slightly mad, she returns to the bedroom to pretend that everything is completely normal.

There isn't an improvisation class on the planet that could prepare her for this.

James is getting dressed. 'Well Miss Sauce Pot,' he says jovially, 'that was a very unexpected and delightful welcome. What say you we get ourselves some fresh air now, blow the cobwebs away?'

He is suggesting they go for a walk! She hasn't a clue where to take him. Why on earth would she go for a walk round here? Walks are for the country, with dogs and wellies. In desperation, she pretends it's a super idea and pulls a random 'walking round Didsbury' outfit together from her wardrobe.

James pulls a face at her jumper, a vast orange and black striped mohair affair. 'Gosh, that's large and loud,' he remarks and, pretending it's just a joke jumper and not her favourite sweater of all time, Fern changes into a form-fitting, simple black V-neck that she can tell meets with his approval because he licks his tiny lips and attempts an awkward wolf whistle. The urge to bite his entire face off is almost overwhelming; she has to busy herself with zipping up her boots in order to resist it.

For want of anywhere picturesque locally, and having no clue where else to go, Fern walks in the general direction of college and James holds her hand. It feels like a shackle and she becomes sweaty-palmed with claustrophobia.

By the time they reach the drama school building the rain spits in their faces, so they pop into the pub opposite for a drink.

The locals are at their worst. A fat woman sits with her legs wide open, her stocking tops on display. Her husband sits next to her, his right hand is bandaged and he has a black eye. As he struggles to roll a cigarette his wife stares into the distance while a bulldog lying at their feet licks a row of angry-looking stitches dotted along a gash on its belly.

'Where's Hieronymus Bosch when you need him?' mutters James in a voice than can never be quiet enough not to hear. He's not an army officer for nothing.

They leave without finishing their drinks, and all the way home he never once lets go of her hand.

Back at number 2 Old Lansdowne Road, Rob and Jill ask them in for a cup of tea, and even though she knows the invitation is inspired purely by nosiness, Fern could kiss her funny, generous, plump best friend.

Jill keeps the conversation bouncing to and fro. She even makes James laugh, and then Rob embarks on a man-to-man rugby chat, which is very boring indeed but takes the pressure off the girls for ten minutes.

Time crawls and all Fern can think of while she sits in the very kitchen where *he* makes his morning cup of coffee and rolls his first cigarette of the day is Charlie. Where is he now? Is he already in the land of dreaming spires? That impossible fairy-tale city where all the women are clever and beautiful, and immediately she visualises a turreted kingdom populated by velvet-gowned beauties, fabulous academic sirens all calling Charlie's name, but probably in Ancient Greek.

'Fern!' James is almost shouting her name and Jill brings her to her senses by slyly kicking her under the table. 'I was just saying, it's probably time we got ready to go out, leave these good people be.' For fuck's sake, he talks like my dad, thinks Fern, smiling benignly and pretending to look forward to a delicious dinner for two, when all she wants to do is go back to bed and wait for Charlie to come home.

He reaches out his hand for her to hold again but she pretends not to notice and moves independently, on invisible strings, up to the top floor. Inevitably they bump into Felicity and Dee on the landing and Fern braces herself for the inevitable awkward encounter. James tries his best, but she can sense every hair on his body is bristling with revulsion. He enquires after the girls' health and tells them in loud and simple phrases that 'it's raining outside', as if they might be foreign or have learning difficulties rather than a penchant for the same sex.

Fortunately they are on their way out – 'lesbian bingo night,' jokes Felicity – so the chat is mercifully brief. As Dee and Felicity clatter down the stairs Fern is convinced she can hear the words 'What a tit', followed by shrieks of laughter.

James is oblivious. 'Well that wasn't too bad,' he smirks. 'As long as they don't try and recruit you into their gang, I can just about cope with them.'

Fern ignores him. Desperately trying to kill time before dinner, she attempts to play some LPs. Sadly it transpires that she and James have very little in common when it comes to music, and the moment he calls Elvis Costello 'a funny little speccy-four-eyed freak' is almost his last.

'So what do you listen to?' she asks and he tells her that his favourite record is actually a recording of Winston Churchill's 'We will fight them on the beaches' speech, which he finds truly inspiring. But as for pop music, apart from a bit of Dire Straits he's not much of a fan. Fern's heart sinks to somewhere behind her knees. Charlie loves music, he's forever popping up to make her listen to some obscure French punk band or some awful electronic synthesisers, and just to piss James off she plays David Bowie's 'Fashion' at wall-shuddering volume, until even she knows she's being ridiculous and removes the needle from the groove.

If only Charlie hadn't swiped the gin.

An hour later, as they are about to leave for dinner, she removes her new red lipstick from its packaging and as she leans into the bedroom mirror to draw it around the bow of her lips a hand reaches from behind and confiscates the tube. 'You don't need it,' James tells her. He's right, without the lipstick she is beautiful, with the lipstick she would be alarming. Madness is buzzing all around her, it seems to be oozing from her skin.

James is a very courteous dinner date. Walking to the bistro, he fetches an umbrella from his car and holds it protectively above her head, even when a suddenly narrowed pavement means he has to wade through a streaming gutter.

As they make their entrance into the restaurant, heads swivel like sunflowers to look at the beautiful girl. The proprietor himself removes her tartan charity-shop coat as if it were mink, while the maître d' directs them with much bowing and scraping to their table.

He'd be great in a Restoration play, thinks Fern, enjoying the fuss. She feels like Grace Kelly. It's so much easier to play the enamoured girlfriend when she has an audience.

She plays her role to the hilt. Over the next couple of hours Fern bats her eyelashes, nibbles suggestively on breadsticks, spits olive stones charmingly into her elegant hand and laughs frequently, throwing back her swan-white neck at the slightest bon mot. She even allows herself to be spoon-fed morsels of her companion's food from the other side of the table. He has the foie gras for his starter, followed by the liver. How peculiar, he's liver mad. She has the smoked salmon followed by the mussels in white wine. The shells give her something to play with between cigarettes. She's not remotely hungry but the staginess of the event is appealing, she is beautifully lit and the wine, warm and bloody, heats the chill of dissatisfaction in her blood. By the time they have ordered a glass of brandy each she is soft with fondness for this man who treats her like a china shepherdess, and it's only when she gets up to leave that she realises she is pissed out of her head and that the tablecloth is littered with individual mussel-shell ashtrays.

Now when James offers his hand she grabs it gratefully. She has no idea how on earth they get home.

There is no more fucking. Fern is sick twice, once in a hedge and once in the lavatory. James is very good about it and blames himself for letting her order mussels.

In the morning he brings her tea and Weetabix, and he is such a picture of freshly washed health and strength that she feels weak just looking at him. He's so straightforward, so black and white. He sits down on the edge of her bed, searching the carpet for his gutter-drenched shoes. Her new blouse is in a heap on the floor, the rest of her clothes in a trail leading to the bed. Once his laces are neatly tied he looks directly at her. 'I've been meaning to ask you . . .' Oh God, she might be sick again. 'I've been meaning to ask you, and you must tell me the truth: your necklace, the one I gave you for Christmas, where is it?' And she lies, straight to his face. It's such an easy lie to tell, she almost believes it herself. The words fall without hesitation from her mouth. 'Oh God, James, I'm so sorry. I wear it every day, but on Friday we had a stage-fighting workshop at college and I put it in my locker for safety, and I'm so sorry but it's still there! I'm such an idiot, but I wanted to pick up some croissants on the way home for your breakfast before the shops shut and I just rushed off.'

He cheers up at the mention of the croissants and she forces herself up to make him breakfast, only to find Felicity and Dee sitting at the kitchen table, with pastry crumbs all over their lips like naughty puppies.

He leaves quite soon after, but before he goes he fetches the second bottle of champagne from the communal fridge and hides it on top of her wardrobe. 'Let's save this for the next time I come – I don't want those greedy old dykes lapping it all up,' he remarks cheerfully, stroking her smelly hair and kissing her despite her mussel-sick breath.

18

Waiting

Sunday is bleak, Manchester sulking under thick black clouds. And, matching the city's disconsolate mood, Fern spends the day flopping in and out of bed. At one point she almost makes it out to the shops, but manages to bribe Felicity to pick up some fags for her instead.

The day seems to be waiting for something to happen. When will he be back? And she dreams fitfully about a brainy sex-starved Rapunzel letting down her golden hair for a rampant Charlie to climb up.

Jill invites her down for a roast chicken dinner, but her stomach is still delicate and she declines the offer, a decision she regrets as soon as the heady scent of stuffing and gravy wafts up the stairs.

Maybe he has decided to stay another night with his sister. Just because he is no longer seeing Fabiana doesn't mean he is now automatically her property. He is a grown man; he can come and go as he pleases. 'But please, Charlie,' she mutters under her breath, 'please, please come home.'

Her senses are on standby all night, hyper-alert to the tiniest sound, and finally, around midnight, she hears it, the soft click of the front door, and her heart races. Will he come up and see her?

Should she go down and see him? She hasn't even given him his birthday present yet, and she needs to get her necklace off him before he loses it. Yes, that's the best excuse, her necklace. She'll give him the hip flask another time.

Grabbing the bottle of champagne from its hiding place on top of her wardrobe, she tiptoes downstairs in a carefully chosen Victorian pin-tucked nightgown that she knows she looks both virginal and wanton in and creeps into his room as quiet as a thief. Charlie is just sitting, half-dressed, in the dark. His curtains are open and a tiny shaft of moonlight illuminates his face. He looks shocking and barely reacts to her presence. 'You look knackered,' she ventures.

He half grins. 'Bit of an understatement,' and wearily he rolls into bed. 'Would you mind if we just sleep?' he asks and she climbs into his grimy bed, feeling suddenly more like a Victorian housewife than a sexy chambermaid.

Charlie seems to be more unconscious than asleep. She tries not to fidget but the bed is lumpy, her nightgown bunched and twisted. At one a.m., according to Charlie's alarm clock, she hears the phone ringing on the landing, insistent and shrill like a spoilt child being ignored. Who on earth would be calling at this time of night? She suspects it might be Fabiana and an electrical current of paranoia passes through her. Eventually, after another burst of furious ringing, there is silence. Charlie's breathing is so shallow she can barely hear it, and for want of anything better to do while she lies there wide awake and unaccountably anxious, she undoes the catch on her fern necklace from the back of Charlie's neck. His Adam's apple bobs dramatically in protest, but he doesn't wake and she gently slides the silvery pendant onto the bedside table, where it glints, all shiny and clean amongst the detritus of Charlie's life. Finally, as the moon slides behind a bank of black cloud, she sleeps.

The phone jars her awake again, then just as abruptly the ringing stops. It's seven o'clock. Moments later there is a hammering on the front door and a commotion in the hall, a scream from Jill and then they are in the room, two uniformed police officers and a third man holding up an official-looking letter.

They have come for Charlie. They want to take Charlie away for questioning. They are not arresting him yet, but he needs to go with them. He sits up blinking. 'I'm sorry?' Fern is asked to leave the room, this is nothing to do with her. Charlie must get up and dressed. He is confused, he doesn't know what's going on, his underpants are pale blue and have a hole in them, his legs are shaking. She allows herself to be manoeuvred out of the room and she sits on the stairs and watches as they bundle Charlie out of the house and into a waiting police car.

'Fuck,' says Jill. 'What the hell?'

Fern feels numb. Something deep down inside her seems to shift and she knows instinctively that from this moment on there is no going back, the dice have rolled and her life has changed for ever. Again the incessant ring of the grey payphone on the landing shatters the stunned silence in the hallway. Fern is the nearest. She hauls herself up and even before she can place the receiver to her ear she can hear her mother's voice, hysterical, weepy, almost incoherent. 'Mummy?'

'Oh thank God it's you Fern. Oh darling, I'm so sorry, but the most terrible thing has happened.'

Oh shit, thinks Fern, not Pippin.

'It's Elise, Elise is dead. Oh Fern, my poor darling sister is in the most awful state.'

Fern slides down the wall and sits on the filthy stair carpet in her ghost white nightie and tries to make sense of her mother's garbled words. The details are sketchy, Rosemarie isn't sure exactly what happened, 'She may have choked . . . she was at a party, a friend of a friend. In Oxford, apparently. Oh darling, your lovely cousin.' Fern lets her mother's grief pour down the line until eventually Rosemarie is spent and Fern is able to put down the receiver and tell Rob and Jill what has happened.

It's Jill who immediately connects the two incidents. 'Your

cousin was at a party in Oxford – isn't that where Charlie's sister was having her party? You don't think . . . '

No, she doesn't think anything. She doesn't want to think anything. It's too much of a coincidence. 'I don't want to talk about this,' she tells Jill. 'I just want things to be normal. I just need to go to college and, please Jill, just don't tell anyone.'

But the news breaks like a giant wave at lunchtime, crashing over the television, radio and evening papers – GOVERNMENT MINISTER'S DAUGHTER FOUND DEAD – and Fern locks herself in the same wooden cubicle she used to hide in when she first arrived at drama school, and howls.

That evening, Jill helps her pack. In the morning she will catch a train back to Godalming. There has been no word from Charlie. 'I've been thinking,' she tells her friend, packing and then unpacking her striped mohair jumper. 'Maybe the police want to question him about stealing bikes.' Jill says nothing.

19

The Aftermath

Elise is magnificent in death. For the rest of the week she is on the front cover of every newspaper, pouting, preening, sticking out her tongue, flicking V-signs and laughing straight into the lens. It is inconceivable that she is dead; she is so very much alive.

DRINK AND DRUGS ORGY KILLS 20-YEAR-OLD BEAUTY scream the headlines.

According to a preliminary inquest, Elise choked on her own vomit before suffering heart failure as a direct consequence of alcohol and drug abuse.

Eyewitnesses state that Miss Landreth had been in high spirits ... fateful night ... a lethal concoction of champagne, heroin, amphetamines, marijuana and lager. The girl's body was found ... desperate attempts to revive the minister's daughter ... tributes paid ... Margaret Thatcher deeply shocked.

Piece by piece, the events of the night unfold. Beneath the tabloid frenzy certain indisputable facts begin to emerge: the party Miss Landreth had attended was held in an Oxford college to celebrate a recent spate of twenty-first birthdays, and the last days of freedom before the onslaught of final-examination revision.

Elise Landreth was not a student at the college, although coincidentally her father had attended Hertford three decades previously. However, she had been invited to the party by a close personal friend. The minister's daughter, who had previously studied fashion at St Martin's School of Art, arrived from London by car, and the festivities began early and lasted well into the night. Brunette Elise had been given permission to 'crash out' in the bedroom of a German count absent from college that fateful weekend on account of his grandfather's funeral in Hanover. On the Sunday morning after the celebrations, her lift returned to London without her. No one was quite sure where she might have ended up – she was a popular and sociable girl.

'They mean she was a slut,' Fern's father mutters over the rim of his Glenfiddich. 'Christ, what a mess.'

By the following weekend the stories are more subdued. There is less hysteria and more in-depth navel-gazing on the subject of privilege and excess. 'The Curse of those who Swap the Silver Spoon for the Silver Foil' is the title of a *Sunday Times Magazine* article, complete with grainy pictures of Elise at her tenth birthday party flanked by her cousin Fern Woolbright and Lucas Spinner, the son of Miss Landreth's godmother Barbara Spinner, and the young man who gave Elise Landreth a lift to Oxford.

Fern stares hard at the photograph. Lucas is a pallid, doughy-faced boy whom she vaguely recalls meeting as a pallid, doughy-faced teen. While Barbara and Aunty Minty were extremely close, Fern's mother Rosemarie had never much liked 'that Spinner woman', finding her overbearing and self-satisfied. 'She's very "London",' Rosemarie once sniped, which is why their paths seldom crossed. The Woolbrights are rather more 'country'.

According to the article, Lucas drove the 'unfortunate' Miss Landreth from London to Oxford and returned the next day without the party girl, oblivious to her fate.

As for Charlie, so far, he is the unnamed twenty-one-year-old male helping the police with their enquiries.

His name is released to the press as soon as he is charged. Charles Sebastian Treadaway, an art student at Manchester and the twin brother of one of the party hosts, Rowena Treadaway, third-year English student at Hertford College, has been released on bail to attend trial in due course.

'They had no idea she was using heroin,' confides Rosemarie. She has been visiting her bereaved sister at Paul's Westminster flat. 'It's a siege,' Rosemarie reports. 'The press are all over the building like rats. They're making out she was a hardened drug user – I'd like to get my hands on this dealer chap. Minty hasn't eaten since it happened, she's lost stones. Stones, I tell you.'

They are eating a lamb and flageolet bean casserole, which Rosemarie unearthed from the freezer. She really doesn't feel like cooking, but they must eat. 'Please, Fern, just a little bit.' She can't, she might be sick.

'An art student from Manchester, would you believe? I knew you shouldn't have gone up there. Apparently the place is full of druggies, and according to the special police liaison officer this chap was arrested in Didsbury. That's where you live, Fern! Imagine, you might even have passed him on the street.'

'I don't think so,' chokes Fern, and she only just manages to say 'excuse me' before she bolts up the stairs and into Mrs Bibby's beautifully polished bathroom, where she is horribly sick, over and over again. This is worse than the night of the mussels, she thinks, and I haven't even had a drink.

She makes it back to Manchester just once before the Easter holidays. It's a couple of days before Elise's funeral and she needs to go back and get some shoes, maybe the pearls her grandmother left her. What do you wear to a funeral? She's never been to one before.

Her mother wants to accompany her but she insists on going by herself. Just one night, she promises. She wants to see Jill, she wants to ask Rob if he knows anything, if Charlie has been in touch.

Before she sets off her mother asks if she has lost that lovely necklace that James gave her. If she has, it might be a good idea to secretly replace it.

'I know where it is,' Fern snaps and she does, and for a second she is back in Charlie's bed. The necklace is draped over a pile of loose change – spilt coppers and a stack of fifty-pence pieces for the meter – a crumpled packet of Juicy Fruit chewing gum, any number of Rizla papers and bits of torn cardboard. Everything is covered in a fine layer of ash; it's as if Charlie creates his own mini-volcano wherever he goes.

The house is weirdly empty when she gets back and she solemnly fills the suitcase she has brought up north with funeral clothes, momentarily wondering if the black skirt with the slit up the side is suitable. Elise would love it, but no one else would approve.

Instead, she packs her black practice skirt, part of her drama student uniform – suitable for all maid work, period productions and, as it turns out, tragic family occasions. She feels ten years older than she did six months ago. She adds the black stilettoes and the V-neck jumper. Churches are often cold, but if it turns out nice then she's got a black silk shirt that will do. She cannot believe she is thinking about Elise's funeral in terms of weather, as if it were Wimbledon. She fills the case with anything else she might need for the holidays. There has been talk of a cruise, of getting away from it all, but nothing has been decided. The court case could be months off.

Exhausted by the awfulness of everything, she sits on the floor in front of her rickety chest of drawers and struggles to open the drawer containing all her Charlie secrets. Just the book, she tells herself, just take the book, but she can't resist tucking the cards he painted for her inside its beautifully illustrated pages, along with the envelope containing his hair.

Once the case is closed she lies on her bed and feels weirdly disconnected to her life here. It's as if a line has been crossed and she can't step back over it.

There will always be the before and after: before the police came for Charlie and after; before the phone call from her mother and after; before Elise died and after.

Her pulse quickens in her throat. It keeps happening – she wonders if it's anxiety – and then remembers she needs to go and fetch her necklace. If Charlie's room is locked then at least she knows where the key is. She creeps downstairs, relieved that the coast is clear, fetches the Pinocchio key-ring from under the stairs and quietly lets herself into Charlie's lair. The curtains are still half-shut and the place feels abandoned. Sitting on the bed, she inhales the scent of his pillow. It smells faintly of him, and even more faintly of her. The necklace is where she left it. Reaching to pick it up, she hears a key in the front door followed by Rob's voice in the hall. 'This is Charlie's room here on the left. I'll just get the key.'

But there's no need. Fern has left the door wide open.

A small, determined-looking middle-aged woman walks in. There is something about the way she carries herself; Fern can only describe it as 'presence'. The woman has tied a Moroccan-style scarf around her throat, and the blunt lines of her severely bobbed hair, brown with threads of silver, accentuate a dramatic pair of cheekbones. A girl is close behind her. She too is all cheekbones, bonier than her mother; she has a large hooked nose and is too gaunt to be properly attractive. She looks like she might recently have cut her own hair: the fringe is short and jagged. Instinctively, Fern knows this is Rowena, Rowena and her mother, Charlie's mother Edwina Treadaway.

Panicking and now feeling as if there is a small bird stuck in her throat, Fern's first impulse is to run, but she can't, the Treadaway women are blocking the exit.

Putting herself into acting mode, she mumbles, 'Oh yeah, sorry about this – just had to pick up something that accidentally got left in here by mistake.' As she speaks, the chain slithers from her grasp, and before she can bend down to pick it up the older woman has it in her hand. 'Here you go, dear.'

Fern all but snatches it back and bolts, her face and neck on fire. She is blushing so hard she is surprised she doesn't just burst into flames on the spot. She doesn't look back, she takes the stairs two at a time until she is safely on the top floor, where she aims straight for her bedroom, closes the door behind her, collapses to the floor and hyperventilates on the carpet.

Eventually, when she is calm enough, she fastens the silver pendant back where it belongs, around her own neck.

Two floors down, she can still faintly hear them, Charlie's mother and Charlie's sister. She edges over to the window. Parked outside the house is a large grey estate car, it might be a Volvo or a Volkswagen. The back seats have been put down and Rowena is loading bags into the boot. More bits of Charlie are being taken away, he is disappearing bin liner by bin liner. By the time she has played the Rolling Stones' *Emotional Rescue* five times on the trot, darkness has fallen and the estate car has vanished.

Jill finds her rooted to the spot. 'Rob said you were back,' and she sits on Fern's bed and Fern sits next to her, puts her head on Jill's lap and sobs while Jill strokes her hair and says 'It's okay, it's going to be okay,' until Fern almost believes her.

They eat a takeaway supper in the ground-floor kitchen. Rob fetches parcels of hot vinegary cod and flabby chips from the chippy round the corner, they drink copious cans of lager and the evening is a cross between a celebration, a last supper and a wake.

Rob fills her in on what Edwina has told him about the 'situation': apparently Charlie's bail conditions mean he has to live with his mother and stepfather until the court case, which will most likely be in September. The art school has decided they no longer want him and the landlord said if he didn't clear his stuff out then he was going to come round himself and have a bonfire.

At this point Jill interrupts him. 'We've decided me and Belinda are going to move in after the Easter holidays. I'll share with Rob and Belinda can have Charlie's room – there's tons of space for her machine and stuff.' Instantly she looks guilty. 'I'm not saying I'm glad, I'm just saying it's a solution.'

Fern nods. The lager is making her head swim, she really isn't handling her alcohol very well at the moment. As for cigarettes, she can't think why she even lit the one she is currently smoking, it's disgusting. Felicity and Dee join them for coffee and more lager, and Fern's heart aches with wishing that things could be different and that Charlie could be here. Dee even has some dope: he would love it. She can see him hunched over a roll-up, grinning like a fox.

'They seemed very nice, his mother and sister.'

Rob's face twists into a grimace. 'They are. They're in pieces: I don't think his sister has eaten since it happened. She looks a bit fucked, to be honest. I have a horrible feeling she saw the body.' There is silence for a moment while that sinks in, but fortunately Felicity gets a pack of cards out of her bag and they end up playing gin rummy till two in the morning.

Lying in the single bed that she and Charlie and she and James have shagged in (and God knows how many countless other couples before them), Fern wishes she could stay until the end of the week. There's a real end-of-term feeling in the air. She has missed this life, she misses college, she misses this flat, she misses her friends. But she can't stay, she has Elise's funeral to attend. How the hell is she going to get through that? Fern nips out of bed, finds the hip flask she was going to give Charlie for his birthday, unlocks her case and stows it away, right at the bottom.

Tomorrow is another day, she reminds herself.

'See you after Easter,' she tells Dee and Felicity, who are making a mess of making French toast in the kitchen, and then she runs downstairs to say the same to Rob and Jill.

Jill hugs her. Who'd have thought it? 'And there was I, thinking you were going to be my mortal enemy,' Fern mutters into Jill's hair.

'Never,' states Jill firmly, giving Fern strict instructions to 'take care'. Rob offers to bring her case down from the top floor, and as he accompanies her up to her room he palms her a piece of paper. 'It's Charlie's London number, just in case.' Fern slides it deep into the pocket of her jeans. 'You never know.'

But she does know. She knows she can never speak to him again, and as the door closes on number 2, with Jill and Rob waving from Rob's bedroom window, and Dee and Felicity waving from the top floor, she is struck by the feeling that this chapter in her life is over and that she is walking away from something she really doesn't want to leave.

20

Grief

Elise's funeral is as bad as expected. Fern has never seen so many grown adults weeping, and she finds watching middle-aged men cry particularly unbearable.

Her dear Uncle Paul sobs silently, his face wet and agonisingly lined. Aunty Minty has obviously taken something: she is a walking statue, her face immobile, shrouded in black, shrunken in grief.

Fern is flanked by her parents. Her mother's hands twist around a sodden lace handkerchief, her father's jaw is set in fury, but during the eulogy it wobbles continuously until, defeated by the sadness of the occasion, he bows his head and tears drop onto his black-suited knees.

Fern is in shock. The coffin horrifies her: this cannot be happening, her cousin cannot be in that box. A wave of claustrophobia swamps her and it's all she can do not to faint.

'Beloved only child, all that knew her, much loved, in the arms of the father, lamb of God.'

Fern loses the thread of the service. She cannot help thinking of the Elise she last saw, crouched in the Harrisons' boot room with a smuggled bottle of Cinzano, a fairy ring of love bites round her neck. Mad, funny, crazy Elise, and she feels a strange sensation in her ears, a rushing noise, a closing-in from all sides.

Her mother is passing a bottle of eau de Cologne under her nose. 'I thought you were going to go, darling, you're terribly white.'

The worst thing is how long it goes on. First the service at the church in Chelsea, then the cremation in Mortlake followed finally by the 'celebration' of Elise's short life at the Cadogan Hotel.

Here, at the hotel where Oscar Wilde was famously arrested, Fern realises she is on show, like a Kennedy after an assassination. She must be gracious, noble, she must be a credit to the family. She knows some of the other mourners: there are girls she vaguely recognises from Elise's parties, older now; some are mumsy and sporting engagement rings.

'Minty had to be very careful about a *certain element* turning up,' her mother hissed at one point. 'Quite a few undesirables from the fashion school needed to be told in no uncertain terms they weren't welcome.' She'd spotted a couple at the back of the church, but security has been employed at the hotel and Elise's more colourful friends have been weeded out. Here are the pink faces and Alice bands of Chelsea and Westminster, the Amelias and Fenellas of Elise's childhood.

At one point, Margaret Thatcher is rumoured to have arrived. She hasn't, but she has sent a wreath. The atmosphere is hushed and strained. Subdued waitresses, aware of the painful nature of the occasion, circulate with crustless sandwiches and slices of Madeira. Tea is served, or pink champagne for those who cannot cope without alcohol.

Fern is sipping a cup of Earl Grey when a young man approaches her. He is not fat, but his body has no definition. His suit fits like loose covers on a small sofa. Something about his face makes her think of silk scarves transforming into white doves.

'I'm Lucas Spinner,' he announces, and she immediately hates his guts. 'We seem to have attended the same parties in the past,' he continues, 'but sadly not in recent years.' Something in her eyes must have made him suddenly conscious of how inappropriate that sounds. 'I mean, God, I'm glad you weren't at the, er, Oxford, um, do – no, no, awful terrible business, poor Elise,' and he blows his nose on a horrible middle-aged man's handkerchief and tries again.

'She was my mother's goddaughter, you know.' Fern nods, she is well aware of Barbara Spinner: she and Aunty Minty were at finishing school together. Lucas's eyes swivel round the room. 'There she is,' and Fern spies a large woman with the biggest hair she's ever seen. There is something of the drag queen about her: she is all bosom and yet surprisingly dainty around the ankle. 'Poor Mummy, it's been hellish for her, and of course it's all been horribly complicated by the fact that – well you know . . . '

Barbara has sidled up. For a big woman, she covers a lot of ground very fast. A moment ago she was on the other side of the room, now she is here, like a glittering-eyed boa constrictor breathing down Fern's neck. 'He's playing it down, of course,' she rasps.

'What?' asks Fern. She genuinely has no idea what this overly perfumed woman is talking about.

'Well, it was thanks to Lucas that they got their man. I mean, it won't bring Elise back, but it's a tiny crumb of comfort for Paul and Minty: at least they know the fiend who killed their daughter will end up behind bars.'

An odd sensation in her mouth, a roar like the sea, a feeling like she is entering the dark mouth of a cave and Fern hits the newly laid fleur-de-lis-patterned carpet in the main function suite of the Cadogan Hotel.

It is a welcome distraction, the sight of a beautiful red-haired girl crumpling to the floor in what looks like slow motion.

'Stand back, everyone, give her some space.' Her father carries her from the room like he did when she was small and she is put to bed in a suite until her parents feel she is fit enough to be driven home.

'I think we might get Doctor Leonard to have a look at you next week,' says Rosemarie, perching anxiously by her daughter's bedside. 'You've been looking very peaky lately. I think you might need a tonic, a little pick-me-up.'

A little pick-me-up, ha.

Fern turns her face to the wall and weeps.

21

The Inevitable

Unbeknownst to Fern, her mother had guessed before the GP even suggests it might be a possibility.

Dr Leonard looks mortified as he brings up the idea that the girl opposite him, whom he has known since she contracted chicken pox as a toddler, may 'possibly, conceivably . . . aha, apt choice of word . . . be with child'.

Fern looks around the surgery. What does he mean, 'with child'? There is no child here. She has come alone on her mother's orders to discuss her feelings of exhaustion and nausea, her sudden inability to eat certain foods, the peculiar overly sensitive sense of smell that she has suddenly developed. What does he mean, 'with child'?

The penny slowly drops and she laughs involuntarily. 'You mean, am I pregnant? No, of course not. I can't be.'

'So you're on the pill?'

'Not the pill, but I do have a, um, Dutch cap, should the occasion arise.'

'And are you conscientious?'

She pauses for a second too long. The doctor continues, 'Insomuch as barrier methods are only truly effective if they are implemented religiously, the – ahem – device must be in position to be efficient as a means of birth control.'

Fern feels the blush travel from her throat to the roots of her hair, and the doctor duly takes note and offers to take some blood to be on the safe side.

She is pregnant, of course she is pregnant. She is nineteen years old and she has ruined her life.

Her mother is white-faced but efficient. 'It's not the end of the world, Fern. What has happened to Minty and Paul *is* the end of the world, but this, this is just something we are going to have to deal with.'

For a moment Fern thinks her mother is going to suggest an abortion. How wonderful to just fall asleep and wake up and the problem have gone, like her tonsils when she was nine.

But an abortion is the last thing on Rosemarie's mind, and in some respects Fern is grateful, because if her mother suggested it she would find making the choice impossible. Better, in some respects, to have no choice.

Rosemarie does, however, have a plan of action, and it very much involves James. 'I'm surprised at him,' is all she says, 'but I have no doubt he will shoulder his responsibilities.'

Rosemarie informs Fern's father of the situation while Fern is safely out of the house.

'Give me a couple of hours,' her mother warns. 'The worst of it will be over by the time you get back.' Her father's temper is like a hurricane, terrifying to witness but eventually blowing over.

By the time Fern returns, he is in his study with his head in his hands. 'I'm disappointed in you,' he says, 'but thank God James is the father.'

She can't say anything, she can't say, 'I don't know. It could be a boy called Charlie Treadaway, a boy who you have only read about in the papers, a boy who may have given my cousin the drugs that killed her.'

No wonder she feels sick all the time.

Telling James is awful. Initially he looks so shocked: 'I thought I was just coming for Sunday lunch,' he stammers, and then he does the oddest thing imaginable: he gets down on one knee and asks her to marry him.

Out of the window she can see her mother cutting tulips for the table. She cannot destroy everyone's life, she might have fucked up her own, but . . . 'I'm only nineteen,' she whispers and he says, 'So is Lady Diana, darling,' and somehow, between the cutting of some tulips and the yellow wobble of her mother's Sunday-lunch trifle, Fern agrees to becoming Mrs James Frobisher.

By the time the dishwasher has been stacked and they are drinking tea in the conservatory, dates are being discussed. 'A June bride, I think,' her mother resolves. 'Of course it gives us very little time, but then we don't really have the luxury of time. Sadly it'll have to be a registry office do, but in the circumstances . . .'

'What about college?' ventures Fern.

'Well, it's a shame,' her mother replies coolly, 'but I can't see the point in you finishing the term when you aren't going back in September. Your father will write a letter.'

'But my flat and my things—'

'I shouldn't worry about that sort of nonsense,' her mother continues. 'I'm afraid one of the side effects of being pregnant is that fitting into one's normal clothes becomes rather problematic. You've brought enough back to cover the Easter holidays, and then we can sort out some maternity wear.'

She feels like screaming, but she knows that she can't. All this could be much worse: they are at least being kind, even if they are controlling every element of her life.

'I'd like to buy you an engagement ring,' James interjects, and he smiles as if he's been practising for hours but still hasn't got it quite right.

Rosemarie breaks the silence that follows: 'Thank goodness James is based at Aldershot – it's only half an hour by car. We can look after you here until the wedding and he can come and visit whenever he can. James, you will want to tell your parents, of course, and I think it might be good if they came for a sherry in a week or so. Please give your mother my number.'

Fern walks James to his car. 'I'm sorry,' she says and he tells her she mustn't be. After all, it's probably what they would have done in a couple of years anyway. 'The process has just been sort of speeded up.'

He hasn't touched her since she told him, but before he gets in the car he kisses her rather clumsily on the cheek and then he drives off very fast.

It's a beautiful evening and there's still time for a ride. She walks over to the livery stables where Bruno blindly munches apples and persuades the stable girl to lend her a 'proper pony', and so the girl saddles up a frisky-looking bay, whom she introduces as Bunty. Fern swings herself into the saddle and rides the mare out into the lane.

As soon as she can, she leaves the bridle path and takes the pony into open farmland, where she pushes the little mare as hard as she can over gates and hedges. If only she could jolt this baby out of her, if only she could fall off and lose consciousness for ever. Eventually Bunty refuses to jump any more. She is tired, and Fern has no choice but to walk her back to her nice clean stable. 'I'm sorry,' she sobs into the mare's hot, damp neck. Bunty is sweating and frothing, greenish foam around her mouth. 'I'm sorry,' but like her father, the pony will not look at her.

'I don't think you should ride again,' her mother says as soon as she walks in the door. 'And if you do, I shall have Bruno sold for glue, do you hear me?'

22

Shotgun

James meets her in town the following Wednesday to buy the ring. If they hurry, he will have time to buy her a celebratory lunch before he has to get back to camp. She chooses a simple diamond solitaire, and the jeweller is more excited by her choice than she is. 'Very nice diamond,' he keeps repeating, 'good choice.'

Over lunch, James raises the subject of their honeymoon. 'What with the wedding being a bit low-key, the least I can offer you is a couple of weeks somewhere romantic, a bit of sunshine,' and for the first time Fern feels a tiny stirring of optimism. A holiday: at least she is getting a holiday out of this. She is also feeling less sick, and her carbonara is delicious.

'How about Greece or Italy, or even the South of France?'

'I won't be able to wear a bikini,' she says, but he doesn't understand she's attempting a joke, and instead of laughing he pats her hand and tries to reassure her: 'That's fine.'

But before the holiday, or honeymoon, as she needs to get accustomed to calling it, there has to be the wedding, and before the wedding there has to be a meeting of the parents. Such is the order of these things.

As soon as they possibly can, the Woolbrights host a tense little meet-and-greet at Three Paddocks for their prospective in-laws, an occasion thinly veneered with good manners and copious amounts of sherry.

The evening is purgatory for Fern. James can't attend, so she is cast adrift, alone on a sea of middle-aged disappointment.

Glenys and Andrew Frobisher seem slightly stunned at the events so rapidly unfurling around them. Their elder son only got married a year ago and they already have a grandchild on the way, and now ...

'Now you have two,' trills Rosemarie. 'Imagine: they can be little playmates. Cousins are so ...' and the words stall in her throat. She cannot say the word 'cousin' without the ghost of Elise appearing in the room.

No wonder the Frobishers look faintly horrified. They must be wondering what kind of family James has gone and got himself mixed up with. After all, it's only been a matter of weeks since a preliminary inquest into the cause of Elise's death cited a cardiac arrest following a lethal combination of heroin and champagne.

Fern is desperate for a drink, but her mother has been very strict about pregnancy and alcohol, so she sits and nurses a sparkling orange Britvic 55, while the grown-ups plot her future.

It is decided that the couple will have a small registry do, followed by a nice lunch. 'But not at the golf club,' insists Andrew Frobisher. 'Because ... well ...' Fern has to bite her tongue before she shrieks, 'Because you don't want all your fucking horrible friends witnessing your son's shotgun wedding!'

Rosemarie chips in quickly with the name of an Italian restaurant with a discreet conservatory tucked away at the back, which can easily seat twenty. She doesn't imagine any more will be necessary.

Fern thinks back to when she and Elise drew themselves as future brides, with fourteen bridesmaids apiece.

'I'd like my flatmates to come,' she interjects, but instantly backtracks as her mother's left eyebrow disappears into her hairline. Of course, the lesbians would add even more shame. 'Well, just Jill, then. Please may I have Jill? I need a sort of bridesmaid.'

Rosemarie, hearing the hysteria in her daughter's voice and fearing a scene, quickly agrees to Jill attending, but as for anyone else, it's close family only. 'After all, we have very recently suffered a family bereavement,' murmurs Rosemarie, and Glenys nods fervently.

This, of course, is the best excuse of all. This is what she will tell her friends when they start asking difficult questions: 'A small private wedding, due to a recent, tragic bereavement, and then a honeymoon in Cap Ferrat.'

'Well that's that sorted,' trills Rosemarie.

Her mother is getting over it. Rosemarie's grandmotherly instincts have kicked in: a baby is her gift to make up for the menopause, for getting old, for not wanting sex with her husband any more. A grandchild is compensation for all the other shit she is going through.

Fern goes to bed, she is exhausted. Twenty minutes later her mother comes up with hot milk and scrambled eggs on toast. 'You might not want to eat,' she tells her daughter, 'but the baby does.'

The Easter holidays are almost over. Gordon writes to the college, informing them that Fern will not be returning for the new term, or indeed ever again. He gives no reason – why should he? It's nobody else's business.

A few days before term is due to start, Jill rings to ask Fern if she fancies seeing a show in London. Her aunt gave her tickets for *Evita* for her birthday; it's a matinée, so Jill can catch an early train down, meet Fern for lunch, see the musical and then catch a train home.

'It's a date,' says Fern, and the girls arrange to meet at the Pizza Express near Leicester Square.

Jill is horrified, she can barely eat her margherita she is so horrified. She keeps repeating, 'I can't fucking believe it. Is it too late to get rid of it? Why weren't you on the pill? Oh Christ, there was me feeling sorry for that poor bitch Diana and now you go and do this.'

Later, sitting in the dark waiting for the show to begin, Fern leans over and whispers 'Will you be my bridesmaid?' into her friend's ear. For some reason this makes them hysterical with laughter and it takes a great deal of tutting from neighbouring seats before they calm down.

Fern sees Jill to King's Cross, and they hug tightly before Jill boards the train, a full, bosom-crushing hug. 'I'll be your bridesmaid, just don't make me look like a prat.'

Fern feels weepy as the train disappears. It takes her for ever to get back to Godalming; by the time she gets a taxi home from the station her mother is white-faced with worry in the kitchen.

'I don't like you gallivanting off to London in your condition,' she snaps, and not for the first time Fern can't wait to be married and out of this house.

23

No Going Back

As the wedding hysteria for the royal groom and his princess bride mounts, plans for Fern's nuptials are also gathering pace. Very subtle invitations have been sent out to a select number, and sixteen accept.

Minty and Paul will 'unfortunately' be out of the country. Gordon's cousin and his wife simply don't respond, but both paternal grandmothers are game and Mr and Mrs Bibby, whom Rosemarie invited when it looked like no one was going to come, are 'positively delighted and greatly looking forward to the event'.

It's been decided that Fern will wear a pastel two-piece, even though there is barely any physical evidence of a baby yet. She just looks fuller, her bras are tight and her face is rounder.

With Rosemarie's help she chooses an ice blue silk ensemble with a cleverly cut jacket that would disguise even the smallest bulge, and a little pill box hat with a half veil. 'Very Diana,' chirps the saleswoman.

Jill is allowed to come and stay on the eve of the wedding. Rosemarie has requested her measurements and bought her a loose-fitting salmon pink shift dress with a dropped waist and a large white sailor collar.

'I can't believe I've barely even met this girl,' protests Rosemarie. 'I vaguely recall seeing her in that play thing you did, but where did you say she was from again?'

Jill arrives in time for supper. 'I've never had quail before.'

'I beg your pardon?' says Gordon. Both he and Rosemarie are having difficulty with Jill's accent and the more self-conscious Jill becomes, the broader her Geordie accent gets. Eventually her conversation at dinner descends into a series of over-excited vowel sounds.

It's only when they are finally in Fern's bedroom that they are able to talk properly.

'Are you sure?' asks Jill. 'Are you positive you want to go ahead with this, because you've still got time to run away. I know where your dad's car keys are – we could just leave.'

But Fern seems resigned to her future. 'Maybe I've got used to the idea, maybe I just fancy a holiday. Bollocks to it, Jill, this time tomorrow I will be on my way to Cap Ferrat. Let's not talk about it any more. Tell me about college and Rob and number 2.'

So Jill entertains Fern with drama-school gossip and the news from Felicity and Dee, and how Belinda has settled in to Charlie's old room, and she notices Fern flinch when she mentions his name so she doesn't mention him again, and anyway, the conversation is terminated by Rosemarie appearing in Fern's bedroom, insisting 'the bride-to-be needs her beauty sleep'.

Rosemarie is wrapped in a caramel silk dressing gown and has cold cream slathered all over her face and neck, but despite the fluffy mules on her pedicured feet there is very much something of a 'don't mess with me' attitude about her. Jill meekly follows her to the guest room.

At four o'clock in the morning Fern creeps downstairs to her parents' drinks cupboard with the pewter hip flask she once intended to give Charlie and fills it to the brim with vodka. Just in case, she promises herself. Just in case you really can't cope, and then she goes back to bed and dreams of her dead dog Smudge. The next time she wakes her pillow is soaking wet.

The wedding is booked for half-past eleven. It's an oddly solemn affair, with a mumbling and disinterested registrar.

James looks handsome, but Fern cannot for the life of her understand why he and his best man have dressed up as soldiers. They look like they fell out of a toy cupboard and she feels ever so slightly hysterical, possibly because she has been secretly swigging vodka since breakfast.

It is over almost as soon as it began. There are no lawful impediments, no lost ring, nothing. Fern grips her bouquet of cream roses so tightly that their heads begin to droop. 'I do.'

The registry office has rules about throwing confetti. It's strictly forbidden, but Mrs Bibby has outsmarted the council, and as the newly wed Mr and Mrs Frobisher leave Godalming Town Hall Fern is hit in the eye by a small shower of uncooked 'lucky' rice.

She has finished the vodka by the time they are seated in the restaurant, which at least takes the edge off her mother removing her champagne glass and saying, 'You may have a *small* glass when it's time for the toast.'

Fern is pissed enough not to understand what she is talking about. 'What toast? Why are we having toast?' They chose the menu weeks ago, smoked salmon and lamb. No one said anything about toast.

Mercifully, the speeches are very short. Her father is vague, the best man inaudible and James to the point.

Just as everyone is about to raise their glasses, Jill clinks a teaspoon against her champagne flute, then stands up. 'Ahem,' she starts. 'I've always wondered why the bride doesn't get to say anything on these occasions, but as her best friend and bridesmaid I'd just like to say, I fucking love this woman, so James, you'd better look after her or you've got me to answer to, and I'm from Gateshead.' A few people laugh politely, Jill flushes crimson and sits down.

246

Fern is suddenly exhausted. Her new brother- and sister-in-law have brought their very recently born baby, a foul-smelling goblin wrapped in a lemon-coloured blanket wet with sick.

Back at Three Paddocks, Jill surreptitiously hands her two paracetamol before leaving in a taxi for the train station. She has shed her bridesmaid's attire and is happily dressed for her real life as a student. Her black jeans strain across her wide backside and Fern clings to her while the taxi outside sounds its horn.

'I think it's time you put Fern down now,' says Rosemarie and Jill leaves. She doesn't look back and Fern knows it's because she is crying.

Having changed into her going-away outfit, the bride sits on her bed and wishes, more than anything, that she could just crawl in and go to sleep. Removing the hip flask from her handbag, she lifts the cold pewter to her lips and drains the last drops of vodka.

'Shit, what have I done?' she whispers as she walks out of the bedroom where, once upon a time, she was just a child reading books about ponies and ballerinas.

24

Mother Nature

Cap Ferrat is beautiful, and for a week the newlyweds bask in a bubble of optimism. Marriage can't be all bad when it means fresh buttery croissants and towering multi-coloured ice-creams. Maybe it's the food, maybe it's the baby, but Fern is noticeably fatter by the time they are due to fly home.

Throughout the honeymoon James is the epitome of gentlemanly charm, ordering snacks of fresh melon and insisting on rubbing sun cream into her porcelain back and shoulders, but he avoids touching her belly and the baby is not mentioned.

When, she thinks. When are we going to talk about the future?

Eventually, on the last night, over a very nice chateaubriand and emboldened by an excellent bottle of claret, he broaches the subject of where they are going to live, 'as of tomorrow'.

'Your mother would like you to stay at Three Paddocks until the baby's born. She thinks it's best someone keeps an eye on you, makes sure you get to all your appointments.'

Fern nods. The idea seems reasonable enough.

'Then, after Christmas,' he continues, 'I'm due for a new posting. I'm pretty sure it's going to be Germany, so we'll move into married quarters out there. Paderborn or Bielefeld, I should think.'

Fern almost chokes. 'Germany? Is there nothing in France, somewhere by the sea?'

He laughs and says, 'It doesn't really work like that.'

She starts bleeding on the flight home, just some spotting at first, but by the time they have landed in Heathrow the awful redness has flooded her knickers and stained the back of her skirt. Thank God she is wearing navy. Waiting at passport control, she eventually tells her husband that she is feeling faint, that something is wrong.

Fern regains consciousness in St Thomas' Hospital. She is lying in bed in a small private room with a grey-skied view over a brown River Thames.

The consultant explains things as best he can. 'Although nothing, Mrs Frobisher, is an exact science ...'

Mrs Frobisher? Fern scans the room for James's mother, but of course she is Mrs Frobisher now. *Fern Frobisher*, what a bloody silly name.

'From what we can gather, you have lost a baby and yet, because we can still detect a heartbeat, we can only deduce that you must have been carrying twins. Now sometimes, in the case of fraternal twins ...'

She is back in Charlie and Rob's kitchen. She is looking at a drawing of two eggs and two non-identical babies, and for some reason she pictures one that looks like James and another that looks exactly like Charlie. 'Fern, listen to the doctor,' James reprimands her. She wants to shout 'I'm not a child', but she knows he is right, this is important.

'When two eggs have been fertilised and both are developing independently in the womb, a miscarriage can occur which will result in the loss of just one baby. Now, usually it will be very obvious that a foetus has been lost, but now and then, apart from some bleeding similar to what you have experienced, the healthy embryo will simply absorb the non-viable foetus ...'

James looks a bit sick.

'Vanishing twin syndrome,' whispers Fern.

'Yes,' the doctor answers, 'this condition is sometimes referred to as vanishing twin syndrome. You see, your body is very special, it can make things appear and disappear,' and the doctor clicks his fingers and laughs. 'As if by magic.'

Fern spends the rest of the summer being wrapped in metaphorical cotton wool by her mother, and really, apart from having this peculiar bulge sticking out at the front, it doesn't feel very different from the summer she spent recuperating from glandular fever when she turned sixteen.

She's still not allowed to ride – in fact, Rosemarie even gets funny about her cycling the few miles into town – but the weeks pass pleasantly enough. She has check-ups to attend, maternity clothes to buy and occasionally she gets to see her husband.

She even manages to catch up with one or two boarding-school friends, most of whom are ghoulishly fascinated by everything that Fern has been through: the death of Elise, the miscarriage, the surviving baby. 'Can we touch your tummy?' they chorus. One even admits to being jealous. 'I'd love to get married and have babies,' sighs Lydia Metcalf, stroking her long narrow nose, which she is convinced is the only obstacle between herself and everlasting happiness.

On the August bank holiday weekend, when James is free, they drive to Manchester and clear her remaining possessions out of number 2 Old Lansdowne Road.

The college has requested that Fern's room should be made available for a new first-year student. Life goes on, after all.

Feeling like a burglar, but with the advantage of keys, she opens the front door and the familiar smell of damp and grease assaults her senses. As she climbs the stairs with James close behind her she conducts a silent running commentary with every step. 'This is where I sat and cried when Smudge died, this is where Charlie pulled my knickers down when I was talking to James, this is where

Dee threw up after a night drinking sangria, here is the missing banister rail, this is the stair that creaks.'

Her room feels like a place she once visited a long time ago and she's glad the mirror is too thick with dust to reveal the expression on her face.

James is instantly Mr Efficient, the army officer on a mission to clear this place of any evidence that she ever lived, breathed or fucked in this room.

Methodically, he fills a large suitcase and several carrier bags with clothes that she can't imagine ever wearing again. At one point the blue plastic case containing her diaphragm falls to the floor and rolls under the bed. There is no point in picking it up.

She leaves the record player and the radio for Felicity and Dee, and a note saying nothing more than 'hello and goodbye'.

The house is mercifully empty, save for the invisible couple on the middle floor. She doesn't see them, she can just hear their television. 'Goodbye house,' she mumbles and secretly kisses her keys before posting them back through the letterbox as the landlord requested.

James listens to the Test match on the radio all the way home. Fern is glad, because it gives her a chance to hate everything about her new life without him noticing.

25

The Inquest

In September, when the balloon of Fern's stomach is pumping up nicely, Rosemarie gets a phone call from Minty. The inquest into Elise's death will be held in October. 'I will be there,' promises Rosemarie. After all, she is Minty's big sister.

As the day approaches, the media sideshow sets up its stalls of gossip and rumour once more. This time more is known about Charlie Treadaway, his innocent past has been rooted out and the first of many pictures of Charlie looking angelic in his chorister's robes appears. Then there's his mother, the well-known children's illustrator Edwina Treadaway, aka Edwina Spinner who, having been widowed young, married the political speechwriter Dickie Spinner.

Copies of some of Edwina's Betsy and Tom illustrations crop up with snide bylines pointing out the chasm between cosy make-believe and sordid reality. Charlie's chequered school history is raked over. 'Top posh school' Wyebourne College refuses to comment on their ex-pupil; as for Glennings, the co-ed school Charlie attended after leaving Wyebourne, a spokesperson states that 'Charlie, like all other children of the school, is a much-loved member of the Glennings family, but sadly drugs are a modern day scourge and not everyone emerges unscathed.'

Scant mention is made of Rowena, Charlie Treadaway's twin and co-host of the notorious party, though several papers declare that the twenty-one-year-old has put her studies on hold, and photographs show a thin girl dressed in black, wearing sunglasses.

Much more attention is paid to the flamboyant girlfriend of the absent German count in whose room Elise's body was found. The girlfriend is unfortunately quoted as saying, 'I saw the girl in his bed and thought he'd been unfaithful. If she hadn't already been dead, I probably would have killed her.'

She is very obviously Russian, right down to the Cossack hat she is wearing when she enters the court.

Fern would rather stay away from the proceedings, but both her parents feel she should show her support and so she duly arrives and sits flanked by her parents, feeling like a prisoner herself.

Many of the details are public knowledge: that Elise choked in her sleep before suffering a cardiac arrest, and that the alarm was sounded by a hysterical Kasia Bogonavitch, who discovered the deceased in her absent boyfriend's bed.

There follows a ghastly description of the attempts made to save Elise's life, during which Rowena, her voice low but precise, recounts how she gave the girl the kiss of life and tried to clear her airwaves by inserting her fingers into Elise's throat. Rowena takes a deep breath before admitting that this was to no avail. 'Her lips were blue,' she finishes.

The next witness called is Lucas Spinner. Fern recoils in her seat. Him, the fucking shit.

Lucas tells the court how he had given Elise a lift from London to Oxford on that fateful day. He describes how he had bumped into the deceased earlier that day and invited her to the party; they made plans to travel down together. Elise had travelled light, she had no more than a leather shoulder bag with her and had been vague about when or if she would want a lift back. In her words, she had told Lucas she 'might get lucky'.

'And what did she mean by this?'

253

'That she might meet someone.'

'And of course she did meet someone, and that someone gave her an illegal substance or substances, including a lethal amount of heroin.' The judge peers around the court over half-moon gold-rimmed glasses. 'Mr Spinner, if you could describe the evening's celebrations?' Lucas adjusts the knot of his tie and continues.

'The party spread around a staircase tucked at the back of the college. Guests piled into any of the rooms that had their doors open. It . . . Well, basically, it was a bit of a free-for-all.'

'So there were young people drinking and smoking. Did you see any drug-taking?'

'Some joint-smoking, your honour, but mostly drinking.'

'So how, in this mêlée, can you be so sure it was a Mr Charles Treadaway who gave Elise the drugs that killed her?'

Lucas stares straight back at the judge. 'Because I was standing by an alcove where she'd left her bag. I saw her fetch her bag and join Mr Treadaway in the opposite corner of the room. I heard them laugh.'

'And how sure are you that the person you think you saw dealing drugs to Miss Landreth was in fact Charles Treadaway?'

Lucas takes a breath and then states loud and clear:

'Because he is my stepbrother, and I have known him since I was eleven.'

There is an audible gasp around the court from those who aren't aware of this final twist in the Elise Landreth saga.

One last witness is called to the stand before the court is adjourned. It's Barbara Spinner, mother of Lucas, who Fern instinctively knows is relishing every second of her big moment. Barbara's hair defies gravity and the delivery of her statement sounds practised; she has obviously spent many afternoons watching *Crown Court* on the television.

According to Barbara, Lucas arrived home on the Sunday while she was out at a luncheon party. She saw his car in the drive but left him to rest as she presumed he'd had a late night and would be tired from the drive. At around five to seven she was informed by her dearest friend and bridesmaid, Araminta Landreth, that a tragedy had occurred: Elise was dead, and drugs were thought to have played a part. 'When I imparted this dreadful news to my son he went as white as paper and admitted seeing Elise being given substances in exchange for money by a certain young man.

'And that young man was Charlie Treadaway.'

'And what did you do then, Mrs Spinner?'

'I called the police.'

At this point Barbara raises her head. If she had crowed like a mighty cockerel Fern would not have been in the least surprised.

Charlie's solicitor takes to the stand on his client's behalf. 'Mr Treadaway, who is of previous good character, is exercising his right to remain silent pending cross-examination at trial.'

All eyes swivel to the hollow-cheeked boy sitting bolt upright in a white shirt and navy suit. His dark curls have been cropped close to his head and he already looks beaten. He is crying, and Fern's heart hurts so badly she worries for a second that she might die. The pull of him is intense; he is a magnet to her soul and it's all she can do not to scream his name. If only she could touch him, if only she could kiss his face. For her own sake she turns her gaze away, but not before their eyes lock and silently she tries to transmit the words 'I love you' across the terrifying divide between them.

At the end of the inquest, Charles Treadaway is officially charged with possessing amphetamine sulphate and supplying heroin to Elise Landreth, and he will be tried by jury on the nineteenth of December 1981.

'Good, should be all done and dusted by Christmas,' says Gordon as they exit the court into bright autumn sunshine.

As the crowd spills onto the pavement Fern panics about Charlie's mother recognising her. Quickly she covers her necklace with her hand and bows her head. She needs to get out of this place very badly.

26

The Reckoning

At last James receives news about his next posting. From January, he will spend three months in Northern Ireland.

'Can't you just swap with someone else?' asks Fern.

'Well, you and the baby aren't going and that's that,' her mother decides and her father agrees. 'We've already lost Elise; we don't want to lose you too.'

'What, so you think I'm going to get myself blown up?' Fern laughs. Her parents are obviously being hysterical, but in some respects it makes life easier: if she stays where she is then her mother can help her look after the baby.

'Yes,' says the voice in her head, which she is hearing more and more, 'and you will never leave home and you will be stuck here for the rest of your life, until you go quietly insane.'

At least James has a whole week off at Christmas. 'Time for the two of you to get to know your baby. You could all move into the spare bedroom over the dining room: it's got twin beds in it at the moment, but I shouldn't think that will be too much of a problem,' her mother says and Fern is silent.

Maybe after Christmas, when James goes over to Northern Ireland, she could leave this baby with her mother and Mrs Bibby to take care of and she could go back to college and drink pints in the pub with Jill and Rob, walk home pissed and eat Felicity's famously awful 'left over' macaroni cheese, 'So called because there's a reason why there's always some left over.'

'Why are you laughing?' her mother asks. 'Maybe the doctor should check your blood pressure.'

The golden walnuts are threaded and garlanded around the tree, all the baubles are in place and Rosemarie has distributed festive bowls of pot pourri around the house. Everything smells of Christmas.

Minty rings Rosemarie to tell her she won't be attending the trial. She doesn't think her nerves will take it and her doctor has advised her to stay away. Nothing will bring Elise back. She and Paul are going abroad for Christmas; they are going to Egypt on the twenty-second. Their barrister is convinced a verdict will have been reached by then, and if it hasn't, they might go anyway. Other people's happiness is too much to bear and, besides, she admits that 'I couldn't stomach a single slice of turkey.'

And Rosemarie feels both a pang of guilt and a sense of relief at not having to see her sister's grief-stricken face. Minty has always been slim, but these days she's positively gaunt, thinks Rosemarie, nibbling on a mince pie (better than last year's).

Gordon has offered to support his brother-in-law for the duration of the trial while Rosemarie stays at home with Fern. After all, *it* could happen any time now. The due date is fast approaching, but as Rosemarie herself says, 'First babies are often late.' Nonetheless, she keeps her car keys about her person at all times and her Mini Clubman has a full tank of petrol. She is ready to ferry Fern to hospital at the very first twinge. An overnight bag is kept in readiness by the front door, containing several nighties and a distressing quantity of breast pads and sanitary towels.

Rosemarie laughs nastily when Fern slips that month's *Vogue* into the bag. 'You really have no idea.'

On the seventeenth of December the paperboy delivers the Woolbrights' *Telegraph*. It's the first day of Charlie's trial and, once again, the media has fired up its cannon of tragic Elise Landreth and wayward Charlie Treadaway information. Family albums have been raided, and Fern gasps at the sight of a fifteen-year-old Master Treadaway in a top hat and frock coat.

'That'll be Braxton Hicks,' her mother says. 'That baby is almost done,' and she looks as smug as when she bakes a Victoria sponge and the top is all golden and springy to the touch.

At lunchtime Gordon calls to say things are looking suitably grim for Charlie. Eyewitnesses place him at the scene and acting suspiciously, other students swear on the Bible that he offered to sell them drugs and, once again, Lucas has been very credible in the witness box.

Gordon is staying over with Minty and Paul. 'They haven't bothered with a Christmas tree,' he whispers to Rosemarie, whose heart tilts at the sight of her golden-garlanded Scots Pine. 'Shouldn't last much longer,' Gordon continues. 'They've done him up like a kipper. The little shit is going down, just you mark my words.'

Mid-morning on the eighteenth, the jury are sent out to deliberate. It's Christmas and a lot of them still have shopping to do – why hang around?

Before lunch, a verdict has been reached. Charles Treadaway is guilty, and is sentenced to a four-year custodial sentence with immediate effect.

'Take him down.'

Fern is resting on the sofa when they interrupt *Pebble Mill at One* with news of the verdict:

'The son of the well-known children's illustrator Edwina Spinner has been found guilty of supplying the daughter of a government minister with a lethal amount of heroin, and sentenced to four years in prison.'

Even though she has been expecting it, Fern is shocked. 'Lunch!'

her mother calls from the kitchen. She's made soup, Fern can smell it, warm and comforting. It's either carrot and coriander or leek and potato.

Fern heaves herself off the sofa, and as soon as she stands upright she wets her pants. She hasn't done that since prep school, what the hell is happening? Dazed, she stands in a pool of slightly vinegary fluid until realisation strikes.

'The baby is coming!' she shouts, and Rosemarie takes the soup pan off the Aga.

This is it.

It's either a girl or boy.

Charlie's or James's.

LUCAS

I

Home?

London, 2015

Lucas awakes queasy and confused. He is jet-lagged and anxious, unsure of where he is and why.

Breathing slowly in through his nose and out through his mouth to quell the rising tide of panic, he reminds himself of what has happened.

He is fifty-six years old and his beloved mother Barbara is dying. That is why he left North Carolina some thirty hours ago and shan't be returning home until the business is done and dusted. Literally, his mother's ashes just that: dust.

Anyway, where is home? Now that he is back in London his life in the States seems preposterous and dreamlike. Does he really live there?

Lucas has always viewed the American version of himself as a sort of cardboard cut-out, a cartoon character over whom he has never really had any control. Consequently, he has ended up unhappily married to a pneumatic, badly dyed blonde with rock-hard breasts.

Once upon a time there was the original Lucas, with a completely different future mapped out, but circumstances conspired and it seemed the only way he could deal with the consequences was to become someone else, only now it's all come unravelled again.

Lucas allows himself a brief self-pitying wallow. His mother, the only woman who has ever truly loved him, is dying, and his delusional American wife finds him physically repulsive. It's not entirely Denise's fault, admits Lucas, kneading the undulating mound of his belly and burrowing for a while between his legs to find his sleepy penis. Sometimes, while his wife works out on the treadmill in their bedroom, he sprawls on the bed in his vest and boxers and consumes a catering pack of ice-cream. The more he licks and slurps, the higher she turns up the dial on the machine. One day, with any luck, she will fall off.

Lucas's penis appears to be in a coma.

She wouldn't come with him, even if he'd begged. 'She's your mom, Lucas, I never met the woman. She doesn't know me from shit.' Lucas is relieved that this is indeed the case. What on earth would Barbara have made of Denise's stringy yellow hair and her skinny tattooed backside, all leathery from the sunbed?

What on earth had he been thinking? Never mind her not wanting to have sex with him: these days, fucking his wife would be like fucking a shoe.

Lucas's stomach churns, he feels both nauseous and starving. The layout of his mother's flat is unfamiliar; he's not actually sure where the bathroom is. Even in middle age he finds it upsetting that he can no longer slip a key into the primrose-yellow front door of River Walk and inhale the smell of the polished parquet hallway before running up the stairs to his old bedroom to touch his things: 'My Lego, my Meccano, my bears, my cars, my books.'

A wave of claustrophobia threatens to engulf him. The flat is poky, a small two-bedroomed apartment squeezed onto the fourth floor of a six-storey block with a prestigious address but neither balcony nor access to a garden. Bartholomew Lodge is an expensive warren of rabbit-hutch-sized apartments.

He is used to American real estate, the sprawling Barbie and Ken mini-mansions of dubious architectural heritage but generously accompanied by sloping AstroTurf lawns and double garages.

For a second he pictures his own eighties-built Dutch Colonial-style clapboard number complete with picket fence and motorised swing on the porch. The house is a perk of his job: Lucas has been working for the same investment company for the past ten years.

Not for much longer, Lucas mentally corrects himself. Let's get our facts straight, shall we, Lucas? Your mother is dying, your wife hates you and you've lost your job.

So far, he has told no one. Lucas has been harbouring the news as if it were some terrible parasitic bug, a bug that makes his bowels churn and his stools turn to water. The consequences are monumental: the company will take the house and his wife will leave him.

That is not in itself a big deal. In fact, her birthday is coming up next month and he might break the news then. Not that it will have any visible impact: Denise has had so much Botox that facial expressions are impossible. She will look exactly as she always does, like a stoned Chihuahua. They have come to the end of the marital road. It was a wrong turning in the first place, and without the adhesive of the house and the cars, they have no reason to stick together.

'I'd have liked children,' Lucas mouths silently, but it transpired his wife had fertility issues, mostly due to being ten years older than she originally admitted, combined with a phobia of putting on weight.

Denise is so scared of getting fat that she sleeps in the spare room in case she acquires Lucas's weight problem by osmosis, which is fine by him. Lucas discovered some years ago that Oreos are a great substitute for sex.

His stomach grumbles at the mere thought of biscuits.

The last time he ate was on the plane, tiny trays of doll's food, some miniature bags of pretzels and peanuts. He now wishes he'd kept a bag of pretzels for this three a.m. emergency.

Lucas gropes for the switch on his mother's bedside table and the room is illuminated through a voluminously swathed green satin shade on an onyx stand. Suddenly it strikes him how much of the bed he takes up. Lucas has been steadily putting on weight since he heard about the redundancy, comfort eating in his car, in backstreet diners, at pop-up Mexican food shacks and sidewalk doughnut stands. America is not the place for an unhappy greedy man. Carbs and sugar have always been Lucas's downfall. He inherited his sweet tooth from his mother, who liked nothing more than afternoon tea, a doilied cake stand of pastries and mille-feuilles, little silver cake forks, whipped cream on the ends of their noses, his mother licking her handkerchief to wipe his jammy mouth.

There is something Oedipal about being in this bed, surrounded by the flotsam and jetsam of Barbara's life. A bottle of Oil of Olay stands sentry on the nightstand just as it always did, next to it is a green velvet-covered tissue box containing lemon-coloured tissues. His mother has thought about her colour scheme; there is a great deal of green and gold throughout.

When he arrived last night, despite the solicitous welcome from the concierge – 'Call me Hastings, sir' – he felt like an intruder, a clumsy burglar, rooting through his mother's possessions, searching for what?

It had been an unedifying experience. Barbara's dementia is evident in the peculiar mixture of order and chaos in these cramped living quarters.

Her handkerchief drawer is pristine, scented with lavender bags, each monogrammed cotton square perfectly ironed and folded as if freshly returned from the laundry, and yet he found thirty tins of tuna at the bottom of her wardrobe, stashed away like Christmas presents.

The mixture of River Walk relics and new possessions is

confusing, it's as if a stranger had gone to a car boot sale and got lucky with some of his mother's old belongings. The magazine rack and the Chinese drinks cabinet, the marble chess set, artificially set out mid-game, the silver cigarette case (empty) and the collection of colourful Meissen birds all belong to another time, but the ugly mechanical recliner in the sitting room and the handrails in the bathroom are clues to a more decrepit recent past, and it makes Lucas feel depressed, which in turn makes him hungry, it always has.

Jesus Christ, he is so hungry he could eat ... what? There is nothing in the flat; the cupboard is bare, apart from the wardrobe, of course.

Unable to stand it any longer, Lucas gets up and mashes a tin of tuna into a cereal bowl. At the back of the kitchen cupboard, alongside an ancient collection of Yellow Pages and a box of spent batteries, he finds a jar of gherkins. The flat has been empty for three years but pickled cucumbers never go off and he sits in the unfamiliar kitchen, where every drawer reveals incongruous items, eyelash curlers in the cutlery tray, clothes pegs in the fridge's salad drawer, and scoffs his fishy snack. It is both disgusting and delicious.

Back in bed with a burning knot of indigestion, Lucas once more battles sleep. He needs to be strong for tomorrow: in a few hours' time he will visit his mother. Dear God, just let him have some fucking sleep.

In desperation, Lucas wanders into the green and gold symphony of his mother's sitting room and scans the bookshelf for something soothing. Barbara has a large collection of Agatha Christie paperbacks, seventies editions with lurid covers.

There is something rather comforting about an Agatha Christie story, thinks Lucas. By the end the guilty are always guilty, there is never any room for doubt, not like real life. He chooses *Sparkling Cyanide* and wanders, dazed and flat-footed, back to bed. If his mother were here she would make him hot milk, it always used to help him sleep, hot milk and honey.

Propped up against plumped-up pillows, Lucas is wondering how long it's been since he read something with actual pages when a letter slides out of the back of the book, a single sheet of writing paper scrawled all over in violet ink. Squinting at the paper, Lucas vaguely recognises the handwriting from long-ago birthday cards containing book tokens, a loose italic hand, similar but more erratic than his mother's.

'My darling Barbara,' It's from his Aunty Minty, not a real blood aunt – there were precious few of those – but one of his mother's dearest finishing-school chums, the accomplished and beautiful Araminta Landreth, rechristened in later life as 'poor Minty Landreth'.

The child has been born. Fern gave birth two weeks ago to a baby girl, her name is Sophie. I shall never be a grandmother but I am a great aunt. Grannie Rosemarie is besotted; she has both her daughter and her granddaughter living at Three Paddocks while Fern's husband is on duty in Northern Ireland. She says it's exhausting and I snapped at her, I'm afraid. She's just so tactless.

I still think I am going to see Elise. Every day I wake up and I think, today, I might see her today – we could have a coffee, and the realisation that this will never happen feels like an icepick to my heart.

Anyway, darling, we are packing again: a couple of weeks in Verbier. Neither Paul nor I seem to be able to stay in one place for long. If we don't keep moving misery will turn us to stone. I suppose we keep going for each other.

The letter is dated January 1982.

Lucas freezes. Just a month after the court case, and once again he is back in the Old Bailey, in his suit bought especially for the occasion. 'After all, darling, all eyes will be on you: you're the star witness.' His mother's eyes glittering with venom and revenge.

That very last day, the culmination of weeks of waiting, of long and boring cross-examination, a snow-flurrying Friday before Christmas, when the long-winded procedure suddenly speeded up, like an LP accidentally played at 45 rpm, a hurried pre-lunch verdict, a tiny crow from his mother's scarlet mouth and within seconds Charlie had disappeared – it was as if a trapdoor had opened beneath the court. His father's face in his hands, his stepmother and stepsister wide-eyed in horror.

His mother took him out for lunch: 'Come on, darling, we must celebrate: justice has been done. I'm going to take you somewhere divine.'

She even ordered champagne, just the two of them in a Knightsbridge restaurant. Thick white napkins, narrow-stemmed champagne flutes and tender chunks of delicious veal that, however many times he chewed, he couldn't swallow.

Lucas's stomach lurches, and instantly he knows he is going to be sick. It's all too much: the flight, his mother, the memories. As mashed tuna and gherkin reappears in his mother's dramatic burgundy-coloured lavatory pan, Lucas acknowledges that, just like osso bucco, he will never eat tinned fish again.

2

Visiting Barbara

Five hours after the unfortunate tuna incident, Lucas treats himself to proper cooked breakfast at a café in Pimlico. He tries to resist ordering the fried bread, but he can't help himself and proceeds to dip the delicious crispy triangles into golden yolks, then asks for another round so that he can mop his plate of baked bean juice.

He needs to line his stomach, he needs to be strong. Today he is visiting his mother in the nursing home that is devouring his inheritance quicker than he can eat his full English.

That's another thing he has avoided telling Denise: the fact that he has been paying for his mother's board and lodging, and has borrowed equity from the flat in order to do so.

Lucas dabs his mouth – his mother would hate to see him with an orange tide of baked bean juice around his lips – leaves an American-sized tip and steps out onto the street to hail a cab. Once he's seen his darling mother he will sort out an Oyster card and stop being so extravagant, but for now Barbara must take priority.

Avondale House is in Holland Park, a sprawling red-brick edifice with a maze of ugly modern annexes tucked around the back.

Lucas is expected. Staff bustle in various coloured nylon jackets; he cannot tell who is important: they all smile, they all walk silently on rubber heels, they make sure visitors are signed in and the front door is firmly closed. 'We can't be losing any of our valuable clients,' laughs a small Indian woman as she leads Lucas through a carpeted reception area complete with fish tank and coffee table piled with the *People's Friend*. Pausing to tap a code into a metal door, she continues down a chilly linoleum corridor and into a lift. The further they walk the more the home becomes a hospital. The smell changes.

Nothing can prepare him for the sight of her. For a moment, he thinks the bedroom has been wrongly labelled. The brass plate on the door reads 'Mrs Barbara Spinner', but lying in the bed is an impostor. This cannot be his mother.

He had been warned that she is bed-bound, that she is barely ever awake, that she won't recognise him, but he didn't expect not to recognise her.

Lucas's mother crouches under white sheets like a balding eagle, hands like claws clutching at the blue satin-trimmed cellular blanket.

It's the hair he can't get over. She used to have such a mass of hair, hair as big as Elizabeth Taylor's, black and glossy, a massive electric-rollered mane teased and lacquered by Terence, a little man off Eaton Square.

Once upon a time Barbara Spinner was an impressive woman, clicking around Chelsea in her patent Bally court shoes, nipping in and out of Peter Jones and having her groceries delivered by Harrods.

Stunned, Lucas sits heavily in a chair by his mother's bed. 'Hello Mum, it's me. It's Lucas.'

Nothing, not a flicker of recognition, she doesn't know who he is, not even him, her best and darling boy. She doesn't speak and her eyes are milky. He preferred them when they glittered so dark they seemed almost black. Surely she can still see him?

Lucas glances around the small, functional room. Some personal touches have been artfully placed to give the impression of homeliness: a small Turkish rug, a few coloured-glass ornaments and, of course, Barbara herself, in all her glory, framed on the window sill.

The photograph was obviously taken at a do. Barbara is wearing a turquoise taffeta frock and, sitting next to her, is a bow-tied Terence, Barbara's loyal hairdresser and, in later life, live-in companion, a decision that initially seemed disastrous but had worked out well, considering his mother benefited from an on-site carer-cum-coiffeur, while the penniless Terence had a roof over his head.

Terence would have been responsible for his mother's hair in the photo. It is a giant edifice of spun black nylon carefully sculpted to incorporate Barbara's own thinning, dyed locks. There is still a box of Wella 'Raven Black' in the bathroom cabinet back at the flat.

He died before Barbara went into the home. Terence's fatal stroke pushed Barbara over the edge and she started wandering the streets of Chelsea at three in the morning, banging on the door of Peter Jones demanding to be let in. 'I need some bias binding and some soda crystals,' she told the nice policeman.

And now she can no longer walk, she is nappied and catheterd, and Lucas wonders, how much longer? How much longer will this limbo between life and death last?

His mother breathes by herself but can do very little else. A Czech girl knocks and enters with lunch on a tray. 'I am Katya,' the girl announces, nimbly bibbing his mother and spoon-feeding her a greenish-grey soup and some tiny buttered fingers of toast.

A combination of anger and upset flares up in Lucas's chest. This is all wrong. Once upon a time Barbara only ate nursery food when she'd attended too many social engagements and needed Disprin and a coddled egg on a tray in front of the television.

His mother dribbles and chokes and Lucas feels like being sick and screaming at the same time. 'It's jelly for pudding,' Katya says. 'Mrs Spinner, she like jelly. Red jelly, she like, it her favourite.'

'How do you know?' Lucas wants to shout. 'How do you know what she likes? She's a fucking shell. You might as well spoon jelly into an empty post box. I'll tell you what my mother liked: she liked the vanilla panna cotta at Daphne's, she liked Le Caprice's tarte tatin. She thought jelly was for children, you fucking imbecile.'

But of course he doesn't. The care workers are incredible, the room is comfortable, the home is better than most. It should be, for the amount it bloody costs.

Lucas can't believe it. The money dwindles by the day, and for what? You might as well lavish a fortune on the mouldering contents of a salad drawer. His mother is completely gaga. Who'd have guessed it would be Barbara whose mind would wander off into a freezing fog and never return?

Katya tips a small measure of liquid into his mother's throat and departs with the lunch tray.

Within minutes Barbara is a sleeping bag of bones. He suspects she has been sedated, and who would blame them? Kinder to switch all the lights out in her head than let her suffer. Her brain has become a circuit board that refuses to function properly. It keeps shorting; eventually this will happen more and more, then one day she will forget how to breathe and she will die.

The matron of the nursing home explained all this to him on a long-distance call two weeks ago. The only question he can't ask is when?

So Lucas sits and waits and wishes he'd brought a book, and for want of anything better to do he idly checks the contents of his mother's bedside locker and finds a random collection of photographs bound in a surprisingly cheap imitation-leather album.

Flicking through the snaps Lucas suddenly realises that Barbara must have put this collection together to remind herself of the big events in her life, her friends and her family. Under each photograph, there is an inscription; his mother's handwriting is more erratic than he recalls. She must have made this as a sort of aide-memoire to her past, it is almost unbearably sad.

It starts with a monochrome picture of Barbara and her friends Minty and June, taken at a summer ball during their debutante season. They look like what they are, three posh little fifties virgins drinking champagne. 'My darling girls,' reads the caption below, 'Minty and June, best friends since Mont B,' which Lucas presumes refers to the finishing school where the three young ladies first learnt the art of finger bowls.

The same trio feature in the next snap, all starched hair and empire-line dresses. Under this photograph Barbara has written 'A bride and her bridesmaids'. They don't look like virgins any more; his mother looks positively honeymoon-ready. There are no photos of the groom, so she must have been compos mentis enough when compiling this album to know that he was long gone.

Lucas features prominently, as he would expect, first as a baby in a black and white photo, being carried from the Royal Brompton Hospital, 'Lucas Peter, born 16th May 1959'. His mother has a large white bow in her hair and is fully made up, complete with white-patent court shoes with bows that match the one in her hair. Typical Barbara: she'd have been planning her leaving-hospital look for months. It's Priscilla Presley meets *Good Housekeeping*.

The next few pages feature the house in River Walk ('My beloved River Walk with roses'), a poodle ('Trigger. RIP') that Lucas has no recollection of and a car he immediately recognises as a Mark 2 Jag.

This photo is in vivid Technicolor. His father must have been very proud of the car; his mother is leaning against the bonnet in a pretty floral skirt, white blouse tucked in to show off her still-minuscule waist. A headscarf and film star sunglasses complete the look, she is channelling her inner Sophia Loren. She will never be this lovely again and she knows it.

Clumsy with sleep deprivation, Lucas drops the album and, reaching to pick it up, he finds his mother at the polo with the Landreths. They are having a picnic out of the back of Uncle

Paul's Jag, complete with bottles of Dom Perignon and a proper wicker hamper. Barbara seems to be laughing slightly hysterically at a scotch egg; they all look so happy. The registration plate on the car ends with a W, suggesting it is 1980. Of course, that's why everyone is smiling: it's the year before everything went wrong.

Lucas is suddenly overcome with jet lag again, and as his head nods to his chest for the third time his eyes close to darkness.

He dreams that he is in a boat that is capsizing in a lake and he knows with complete certainty that he is going to drown. There is no one to save him.

The Czech girl, Katya, wakes him up by coming in several hours later with a tea tray. 'Feeding time at the zoo,' jokes Lucas. She doesn't smile; briefly, she looks insulted.

It's a phrase, he tries to explain, only she appears not to be listening. Lucas picks up his jacket, tucks the photo album under his arm and reassures Barbara, 'I'll be back.' He doesn't kiss her. She smells like she is going off and it upsets him.

3

River Walk (With Roses)

Lucas gets a cab back to Chelsea and stops off at the newsagent's round the corner from Bartholomew Lodge for some basic provisions. He will do a proper shop later, but for now he buys tea, coffee, milk, sugar, biscuits, cereal and a tin of Ambrosia creamed rice, which, once spotted, sent his gastric juices into overdrive. There are some things America cannot do, and tinned rice pudding is one of them.

Back in his mother's flat Lucas takes a cup of coffee and the photograph album into the sitting room and experiments with some of the settings on the recliner. It might be ugly but it's incredibly comfortable and, finding a position somewhere between upright and recline, Lucas opens the album and stares hard at a photograph of the house where he grew up.

A pretty white-washed thirties semi tucked away in a quiet street in Chelsea, just a stone's throw from the river. The front door is yellow and surrounded by fat cream-headed roses. Suddenly he remembers the bees: there were always bees in the garden and, for a long time, being stung by one was the only bad thing that could possibly happen to him.

Behind the yellow door he was safe, his mother arranging flowers in the kitchen, his father smoking a pipe in the sitting room. Was that true? Had his father ever smoked a pipe, or is he getting mixed up?

Whatever, I was a very privileged little boy, Lucas acknowledges, remembering cycling along the Embankment and boating on the lake in Battersea Park. If he thinks hard, he can remember being very small, walking down the King's Road between his mother and father, all three of them holding hands and his parents swinging him off his feet, one, two, three, *wheee*. Back then, life seemed to be a series of treats, of snakes and ladders and mugs of cocoa and *Dr Who* in his pyjamas.

Of course, it all started to go wrong when he was ten and his father left River Walk for good. Lucas knew other boys at his school whose parents were divorced, but he hadn't expected it to happen to him. Almost half a century later, whenever he hears or sees the word *divorce* Lucas feels like he needs to pee very badly.

His father told him in the car. He'd picked him up from his prep school, and on the long drive home decided to break the news that whereas Lucas would be going home as usual for half term, his father wouldn't be there.

It was such a serious man-to-man chat that Lucas didn't dare tell his father that he needed to stop and wee. He just held on until his father pulled up outside the house on River Walk and then, without saying goodbye, he'd bolted for the safety of the yellow front door. Finger on the buzzer, the other hand clutching the front of his shorts, Lucas hopped on the doorstep until the housekeeper eventually let him in. By the time he'd finished in the bathroom his father's old black Bristol had driven away. He hadn't even washed his hands before his father had gone.

His mother was lying down. She spent most of half term lying down while Lucas read comics and played with his science kit – which mostly involved looking at his own bodily fluids through a microscope, smearing the glass slides with wee, poo and bogies.

When she did surface, it was to receive her friends. He recalls her white, over-powdered face, lipstick bleeding into all the little grooves around her mouth, staining the gold-tipped filters of her cigarettes deep geranium; heaps of stinking butts smouldering in ashtrays; drinks in the afternoon; Minty and June shrill and hysterical on her behalf; while upstairs he magnified his tears.

At the end of the week his father arrived to take him back to school. He didn't come in, he just tooted and the housekeeper saw Lucas out. His mother didn't even wave from her bedroom window, but he knew she was up there. He'd heard her crying.

It was on this return journey that his father explained that he'd left Lucas's mother for another woman, called Edwina. His father's face changed when he mentioned Edwina, it was as if he couldn't get enough of saying her name. He never referred to Barbara by her Christian name, she was always 'your mother', and when he spoke about 'your mother' he always looked like he had a headache.

'I have fallen in love with a woman called Edwina, Lucas, and I am sure you're going to love her too.'

How? Why should he?

At school, he pretended nothing had happened, but he had a tummy ache for the rest of term, a dull emptiness that only felt a tiny bit better when they got sponge pudding with custard for lunch.

That Christmas, when his school broke up for the holidays, his mother had arranged for an older boy's parents to drop him back to Chelsea.

Lucas felt crippled with shyness on the journey home and the older boy did nothing to help, sitting in the front seat with his father, discussing their exciting holiday plans and entirely ignoring the boy on the back seat.

'Give my regards to your mother,' the man said, waving a leather-gloved hand out of the car window.

He could no longer smell his father. That's what Lucas recalls all these years later, how the yellow door looked the same but inside it was different. His father's scent had gone and every trace of him had been removed, right down to his mouthwash from the bathroom.

A few days later Mrs Glynne, the housekeeper, took her annual leave. She always went back to Ireland for a fortnight over Christmas, it was the tradition, but before she left she issued Lucas with a front-door key for emergencies. 'I don't suppose you'll ever need it,' she said, but one day he did.

Lucas vaguely remembers being taken by friends to the Science Museum that day, but the details are hazy. All he knows for sure is that when he came home the lower part of the house was in darkness and he immediately came to the conclusion that his mother must have been out buying him presents.

He remembers finding the key in his coat pocket and feeling eminently grown-up and sensible when the Yale turned the lock and he was able to open the door. This is what being a man must be like, coming home to your own house, dinner cooking, slippers by the fire.

It was cold in the hallway and his mother was yet to put the decorations up, even though everyone else seemed to have done so already. He trudged upstairs, trying not to be frightened.

Someone had left a light on in the bathroom. Lucas pushed the door open and his first impression was that his mother was marinading herself in red wine. He'd seen her do this plenty of times in the kitchen – coq au vin was one of his father's favourites. Only there were no onions and carrots in the liquid, and his mother was naked and unconscious.

Lucas phoned the police, and they said he was a very clever and brave little boy. A neighbour stayed with him until his father arrived. 'It's all right,' Dickie said, 'I'm here now. I'll take care of things.'

In the midst of all the awfulness, Lucas recalls how thrilled he was to have his father back in the house, only Dickie had no intention of staying. 'Under this bloody roof? You can see that, can't you son? Your mother has made it impossible. Now, fetch a case and pop your pyjamas in it, and some spare clothes, and let's skedaddle.'

While Lucas packed his father tried to swab down the bathroom. It was still rather pink when they left and there were drops of blood on the landing carpet and all the way down the stairs.

'Bloody hell, Barbara,' his father kept muttering.

It was very dark by the time they got to Kennington. The house was tall and brown with railings; a woman was waiting at the door. 'This is Edwina,' his father told him. She tried to hug him but he got away.

He slept with his father that night in a strange wooden double bed like a boat, and in the morning he was ferried back to Chelsea, where his mother's friend Aunty June had taken up residence at River Walk.

'Listen, Lucas,' his father urged quietly, 'it's probably best you don't tell your mother we went back to Kennington last night. Let's just pretend I stayed here. Least said, soonest mended.'

But of course it wasn't the last time Lucas crossed the river. After all, his father had rights. 'You can't stop me seeing him, Barbara, I'm his father.' Raised voices in the dining room.

And so it began. For the next eight years of Lucas's life he felt he had very little control over where and with whom he should be. Consequently, he always felt out of context.

He didn't know which was worse, being at home with his mother who was crazy and sad, or staying with his step-family, where his father mooned after 'that woman'. He was better off at school, where at least everyone was consistently horrible, so you knew where you stood.

'Kennington!' his mother spat. 'Who lives in Kennington?'

Certainly no one Lucas knew. He'd been brought up to play on the sloping green lawns of Kensington Gardens and Hyde Park. According to his mother, Kennington consisted entirely of council estates and bingo halls. Lucas kept quiet about the Imperial War Museum, a mere ten-minute stroll away. Extolling its virtues would be disloyal, so he kept his trap shut.

Then there were the other children, Edwina's son and daughter, twins who looked both identical and nothing like each other, the girl with glasses and hair so fine you could see straight through to the white of her scalp and the boy— Well, Lucas can never really recall Charlie's childhood face, it turned and twisted with every mood, a face that could both open and close, change from handsome to ratty. From different angles the boy could look like an entirely different child. Only his hair remained the same, an unruly tangle of black curls.

Lucas was their senior by almost a year but they didn't seem to care, they simply weren't interested in what he thought or said. The girl read books all day and the boy drew pictures and they both played made-up games, which Lucas was too old to join in with. They made him furious, and what made it worse was that Edwina just laughed at him. She thought he was funny when he wasn't even trying to be remotely humorous, and when she laughed at him he felt like kicking her.

'He's a funny, priggish little thing,' he once heard her describe him, and just to spite them all he'd smashed up a stupid model that the idiot Charlie had spent all weekend pulling his stupid concentrating monkey face over, and as a result his father had had a word on the way home. 'It's just not cricket, Lucas. You're not playing the game, son.'

The trouble with his father was that he liked people to get on. He was a very nice, polite man. In fact, leaving his wife was the rudest thing he'd ever done, and deep down Lucas knew he wouldn't have done it if he hadn't fallen madly in love with Edwina.

He just couldn't understand why. While his mother looked like something out of a magazine or a woman on the Eurovision Song Contest, Edwina looked like she lived on one of those houseboats down by the river. She wore jeans and pumps, and tied her hair back in a ponytail and barely bothered with make-up.

Lucas was surprised his father wasn't embarrassed by her, and was relieved when she was forbidden to attend any events at his prep school. Most of his school friends' mothers looked a bit like Barbara. Some were shorter, others thinner and some were the same, only blonde. They were all comfortingly elegant and groomed, apart from Miles Gordon Russell's mum, who looked like a prostitute.

What was most scandalous about the whole affair, Barbara said, and Minty and June agreed, was that Dickie had just moved straight in with the woman!

One would have imagined he'd rent a flat, wait until things were above board. 'What kind of example is it to set to the boy?'

'I hear she's a widow. They're the worst, of course – after any-thing in trousers.'

The only other thing he remembers about that Christmas was that his mother bought him a G.I. Joe Astronaut complete with space capsule. It was the best present ever.

Lucas reclines the chair to sleep mode. He's not sure if his jet lag is physical or emotional.

4

Godmother to Darling Elise

By the time Lucas wakes up it is dark and he feels disorientated. Unable to face the prospect of going out to eat, he phones down to the concierge for pizza-delivery advice. Hastings is most obliging: 'Of course, Mr Spinner, and I have many other delivery services that I can personally recommend.' Lucas is momentarily stunned. Is Hastings offering to supply him with an escort service? To be honest, he'd much rather have a twelve-inch capricciosa.

While he waits for his cheesy meat feast with extra garlic bread, Lucas continues to flick through his past. The photo album acts like a portal: one minute he is a naked toddler sitting in a paddling pool in a sun-dappled garden, the next he is wearing a balaclava and perched on Santa's lap in a mid-sixties Harrods grotto.

Even with his front teeth missing and chicken pox, he is obviously the apple of his mother's eye, her 'darling and best boy'. An adored only child who, in hindsight, was completely unprepared for what was to come.

His mother's goddaughter is the only apparent rival for Barbara's affection. Elise first crops up between the plastic sleeves of the album in a black and white photograph taken at her christening.

His mother looks like a Pan Am air hostess and is holding a bundle of baby; on either side of her are Minty and June. The snap has been trimmed with pinking shears and is titled 'Godmother to darling Elise. Christening St Saviour's Church, Chelsea'.

From what Lucas can glean from the picture, Elise as a baby was a furious-looking turnip with a tuft of black hair.

She certainly wasn't a pretty pink-cheeked Pears soap baby, but nonetheless his mother was besotted with her – 'the daughter I never had' – and she crops up at regular intervals.

Here she is as a cross-looking toddler ('Miss Bossy Boots'), there she is on a pony ('Elise riding Rex'). Lucas feels a sudden pang of jealousy and has to reassure himself of his mother's devotion by staring at himself eating a vast banana split with the Italian Lakes in the background ('Adorable Lucas and his favourite pudding, Lake Como 1964').

Oddly enough, the picture he finds most poignant is the one that looks the least like her. It's a school photograph taken against a pale blue background. Elise must be about eight, her wild curls have been tamed into two thick plaits and her new adult teeth are still working out their positions in her mouth but she is grinning, her brown eyes wide and friendly. She looks like what she is, a little girl, just a little girl.

From behind this photograph Lucas removes a folded square of paper, a page torn from a magazine. The paper is glossy and Lucas has a feeling he knows what it is before he even opens it.

His instinct is correct: 'Miss Elise Landreth celebrates her tenth birthday at the Park Lane Hilton, Mayfair'. He has seen this photograph many times, mostly reproduced in grainy black and white newsprint, but the *Tatler* original, in colour on good-quality paper, still shines.

Elise is standing up in a sleeveless yellow dress. In front of her is a cake, a magnificent chocolate edifice fizzing with sparklers at each corner. Ten candles flicker in the middle of the cake and Elise is taking a breath in. Soon she will blow out all the candles and everyone will applaud, but now, right this minute, she is breathing in.

Two other children sit either side of her. One is a wide-eyed twelve-year-old boy staring at the cake, the other is a younger girl wearing a dark green velvet dress with a white lace collar. She has a face that could be found in any painting from Titian to Rossetti, an angel perched on a cloud, a pretty serving wench, the spoilt child of the aristocracy. She is red-haired and her eyes are raised to Elise in adoration.

Elise, Lucas and Fern.

In the corner of the picture, if you look very closely, is the tip of a dove's wing. Lucas refolds the paper and carefully places it back inside its plastic protector.

He feels hot and uncomfortable, the past is dragging him back as surely as if it had a finger hooked around his collar.

It is 1971, he is in his last year at Witterings and his father is marrying 'that woman'. His mother is spitting with rage during the day and weepy and maudlin by night.

Lucas cannot go, of course he can't, and anyway he doesn't want to. It's not a proper wedding anyway, not like the ones in the magazines that his mother reads, society weddings held in country churches with elegant brides and handsome grooms. 'A dirty, sneaky registry office do,' his mother snarled.

Barbara was officially a divorcee and yet she clung on to her married name. 'I will always be the original Mrs Spinner. Your father will live to regret this, mark my words.'

Had he? wonders Lucas. Were there moments in his father's later life when he regretted his decision, when he wished he'd stayed with Barbara and Lucas in the sunny gardens of River Walk?

The wedding was planned for a Saturday in May, 'A cherry-blossom wedding,' Edwina enthused. 'I might wear some in my hair.' She really was the most ridiculous woman.

Brides didn't pick stuff off trees to wear in their hair, they wore buns and tiaras and veils. This woman seriously didn't have a clue.

Dickie was keen that Lucas should be allowed to attend, which made Barbara blaze. 'Over my dead body,' she ranted, clawing at the silk scarf knotted around her throat. Just the mention of Edwina brought her out in hives, her neck aflame with angry red lumps.

The twins were eleven and Lucas just turned twelve, and even though a church ceremony was out of the question Edwina said Rowena and Charlie could dress up as bridesmaid and page boy.

'You can't be a bridesmaid in glasses,' Lucas told Rowena, who just blinked back at him. 'I can do what I like, Lucas.' Charlie was even worse: his mother found him some buckled shoes, the sort usually seen only in pantomimes, which he decided he'd wear with a velvet waistcoat and a cravat. 'A hat would be good too,' the boy threatened. Lucas wasn't sure why he felt so horrified by all these silly plans; it wasn't as if he was going to be there.

As luck would have it, Lucas had a prior engagement. He'd been invited to the birthday party of his mother's goddaughter Elise, daughter of Aunty Minty and Uncle Paul, who was of course a Tory Cabinet minister and therefore rather important.

Barbara was increasingly jealous of Minty; her husband had pursued his political career with rather more vigour than Dickie had and now look at him. He was an important man and Minty was never out of Harrods' hat department. Minty pretended the amount of functions she had to attend with her handsome clever husband was an utter shoe-pinching bore, but Barbara didn't believe her for a minute, for starters she didn't half go on about the canapés at Chequers.

Lucas is awash with memories, he'd need the mental equivalent of the Thames Barrier to stop them flooding in.

His mother organised a taxi, she wore a pink hat with what looked like petals all over it, she looked very beautiful, but her eyes were red-rimmed; he carried the parcel, it was all wrapped up and tied with a bow; 'I don't think she's too old for dollies,' his mother said. She was anxious and chattered nervously all the way to Park

Lane. 'My goddaughter's birthday party,' she told the cab driver. 'At the Hilton.'

Lucas couldn't really hear the driver's response, but it sounded suspiciously like 'more money than sense'.

He felt a little bit self-conscious. There had been some wrangling with his mother over whether he could wear long trousers, but Barbara wouldn't countenance it, not until he had left Witterings and was heading for Wyebourne College. 'That is when long trousers will come into the equation,' she snapped. His shorts were slightly too tight and slightly too short, and his knees were very pink above his long grey socks. He also wore a white shirt and a tie which he'd done himself – he had to, because his father was marrying that woman and wasn't there to help.

A receptionist pointed them in the direction of the function suite where there was a cloakroom purely for the guests of Miss Elise, and a long table in the corridor where gifts for the birthday girl could be left.

Many of the details of that day have blurred with time. Lucas vaguely recalls a live band and some party games which were a bit silly, and he remembers the shame of being coerced into musical statues. But the birthday tea was phenomenal and all the parents stayed in a huddle on the far side of the room, drinking and smoking and eating canapés.

After tea and before the cake a master of ceremonies, all dressed up like a ringmaster in a red jacket, announced a magician and all the lights suddenly turned different colours. The band played dramatic music and, in a puff of green smoke, a man in a top hat arrived on the stage, and even the parents put down their Camparis and cigarettes as he drew doves from his sleeves and a large white rabbit from his hat.

He had an Italian accent and Lucas just knew he was going to pick on him, he could feel his eyes lasering in on him. 'He's a member of the Magic Circle,' someone whispered.

'Pick a card, any card,' and Lucas picked the six of clubs and wrote his name in felt-tip pen on the back. Five minutes later it turned up all rolled up inside a tennis ball. He kept that card for a long time. Rowena and Charlie might have been to a stupid wedding with his dad and his new stepmum and eaten knickerbocker glories in Knightsbridge, but he had a rolled-up six of clubs with his name on it, and anyway, they'd had ice-cream and a massive cake at the party, a cake with sparklers stuck into it, a cake that was so big it had to be wheeled in on a trolley while everyone sang 'Happy birthday dear Elise' and a professional photographer who was renowned for taking pictures at all sorts of important society events, such as Ascot, captured precious moments on a big black flashing camera.

Snap! He is sitting next to the birthday girl and she is about to blow out the candles. Snap! They are eating the cake and laughing. 'Smile for the dickie bird,' says the photographer. Snap! Three of them, Lucas, Elise and her cousin, the one with the bright orange hair.

Fern she was called, she was only nine.

After the cake there was disco-dancing and some of the parents joined in. An escaped white dove from the magician's act got upset and started dive-bombing the sparkling stage curtains and shitting over the dance floor, and all the women covered their heads and started screaming and running.

That's when he noticed the little girl with the red hair. She was rooted to the spot on the dance floor, sobbing, so Lucas reached for her tiny starfish hand and led her away, and in doing so, for the first time in his life he felt brave and good, like a superhero. 'I was upset because the bird was so frightened, I thought it might die,' she told him, her blue eyes continuing to brim. He gave her a napkin to wipe them with.

That was the bit the twins were interested in when Lucas told them about the birthday party. They played the bird shitting on the guests game all weekend, taking it in turns to be a great squawking monster bird, jumping off the furniture and pretending to crap on cowering guests over and over again until it wasn't a bit funny, and even Edwina told them to put a sock in it. She was wearing her new wedding ring, it was very shiny and very golden, and Lucas hated the very sight of it.

His mother still wore hers: 'You get better service in shops if you're a married lady,' she explained. 'People feel sorry for spinsters because they seldom have any money and no one trusts a divorcee.' Edwina and Dickie didn't have a honeymoon. 'How peculiar,' sniped Barbara. 'He took me to Capri.'

The doorbell interrupts Lucas's memories. His pizza has arrived – good. For pudding he will have that tin of Ambrosia creamed rice.

5

Lucas in Long Trousers

Supper was most excellent and, Lucas decides, if he is ever on death row that is exactly what he would choose for his last meal: pizza and tinned rice pudding. Replete, he settles himself back into the recliner and returns once more to the edited highlights of his mother's life.

Most of the photographs are in a vague chronological order, although occasionally Barbara has opted for a theme, such as summer holidays, and suddenly there are jumbled holiday snaps careering from the eighties back to the fifties with dizzying speed, and it's bewildering and slightly disturbing to find his mother look-ing oddly sexy in a white bikini ('Saint-Tropez, 1966').

Embarrassed, Lucas quickly turns the pages until once again he is staring at himself, a plump boy in long grey pinstripe trousers pinned up at the hem. He can see the indentations where the pins have pierced the material, he can feel the scratchiness of the polyester/wool mix.

The trousers were a good eight inches too long. He had to stand on a chair while Mrs Glynne the housekeeper shuffled around him on her knees taking them up. He is beginning to look tubby, wider than he is long.

The boy in the photograph looks back. He is excited and nervous and scared, his time at Witterings is over; in September he will be going to Wyebourne, his father's old school, where Dickie had excelled in all subjects and eventually won a place at Brasenose College, Oxford.

'No pressure, then,' mutters Lucas, feeling a wave of sympathy for the boy on the chair who was yet to meet failure head on.

His mother was in her element, poring over the uniform list and gleefully proclaiming, 'Fencing, darling, how exciting! You'll be just like Errol Flynn.'

But before Wyebourne, there are eight weeks of summer holidays.

'School's out,' screamed Alice Cooper, much to his mother's disgust.

The summer of 1972, they went to Ibiza – it literally was just a fishing village back then. Barbara hired a villa with friends, women who screeched like parakeets behind huge sunglasses, smeared their orange lipstick around cocktail glasses and flirted with foreign waiters when they went out for dinner.

There was no one his age there, and for most of the holiday he felt fat and uncomfortable. His figure was starting to give both him and his mother cause for concern. He heard her talking about it to her friends, 'You don't think he's fat, do you?' The answer from the sun lounger next to his mother was reassuring: 'It's just puppy fat, darling. As soon as he goes to school it'll drop off him.'

Lucas refused to take his T-shirt off or go in the pool. He developed prickly heat and spent most of his time fully dressed, trying to burn ants in the grass with a piece of broken mirror.

The food was the highlight of the holiday: the villa was fully staffed, and at one o'clock a running buffet lunch was laid out. It was like going to a wedding every day for two weeks.

'Darling, when we get back it's going to be nothing but Ryvita and celery.' Barbara was good at starting diets. She took them very seriously, bought books and joined slimming groups, but her weight continued to yo-yo. She was either too unhappy to eat, or too unhappy to stop eating. 'It's a vicious circle,' she explained to Lucas, and in desperation she installed a plug-in vibrating weight-loss machine in the bathroom at River Walk and would spend hours with a broad canvas belt hooped around her waist or thighs, oscillating away the excess flab.

'It's a miracle,' she informed Lucas. 'Between the machine and a good girdle, there'll be no more tummy bulge for Barbara.'

Lucas tried it once, it was the first time he got an erection and he was far too fearful of it ever to have another go.

That was another thing about not having a man about the house: there was no one to talk to about things, the willy things, and hair.

If he wanted to talk to his father he had to wait until it was a Kennington Road weekend, and while Lucas looked forward to seeing his father, he could never step into 137 without feeling he was walking into quicksand.

The twins unnerved him. They were peculiar, with their boy/girl bookend looks and unspoken understanding of what the other might need. Everything they did was odd, the way they layered lime marmalade over peanut butter, their silent freakishness followed by bursts of hilarity. But most of all, Rowena's terrifying intelligence and Charlie's mercurial talent made him feel lardish and slow by comparison.

The balance was all wrong, two against one. If only he'd had a younger brother, a boy who looked a bit like him, a companion and ally, but as it was he felt alien and lonely in a house that smelt strange, surrounded by people he didn't really like and who, compared with his mother, didn't seem to rate him particularly highly.

Of course his father tried his best, Dickie made it quite plain that he thought Lucas was a good chap with a fine brain and seemed completely confident that his son and heir would follow in his footsteps, matching him stride for stride. Wyebourne followed by Oxford (preferably his father's old college), before putting a tentative toe into politics.

'And what would *you* like to do, Lucas?' his stepmother asked, dishing out some awful slop one Saturday lunchtime. Edwina didn't really cook very much, she wasn't interested. A lot of the meals were made by a black woman who helped keep the house and terrified the living daylights out of Lucas.

'A black woman, Lucas, are you sure?' asked his mother. Her eyebrows, which she pencilled on, almost disappeared into her hairline.

'Come on, spit it out. When you leave school, what would you like to do?'

Edwina left him tongue-tied a great deal of the time. She was so different from his own mother; she behaved like a teenager, walking round the house with no shoes on, flicking ash wherever she went, playing pop music too loudly and never asking the twins if they'd washed their hands before sitting down to eat (which Lucas was sure they hadn't).

'I'd like to work in a bank,' he replied. Edwina had laughed at that. 'Really, Lucas, is that it? Is that the pinnacle of your ambition, to work in a bank? I thought you liked space – don't you want to go to the moon, discover new galaxies, experience zero gravity?'

At this point Charlie put a colander on his head and started talking like an alien and Edwina didn't bother to tell him to shut up.

'Is there any meat in this dish?' asked his father.

'No,' replied Edwina. 'We're having a vegetarian weekend. It's chilli chick peas.'

It was awful.

Edwina was very keen on allowing one's imagination to run free; that was why she didn't really mind things like drawing on the wall or Charlie wearing her lipstick. 'I want to encourage you to expand your artistic horizons, experiment, be whoever you want to be.'

'Well, I want to be a bank manager,' Lucas insisted.

Suddenly he wonders if he has spent his entire career in finance in order to spite Edwina. What had he really wanted to be? Lucas looks again into his own thirteen-year-old eyes.

I wanted to be taller and funnier and sportier and really popular, but most of all I wanted to be comfortable inside my own skin, and I wanted to be thin, like Charlie and Rowena.

In hindsight, Lucas wasn't unpopular as a child. At school he had a lot of friends, it was just difficult making arrangements to see other boys when he was home during the holidays. He seemed to spend most of his time being ferried from one side of the river to the other.

Also, he was a bit embarrassed about how things had turned out. There was something rather disreputable about the situation, something extra scandalous because a lot of people knew who Edwina was. She was 'that famous illustrator lady – you know, the Betsy and Tom books'.

Lucas simply went into denial about Edwina's talent. He refused to enter her studio and blocked any attempts at doing anything creative on the kitchen table.

'I hate drawing.'

'You can't hate drawing.'

'I can, I hate it, drawing and painting and all that rubbish. It's for babies.'

Lucas feels a prickle of guilt. He'd been quite difficult about trips to galleries, dragging his feet through the Hayward Gallery, refusing to look at anything other than his shoelaces.

Once he heard her sobbing onto Dickie's chest, 'I can't do anything with him, darling, I just don't understand him.' His father simply smoothed her hair and said, 'It'll take time, that's all. He just needs to grow up a bit.'

And he was growing, at least outwards. The evidence is frozen in front of him: a fat, immature teenager in trousers that are far too long for him.

His hair needed cutting before he went away. Edwina offered to put a pudding bowl upside down on his head and trim around it like she did with Rowena. She even picked up the bacon scissors and made snip-snipping noises by his ear. God, sometimes he really hated her.

When he was a little boy his mother took him to her salon to have his hair cut. Terence would balance a plastic stool especially for children on one of his normal salon chairs.

He was happy to cut little boys' hair but drew the line at adult males, so when Lucas turned thirteen he was taken by his father to his barber in St James's, where Lucas watched as Dickie was lathered up for a proper cut-throat razor shave.

As the barber scraped at Dickie's foam-covered throat with a steel blade, his father's Adam's apple bobbed precariously and Lucas had felt sick. His relationship with razor blades was an unhappy one and he had to go outside to breathe in a lungful of fresh air and pull himself together. He was off to Wyebourne in a couple of weeks and they wouldn't stand for any limp-lettuce nonsense.

His parents took him out for lunch before he went. It was a rare show of unity and certainly the first time Lucas had seen them together since Dickie had left home.

They went to Simpson's on the Strand. His mother's hair was a triumph of black curls. Terence had incorporated several 'pieces' into the construction and the result was magnificent. From a distance, she looked ready to win Miss World.

His father had behaved impeccably and so had Lucas. They all ordered the steak, it was delicious, but Barbara didn't eat hers. She had left her prawn cocktail too. She just looked at Dickie and her eyes brimmed with tears, she twisted her wedding band over and over and said, 'What was it all for, Dickie? The vows on our wedding day, my bridesmaids all in lemon chiffon. Don't you remember? You've ruined my life.' At which point his father tried to change the subject, and mentioned the cricket and a new West End musical.

'I don't really go out these days,' his mother sniffed, which was utter rubbish: she was forever going to charity balls and bridge club meetings.

In between sips of champagne – 'After all, this is a celebration' – Barbara would scratch at the scars on her wrists. Lucas was relieved when the waiter took away her barely touched main course because he didn't really trust his mother with the serrated edge of the steak knife. What if she should do something silly? The table-cloths were so starched and white, he couldn't help imagining how awful they'd look if any blood got spilt, and how everyone would notice and stare at them.

His father wanted him to have a knickerbocker glory, but all he could think about was how the twins had crowed about the knickerbocker glories they'd guzzled on Dickie and Edwina's wedding day. Suddenly he felt faint and wanted to go home.

His mother cried all the way back to Chelsea. He'd held her hand in the back of a black cab and promised never to leave her, which was ridiculous considering he was off to Wyebourne in three days' time.

When they got back to River Walk his mother went to bed with a cold compress on her forehead while Lucas repacked his trunk for the tenth time.

It was a super-smart trunk; his father had bought it for him from Harrods. 'You're going to have such a splendid time,' he promised. Dickie had paid for Lucas's initials to be printed in gold on the burgundy leather lid: L. P. S. – Lucas Peter Spinner. 'Just because I don't love your mother doesn't mean I don't love you,' his father told him.

That reminds me, thinks Lucas, woozy now with tiredness. Where is the trunk? For years it was in his bedroom at River Walk, and once again Lucas feels nostalgic for a time when he had a bedroom with models of space rockets on the window sill and a giant poster of all the planets on his wall. Getting ready for bed he tries to remember everything he used to know about the solar system and falls asleep with the words 'thermonuclear fusion' on the tip of his tongue.

6

The Trunk

Lying in bed wishing he'd ordered a spare pizza for breakfast, Lucas comes to the conclusion that it was the trunk that spoiled everything. To this day, Lucas still can't fathom out why his father actually did it.

With the benefit of distance and hindsight, he can see now that Dickie probably didn't give it a moment's thought. A trunk was a trunk.

Lucas's was burgundy. His mother took a photograph of 'My grown-up baby' standing with one foot on the vast leather box, as if he'd just shot it on the front lawn of River Walk.

Just moments later his father pulled up outside the house and tooted the horn three times. This was it: for the next five years he would be a Wyebourne boy.

His mother dabbed at her eyes, told him that she loved him and was very proud of him, kissed him clumsily on his nose and then fled indoors, slamming the yellow front door so hard the windows rattled in their Crittal frames.

If Dickie noticed, he didn't say anything. His father was a very even-tempered man, nothing really fazed him. It would not be until a decade or so later that Lucas would see him unravel.

On the journey to school, Dickie filled Lucas in on all the scrapes and high jinks that he'd got up to during his time at Wyebourne.

His father was in an expansive mood, window rolled down, cigarette ash drifting in and out. 'I'm jealous, old boy, it's all ahead of you: all the fun, all the excitement.'

Lucas made a pretty good fist of being the confident teenage son looking forward to a new school and all the adventures that entailed, but inside he was petrified. What about wet dreams, what about his voice breaking, what about his testicles?

Instead of tackling these thorny issues, father and son skimmed the surface of any real emotion, and in the two-and-a-half-hour drive they managed to avoid anything gloomy or peculiar, with chats about the school sporting calendar and the merits of each house.

Dickie had been in Milton, Lucas was destined for Bunyan, which his father reminded him was spelt with a 'y' after the Christian author of *The Pilgrim's Progress*, rather than 'bunion', the medical abnormality of the foot.

It didn't really matter what his father said, Lucas soon realised that at Wyebourne boys in Bunyan were (not entirely) affectionately known as 'lumps'.

Approaching the school's gravel drive, Dickie suggested that Lucas try his hand at rowing, and Lucas was quiet for a second. Was his father mad? Fat boys don't row. He'd sink the boat.

'Basically,' his father continued, 'join in. No one likes those boys who skulk around in the shadows. Make an effort, put your hand up, volunteer, be a good sport and everything will be just dandy.'

And it was, sort of. Lucas thinks hard about Wyebourne. Despite ignoring his father's advice, most of the time he was neither happy nor unhappy. He was used to boarding and it was refreshing to be away from his mother and her deranged loneliness for a while. The food was all right, the masters were all right, work was all right. The main thing was he didn't stand out. He even missed out on a weight-based nickname, thanks to a pair of morbidly obese twins in his year who were imaginatively re-christened Fatty and Fatso on the very first day.

He was just Spinner, and he wasn't even the only Spinner: there was another who had earned the moniker Sycamore. It took Lucas a while to get the spinning connection, and when he did he was jealous. Why had that boy been chosen to get the special name and not him?

On refection, it seems like he drifted through his entire Wyebourne career without being chosen for anything. Forty years later, Lucas wonders if he could have tried harder, taken advantage of what was on offer, joined in, made an effort.

But at the time he just wanted to coast. He was chronically self-conscious, about his weight, about his breath – how did one actually know if one had halitosis? He spent many private moments breathing into his cupped hands, but disguised his paranoia by pretending he didn't care about anything. He practised this air of nonchalance to such a degree that it became impossible to shake off: of course he wasn't going to audition for the choir, why would he bother joining the photography society, or the Wednesday evening philatelists, or chess club? This attitude hardened over time into a cross between apathy and lethargy, and eventually Lucas barely did anything. He was literally a Bunyan lump.

In fact, the most dramatic thing to happen to him at Wyebourne was the arrival of his stepbrother Charlie. It was almost unbelievable and the second most awful thing (after leaving his mother), that his father had ever done to him.

There is a letter from Dickie somewhere, probably stowed away in his trunk, explaining the situation. Something along the lines of:

Look here, old boy, young Charlie seems to have come a bit of a cropper in terms of schools. Fortunately Wyebourne has been persuaded to take him on. Now, I know this might not be easy for you, but I'd very much appreciate it if you could keep an eye on him, there's a good chap.

His father's beautiful black-ink handwriting on crisp vanilla-coloured paper. If there were kisses, he can't for the life of him remember.

Lucas wanted nothing to do with Charlie. He was only in his second year at the school and didn't need things complicating. There was nothing obvious that linked the two of them, they didn't share the same surname, so why couldn't they just keep the thing quiet? Plenty of boys at school ignored their brothers, even when they were real ones and not step-halfwits.

Dickie drove Charlie down a week or so after the Michaelmas term had begun. Lucas watched aghast from his dorm window. What if Edwina got out of the car too? She'd recently adopted a horrendous, stinking afghan coat. What if she was wearing that? The potential for shame pricked at his every pore.

As luck would have it, only Dickie and Charlie emerged from the Bentley, followed by Charlie's trunk. A brand-new trunk that, apart from being pale blue, looked horribly similar to Lucas's.

Once again he feels the twist of rage in his guts, the sudden need to go to the lavatory. Damn fucking Charlie.

A porter came out of the lodge to take the trunk to Charlie's boarding house (he was in Milton, of course), and as he wheeled it directly under Lucas's dormitory window he knew instantly that it was the same, exactly the same, only instead of his initials it had C. S. T. emblazoned in gold across the lid. Charlie Shithead Tosser.

Did his father have no idea what this meant?

It meant that he and Charlie were equal, that his father cared as much for that simpering idiot as he did for his only son.

In a fleeting second of hate, Lucas was glad that Edwina's baby had died, glad that it ended its life down the toilet like a bleeding fairground goldfish.

His father had eventually told him about the pregnancy some months previously, mostly because he wanted Lucas to be kinder to Edwina. They were both still 'suffering from the disappointment,' he confessed, and added, 'There is nothing sadder than a lost child.' At the time, Lucas had felt a tug of sympathy, but now he was pleased. His father didn't deserve any more children,

Charlie caused a small stir at Wyebourne, arriving late with his hair in his eyes and his shirt open at the neck. It was as if a teenage film star had landed from Hollywood. Who was he?

Lucas was summoned by the housemaster of Milton and instructed to introduce the newcomer to the customs and traditions of the school, particularly those concerning uniform.

'What a lot of silly shit,' was Charlie's response. From then on, Lucas avoided his stepbrother. It wasn't difficult: if Charlie wasn't in class then he was usually in detention, and, as it transpired, it was in detention that the *thing* happened.

It was the only time Charlie ever came to him for help. One wet day in November, when the trees were dropping their rust-coloured skirts, Lucas returned from double divinity to find his stepbrother waiting for him outside his dorm. Typical Charlie behaviour, thought Lucas, bored with his tedious recalcitrance. Surely he'd been at Wyebourne long enough to know that visiting Lucas's boarding house without permission meant he was out of bounds.

'I don't know what your problem is,' Lucas had hissed at Charlie. 'It's as if you're looking for trouble,' and then Charlie told him.

At the time, some of the details didn't make sense. If Lucas was an innocent regarding women, then he was just as naive when it came to relations with other boys, or indeed older men.

And now, forty years on, he knows he made a mistake when he

simply told Charlie to his thirteen-year-old face that he was a fantasist and a liar, and how dare he make up such a load of tosh about Mr Robbins, who was an old schoolfriend of his father's. 'We get Christmas cards from him, Charlie. Do you think a man who sends a Christmas card to his old schoolfriend is capable of such beastliness?'

'But Lucas, he made me suck him off,' Charlie responded, and to this day Lucas cannot decide if his stepbrother was smirking when he said it. 'He took me into the stationery room, Lucas, and he told me that I was special, and all the time he was playing with himself, and once he was as stiff as a broom handle he made me take it in my mouth and ... Well, I was just wondering who I should tell.'

'You don't tell anyone, you fucking freak,' Lucas shouted, but Charlie did tell. He told matron, who already had her suspicions, and then two other boys came forward and told similar stories, and by the time they broke up for Christmas both Charlie and Mr Robbins had left the school for ever.

Wyebourne managed to hush it up. There was a small flurry of news activity when Robbins hanged himself, but most people thought he'd finally done the decent thing.

Oddly enough, Barbara had been uncharacteristically sympathetic. 'Poor man. Don't get me wrong, Lucas, what Robbins did was heinous, but don't tell me those boys weren't somehow to blame. Flaunting themselves, no doubt.'

Of course, after the Robbins debacle Charlie went to some ridiculous 'experimental' boarding school where, in stark contrast to the furtive after-lights-out activity at Wyebourne, pupils were allowed to openly explore their sexuality, and homosexuality was widely accepted.

'If not positively encouraged,' mutters Lucas bitterly, glad that the place burnt down in the nineties, no doubt due to someone exploring their inner arsonist and experimenting with matches.

Personally, he had no first-hand experience of 'that sort of thing' in all his years at either Witterings or Wyebourne but now, forcing himself to dredge deep along the seabed of his boarding-school memories, he does recall pretending to be fast asleep while peculiar barnyard-type noises emanated from a squeaking bed at the far end of his dorm, covering his ears against an outburst of hysterical laughter followed by weeping.

Right, enough of that, thinks Lucas. It's time to get up and crack on with the day, starting with a bath. Some of his schoolboy memories have left him feeling distinctly unclean.

7

My Roly-Poly Best Boy

Lucas catches sight of himself naked in the bathroom mirror. He looks like a grotesque Gollum; his weight has plagued him all his life. As he lowers himself into the bath a tide of displaced water washes over the edge of the tub and soaks the carpet.

Even his mother thought he was fat. One of the photographs in the album is inscribed 'My roly-poly best boy.'

Of course, a great deal of it was her fault. Whenever he was back at River Walk Barbara treated him like a spoiled lap dog, an overgrown Pekingese, un-walked and constantly fed. Barbara's love was wrapped up in sugar, coated with cream and topped with chocolate. It was an endless cloying love that Lucas both craved and resented.

'Get off me, Mum, I'm not a baby.' But he was her baby, her great big baby.

When Lucas turned fifteen he stood on his mother's scales and immediately jumped off. His weight in stones was exactly the same as his age. Even the dial shuddered in horror.

Some weeks later the school matron phoned Barbara to inform her that Lucas needed a special talcum powder in order to deal with the skin fungus that had developed between his legs due to his thighs chafing, and that the cost of the talc would be an 'added extra' on his fees.

Barbara was incensed. This was the same woman who had blown the whistle on poor queer Robbins. 'Interfering cow. She needs to take her big fat nose out of other people's business.'

However, the fact was undeniable: Lucas's natural tendency to pudginess had now progressed from chubbiness to solid stretch-marked flab, and sometimes when he stood next to Fatty and Fatso, the sumo wrestler-sized twins in his year, he felt like their long-lost triplet.

Something needed to be done, so Barbara took him to a place in Harley Street for some diet pills in order to kick-start his weight-loss regime.

Lucas squirms at the memory of being weighed in his underwear, callipers measuring the circumference of his meaty upper arms, his mother saying 'I can't understand it, we eat very healthily, but of course his father abandoned us and I think the shock of it might have affected his metabolism.'

She was a Harley Street aficionado, and a big fan of the quick fix. Lucas can remember her first face-lift, how she returned home from a health farm swathed in bandages, looking like she'd fought Joe Bugner.

The scars are still visible, even more so now that her wonderful hair has gone. The knotted purple scars behind each ear are cruelly evident.

What was it all for, Ma? wonders Lucas, the face-lifts and tummy-tucks. There were no more men after Dickie. In some respects, it was only when Terence moved in that she could really relax. After all, being both homosexual and penniless, Terence wasn't likely to stray. Finally Barbara had her loyal companion and pet.

As for Lucas, a combination of prescribed amphetamine sulphate and a sudden growth spurt meant that, although by no means slim, by the time he was sixteen his 'annus fattus' had been consigned to the photo album.

Until now, he thinks ruefully, slightly relieved that his mother is too gaga to realise that her rotund visitor is her son and not some passing chubby orderly.

Edwina was much more into health and nutrition than Barbara, who could never resist the sweet trolley. His stepmother was a big fan of brown rice and lentils. She also approved of long walks and fresh air, and letting off steam. 'He just needs to run around more,' he heard her tell Dickie, and he felt himself burn with embarrassment and rage. He wasn't some nine-year-old kid and anyway, as his mother said, it was his 'Glands, darling, you'll grow out of it, and anyway it's a well-known fact girls don't like skinny boys.'

Which was a lie: girls did like skinny boys. They were all over Charlie. Charlie's prowess with the opposite sex was infuriating. He was so casual about his conquests: girls were always phoning 137 in tears and asking for him. 'Tell her I'm not in,' the teenage Casanova of Kennington would frantically whisper, tiptoeing away from the phone as if it contained a mad snake. Rowena would lie for him, but Lucas wouldn't.

'I'm afraid he doesn't want to speak to you. Don't bother calling again.'

Charlie was promiscuous from a very tender age. He was a year younger than Lucas, but had already displayed love bites and once informed Lucas that he might have crabs. At first Lucas didn't know what on earth he was talking about, how could he get crabs without going to the seaside? The boy was ridiculous.

Rowena had to explain. 'He means pubic lice,' she said in a bored tone, and then added, 'Well, I tell you Charlie, I'm not raking through your manky pubes with a nit comb. You're on your own, mate.'

In Lucas's feverish imagination, Charlie lived some kind of Bond existence at his boarding school, fobbing off women who all looked a bit like Britt Ekland in *The Man with the Golden Gun.*

By stark contrast, the girls who were bussed in from neighbouring girls' boarding schools for sweaty-palmed Wyebourne dances were either too pretty for Lucas to look at or as awkward and plain as he felt, and the only other girl he ever came into close contact with was his stepsister.

Clever, watchful Rowena with her sharp tongue and her complete lack of interest in anything she considered a bit silly: clothes, shoes, pop music. Rowena ploughed her own furrow, she read difficult books, listened to peculiar music and, until she left home for college, wasn't particularly sociable. At her London day school Rowena had a couple of close friends: a very small girl with some kind of condition that affected her growth and a silent Chinese girl who was apparently some kind of maths genius.

Compared with the girls in Lucas's imagination, Rowena wasn't really particularly female. Indeed, Lucas knew for a fact that she occasionally wore a pair of Charlie's underpants, and only very infrequently bothered with a bra. Because she hated food and barely ate, her spine was knobbled, at no point did her thighs touch, and her breasts hung like empty purses.

Really, all things considered, she was a rubbish stepsister to spy on in the bathroom.

His social life improved when he spent most of his post O-level summer holidays with his mother in River Walk. Barbara was a sociable woman and her network of contacts across the Royal Borough of Kensington and Chelsea was as intricate as a spider's web. Barbara was very keen that society should take note of her eligible son and hence, from the age of sixteen, Lucas seemed to be on some list of boys who could safely be invited to house parties.

'After all, darling, you're not going to steal the silver.'

Most of these parties were interchangeable: privileged children who once went to nursery school together met in the basements of white stuccoed houses and drank measured amounts of beer and cider. Miniature bottles of Babycham were provided for the girls and an adult would occasionally patrol the party area, turning lights up and music down.

At these parties Lucas eventually plucked up the courage to snog girls who often turned out to be the sisters of boys he knew from Wyebourne or Witterings, pink-faced fifteen-year-olds experimenting with blue eye shadow and platform heels, chubby little virgins with garlic breath and no intention of allowing anything beyond a top-half grope into often disappointingly empty bras.

Try as he might, he couldn't get a single one of these nicely brought-up girls to touch his willy. Of course there were apocryphal stories of girls that would go all the way, and occasionally the name Elise Landreth would crop up. Lucas never knew whether to claim ownership of Elise: on the one hand, she was his mother's adored goddaughter, but on the other hand, rumour had it she was a bit of a slag.

The water around Lucas has turned scuzzy and tepid, it's like sitting in a cold vichyssoise. The hot water tank is obviously empty, so he heaves himself out and wraps up as much of himself as a bath sheet can manage.

There is a photograph in his mother's album that dates Elise's transition from innocent to Lolita. Lucas leafs through the snaps until he finds what he is looking for, in the holidays section of his mother's photographic aide-memoire: 'Elise aged fifteen, Turks and Caicos'.

At fifty-six, Lucas has no idea where the Turks and Caicos are, but what he can glean from the photograph is that the girl in the tie-dye bikini bears no resemblance to the pig-tailed, gap-toothed kid she used to be.

Packed away to a girls' boarding school in the country at the age of eleven, Elise had obviously spent the last four years marinading in some heady brew of oestrogen and metamorphosed into a slim-hipped, long-legged, busty looker.

Part schoolgirl, part woman, her body is beaded with pool water, and behind a mass of wildly curly hair, Elise is laughing. There is something untamed about the teenager, and Lucas notes sadly that she is both lovely and already slightly spoilt. In hindsight, it was probably already too late to save her. Elise did what Elise wanted.

Lucas wanders back through to his mother's bedroom. Surely she has some talc. That wretched fungal infection seems to be back.

8

Elise Sweet Sixteen

Lucas talcs his thighs with some 'mildly medicated' Cuticura powder. After breakfast he will go for a stroll up the King's Road, visit Marks and Spencer and get some decent-quality food in.

His mother isn't exactly clock-watching; he can take his time, have another cup of coffee and contemplate the slightly unnerving photographs that chart his own teenage transformation.

The change is nowhere near as dramatic as Elise's, but nonetheless, there is some improvement.

Lucas stares hard at the seventeen-year-old him. He has obviously had a growth spurt as the trousers of his dinner suit are slightly too short. There is something both arrogant and shifty in his expression: he looks sly, but his mother is obviously very proud of him. 'My Wyebourne sixth former'.

Peculiar as it might seem, black tie was compulsory for certain school events, such as Founder's Day and end-of-term formal dinners. Appropriate dress was considered an important part of learning to be a gentleman, along with passing the port to the left, spitting out 'shot' delicately while eating game, not choking like a child on a panatella, and knowing one's way around a gaming table.

Poker was the game back in the mid-seventies. Gambling with cash on school premises was strictly forbidden and matchsticks were considered a much more sensible option, but what with some of his peers coming from ridiculously wealthy backgrounds, sometimes it was hard to stick to the rules.

Lucas looks at the cocky sixth former again. Behind the haughty demeanour he can sense a tension. I've never been particularly good at self-control, he admits to himself, eating a biscuit. If it wasn't food, it would be something else.

He hasn't been near a poker table or a casino in years, at least that's something to be proud of, but he quickly turns the page away from himself. The photograph has unsettled him and he feels anxious for the boy who is so obviously heading for a fall.

He distracts himself with a few Christmas snaps, of gifts piled high under a glowing tree, all for Lucas. He was a very spoilt young man. But not as spoilt as ... there she is again.

When Elise was sixteen her parents commissioned a semi-famous photographer to take her portrait, and Barbara was sent a cut-out from the contact sheet of the image the Landreths eventually had framed and hung above the mantelpiece in their dining room.

Elise's shoulders are bare, giving the impression she is topless. ('She wasn't,' Minty insisted, 'she wore a towelling robe throughout the shoot.') Her nose is obviously too big and has been crudely shaded by a make-up artist to look smaller, and her tangled mane has been straightened and blow-dried beyond recognition, but it is her eyes that draw one in. At sixteen, Elise's eyes are already full of stories. 'Sweet sixteen!' his mother has written underneath. Lucas would have added several more exclamation marks.

He transports himself back to the year this photo was taken. Naughty Elise had just been expelled from her boarding school deep in the English countryside, where Scottish dancing and calligraphy were on the curriculum. Her crimes, unimaginatively, included smoking, drinking and setting off a fire extinguisher. As a result, she was being moved to a day school in Kensington – which, rather than a punishment, had been her intention all along.

They should have kept her in the country in her tartan-pinafore uniform and white Sunday gloves. In fact, had they known what was to come, Paul and Minty Landreth should have locked her in a tower and thrown away the key.

Some years later Elise told Lucas that she'd fucked the semi-famous photographer in his studio, confiding that she only mentioned it now because said photographer had recently taken a portrait of Lady Diana and she wondered if the princess-to-be had fucked him too. 'He was very old, but there was nothing wrong with his cock,' she added.

Barbara was firmly on Elise's side. So what if she had been expelled – what did Minty and Paul expect? Her goddaughter was a free spirit and didn't deserve to be buried alive in the graveyard of the English countryside!

Being a day girl in London was a much more suitable option, and Barbara aimed to see as much of her 'favourite girl' as possible. 'Imagine,' she told Lucas, 'she's practically on my doorstep. I can take her out for lunch and I shall make sure she has no more than one small glass of wine before she goes back to school.'

Only, unbeknownst to Barbara, Elise rarely bothered to go back to school after lunch. The charms of the King's Road in 1977 were a lot more appealing than double geography back in Kensington Gore.

But, for a while, her scholastic absence went unnoticed, and Elise and Paul decided to throw their daughter a sixteenth birthday party. It was both a celebration of her birthday and a means of introducing their daughter to the young and eligible Kensington and Chelsea scene.

'We want lots of lovely young people from nice families,' vouched Minty, and Barbara promised to help. 'How about ice-skating followed by a lovely meal?' she suggested.

Ice-skating was such fun and it gave the boys a chance to be chivalrous. Barbara quivered with the romantic potential of it all. 'Oh Lucas, darling, you'll love it. Minty, June and I had such a hoot when we used to skate in Switzerland. I was actually rather good, even though I say it myself.'

Unfortunately Lucas hadn't inherited his mother's natural grace on the ice, and even though he was a good deal slimmer than he had been as a young teen, he was still a chunky boy, and he spent most of the afternoon clinging to the wooden sides of the rink and feeling like a prize chump.

By contrast, Elise was fearless, flying around the ice in a white leotard with a matching crushed-velvet miniskirt. Of course she owned her own skates, which was obviously an advantage. Lucas can still remember the orthopaedic look of his hired skates and the feeling of shame as he sat down heavily, time and time again, on his bottom. 'At least you've got some padding,' laughed Elise, and in that second he hated her. She was a bitch; she wasn't even very pretty or nice. She was just exotic-looking, with a great deal of hair, which she hid behind because actually her nose was fat and greasy and, if you looked closely, her chin was pitted with black-heads.

There was only one girl who shone brighter on the ice than Elise, and that was Fern. Lucas managed to forget his soggy cor-duroy bottom for a second as he recognised the girl he had sat next to at Elise's tenth birthday party, a girl whose hand had once held his. Maybe they were destined to only ever meet at these occasions.

If only he could attract her attention, but unfortunately he didn't really get a chance to talk to her because she spent the entire afternoon gliding, racing and spinning around the middle of the rink, a cloud of red hair billowing behind her. Sometimes she put one leg up quite high, and she could also go backwards.

A fellow plump non-skater, who introduced herself through the spittle of her braces as Clem, confided Fern's secret to Lucas as their legs buckled in harmony and they landed in a heap on the ice: 'It's easy for Fern, she does ballet and tap.'

The plump girl had been interested in him, he could tell. She managed to sit next to him when they went for the birthday meal and laughed at every single thing he said, and the sound of her laughing eventually began to grate.

Far away at the other end of the table sat Fern. She had changed into a black velvet dress and her skin was the colour of a certain type of creamy rose that grew round the door at River Walk, and he wanted more than anything to tell her this and simultaneously smell her neck. But suddenly, while they were ordering pudding, she disappeared and the plump girl with the big spitty teeth glee-fully informed him that Fern had passed out in the ladies', and Elise's father's chauffeur had been dispatched to pick her up and take her home.

Lucas couldn't imagine how she'd managed to get so drunk, con-sidering the only alcohol on the table had been beer for the boys and cider for the girls. But apparently Elise had smuggled in a bottle of vodka and the two of them had been topping their cider up with Smirnoff.

'She was a terrible mess,' added Horse Teeth gleefully. 'Sick all down her nice dress.'

Lucas's memory of the rest of the night is hazy. All he can remember is catching sight of Elise in the kitchen. She was sitting on the worktop with her tights and knickers around her ankles, while one of the waiters buried his head beneath her skirt.

Today, health and safety would have a field day with that sort of behaviour. Not only were Elise's naked buttocks grinding down on an area where food was prepared, but she was also smoking.

Three weeks later Elise was expelled from her nice girls' day school for truanting and stealing, and even his mother looked worried.

'She was caught shop-lifting when she was meant to be at school, Lucas. What on earth possessed her? A tin of hairspray and an eyeliner – why didn't she ask me? I would have bought her those in a flash.'

He didn't have the answer, not one he could tell his mother. He could have said, 'Because sometimes we all do stuff for a bit of excitement, Mum. Things we shouldn't do, just for the thrill of it.'

Lucas feels himself overheat in the confusion of all these memories. It's time he headed out. He needs some fresh air to blow away the cobwebs of his past.

9

Lucas the Undergraduate

Lucas walks up to Marks and Spencer and then back to his mother's flat. The King's Road is both exactly the same and totally different. The Duke of York's playing fields are still in situ, but the Headquarters are now an art gallery.

Maybe he will visit. He wonders if his mother ever bothered. She was quite specific about what she liked: impressionists mostly, and nice pictures of flowers in vases, fruit in pretty bowls, things one could easily recognise, none of your abstract nonsense. Unlike Edwina, Barbara had a loathing for anything avant-garde or, as she called it, 'silly'.

The streets around Sloane Square are still full of tiny uniformed children being walked in crocodiles. In fact, once upon a time he attended a kindergarten just a stone's throw from where he is standing right now. From the age of three his academic future was charted as if he were a small ship, from Drake House to Witterings to Wyebourne, before landing safely in Oxford.

Only somehow he got lost, and the winds of academia blew hard against him. Lucas unpacks his groceries, kicks off his shoes and takes a bag of Percy Pigs and the photograph album over to the recliner.

By rights these pages should feature snaps of Lucas standing in front of a gothic stone college with a black and gold striped scarf garlanding his neck.

Only it all went slightly wrong, and the Lucas staring back at him now is wearing the black, red and white college scarf of his alma mater, Warwick, a modern campus university situated horrifyingly close to Coventry.

If Lucas looks slightly stunned in the photograph, it's because he is about to embark on an adventure that will, for the first time in his life, involve mixing with 'other' types.

People from all sorts of backgrounds went to Warwick. Rumour had it there was quite a lot of donkey jacket wearing and protest song singing.

Being little more than a decade old, Warwick had neither dreaming spires nor oak-panelled dining rooms. Indeed, from now on Lucas would be eating in a cafeteria. 'You don't mean one has to queue up with a tray?' queried Barbara.

He'd been warned, of course, that Oxford wasn't a shoo-in, that competition was fierce, but neither Lucas nor Barbara had taken the warnings seriously. They both presumed that he'd pull it off; like a conjurer pulling a stream of silk handkerchiefs from his sleeve, Lucas would triumph at the last minute.

His mother thought he was a genius. The one time he appeared in a school play she thought he was better than Laurence Olivier; when he swam a length in a hotel swimming pool she insisted he was the new Mark Spitz. His mother really saw no reason why he couldn't be a fighter pilot, a heart surgeon or even an astronaut.

At difficult parent-teacher evenings, one of the few occasions when his parents joined rank, Barbara highlighted the positive comments and glossed over any criticism. 'They're just being particularly hard on you because they know how clever you are,' she insisted.

His father was slightly more phlegmatic. They would have long talks about his school reports, conversations held in the dining room in Kennington Road, his father sitting at the desk that had once belonged to his father, scrutinising the comments made by various masters: 'lacks commitment', 'prepared to coast', 'half-hearted'.

'Well, Lucas, what do you have to say for yourself?'

Lucas blushes at the memory. Dickie had been so disappointed when the crested letter of rejection eventually arrived from Oxford, whereas his mother had been furious on his behalf: 'They've made a mistake. Mark my words, Lucas, you'll show them. When you're a great big success, they'll have to eat their words, the fools.'

For a split-second Lucas wishes he could go to his mother and find her as she used to be, in the sitting room at River Walk, ankles elegantly crossed in twenty-denier stockings, a gin and tonic on a coaster by her side, and tell her that he has lost his job, because it would be nice to hear her say, 'Well it was never good enough for you, darling. You need to be doing something more exciting than being stuck in that boring old bank. Have some nibbles.'

And just for a minute he might feel like there was something better for him out there, that he could dare to hope.

There are very few photographs of Lucas at Warwick in the album. Barbara visited once and tried not to cry when she saw his living quarters. 'It's just so impersonal, darling,' she wailed. 'All nasty Formica and lino, I can't bear it. Why is the lighting so unflattering?'

As for Lucas himself, without photographic evidence to prod his memory the uni years are vague. He grew his hair a little longer to fit in, stopped wearing shirts with cufflinks because no one else did, and tried his hardest to find a pair of jeans that he didn't look completely idiotic in, which turned out to be impossible.

Fortunately there were plenty of other students at Warwick who weren't achingly trendy, so Lucas was able to blend in with an amorphous mass of pasty-faced, hairy young men and women in baggy corduroy trousers.

He naturally gravitated towards the braying classes, fellow ex-boarding school types and rugger buggers.

As for women, he avoided the angry feminists because he couldn't understand what they were on about or why they didn't want to look nice, and concentrated on less secure women, usually the plainer friend of the popular beauty, and with this tactic he managed to lose his virginity in the second term of his first year.

Lucas checks his penis, to see if the recollection of this momentous occasion is giving it any ideas, but it seems not.

Lauren was an ex-grammar school girl from a place Lucas had never heard of called Lytham St Annes. She and her long-term boyfriend from home had made a pact to stay virgins until they got married after graduating, only she found out that he'd broken the pact, and had been carrying a packet of condoms in her handbag ever since.

That it was a tit-for-tat tryst didn't bother Lucas in the slightest, they were both doing each other a favour, and Lucas soon discovered that sex was more enjoyable in the aftermath than in the act itself. In fact, the bit he liked the best was telling his male friends about his conquests in the student union bar. Women were still an alien species to him, and yet there were a sufficient number who agreed to sleep with him.

Sometimes when a female took her bra off he would have a flashback to seeing his mother's blood-stained breasts in the bath and he would instantly lose his erection, which was embarrassing. However, Lucas soon realised that most girls thought flaccidity their fault and learnt to insist the problem had 'never happened before'.

If he were honest, Lucas found the naked female form a bit shocking. He liked women best when they were safely zipped into evening gowns with little fur stoles around their shoulders. What he didn't like was all the paraphernalia that went with being intimate with the opposite sex: he didn't like condoms, was horrified by the sight of a box of tampons in a girl's bathroom and almost threw up when an overnight female visitor used his razor to shave her legs.

There was something unclean about a lot of women, he decided, and sometimes his subconscious would conjure up a pair of cream shoulders and the stem of Fern's delicate neck in that black velvet dress. No one ever really matched up to her, the pictures he carried of her in his head, the weeping nine-year-old who needed rescuing, her small hand in his, a blaze of angel-red hair.

Possibly Lucas's bleakest moment at Warwick was hearing from his father that Rowena had gained a place to read English at Hertford College, Oxford.

He remembers sitting on his single bed in the sliver of a room that he had been designated, with its ugly blond-wood desk and Anglepoise lamp, and wanting to smash the place up.

Typical: fucking skinny weird Rowena who wouldn't eat potato or custard or pastry or gravy had got into fucking Oxford. Where was the justice in that? She wasn't even eighteen.

Lucas dimly recalls getting horribly drunk on real ale that night and throwing up over and over and over again into a wastepaper basket by his bed. If he thinks back hard enough, he can still conjure up the horrific stench of puked-up yeast in his nostrils. Of course, in years to come the bedside puke bin would be an occupational hazard.

On a happier note, he celebrated his twenty-first while still at Warwick, although obviously the party was held in London. His mother took charge of the arrangements; she was in her element, fussing over the invitations, eventually opting for a sophisticated silver font on shiny black card. The envelopes were black too, which meant they needed to be addressed in a special silver pen, which then leaked all over the dining-room table.

Dinner for thirty at Claridge's, followed by a trip to a West End nightclub, and Lucas has a sudden vision of his mother disco-dancing wildly in the middle of a mirrored dance floor, multi-coloured lights spinning behind her, hairpieces flying.

A photograph of Lucas and his mother taken hours beforehand is titled '21 today'. They are sitting side by side, Barbara in an easy chair with Lucas perched on the arm. Someone must have taken it for them. Considering the enormity of his mother's hair, it was probably Terence.

Lucas is back in black tie; his mother had bought him a new dinner suit for his birthday. The satin lapels are wide and glossy, matching the stripe down the outside of his trousers. He is wearing a cummerbund and the effect is quite pleasing.

His mother certainly looks delighted. She is gazing adoringly at him; the window sill behind them is crowded with birthday cards.

Rowena sent him one, postmarked Oxford, of course. It was a portrait of Virginia Woolf. 'How peculiar,' his mother commented. Charlie didn't bother, but Edwina had parcelled up a rather pretty little landscape, or 'a muddy little daub', as his mother described it.

Lucas remembers being rather nervous about the whole event. In fact, even now the memory evokes a feeling of unease. He'd invited a select group of Warwick mates down for the occasion, including Lauren, whom his mother was rather disappointed in. 'Northern, darling. Lytham St *where?*'

But apart from Lauren not passing muster, the evening had been a roaring success. Barbara had put together an elegant mix of old and new friends, and even Dickie seemed in his element, catching up with old friends, cigar in one hand, Jack Daniel's in the other. For one glorious second Lucas thought his parents were going to dance together, but the moment passed and instead his father looked at his watch and muttered, 'Lord, have you seen the time? Edwina will think I've got lost, stolen or strayed,' and with that he vanished.

Elise was there, with her parents keeping a hawk-like eye on her. 'She's been a bit of a silly billy lately,' his mother whispered, 'but the good news is that she's studying fashion at St Martin's. You wait: she'll be the new Zandra Rhodes.'

As usual, Elise looked fabulous from a distance. It was only close up that her skin seemed grey beneath her make-up, and she kept needing to go to the lavatory during dinner. 'Cystitis, I expect,' his mother said. 'Her mother used to be a complete martyr to it, poor Minty.' It was the first time he ever heard his mother refer to his Aunty Araminta as poor Minty, but it wouldn't be the last.

Flicking further through the album, beyond his twenty-first, Lucas stops at a photograph simply titled 'My son, the graduate'.

The photograph is slightly blurred. Lucas has to peer hard at the picture to make sure it's him, but the beard is a clue. He was so proud of it, even though Charlie once told him it made him look like Peter Sutcliffe, the Yorkshire Ripper.

Wearing his mortarboard and gown, he looks remarkably like a million other recently graduated students, but on closer inspection there is a palpable sense that he's relieved it's all over.

His parents attended the ceremony held at Warwick's Butterworth Hall together. 'Very nice,' his father said in a slightly patronising tone. 'At least I understood every word. At Oxford, the entire graduation ceremony is conducted in Latin.'

'Well, how ridiculous,' his mother replied. Ever since Lucas failed to get in to Oxford she'd taken violently against the place, to the point that when she watched the Boat Race on the television she cheered on Cambridge. Years later she admitted to Lucas that when Warwick beat an Oxford college on *University Challenge* she opened a bottle of champagne.

She insisted on some fizz with their lunch. 'I'm not sure a two-two really warrants a Laurent-Perrier,' Dickie pretended to joke, unable to conceal his very real disappointment. But it was bearable, his mother ate all her lunch and there were no tears.

Maybe everything really could be all right.

Lucas feels suddenly terribly sad. The bag of Percy Pigs is resolutely empty and he turns on the television to distract him from his past.

10

Work Hard, Play Hard

There has been one message from his darling wife. Lucas checks his phone again; it's short and to the point:

WTF?

What the fuck what?

He deletes it. He doesn't need to deal with Denise, he has enough on his plate and Lucas wonders for a moment if he might just stay here for ever, back at Mummy's again.

It's where he ended up after university. It wasn't intentional, rather that he had nowhere else to go, and as his mother always said, 'My home is your home.'

He vaguely expected his father to buy him a flat but the offer wasn't forthcoming. On the contrary, it seemed his father intended him to work for a living, and Dickie was very much instrumental in securing Lucas his first job in the City.

Barbara was of course delighted to have her 'man of the house' home and insisted on taking a photograph of him on his very first day in gainful employment. Lucas finds the photo halfway through the album. Barbara has marked it 'My young professional', but all

Lucas can see is a twenty-one-year-old boy with a ridiculous beard looking slightly sheepish in a new shirt and tie.

She was more excited than he was. 'Just think – I can cook you a proper breakfast every day, and every day you can come home and tell me all about work. Now come on, darling, smile. Don't forget, the world is your oyster.'

Unfortunately, oysters aren't always what they're cracked up to be, and within weeks Lucas knew he hated his job.

Middle-aged Lucas feels a pang of sympathy for the young adult in front of him, recalling how he spent most of his time at work hiding in the toilets, taking two-hour lunch breaks and slipping out of the office as early as possible.

To all intents and purposes Lucas became a full-time shirker, but obviously he hid the reality of his working life from both of his parents, managing to convince Barbara that it was only a matter of time before he was invited onto the board.

Lucas recalls London in 1980 semi-nostalgically. A new decade might have dawned, but the streets around Aldgate still teemed with furled umbrellas and bowler hats. In fact, there were still plenty of men on his morning commute who were a dead ringer for the banker dad in *Mary Poppins*.

Another time, lost now.

But if the City clung to its traditional past, Lucas's home borough was rapidly becoming the boozy playground of the newly identified Sloane Ranger. Wine bars were springing up all over the postcode and for once, at least out of office hours, Lucas seemed to be in the right place at the right time.

He went out most nights. As soon as he got home from work he would shower, change, eat and then hit the mean streets of Fulham. Thanks to his mother refusing to take any rent, he could afford to cultivate the image of a part-time playboy; the drinks were frequently on him.

Barbara was a little bit clingy: 'You're not going out again, Lucas, you'll get ill.' She cooked exotic meals complete with fancy puddings, which Lucas had to refuse as suddenly people were becoming very body-conscious and London was buzzing with aerobics and Lycra.

'But it's your favourite,' Barbara would bleat. Honestly! Sometimes Lucas imagined his mother would only be happy when he turned into a *National Enquirer* story: FAT MAN LIVES AND DIES ON MOTHER'S SOFA.

He joined a gym but only used the sauna, met up with old friends from Wyebourne, most of whom seemed to have gone into 'the family business', whatever that might be, and hooked up with a couple of Warwick alumni who'd made the move to London and were renting a flat in Earl's Court.

Eddie and Joe had set up a mobile sandwich business delivering exotically filled baguettes and bagels around Soho and the West End. 'Sandwiches?' his mother remarked disdainfully. 'I'm so glad you've got a proper job, Lucas. There's earning a crust and there's earning a crust.' At this point, his mother became slightly hysterical at her own wit and only stopped laughing when she started choking and Lucas had to hit her hard between the shoulder blades. That she should choke on her own words was oddly prophetic: Eddie and Joe made an absolute killing and the last Lucas heard, they'd taken early retirement and were dividing their time between various philanthropic projects and their ski chalet in Aspen.

Talking of which, here is Lucas in his black salopettes, looking like a rather plump Milk Tray man. He has all the kit, right down to his shiny reflective goggles. 'Lucas hits the slopes', his mother has titled the snap; her handwriting is still legible and strong, 'January 1981'.

He had been working at Hargreaves Benedict for nearly six months and survived his first office Christmas party. Fortunately there is no photographic evidence of that occasion, as he behaved rather badly and was almost caught pissing in the office yucca plant.

A bunch of them had decided to go skiing in the New Year. The party was a mixed bag of uni chums, including Lauren, a couple of old school mates and several Fulham faces Lucas vaguely recognised from various parties and wine bars.

The chalet slept ten comfortably and was satisfyingly pine-clad and log-fired. Antlers and elk-hide rugs abounded, and in the dining room a stuffed moose head looked down balefully over a baronial table.

This is the life, Lucas remembers thinking. No work and pure play for ten days under glorious blue skies and, best of all, no waking up to find Barbara sitting on the end of the bed, waiting to pass him his morning cup of tea.

In truth, he enjoyed the après a great deal more than the ski. He found the ski lift traumatic and was much more inclined, once he got up the bloody mountain, to hang out in a restaurant enjoying the view. After all, once you'd skied down the bloody thing one only had to come back up again. Much better to sit outside in the fresh mountain air and lark about with other people who could afford to buy startlingly overpriced Glühwein and delicious cheese fondue lunches.

Lucas's stomach rumbles at the memory. God he loves fondue, any type of fondue: cheese, meat in hot oil, or chocolate, and preferably all three.

Halfway into the holiday, and completely by chance, he bumped into Elise. You couldn't really miss her: she was wearing a shocking pink all-in-one ski suit and a massive fox-fur hat.

She was staying in a chalet just down the hill from where Lucas's party was staying and had already fallen out with most of her friends, whom she dismissed as 'uptight and boring'.

Elise was as fearless on the slopes as she had been on the rink. She was forever hurling herself down black runs and going off piste. The general consensus on the resort was that she was 'lucky not to have broken her neck'; meanwhile Lucas couldn't even manage a flaming sambuca without burning his lips.

Occasionally Elise would join Lucas and his assorted pals for lunch. She was a terrible scrounger and never seemed to have any money for things like food or buying anyone else a drink, and yet she could afford to be here. It didn't make sense.

'Well, Elise is very fond of the white stuff,' a cocky little Australian stranger dropped into the conversation.

'Obviously, otherwise she wouldn't be here,' Lucas replied. Who was this shifty-looking oik anyway? Elise had a habit of attracting a terrible bunch of hangers-on and honestly, some of the new snowboarding fraternity were beyond the pale.

'She's terribly easily led,' his mother's voice echoed in his head.

Which is presumably why there was that incident in the chalet where she was staying. Elise swore blind she wasn't even there when the fire broke out at four in the morning, which raised the question where the hell had she been? But the fact was her father had to claim on his insurance, and yet again Elise was in the dog-house.

Strange how all these memories can be triggered by just one photograph, thinks Lucas, suddenly exhausted, his mind a whirl of raclette and reindeer meat. That was the holiday Lauren had more-or-less thrown herself at him on a very drunken first night, but he'd fobbed her off. She was a nice girl, she was doing well, she had a company car and an expense account, but her northern accent was a tad embarrassing and her gums too big and too pink. He ignored her, he made her cry, he ignored her some more, and by the end of the holiday she'd paired up with Tim, one of the Fulham wine bar faces, and six months later Lucas heard they were engaged.

His mother was right, Lauren wasn't the girl for him. Deep down, Lucas knew there was only one girl for him and the older he got the more convinced he was that fate would bring them back together.

Lucas cannot decide whether to attempt a wank or lunch. Lunch is probably easier, he decides: he'd bought a selection of rather fine ready meals at M & S.

11

Just Before it Happened

Thanks to Marks and Spencer, Lucas enjoys a very good Cantonese chicken accompanied by duck spring rolls and egg fried rice. His hands are very sticky and he makes sure he washes them thoroughly before delving back into the album. Barbara has collected precious memories like a sentimental magpie and occasionally, squeezed between the plastic leaves, are theatre and opera ticket stubs, invitations to charity balls and birthday parties at smart venues. Lucas roots out a piece of pink paper, a note folded into quarters. It is from Elise.

It was written just a few weeks after the skiing trip to say a belated thank you for Barbara's lovely Christmas gift. The details of the gift are vague, suggesting Elise has forgotten what on earth it was. But then, Christmas had been and gone some time ago.

Her handwriting veers all over the page and she seems to have used a green felt-tip pen. The note is full of apologies, of thank-yous and gossip from the holiday, how great the snow was, how brilliant the weather and, finally, how seeing Lucas was 'the icing on the Alps!'

The letter is peppered with exclamation marks, and above the 'i' of her name she draws a circle with a smiling face inside. She doesn't mention the blackened chalet kitchen or the girl who ended up in hospital suffering from smoke inhalation, but she does say that she aims to knuckle down this year, and that 'trying harder at college' is just one of her many resolutions.

The letter is dated the tenth of February. Within weeks, she will be dead.

Lucas's new year's resolution was to move out. It would upset Barbara, but it needed to be done, and Lucas remembers making his mind up to approach his father about the possibility of helping out with funds to buy a flat.

Slipping Elise's letter back into its plastic sleeve, he rifles through a few more pages of the album until he discovers a Polaroid, both blurred and faded, that he has no recollection of ever giving to his mother.

It was taken on the twins' birthday, their twenty-first. His father had been very generous and bought them each an instant camera.

After a celebratory roast, one of Edwina's finer culinary moments, Dickie loaded up one of the cameras with a cartridge of film and began to show Rowena and Charlie how to use it.

The twins crowded behind him, watching as he pointed the lens at Lucas. Snap! Then a slight buzz followed by a short whirr, and within seconds the photograph fell from the camera's mouth onto the table.

No one else wanted it, so Lucas picked it up and watched his face emerge from a pale grey square of nothing. It wasn't a bad picture, though he was still in two minds over his beard. They weren't fashionable, but he still thought it made him look thinner.

The beard is now all that remains of the photograph. Lucas is a pale featureless blob behind it. Beneath it Barbara has written 'Last outing for the beard'. Of course, that was the weekend he shaved it off. He suspects now that she didn't like it.

For him, it's a reminder of the last time he ever sat at the table at Kennington Road. He was surprised to be invited to the twins' birthday lunch and imagined it was Edwina's ironic way of getting back at him for not inviting the twins to his Claridge's bash the previous year.

Whatever the motive, it hadn't been as excruciating as he'd expected. Rowena, with her ironing-board chest, at least made an effort to eat, while Charlie, with his dreadful table manners, fork in his right hand, knife in his left, clumsily cleared every scrap, peas ricocheting off the plate.

'It's only because he's left-handed,' Rowena always insisted, but privately Lucas thought it was the bog Irish farmer in him. After all, Rowena and Charlie came from rather rackety stock. 'Gyppos,' his mother would occasionally mouth when he returned from Sunday lunches in Kennington. 'I'm surprised she didn't roast you a hedgehog.'

Actually, Edwina had done lamb and it was very nice. In fact, the whole occasion was almost enjoyable. A civilised conversation was conducted over a couple of bottles of good red wine, Rowena spouted off about feminism, Charlie allowed himself to be teased about wearing a girl's silver necklace and Lucas managed to voice some of his opinions about the financial market without being shouted down.

It felt like something had shifted, as if the usual shadow of tension and resentment had lifted. Both his father and stepmother wore the same expressions of delight and relief throughout the meal.

We so nearly made it, Lucas realises and his chest tightens and tears spring to his eyes. We might have been friends in the end, there was a chance.

As usual, it was Rowena who held out the olive branch. 'Um, Lucas, I'm having a joint sort of celebration do, a kind of twenty-first cum pre-exam bash next weekend. You'd be very welcome. It's in Oxford.'

He can see again the flicker of surprise in Charlie's eye, Edwina pausing as she poured coffee from the silver jug, her hand freezing momentarily. This was a breakthrough. His father's tiny intake of breath before Lucas responded, 'That's very nice of you, Rowena. If I haven't got anything else planned, then why not? Sounds fun.'

His father breathed out, Edwina finished pouring the coffee and Charlie blinked in surprise.

'You see how fucking mature I can be?' he wanted to yell. But the words he allowed out of his mouth sounded like 'Yes please, I'd love some coffee.'

This is how being an adult feels, he decided, and chose to drink his coffee black, in keeping with his new-found status.

An hour or so later, once the twins had disappeared in a whirl of coats, he and Dickie retired to the living room for a man-to-man chat.

Lucas blushes at the memory. He really hadn't imagined it would be such a big deal asking his father for a flat.

But Dickie had taken it badly. 'Is this why you've been so accommodating?' he asked. 'Trying to butter the old man up? Well, I'm very sorry, Lucas, but there'll be no handouts from me.

'I've told your mother that, since you've finished full-time education, I don't have to keep paying her as much as she's used to. She's going to have to start economising. Now, I know she lent you money for a car and I have no idea where she got that money from, but I'm telling you, Lucas, I'm not a bottomless pit and I'm afraid a flat is completely out of the question until River Walk is sold.'

Lucas couldn't believe his ears. Essentially, his father was saying that until Barbara was ejected from River Walk he didn't have a cat's chance in hell of getting a flat.

'Anyway, son,' his father continued, 'you don't need my financial help. You're a bright young man with a good future, you can do this on your own, you don't need me. Cigar?'

Lucas recalls choking on a panatella, feeling dizzy and making his excuses to go home. He cannot remember if he thanked Edwina for her hospitality; all he knows is that, once again, he couldn't get out of that house fast enough.

Poor Barbara, he couldn't ask her to leave the home she loved.

Why should his mother have to move into some crappy little dive when Edwina had that massive place on Kennington Road? Why couldn't his father and Edwina sell up? Why did it have to be him and his mother who always got the shitty end of the stick, time and time again?

'How was it?' asked his mother when he got home.

'Awful,' he replied.

'Oh good,' she smirked, licking meringue crumbs off her lips. 'There's a Pavlova in the fridge.'

She'd sold some jewellery to help finance his car. She insisted she wasn't fussed: 'There's such a lot of good paste around these day, Lucas. Anyway, it's not what you've got, it's the way you wear it.'

He realises now that she must have sold it all before she gave up River Walk. That's why there's nothing left, not a diamond, emerald or sapphire. Like the Percy Pigs, the jewellery is all gone.

12

Lucas's Fabulous Wheels

He was intending to visit his mother this afternoon, but what with the Chinese feast at lunchtime and the stinging realisation that Barbara never liked his beard, Lucas decides that all he is fit for is a nap.

Memory lane has turned out to be far more traumatic and nerve-racking than he expected.

Any good American shrink would tell him that he hasn't managed to *process* the events that happened all those years ago, and they would be right. Setting the recliner to a 'dozing' position, Lucas lies back and tries to marshal his emotions.

In some respects, the aftermath of Elise's tragic death is like shattered glass. Just when you think you've swept it all away, another tiny shard tells you that you haven't.

So much is implicated in the story, it runs through all their lives in the same way the Thames snakes through London, shaping and forming their futures. For over thirty years he has been struggling with one question: was it my fault?

Where does the chain of guilt begin and end? Elise died because she took drugs, but in reality she only died on that particular night because Lucas invited her to that particular party.

He pauses for a second, but if his mother hadn't given him the money he wouldn't have bought the car. If he hadn't bought the car he probably wouldn't have bothered with Rowena's stupid party.

But she did and he had.

He can still hear the delight in his mother's voice as he posed with his new car outside River Walk. It was early spring and the forsythia was budding. 'Just one more with your sunglasses on, Lucas, you look like a pop star.' He didn't, but his smile as he casually perched on its shiny streamlined snout says it all: it was his pride and joy. The picture inevitably appears in the album, inscribed 'Lucas's fabulous wheels'.

A Triumph TR8, a nippy little scarlet convertible coupé, just the thing to turn girls' heads while cruising around Chelsea, which was precisely what he'd been doing that Saturday morning in March when he spotted Elise.

She was weaving her way across the King's Road without bothering to use the zebra crossing, which was a mere yard away.

He sounded his horn and she flicked him a V-sign. He tooted once more and this time she recognised him and gleefully yelled instructions that he should pull up on Flood Street so they could have a catch-up.

Five minutes later she was in his car, fiddling with his stereo, touching buttons and knobs that he'd rather she didn't touch. She smelt slightly pole-cattish and complained about not having had any fun since Val d'Isère.

Something about the car gave him a confidence he didn't normally feel, and Lucas surprised himself by asking if she had any plans for that evening. 'Nothing special,' she admitted. 'There's a house party in Ealing, but seriously, Ealing? I don't think so.'

'I'm meant to be schlepping all the way to Oxford,' Lucas responded.

'I love Oxford,' Elise gushed, and pressed him for more details.

He remembers blushing as he explained that Rowena was having a party.

'Oh, of course, one of your mysterious step-family who must never be mentioned,' she laughed. 'Well, as luck would have it, I know quite a few bods at Oxford. There's a German bloke, a Count something or other, but we call him the cunt. I can always crash in his rooms. What time are you setting off?'

Lucas hadn't really thought about it, because deep down he had no intention of going. He had a sneaking regard for Rowena, but not enough to make a round trip of approximately a hundred miles. That said, it might be rather fun to take the Triumph for a proper spin. He was dithering, and so Elise made his mind up for him.

'Pick me up at Daddy's Westminster flat at five. I'm staying there for the time being – had a disaster with my last place. We can have a bite to eat in Oxford and then move on to the party.'

His mother was slightly taken aback: 'Oh, I thought we might go out for supper, there's a super new Italian round the back of Harrods. I was going to treat you – apparently the osso bucco is to die for.'

For a moment he was tempted. Elise was rather hard work and he had a horrible feeling she would smoke all the way to Oxford in his lovely new car, and anyway, when he got there he wouldn't know anyone and Elise would disappear and he'd be stuck in a corner feeling unpopular.

But when he told Barbara he had arranged to take Elise she completely changed her tune, 'Well, then you must go. Elise might meet someone eligible at last: it's high time. Poor Minty says she's been associating with some terrible riff-raff, but as long as she's with you she'll be safe. You will drive carefully, won't you, darling?' and he assured her that he would.

As instructed, he arrived at her father's Westminster flat on the dot of five, but she wasn't ready until six.

She didn't know what to wear and so she dragged him into her bedroom to help her choose. Elise's wardrobe looked like a badly organised theatrical costumier's. Clothes were strewn everywhere, on the bed, all over the floor, hanging out of drawers and closets.

In the end she opted for a thirties silver-sequin evening gown – 'darling Grannie's' – on top of which she threw a rather peculiar purple leather jacket, then nipped into her mother's room to borrow a spectacular pair of amethyst earrings and a cashmere cardi, 'to be on the safe side'.

Lucas, who thought he was being rather daring by wearing a Hawaiian shirt from Flip under his second-best linen suit, felt slightly unnerved. Elise was an overly excitable date, the kind of girl who would suggest doing a runner from a restaurant. He felt a sense of impending doom and wished he had some aspirin. She had already succeeded in giving him a headache.

Before they left, she rummaged for a bottle of red wine in the dining room and removed the cork before locking up. 'I think Mummy and Daddy are at Chequers this weekend. Not sure.'

The Westminster flat, with its extraordinary views over the river, was not the only Landreth residence. Paul also had a country seat in his Norfolk constituency, not to mention a little place in Portugal. Of the three girls who had been one another's bridesmaids, Minty had definitely done the best out of marriage and suddenly Lucas felt sorry for his mother, spending another lonely night watching television in River Walk. June, he recalls now, never married. His mother was convinced it was because she had size-eight feet, 'like canoes, darling'.

The concierge tipped his cap at the two of them as they left the building. 'Good evening, Miss Landreth, good evening, sir.'

As predicted, the first thing Elise did when she got in his car was get out a packet of cigarettes. Oh well, thought Lucas, I suppose if you weren't meant to smoke in this car, it wouldn't have an electronic lighter. And he pressed the requisite gadget, which popped out glowing red just a couple of seconds later. 'Cool,' breathed

Elise, exhaling a lungful of Peter Stuyvesant as they headed out of town.

He had been slightly worried about conversation drying up, but they had enough people in common to keep the bitching going until they hit the M40.

For a while, when they were stuck in traffic and Elise had only just started swigging the wine, she turned philosophical. 'What do you want to do with your life, Lucas?' And he answered as honestly as he could, 'I want to be rich and successful,' and 'thin,' he added silently.

'I think I'm already rich,' Elise observed. 'I've got trust funds that kick in when I'm twenty-five. Until then, Ma and Pa keep me on a financial leash, but I don't think I'll ever actually have to get a job. Which is a shame, really, because having a job, having a purpose in life, might actually be quite interesting, don't you think, Lucas? That it might be quite interesting to actually be a bit fucking useful?'

He didn't really know what to say to this, so he pretended to be concentrating on the road. Elise continued, 'I mean, obviously I'd like to get married and have children one day – that's if I still can. Thing is, I had an abortion, Lucas, and sometimes these people can be rather clumsy and, well … God knows if any permanent damage has been done. Not that I'd make a particularly good mother, but then that's what nannies are for. I'd rather have boys than girls, though. Girls can be such hard work: I've been a complete bitch to my mum, poor cow.'

Again Lucas was struck dumb; this was all terribly intimate. To cover his embarrassment he slid a cassette into the stereo system and Pink Floyd's 'The Wall' momentarily drowned Elise out, until she pronounced it 'shit' and ejected the cassette.

'I mean sometimes, Lucas, I think I should do some volunteering, give something back. I'm a very privileged girl, as Mummy and Daddy never stop telling me. Maybe I should go and help somewhere, like in the Third World.'

Lucas had a sneaking suspicion that Elise thought the Third World was an actual country.

On and on she droned in that typically nasal posh London girl drawl. Lucas attempted to tune her out by concentrating instead on the throaty drawl of the car's engine, but unfortunately odd snippets of her monologue still broke through. 'Spiritualism, Lucas, there's got to be a reason for all this. I'm not saying it's God, but there's got to be someone in charge ... Blah, blah ... Maybe I'm not easy to love? Of course, a lot of girls are just jealous of me ... blah ... the truth is, I love animals, but there's nothing duller than walking a dog. Doesn't matter what kind of dog, walking any dog is boring.'

At this point Lucas almost interrupted. 'No Elise, dogs aren't boring, but by Christ you are. You are the dullest, most self-centred girl I have ever had the misfortune to be squashed in a two-seater sports car with.'

The journey seemed interminable. Elise continued to swig red wine from the bottle, and as a result became increasingly animated, repeating the same stories several times before finishing the bottle and mercifully falling fast asleep with a lit cigarette still in her hand. Lucas removed the smouldering Peter Stuyvesant and came to the conclusion that women were, on the whole, frightful. Apart from one, of course.

Lucas shifts on the chair and considers Fern's involvement in the story. In some respects it's thanks to Elise that he met her. It was so long ago but he's never forgotten it: fireworks and music, doves and silk handkerchiefs. Lucas fell in love when he was twelve years old and her name was Fern Woolbright.

Flame-haired Fern who sat next to him at Elise's tenth birthday party and had seen him cry. Imagine his humiliation. A great big twelve-year-old boy crying because his father was marrying another woman, who wasn't his mum, and all she did was simply hold his hand. A small collection of tiny anemone-like fingers curled themselves tightly round his hand and she said, 'I'm here, it's okay.' He had completely forgotten this incident until now, lying here on a green Dralon button-operated psychiatrist's couch – talk about Freudian. But suddenly his infatuation makes sense: no wonder he'd been so keen to rescue her from the shitting dove.

Of course, the next time they met it was pretty obvious she hadn't a clue who he was. In fact, on that occasion, Elise's sixteenth birthday party, they didn't even speak. He'd just about plucked up the courage to go over to her and re-introduce himself when she disappeared,

If only he'd gone to help her, like she'd helped him. If only he'd barged into the ladies' lavatory and held her hand while she puked and said, 'I'm here, it's okay.' But he didn't, and on that drive down to Oxford, with Elise snoring gently in the passenger seat, he realised it was five years since he had last seen her.

He knew she'd gone to drama school, because Aunty Minty had told Barbara, and there had been much discussion in the sitting room at River Walk as to whether the Woolbrights had been mad to let her go. 'It wouldn't be so bad if it was a London school, but it's Manchester,' Minty despaired.

'Ugh,' Barbara shuddered, 'the frozen north.'

Elise slept until they reached the outskirts of Oxford, when she suddenly awoke, as refreshed as a princess in a fairy tale. The empty wine bottle rolled around in the footwell. 'I should have brought two,' she tutted.

'Nearly there,' Lucas responded, more cheerfully than he felt, and then, as if it were an afterthought and not something he'd been desperate to ask for hours, he added very casually, 'How's your cousin, by the way?'

'Oh, you mean lovely little Fern?'

'That's the one.'

'I last saw her at Christmas, but we speak on the phone occasionally. I keep promising to go up and see her, but really, it's Manchester. Anyway, I thought you'd know exactly what she was up to, considering you know what.'

'No, what?' She really was infuriating.

'Considering she's fucking your stepbrother.'

Something happened to Lucas's brain at that point, and for a split-second he no longer knew how to drive the car. Instinctively his foot pressed hard down on the accelerator and Elise screamed, 'Fucking hell, Lucas, slow down! I don't want to die just yet, thank you very much,' and he had to force himself to remember how to use the brakes.

He was sweating when they finally slowed down. 'Sorry, Elise, the, er, clutch went a bit funny.' But she brushed aside his apology and they crossed the bridge over the Cherwell and on to the High Street without further incident. 'Right now,' she commanded, 'we need to find somewhere to eat, and then we can go and find this party. Shall we do the Randolph? Their grill room is quite good.'

Lucas braces himself in his mother's automatic reclining chair. The story gets worse. By now, it was completely out of his control.

13

That Night

They ate steak, he seems to remember. Elise ate like she hadn't had a proper meal in weeks. She told him she'd had to move back into her parents' flat because things had got 'a bit heavy' with a landlord in Pimlico, and while she couldn't stand her mother watching her every move, it was great to have constant running hot water and free booze on tap.

After the meal, Lucas would have quite liked to drive home. He was possibly over the limit but not by much; Elise had drunk the lion's share of the good bottle of Beaujolais he'd ordered, and he'd had to dissuade her from ordering another.

'I suppose it's party time?' he said, at which point she took her purse out of her handbag in some coy attempt at pretending to contribute to the bill. 'Oh God, sorry Lucas, I haven't got my credit card with me,' she blathered, which was a ridiculous excuse considering her purse was visibly bulging with notes.

As she pretended to rummage a small polythene bag fell out of her bag, the sort of thing his mother used to freeze small amounts of food. 'My party supplies,' she sniggered. 'Got to have something to keep me going, though to be honest I'm running very low. I don't suppose you've . . . ' His face must have been enough of an answer; he could feel his nostrils flare with disapproval and she shoved the polythene bag back inside her handbag, zipped it shut, leant over the table, squeezed his cheek and said, 'Oh Lucas, you are such a sweet and simple boy.' Then he paid the bill and they left.

The party was pretty much as he expected, full of people who made him feel inferior, either academically or socially. He wasn't clever enough, cool enough or weird enough to be there.

Rowena was pleasant but distracted. She seemed surprised he'd bothered to come. 'I wanted to give the car a run out,' he explained, at which point she waved her hand dismissively and asked, 'Do you know Penny?'

Of course he didn't know Penny; she was a harp-playing third-year biochemist at St Hilda's, who enjoyed ancient languages, particularly Sanskrit. Penny was a very dull woman, but not as dull as Elise, because she did at least understand the basic principles of a conversation. She was polite enough to ask him a couple of questions before they parted ways, mutually drifting away from each other like spaceships undocking.

He then spent a good twenty minutes standing with his back against a wall, pretending to be deeply lost in the music. He visited the bathroom three times, and for once in his life he wished he smoked because it would at least give him something to do.

Charlie must have arrived about ten. People had started dancing but Lucas still felt self-conscious. He'd had a lot to drink by this time and was having difficulty keeping himself awake. None of the girls were his type and he didn't know how to talk to the men; after all, these were the chaps who had got in to Oxford when he hadn't. He imagined being grilled on his A-level results.

Sitting on a chilly stone step he watched as Rowena threw her arms around her twin and dragged him around, introducing him to anyone who was still upright. Charlie was his usual slightly stoned, good-natured self, he shook hands and kissed girls on the cheek and seemed to laugh a lot. A grey cloud of cigarette smoke bloomed with his every move. He really was the most awful stinking shit, and the thought of him touching Fern with his vile bitten fingernails made Lucas feel sick. He would like to fight him, but he wouldn't know how to start. He'd like to just walk up to him and punch him unconscious, but then he would be the one in trouble and how could he make anyone understand, even himself, that he was fighting over a girl he fell in love with when he was a boy?

From a distance, he watched Charlie and Elise orbit each other before eventually colliding. Within minutes they were deep in conversation, dark heads almost touching. She kept grabbing his arm; he kept gently shrugging her off. It was like watching animals engaged in a ritual, a dance of some kind. Charlie seemed to have something Elise wanted very badly, enough to make her run around desperately trying to find her handbag, which once she had unearthed it from under a pile of coats she clutched to her chest as she scurried back to Charlie.

Lucas watched as the two of them huddled close and turned their backs on the party. Some sort of exchange was taking place, and as soon as it was completed Elise proceeded to hug Charlie so tightly he had to physically unpeel her hands to make his escape.

By midnight Lucas could barely stand. Elise was out on the lawn in her glittering gown, playing candlelit croquet in the rain. Couples were pairing off and a fair amount of necking and indeed some heavy petting was going on in the dark corners of Rowena's shared sitting room.

Increasingly he was feeling there was nowhere comfortable for him to be. If he drank any more he'd be sick, and the chance of getting off with any of these terrifying young women was practically nil, so Lucas wandered out into the Oxford night. On being told by the night porter at the Randolph that there was no room at the inn, he spent an extremely uncomfortable night curled up in his car. For the first time since he'd bought the thing, he wished he'd gone for something bigger, like a VW estate.

He awoke the next day feeling like someone had attacked him with an iron bar, his linen suit crumpled and stained. All he wanted to do was eat, get home, shower and change.

His mother would be livid at him for leaving Elise. 'That's not the gentlemanly thing to do,' he could imagine her saying, to which he'd have to reply, 'But she's no lady.'

On the off chance, and because he was already feeling guilty about his plan, he drove past Rowena's college three times in the vague hope that he would spot Elise. A few students stumbled out of the ancient wooden gate, but whether they were casualties from last night's party Lucas couldn't tell.

He drove off. It was as simple as that: he couldn't find her. He'd looked and he drove off. He felt dreadful, hungover and gritty. It was eleven o'clock on a Sunday morning and he drove to the first available motorway service station, where he had a delicious full English breakfast plus two cups of coffee and a Coca-Cola and then, feeling slightly more human, he pootled his way back to London playing the Pink Floyd tape that Elise had so rudely rejected the day before.

Back at River Walk his mother was out for lunch and he enjoyed having the house to himself. He bathed, read the Sunday papers and luxuriated in starting to feel better. It wasn't a bad life; his mother's housekeeper did his laundry and, hanging up in his wardrobe, were five neatly pressed work shirts. He chose ties to go with each shirt and made himself a cold roast beef sandwich. He might take his mother out tonight: they could try the osso bucco at that new Italian place.

He was napping on the bed when he heard her come in. It was around five; maybe they could just stay in and have scrambled eggs on their laps and watch some television. It would be good to feel completely refreshed for work tomorrow. He'd made some silly mistakes lately, and consequently been warned that he was still very much on probation.

*

He didn't actually hear the telephone, but it must have rung because at about seven that evening he heard his mother calling for him. There was something in her voice that reminded him of the time she lay swimming in a bath of her own blood, a hysteria he hadn't heard for years. He put a dressing gown over his pyjamas and padded in his slippers from his bedroom down to the sitting room.

His mother was rocking backwards and forwards in an armchair. 'Oh God, Lucas, it's Elise. I thought she was with you, I thought she was safe.' Immediately he felt guilty; he must have done something awful, but he had no idea what it could possibly be. He fetched his mother a brandy from the drinks cabinet and thrust it into her trembling hands. Barbara's face twisted, she looked terrifying, like a Francis Bacon painting. Her mouth flapped open and closed, she couldn't seem to get her breath, she tipped brandy into her mouth and without swallowing it spat out the words, 'Elise is dead. Minty and Paul have just got back from Chequers, they had a police escort. Imagine the horror of it. Oh dear God, Elise is dead and they say it might have something to do with drugs.'

Brandy dribbled down her chin and neck.

Lucas stood in the middle of the carpet with its golden grooved swirls. He looked at the slippers on his feet and at the pattern on his pyjamas and he could not believe what he was hearing.

'You were with her, Lucas, why did you leave her? Why was she alone?'

His mother was never cross with him. He couldn't bear her to be cross now, it wasn't his fault. He felt like he did when he was four, which was quite possibly the last time she told him off, for scribbling on the wall, and for an agonising second he thought he might wet himself.

'I saw him,' he stammered, 'I saw the man who I think might have sold her the drugs. I didn't think anything of it at the time, but I know I saw her give him money, this man, and I saw him give her something in exchange, something in a plastic bag.'

345

His mother wiped the brandy from her throat and stared at him.

'It was Charlie, Mummy, the man who gave Elise the drugs. It was Charlie Treadaway.'

'Are you sure?'

'I'm positive.'

'Then I shall phone the police,' and he watched his mother walk out of the sitting room and into the hall. Through the open door he watched her sit down at the telephone table and pick up the receiver, and he did absolutely nothing to stop her.

Lucas is suddenly cold on the recliner. He reaches for the controller and tips himself out of the chair.

14

After

Lucas turns on the electric fire and waits until the illuminated fake coals warm his bones. He doesn't need photographs to remember what happened next. It was simple: there was a before and an after, when all the dominoes began to fall.

Once his mother blew the whistle on Charlie, Lucas could never go back to Kennington Road. He still saw his father, stilted conversations over barely touched lunches. Dickie was heavily lined and his hairline suddenly receding; the occasions were painful for both of them.

His father wasn't invited to Elise's funeral. 'It wouldn't be appropriate,' his mother had snapped, majestic in black. 'Would you like half a Valium, darling, just to take the edge off?'

He noticed her hair first, her red hair, getting out of the second funeral car. He couldn't see her face, her head was bowed, the church was full. He lost sight of her until after, at the hotel, her white face, the fleeting look of shock on her face when she recognised him. His mother coming over and then, without warning, she collapsed, a heap of black clothes and red hair on a blue carpet and her father shouting 'Stand back!'

The instant mayhem, the welcome distraction. 'She just fainted – overwhelmed, poor thing. Such a sad occasion.'

'Silly girl probably hadn't eaten' was all the sympathy his mother could muster, but he couldn't get the image out of his head, like something out of a terrible fairy tale: Fern unconscious, with a silver necklace around her throat.

He recognised it immediately.

His head echoed with the snippets of a conversation.

'Charlie, are you experimenting with queerness?' Dickie being jovial, his own snigger, a sigh from Rowena, a bowl of buttery Jersey Royals, a whiff of hyacinth.

A silver fern-shaped necklace around Charlie's neck, his crooked yellow-toothed smirk, twenty-first-birthday cards on the mantelpiece.

And then he knew that Elise had told the truth: they were fucking. Why else would Charlie have been wearing her necklace that Sunday lunchtime, the cunt?

Waiting for the trial was interminable. To make it easier, his mother took him away for the summer. They went to Naples and stayed in a five-star hotel; his mother treated him like an invalid. 'He's been through a very traumatic experience,' she told everyone, until even the waiters regarded him as if he were some kind of fragile imbecile.

That was the summer that Fern got married. Barbara informed him in Naples, when they were having brandies on the terrace after dinner, looking out at Capri where once she'd honeymooned with Dickie.

'Very quiet, a simple little registry do, obviously, what with the family being in mourning, Minty told me. She and Paul didn't go, she said it would have been too painful, because of course had she lived Elise would have been a bridesmaid,' and Barbara started crying into her Courvoisier, weeping for the Elise that was never going to be, the bridesmaid, wife and mother.

'It's unbearable, darling. If anything ever happened to you I would simply walk down to Sloane Square Tube and throw myself under a train. With your father gone, you're the only thing I have left to live for.'

In some respects it was a relief to go back to work in the autumn, but one day he came down from his office to find Edwina in the foyer. He didn't want to speak to her, so he immediately got back into the lift and ate biscuits from the boardroom rather than go out for lunch. He was relieved that she couldn't infiltrate the inner sanctum of his workplace. Security in the world of finance was fortunately very strict.

Some days he felt he couldn't breathe with the all-consuming pressure of it, and he used to take the car out late at night and drive around London, the same question spiralling round and round, digging deeper and deeper into his brain: 'Why? Why, if she'd been fucking Charlie, had she married someone else?'

The answer became evident when he saw her at the inquest. Walking into court with her parents, her coat had fallen open to reveal a small neat bulge. Of course, she was pregnant.

'Yes,' his mother had confirmed, 'I believe that's why the wedding was what I'd call a "shotgun" affair, but as luck would have it, he's a very nice man. Army officer – not a squaddie, a Captain Frobisher. I hope they'll be very happy.'

And that was it: she was married, she was having another man's baby. Another man's baby. It's been bothering him for years: did Charlie ever know, and if he did, did he care?

He was glad when she didn't turn up for the trial, glad that he didn't have to lie in front of her. The whole truth and nothing but the truth, that was a joke.

In the end, it all happened very quickly. A man went to prison and a baby was born, so what? It happens every day, and Lucas is haunted once more by the way Charlie was instantly swallowed up the day he was sentenced, how he just disappeared, leaving the gallery agape.

Of course he appeared again. Three years later Charlie was released from prison, but by this time Lucas was safely in America courtesy of a grateful Paul Landreth, who pulled lots of strings to make sure Lucas was transferred to the New York branch of his company and placed in an office where he could do very little harm.

A fresh start.

Lucas's curiosity gets the better of him, and he reaches again for the plastic scrapbook of memories that his mother compiled while her brain still recognised faces and her hand could control a pen. Which photos of his American reincarnation has his mother chosen for her album? Ah, the clean-shaven, preppy Lucas, raising a bottle of Budweiser to an unknown photographer. 'Living the dream', his own handwriting scrawled in marker pen across the snap.

Lucas was happy in the Big Apple, reinventing himself was easy: he had a posh English accent and didn't look entirely dissimilar to Prince Andrew. The past was another country, a cold, grey miserable one where it rained all the time.

He came home infrequently. After all, why go back to a place that made him feel bitter and sad?

Instead Barbara and his father flew out to the States (separately, obviously) once or twice a year and his mother took to the shopping, theatre and dining of New York with alacrity: 'I mean, Regent Street is lovely, darling, and Liberty's is the best shop in the world, but there's nothing quite like Fifth Avenue.'

And there she is. A picture of his mother posing with a Bloomingdales shopping bag is titled 'Spend, spend, spend'.

His father always arrived looking exhausted. He wasn't ageing as well as his mother, who seemed sprightlier with every visit. By contrast, Dickie was a stooped and greying figure who once admitted that at least when Charlie was in prison he and Edwina could sleep at night, they had some peace: they knew where he was and that he was safe.

As for Rowena, Dickie informed Lucas that in her twin's 'ahem, absence' Rowena had eventually recovered enough to transfer her degree to UCL and finish her course while living at home.

She got a first. 'Of course she did,' muttered Lucas and his father nodded. 'She was like a hermit, didn't do anything but work. No men, no life, just books.'

When his father was back in London he religiously called Lucas once a week, and one evening Lucas listened patiently as his father told him how, just weeks before Charlie was due to be released from prison, Rowena had quit her job in publishing and upped sticks to Australia.

Poor Dickie, he sounded in torment as he explained to Lucas that he didn't blame Rowena for needing some space between herself and her twin, that he understood she needed to be free to get on with her own life, but that Edwina didn't agree. She felt Rowena was abandoning them.

Lucas was tempted to interrupt his father and ask, 'Why do our conversations always have to be about him?' But he bit his tongue, suddenly realising that he was the only person his father could confide in.

Some months later his father came over for a visit, and after dinner and a movie in town he filled Lucas in on the latest events back in Kennington. 'It's pretty grisly stuff,' warned Dickie. He was smoking heavily and Lucas remembers being transfixed by the growing pile of cigarette butts in the ashtray as his father talked.

'When Charlie finished his sentence,' Dickie began, 'he refused to come home as Edwina had suggested. Instead he went to live in a squat with some musician friends in Camden, and for a while he was in a band and was doing all right. We subbed him, obviously,' Dickie admitted as the two men sat overlooking the Manhattan skyline from Lucas's shiny new apartment on the twenty-third floor of a shiny new high-rise.

The evening was becoming increasingly soaked in red wine. Dickie topped up his glass before continuing.

'But it wasn't enough. There were constant requests for more money, for driving lessons, for a car. I used to dread seeing him, but Edwina refused to give up hope. She begged him to try and get a place in a London art school, to volunteer backstage in a theatre, painting sets. She bought him clothes so that he wouldn't go around looking like a tramp, but he stopped shaving and washing his hair. You remember he was always a *bit* smelly?

'But I tell you, Lucas, he started to stink. Edwina wouldn't give up, she paid for him to have expensive dental work when he got into a fight and lost his two front teeth. She picked him up from God knows where when he phoned her crying from a phone box at three in the morning, she brought him home and fed him soup and didn't question when he left without saying thank you. It seemed she would forgive him anything.

'But of course,' his father went on, 'there is always the last-straw scenario.'

Dickie refilled his glass once more before he began the next instalment of the saga. 'It was a Tuesday or a Thursday – it doesn't really matter, a weekday in September. Things had been quiet for a number of weeks, London was ablaze with autumn. Remember, Lucas, how the leaves suddenly turn at that time of year? I was at work and Edwina had gone into town for a meeting with her agent to discuss some potential commissions. She was hoping to meet Charlie in town, buy him lunch, maybe some shoes. He swore blind he'd be there, but he didn't turn up.

'She waited until four o'clock, then she finally gave up on him and made her way home and that's when she found ...' Dickie took a breath. 'She found Alicia lying in agony at the bottom of the stairs. It was Charlie, he'd come into the house and helped himself to a selection of highly desirable, easy to sell antiques, including some silverware and couple of framed landscapes that he knew were valuable. Anyway, not to put too fine a point on it, he'd filled a rucksack and was about to make his getaway when he was apprehended by Alicia.'

Dickie rubbed his face with his hands. 'There was a stand-off on the stairs, and whether she was pushed or whether she fell isn't the point, he didn't stop and help her. He ran, he ran and left her, and with that he broke his mother's trust completely and utterly. She ... she ... Well, let's just say Alicia was very badly hurt, smashed-up hip and collarbone, terrible business and Edwina had the locks changed. It was like someone had slid a bolt across the bit of her heart that had been for ever Charlie's.

'And it has remained bolted. She can't forgive him and she's convinced now that he stole her jewellery box all those years ago, and that in fact he's been lying to her for years. She says he has broken all the love and trust.'

Lucas squeezes his eyes shut at this memory. At the time he hadn't dared to look at his father in case the old man was crying. It was one o'clock in the morning; his father was drunk and exhausted, and needed to be helped to bed.

15

Destiny

He misses his father. The realisation hits him like a truck and suddenly Lucas is swamped by a terrible loneliness.

His mother will never recognise him again and his father is dead.

It was the smoking that killed him, the smoking and the worry, mostly about Charlie, of course. Bloody Charlie, casually wrecking everyone's lives and leaving a trail of devastation in his wake.

Lucas fetches himself a cup of coffee. He puts three sugars in and the sweetness is instantly comforting.

Back in Barbara's album a new decade has dawned, 1990, and according to Barbara's photographic record of significant events, Lucas 'The Wall Street whizz kid' is wearing a pair of thick red-framed glasses with matching braces. Lucas smiles, it didn't matter how many times he told his mother he didn't actually work on the stock exchange, she refused to believe him. That was the year his mother slipped on ice leaving a fundraiser at June's, and captioned a photograph featuring herself on crutches with the words 'accidents will happen'.

You're not kidding, thinks Lucas. January 1990 and New York

was thick with snow when Dickie phoned Lucas's apartment. He sounded uncharacteristically cheerful.

'Charlie's gone to Thailand,' he said. 'Rowena paid for him to go, she's meeting him out there. She wanted him to go to Oz but he couldn't get a visa because of the prison sentence. They're going to spend some time together on the beach. You never know, it might be the making of him.'

Lucas remembers thinking he wouldn't mind swanning around Thailand for a few weeks. Typical Charlie, landing on his feet with a beach holiday paid for, no doubt, by his twin.

Six weeks later his father called him to say that Charlie was dead, that he'd been cremated and that no, there was nothing Lucas could do. Dickie would come over and visit when he could, but for now he needed to be with Edwina. She was in pieces, mad with grief, not eating not sleeping, he couldn't leave her.

Barbara responded to Lucas's letter breaking the news with a typically venomous reply. 'Divine judgement, if you ask me, Lucas,' she scrawled gleefully in purple ink. 'That boy deserved to die, he should have been hanged years ago. I can't say my heart bleeds.'

As for Lucas, he felt a combination of horror, relief and complete numbness. He tried saying the words out loud: 'Yeah, like, bummer, my stepbrother died, he took an overdose,' but he couldn't.

It was unbelievable, Charlie was younger than him. It felt like a hoax.

Eventually Dickie managed a short visit some months later and Lucas barely recognised him. His father's eyes were red-rimmed and his post-flight stubble the colour of ash.

For most of his four-day stay his father slept. He had arrived with a chest infection which he couldn't seem to shake off, and rather than take him out on his last night in New York Lucas ordered in and tried not to be surprised when a coughing Dickie insisted on nipping out to the drugstore to buy a 'medicinal' bottle of Jack Daniel's.

Barely bothering to pick at the food, Dickie opened the whisky and proceeded to tell Lucas all the gory details of the Thailand trip and its disastrous consequences.

Lucas had no great desire to hear this tale. He was embarrassed by his father's proximity to tears and anyway, he already knew how the story ended, but Dickie obviously needed to unburden himself to someone, and who better than his own son?

Between coughing fits and sips of whisky Dickie told Lucas what had happened and how it had all gone wrong.

Charlie turned up at Kennington Road to fetch his passport. Edwina was still refusing to see him, but she'd bought him some bright orange swimming trunks. Charlie was really excited, couldn't wait, said he wanted to snorkel, maybe do some diving. If he liked it, he might learn how to do it properly, stay out there and join a dive school.

Typical junkie rubbish, thought Lucas as he loaded his chopsticks. The story had a horrible inevitability about it.

'But,' continued Dickie, 'of course his mother needed to cling to something. She put all her faith in Rowena, she seriously thought that if anyone could help Charlie it would be his twin and Rowena was confident too, said he just needed time and sleep and good food. She had all sorts of plans, yoga and meditation courses, they'd read lots of books, eat barbecued fish on the beach and swim every day. Thailand was one of those healing, spiritual places, she said. We even got a postcard.'

Dickie reached into his wallet and showed Lucas a postcard of the sun setting over the sea. Rowena's neat handwriting on the back briefly outlined all the things they'd been up to, the trips to fabulous food markets and incredible Buddhist temples, their beach hut, just inches from the sea, the fact that Charlie had the best tan ever. She finished off by hoping they were well and then obviously handed the pen over to Charlie. 'Having the proverbial!!' he scrawled, and filled what little space was left with kisses. The postcard had been ripped in half and mended with Sellotape.

They had such high hopes. According to Rowena, he made friends wherever he went. He was sober and healthy, and his new white teeth shone in the sun. Everyone loved him.

'I didn't,' Lucas could have said. 'I hated his guts. He spoiled everything. Even if he didn't actually kill Elise, it was his fault.' But he remained silent.

Dickie admitted being angry with him too. 'I can't understand why he wasn't more grateful,' he rasped, 'why he couldn't have tried harder. It was such an opportunity; he seemed to be getting better every day. But then Rowena had to get back to Australia. She had a job, responsibilities, everything that Charlie should have had, so she left her brother with enough money for a return flight on the proviso that if he stayed in Thailand he'd keep up the regime – the yoga and meditation – that he'd eat healthily and only have the very occasional beer. And he did, he kept it up for almost a week, but then he fell in with some travellers, moved to a rougher end of the resort and, ten days after Rowena arrived back in Australia, Charlie was found dead in a backpackers' hostel with a needle hanging out of his arm.'

Dickie took a big gulp of whisky at this point, spluttered and continued.

'He was cremated in Thailand, and Edwina carried the ashes back home on the plane as if the urn were a small child.'

Lucas hoped that would be it, that at least now they could go to bed, but his father hadn't finished. He carried on talking, with his eyes tightly shut.

'The worst of it all, of course, is that Edwina blames Rowena. She said she should have known how vulnerable her brother was, that if she had stayed with him he wouldn't have died. She said she might as well have killed him herself. I'm too old for all this upset, Lucas, it's almost too much to bear.' And at that point his father apologised for being a nuisance and stumbled off to bed, where Lucas could hear him coughing into the night.

In the morning, his father had already set off for the airport by the time he woke up. He'd left a note in the kitchen: 'Thought you'd better sleep it off, with love, your father.' There were definitely kisses; he can see them to this day, three neat kisses.

The bottle of Jack Daniel's lay drained of its contents on the living room floor. Lucas couldn't remember finishing it but he must have done. His father's carton of pad Thai, however, was largely untouched. 'Shit,' muttered Lucas, what on earth had possessed him to order Thai? No wonder his father had gone off on one.

He was late for work, felt like hell and when someone offered him a quick toot in the toilets to help him through the day he said 'yes'. He hoovered up a short, fat line of cocaine through a hastily rolled ten-dollar bill and then, with one big sniff, he was free.

For the first time in eight years he felt no guilt. He felt nothing except a supreme sense of utter confidence that he was in the right, that he'd always been right and that actually standing up in court and ultimately signing Charlie's death warrant was not the wrong thing to do.

And so it had begun, the drinking and the drugs, years of it and neither of his parents ever guessed. Their version of his life in New York was very different from the reality. Unlike Charlie, he was a fully functioning addict, he even managed to go to the gym between binges. In fact, when he wasn't staggering around having nosebleeds he was physically in the best shape of his life.

It meant that nothing ever touched him, he never really thought about anything but work and getting high. Women didn't come into the equation because he couldn't be bothered to invest in a relationship and he was too squeamish to use prostitutes. It was an oddly monastic lifestyle, he barely went out, he rarely socialised, he just sat in his immaculate apartment night after night and got off his skull.

Now, of course, he wonders if he was punishing himself. Both Elise and Charlie had died of drugs, so why shouldn't he? Surely it would make things fair: if he died then the circle of guilt and blame would finally be complete. So every day he played Russian roulette with his system, but of course nothing worked. He still woke up every day, feeling like death but alive, and the whole cycle would start again. He must have had the constitution of an ox. Of course, he'd always been well built, whereas both Elise and Charlie were scrawny, and Elise's heart had been weakened by an early teenage eating disorder.

He also never succumbed to heroin, it was a dirty drug that involved needles. Of course Elise had died after snorting heroin, whether intentionally or not, but Lucas knew that would never happen to him. He preferred to think of himself as a drug connoisseur rather than a helpless junkie: he drank the best vodka out of expensive crystal glasses and snorted the finest grade cocaine through a crisp fifty-pound note, which he misguidedly thought added a touch of class to the proceedings.

Lucas comes out of this memory feeling like a boxer. He is exhausted and bruised, he barely has the strength to microwave another meal before flopping into bed with meatballs al forno on a tray.

16

Unravelling

Lucas wakes up. There is spaghetti sauce on his pillowcase, Denise would go mad.

He fetches himself a cup of tea and the photo album. He's down to the last few pages.

Now that Lucas is literally out of the picture, Barbara's photo collection begins to feature faces he doesn't instantly recognise. Her Friday morning bridge club cronies, optimistically entitled 'The Girls', features a group of flint-eyed gorgons in their eighties.

Then there is Terence of course, with his Errol Flynn pencil 'tache, his slicked-back hair as unnaturally jet-hued as Barbara's.

Lucas suddenly has an image of them both dripping Wella 'Raven Black' hair dye over the bathroom sink. It would explain the number of discoloured towels in the laundry cupboard.

Bless Terence, he looked after his mother when Lucas was too stoned or selfish to care.

The one thing he is grateful for is that both his parents were spared a ringside view of his decline – their visits through the nineties trailed off dramatically, which was a relief because it meant they never saw the state in which he lived, the shit-splattered lavatory bowl, the smeared mirrors and the fridge full of rotting food.

His father no longer came because Edwina needed him in London, while for the first time in her life his mother was 'a teeny bit strapped for cash'.

River Walk had been sold and what little funds she had left over were required to make the new flat habitable. The soft furnishings she chose back then are still in situ today, green watered-silk curtains, fringed, swagged and draped, a testament to Barbara's expensive, if somewhat 'Queen Mother', tastes.

Trapped in his bubble of selfishness, Lucas chose to be oblivious to the severity of his mother's financial difficulties and the fact that she was lonely. He curtailed Barbara's transatlantic telephone calls the second she mentioned being 'a bit blue, darling', lying down the receiver about important meetings and fictional hot dates. When in fact the only date he had was with Captain Smirnoff.

His mother usually phoned on a Sunday. His father tried to catch him mid-week, and several years after Charlie died, when Lucas was living like a character in a Bret Easton Ellis novel, Dickie rang to tell him that Rowena had written, saying that she'd retrained as a counsellor and was currently working at a centre for young women with eating disorders in Melbourne. 'But this is the really interesting bit,' his father continued, blissfully unaware that the only thing Lucas was remotely interested in was the gram of coke artfully hidden in his Gucci sunglasses case. 'Get this,' his father pressed on and, gurning silently, Lucas listened.

Apparently his stepsister had bought a small house near the beach in St Kilda and had enclosed a photograph of herself and her partner Pat – who turned out to be a pleasant freckle-faced blonde woman with plump arms wrapped around Rowena's waist.

'I can't say I was surprised,' Dickie added drily. 'Anyway, thought you should know. Speak next week – I've got work to do.'

He only ever called from the office and Lucas knew better than to phone him at home. He attempted it once, but Edwina very coldly refused to acknowledge his existence and simply told him he had the wrong number.

The only time Edwina called him was to inform him that his father had died. She left quite a long message on his answer machine, detailing the time and date of Dickie's death and the time and date of his burial.

That was the last time he saw his stepmother, at his father's funeral, but they didn't speak. It was easy not to, he was with his mother, she was with Alicia, and in true Montague and Capulet style they kept to opposite sides of the church.

'She hasn't even bothered with a hat,' his mother remarked. 'What kind of widow can't be bothered to wear a hat?'

Barbara, on the other hand, was sporting a magnificent black swan-feather number. The only person who'd out-hatted Barbara was Alicia. Constantly at Edwina's side, her enormous orange and green jungle print turban blocked the view for anyone unfortunate enough to be sitting behind her. 'Who is that black woman?' Barbara had hissed. 'And what the hell is she doing sitting on the front row with that ridiculous thing on her head?'

The rest of the day is just a blur. The odd memory of his mother's claw-like grip on his suit sleeve, glass after glass of gassy, bitter funeral champagne, and line after line of something white and powdery, which was more likely to be speed cut with talcum powder than the pure class-A narcotic he'd paid for.

By the time he boarded his flight back to New York he was very drunk, and his suit was covered in canapé stains, mostly egg and smoked salmon.

Being violently sick in a tiny toilet cubicle thirty thousand feet above sea level during horrendous turbulence, Lucas reached rock bottom. Suddenly, as he puked for the umpteenth time, he was hit by a blinding revelation: he wasn't having any fun trying to kill himself any more and anyway, he didn't want to die.

Back in the States, he enrolled himself on a twelve-step programme and began a very wobbly progress towards cleaning himself up.

Lucas remembers how often he nearly called his dealer and how many times he nearly bought a bottle of vodka and how on a beautiful blue-sky day, on the 11th of September 2001, he saw the Twin Towers come down.

He watched from the window of his own high-rise apartment block, sinking to his knees and weeping on the floor as the mighty towers crashed to earth. The sight was unbelievable and sickening, and yet oddly enough, the weeks that followed were the weeks that made his recovery possible. His resolve hardened: if other people could pick themselves up, if a whole city could heal itself, then it was the least he could do to keep himself clean.

He had a choice; the people who were killed that day didn't.

Lucas is not a brave man, but at least he recognised he had a duty to keep himself alive.

Rowena got in touch with him after the attacks. She tracked down his email address and sent him a long, rambling message full of kindness.

She said she thought of him as she watched the horror unfold on the television and she wanted to apologise for not attending Dickie's funeral. Thinking back, Lucas had been surprised by her absence but unbothered. After all, what did they have to say to each other? The only person they ever had in common, his father, was dead. Anyway, given the state he'd been in that day, if she'd flown in on a giant pig he wouldn't have noticed.

In her email Rowena explained that she would have been there had she been able, but her partner was being treated for breast cancer and she decided not to leave her. She added that she and Edwina were still estranged, but that one day she hoped they could be reunited.

I have no other blood relatives and, as the world has seen recently, life is too short not to say I'm really sorry.
   With love, Rowena

The phrase has followed him for over a decade. There is something he needs to do and something he has to find.

17

Find and Seek

It's been bothering Lucas ever since he arrived back in London. Something is missing from his mother's flat, something he keeps expecting to find.

She must have brought it with her; he can't have looked properly. Odd that he hasn't tripped over it, though.

His mother's flat is a series of small boxes with neat corners. There are no hiding places, not like Kennington Road, and suddenly Lucas is once again squashed under a strange-smelling wooden bed, where his father now sleeps with 'that woman'.

He shouldn't be here, the grown-ups' bedrooms are out of bounds, but he can't move, he is hiding. One of the twins has to find him. Hours spent staring at a pair of slippers that aren't his mother's, choking on the dust, waiting and waiting.

Eventually his father came in and said, 'Lucas, the twins are downstairs having their tea. What on earth are you doing sulking under the bed?'

Chick peas. Edwina made him eat chick peas and lumpy lentil soup, but she still didn't deserve what you did, he reminds himself, and once again his brain starts to spin in the same old circle: what if?

Lucas has had enough. He cannot spend the rest of his life agonising over the things he has done.

Guilt has shaped his entire life, for good and for bad. When Charlie died guilt made him drink and take drugs, and then when his father died guilt made him stop.

But the nagging persists. He wants to put some small bit of the story right. He can't fix all of it – too much damage has been done, it would be like putting a new pane of glass into the window of a derelict house – but he knows he has to do something. 'Just make an effort, son' – his father's voice.

So Lucas makes himself a hasty breakfast of cereal and M & S miniature sausage rolls and searches the flat again. He looks in places where it can't possibly be, behind the sofa, in the gap between the wardrobe and the ceiling which is much too narrow, and then suddenly it strikes him: none of the flats in the block have any real storage space; the cupboard in the hallway is only just big enough for the boiler and a Hoover. Where are his mother's suitcases? Everyone has suitcases. The people who live in this block are rich, they go on holiday, there must be some suitcases somewhere, so where?

Hastings is most obliging: 'Yes sir, of course we have a storage facility in the basement, where our residents each have a designated space for luggage, wetsuits, skis and suchlike. Yes, of course I can take you down, sir.'

Hastings is the closest thing to a friend that Lucas has made since arriving in London.

A light flickers down the concrete stairwell, a whiff of Jeyes Fluid reminiscent of Wyebourne catches at the back of his throat. What if it's not there?

Barbara's space is tucked away in the far corner, and is blocked with unfamiliar items. Hastings looks stricken. 'Your Mum, she hasn't needed access for a long time,' he says, shoving aside a folded-up baby buggy and a large roll of plum-coloured carpet.

Lucas finally manages to exhale. It's there, he can see it,

underneath his mother's matching suitcases, a glimpse of burgundy leather beneath the dust and cobwebs.

Barbara's luggage is stacked in order of size, with her small navy wheeled cabin bag at the top. Instantly he is in the arrivals hall at John F. Kennedy Airport and he can see his mother's gloved hand waving. 'Here I am! Over here, darling.'

Lucas tells Hastings he can sort out what he needs from here. The concierge brushes down his smart uniform and whistles his way back upstairs.

It's padlocked, it always was: a boy's trunk is a repository for all the things he might not want other boys, matron or his mother to find.

Until his mother moved here, to Bartholomew Lodge, the trunk was kept in his bedroom at River Walk. Barbara was a snooper; it was the one place she could never gain access to. He's sure she has tried: it would have driven her mad, her scarlet talons twisting and turning the dials, guessing at random numbers, trying out birthdays, significant historical dates and postcodes. To Lucas's knowledge, she never guessed the correct four-digit sequence, and yet to him it was obvious.

In 1969, Apollo 11 touched down on the moon and his father decided to divorce his mother: 6-9-1-1.

The wheels of the combination turn, the basement is dry and the lock is only slightly rusty: 6-9-1-1. The same number unlocks his smartphone. He unhooks the device and opens the monogrammed lid.

The first thing he encounters is a stash of early eighties porn. Pouting girls with false eyelashes, orange panstick make-up and floppy tits stare dolefully up at him, un-airbrushed women with pubic hair.

The fifty-something Lucas feels a pang of sympathy for poor twenty-something Lucas, desperately trying to masturbate while his mother knocked on his bedroom door, offering him 'lemonade, or a perhaps a biscuit'.

Under the wank mags is a stash of old exercise books, kept for what? His lack of commitment to the education that had cost his father the price of a small house is evident. Lucas has a quick browse through his history O level essays. Every so often his tutor has slashed though a page in red biro and written 'SEE ME' in the margin.

Poor Dickie, no wonder he got so upset.

Lucas rummages deeper in the trunk. There's a lucky-dip element to it, and the next three items he finds are a plastic cricket box (cracked), a Walkman and a yellowing cricket jersey. The wool has become brittle with age.

Lucas continues to dig, unearthing a plastic bag full of novelty ties, *The Hitchhiker's Guide to the Galaxy* and a stuffed felt elephant. The elephant was the mascot of a short-lived men-only private drinking club, a sort of campus Bullingdon Club overseen by Lucas as the self-appointed president, which the WoWS (Women of Warwick Society) closed down within the week.

A pair of girl's tights emerges; he suspects they might have been Lauren's. Once upon a time he could persuade himself they smelt of nubile young cunt, but not any more, and then suddenly there it is: a scrap of material, floral, faded now from its original vivid riot of seventies pink and purple. He grasps the corner of the fabric and proceeds to pull out a pillowcase containing something hard-edged from the depths of the trunk.

He tips the pillowcase upside down and a box spills out on to the flaccid tits of a *Penthouse* cover girl. The red leather is cracked, the tiny gold catch badly discoloured.

He knows that it's almost empty. The contents were sold long ago to a man who knew a man, a man with contacts, happy to take unfashionable post-war garnets and oversized pearls, a grubby-fingered man who met other grubby-fingered men in pubs and eventually swapped his stepmother's jewellery collection for a pile of crumpled five-pound notes.

He recalls counting them all out, six hundred and fifty pounds.

It was a gambling debt, he had to pay. He was in the sixth form, his father expected him to go to Oxford, he couldn't get expelled, not at the last hurdle. No wonder his grades were slipping, he was worried sick. And then he was offered a solution.

It was all so simple: all he needed to do was to hand over the keys, guarantee the house was empty, and no one would ever find out, and they didn't.

The only evidence that could possibly link Lucas to the robbery at Kennington Road was this box, ransacked save for the things no one in that kind of business could possibly want.

A wedding ring too skinny to warrant weighing, a lock of hair in a matchbox, a creased photograph of a family on a sun-bleached beach and, weirdly, a Parma violets tin that rattled not with sweets but with baby teeth.

Lucas wipes his eyes on the pillowcase. It's all too little too late, but he has to do something. He cannot spend the rest of his life feeling ashamed of some of the things he has done; he wants to do something right for a change.

He picks up the box and puts it back in the pillowcase. Who knows what she might want back? He is going to see Edwina. He needs to do this and move on, he cannot take back what he said in the witness stand, he cannot give her back her son, but he owes her this at the very least.

18

Confession

Lucas takes a black cab to Kennington. Some of the London land-marks on his journey are reassuringly familiar; the twin golden galleons still shine on the balustrades of Chelsea Bridge, Battersea Park and the Dogs Home are exactly where they should be, but south of the river along Nine Elms, where nothing used to be, a whole new glass city seems to be emerging, a skyline of cranes, a new London. Even Battersea Power Station is being converted into flats. The hoardings surrounding the building work promise high-rise living for high-flying people, and Lucas feels sad for the disappearing London of his childhood, the motorised milk floats and the French onion seller, the rag and bone man trotting his cart through Kennington and the punks and Sloanes of the King's Road. He thinks about Princess Diana, her wedding and her funeral. So much happens in a lifetime, all those split-second decisions that can end in tears.

At Lambeth Bridge the driver swings right towards South London and Lucas feels a familiar knot of tension in his stomach as the Imperial War Museum looms into view. They are minutes away, they are seconds away ... the taxi pulls up to the kerb.

He recognised the house the first time he saw it: it was Betsy and

Tom's house and he had no idea why his father should have a key. That was the night of the blood in the bath. The night he slept with his father in an unfamiliar wooden bed, his head on a strange-smelling pillow.

'I've cleared out some of your baby books,' his mother informed him some weeks later. 'I thought we could make space for lots of lovely new grown-up ones.'

All his Betsy and Tom books had vanished, and yet his Noddy collection was still entirely intact. 'Yes, well, Noddy is a classic,' his mother insisted. She had finally removed the dressings from her wrists.

Lucas gets out of the cab into a misty rain, pays the driver and hovers on the pavement. Number 137 Kennington Road seems somehow diminished, as if it has misplaced a storey over the years, and the paintwork is peeling. A 'For Sale' sign nailed to a post by the front gate leans at an angle, and for a moment he wonders if she might have already gone.

The house looks too tired to keep its eyes open. The window panes are thick with grime and the steps up to the front door are cracked and filled with weeds. There is an atmosphere of sleep around the place, and like an unsuitable prince in a fairy tale, Lucas has to fight the urge to turn on his heel and leave.

Instead, he pushes the bell and strains to hear it ring. She may not be in. He is on the verge of peering through the letterbox when he hears someone on the other side of the door.

His first impression is that Edwina has shrunk. She is little more than eight stone of cheekbones, although unlike his mother, her eyes are still bright and her hair is a well-cut silver crop.

But she doesn't recognise him; why should she? It's been fifteen years since his father died, and he is possibly three stone heavier.

A second of silence before he introduces himself. 'I'm Lucas, please may I come in?'

She steps back; her hand is at her throat. It strikes him that she might be frightened and that embarrasses him: it's one of the worst things about being big, the implication that he could use his size to do harm.

He makes sure he walks in front of her, gives her plenty of space and begins to justify his presence: 'I was just passing, I saw that the old place was up for sale.'

'I don't suppose you want to buy it?' she asks. He's not sure if she is attempting a joke, but he laughs anyway.

He has the pillowcase in a battered Selfridges carrier bag that he found in his mother's kitchen. His palms are sweating. The hallway of the house is the same but different, the oil paintings hang where they always did but the stair carpet has disappeared. He feels slightly dizzy, as if the whole house is tilting.

She motions for him to go on down to the kitchen. The staircase is almost too narrow for his bulk and he'd forgotten how low the ceiling is down in the basement. He is a giant in a doll's house.

'Tea?' Her voice is the same, and she still carries herself well: her back is ramrod straight as she fills the kettle at the sink.

The breakfast room is even more cluttered than it used to be. The drawers of the dresser hang open, revealing a tangle of string, tape measures and wool, and he nearly trips over a bin liner stuffed with rolls of dusty, torn wrapping paper. Out of habit he checks for clothes dripping from the rack above his head. It is empty and he realises she probably doesn't have the strength to operate it any more.

Lucas perches clumsily on the sofa, feeling as if everything he accidentally touches might break.

'I can't remember how you take it, your tea,' she says. He half expects her to throw it in his face, scalding and black, but he answers, 'White, one sugar.' He likes two really.

Edwina tries not to appear flustered. She has no idea why he has come, this fat man who used to be Lucas. She is not sure she can still see the boy she once knew under his new coat of flesh, but there is something about the way he sits, his discomfort. It is Lucas. So this is the man he has become, well, well, well.

She seems to be operating on two entirely separate levels, making a cup of tea with her hands while her brain wonders if she should find a knife or some scissors just in case.

She fills the old brown teapot and lifts two mugs down from the hooks in the cupboard. One of them is slightly chipped.

Lucas shifts and the sofa creaks.

'I'm staying at my mother's place. She's in a home and, well, she's not, er, got long to live.'

She reaches for the milk. So she's dying, the terrifying creature from over the river is finally roaring her last. Edwina always saw Barbara as half-woman, half-dragon, a fire-breathing termagant in a patent court shoe. What can she say? The woman must be ancient.

She pours the tea, adds milk and sugar to his. 'I see ...' She tidies some papers, makes a nice neat pile, places a mug within his reach. 'That's why you're here in London?'

But why has he come here, to the house? What does he want? He probably wants a biscuit but he's not getting one; she always encouraged him to eat healthily, she did her best, but then of course he'd go back to that woman who would cram him full of pastries and cake. He wants to watch it: fat people die young too. Not properly young, of course, not before they're thirty. Charlie was only twenty-nine.

Barbara must be ninety. Honestly, what does he expect? No one lives for ever, it's the natural order of events. So his mother is dying, that's normal; your child dying, that's not normal.

She is looking at the picture of the hands, Charlie and Rowena's nursery-school hands, tiny red- and blue-painted hands criss-crossing each other over dark grey sugar paper.

Lucas knows what she is thinking; she may as well write it in marker pen on the wall. He is fifty-six years old, but he feels like he is falling back into the quicksand of his youth.

Oh Christ, this is all so difficult. The Selfridges bag is very yellow at his feet; maybe he could just walk out now and leave it.

Let her find it for herself. The job would be done and neither of them would have to say anything.

But then nothing would get said, and anyway, what's he really got to lose?

'The thing is, Edwina . . .'

She looks startled. He has never called her by her name before, how strange it sounds.

'. . . there is something I need to give back to you.'

'And what might that be?' She is not going to make this easy, she is not bending.

He takes a breath. 'I need to make some sense of everything, me and this house. I want you to understand that when I was young I thought that every time I came here my mother might try and kill herself again, cut her wrists, jump off the roof, put her head in the oven. I used to lie upstairs in the attic bedroom and imagine all the ways she could do it: knives, rope, poison. Then in the morning I'd wake up and I'd have pissed the bed again, and you would just laugh.'

She sips her tea.

'What was I meant to do, beat you? I wasn't that kind of step-mother. I tried, I painted you the moon and you scribbled all over it, you slammed doors in our faces.'

The tile on his bedroom door with his name on it cracks once more in front of her eyes. She sees again the untouched Christmas gifts, the scowls and silences and no wonder, the poor little sod was terrified that every moment he wasn't there to keep an eye on her, his mother might be busy killing herself. But that wasn't her doing, it was Barbara's madness.

For a moment he senses that she is angry.

'Go on then, Lucas, tell me how it was all my fault.'

But that's just it: he doesn't want to blame anyone. That's what has been going on for too long, the blame followed by the revenge and then the guilt. It's time for it all to stop.

Lucas takes his scarf off and Edwina remembers Dickie having something similar, a yellow and red paisley fringed number; maybe it is Dickie's. Everything is getting so jumbled up, the man that used to be her stepson is quite red in the face, he's obviously het up. What if he has a heart attack? Would she give him the kiss of life? And what if he were drowning, would she hold his head under?

Lucas holds his hands up and sighs.

'That's just it, it isn't anyone's fault, but I don't think any of us dealt with the situation very well. For starters, I couldn't cope with the twins, they were such a force of nature and neither of them needed me. I felt like a big, fat sore thumb all the time and I didn't like sharing my father. I didn't like the way he slept in this house with you and them. I always felt like I was in the wrong place: when I was here I wanted to go home but when I was at home I missed my dad. I was so pissed off by it all because it felt like I had half as much of everything that I used to have before, and to be honest I didn't like your food.'

Ha! He's definitely not getting a biscuit now. The cheek of it.

'Your father didn't marry me for my cooking.'

'And I didn't like Alicia.'

'And she didn't like you. She thought you were stuck up.'

'I probably was.' Lucas searches for the words to defend himself. 'Because I went to the kind of schools that didn't believe in women like Alicia or you, I was wired to believe in things I no longer care about. All I know, Edwina, is that some fucking awful things happened and I can't change what happened in that court, I can't bring back Charlie or Elise, but I can give you this.'

He reaches for the pillowcase.

She recognises the fabric as soon as she sees it. Many years ago she bought a set of pillowcases off a market stall: floral, 'All the rage,' the stallholder shouted, 'one shilling and thruppence.'

Something pretty for the nanny's room, which then became Lucas's room, which then became a spare room with maps on the wall. And now Lucas has come back from America with a pillowcase she hasn't seen for decades.

She watches as he reaches inside the slip and places something on the table.

It takes her longer to recognise this: it has aged badly, the thin leather is worn and the colour dimmed, it used to be such a red red. The golden clasp no longer shines. Eventually she reaches for the box, and as soon as she picks it up she fears the worst, it's too light. Everything has gone, the ugly garnets, the smoky pearls, but out of habit she flips the fastening open and the box concertinas out. All the compartments are empty apart from the drawer at the very bottom of the box. All the treasure is in this last drawer.

Her tiny wedding ring, his glorious hair, the children's baby teeth and the photograph, that very last day photograph.

Lucas talks with his head in his hands, his voice is low but steady. 'It was me: I had the box stolen because I was in trouble at school. I owed money to someone who wasn't going to forget it, and so when that someone offered me a solution I took it. I handed over the keys to this house and told them when it would be safe to come in and, well, it worked. I got the money and no one got hurt. Only in the end we all got hurt.'

She can't speak, she can only tremble, and she presses her fingers hard against her mouth for a long time and tears run off her face.

Lucas stands up. He can go now; he has other things to do.

She grabs his hand as he makes for the door. Her grip is fierce. 'Thank you, Lucas.' She doesn't apologise, she can't. He doesn't look at her and she doesn't look at him. Their business is done.

19

Vigil

Lucas leaves Kennington Road. He might weigh two hundred and fifty pounds, but he feels lighter. A sort of peace has been made, an understanding at least, and he hopes his father would be proud of him.

Of course he hadn't mentioned Fern, but what was the point of complicating things further, of spinning unknown facts into yet another web, and anyway, what was the truth in all that?

Charlie fucked a girl who wasn't his to fuck and she got pregnant and had a baby who may or may not have been Charlie's, but probably wasn't.

They have stuck together for years, Fern and Whatsisface Frobisher. Surely if the man had any inkling that the child wasn't his the marriage would have crumbled. And you'd know, deep down you'd know, if a child wasn't your own flesh and blood.

In some respects Fern has been lucky. Let's face it, James Frobisher, decorated Falklands hero, turned out to be a much safer bet than jailbird junkie Charlie.

His mother sent him some cuttings from the *Daily Mail* back in 1982. The report detailed how, at the tender age of just twenty-three, Captain Frobisher was commanding a platoon of soldiers carrying ammunitions to Port Stanley when the landing ship was bombed by the Argentinians and all hell broke loose. Men were trapped, burned and drowned. Pictures of his handsome shattered face appeared on the front page of every broadsheet; his mother was beside herself with the gossip.

'I don't know if you remember Elise's little cousin, the red-haired girl who went to drama school but left to get married and have a baby.'

Well, her husband was blown up on a landing ship at Port Stanley. Survived, but terribly badly wounded. Minty says he's quite disfigured, blind in one eye. There's talk of a medal, apparently he was incredibly brave.'

More cuttings followed a year or so later of the Captain standing outside Buckingham Palace with his DSO, eye patch, beautiful wife and eighteen-month-old daughter.

Out of a fit of – what, jealousy, bitterness, spite? – Lucas forwarded that cutting to Charlie in prison. I was still very angry, he admits to himself. I was still very hurt.

Of course, in these days of modern technology it's very easy to keep tabs on the names and faces of your past. Lucas will still occasionally type 'James Frobisher' into an internet search engine and within seconds there he is, the noble ex-soldier, Falklands survivor, intelligence consultant and, most recently, security adviser to the government. Below the details of his education (Stowe, Sandhurst) and his military career are those of his personal life: 'married with one daughter'.

Fern Frobisher only exists in conjunction with her husband. She is the 'wife of' at charity dinners and fundraising galas; now and again she can be seen pinning rosettes to ponies at horse shows. The would-be actress Fern Woolbright has ceased to exist, and now, in her fifties, Fern is apparently immune to Facebook or any other type of social networking.

By all accounts, she retired to Wiltshire and threw herself into the role of loyal army wife, devoting herself to James and

Sophie. He imagines they live in a large yellow stone rectory with a black Labrador. Sophie must be a woman of thirty-something by now.

Lucas is surprised to find himself at his destination. He has been in a daze since he left the other side of the river, but all of a sudden he is here, shouldering open a heavy brass door into Peter Jones.

He's had an idea and it might be stupid, but it doesn't matter. From now on he is going to only do things that make him feel better about himself. Who knows, he might even buy some swimming trunks and start exercising. He is certainly not going back to his wife.

There is something enormously comforting about being in a well-ordered department store; everything in this shop is how real life should be. The bed linen is crisp; jewel-coloured towels are neatly folded in regimented piles; lavatory brushes are clean enough to brush your hair with. Everything is perfect, no cracked glasses or chipped mugs. He feels calm. It's better than church.

Taking the escalator to the first floor, Lucas can't help thinking of all the times he had his feet measured in this shop, how often he waited, bored, as his mother fingered rolls of material and wondered out loud if roller blinds in the downstairs lavatory would be a good idea. Time seems to have both leaped forward and stayed exactly where it always was. Two elderly, matching sisters pass him by, arm in arm. One has a rabbit's foot brooch on her lapel. For some reason, the sight makes him feel weepy.

With help from a white-coated girl, who finds him exactly what he is looking for, Lucas makes his purchase, takes the escalator back down to the ground floor and goes out into Sloane Square.

How much time is left? He has no idea. But Lucas feels a sense of urgency as he walks back to his mother's flat to pick up the album.

It obviously means something to her. Her furs and jewellery disappeared long ago; in the end, the bits of Barbara's life that really matter lie between the pages of this cheap little leatherette album. It belongs by her side. He needs to get back to the home.

His mother is much as he left her, the little shape of what is left of her shrouded under pale blue sheets. He places the album on top of her blankets and sprays the Diorissimo atomiser around her pillow. For a second he allows himself to fancy she smiles. He pulls the chair up close to the bed and holds her hand. There is nothing else that can be done.

'I'm here, it's okay.'

Blood is strong. She is the only relative he has left, and maybe she loved him a little bit too much, but maybe that's what mothers do.

He would like Barbara to simply drift away imagining that she is lying on a sun lounger on the patio at the back of River Walk; the French doors are open onto the dining room, a pitcher of something chilled and delicious and one of her cherry-topped cakes are close to hand. His father is there and he is a boy home from Witterings for the summer holidays. His father is bowling, he is batting, the sun is shining and it is one of those golden moments before everything goes wrong.

Crack, leather on willow, the sun shines and for a second everything is perfect . . .

EDWINA

Endings

Edwina hears the front door slam. She doubts she will ever see Lucas again, but she will make sure things are fair. He will receive his share of the money from the house sale, and his father's desk, of course.

She looks hard at the photograph of her little family on the beach. Ollie has Rowena on his lap while she clings to Charlie as he reaches for the sea. She was always so scared of him drowning, because deep down Edwina knew that one day she would lose her son. She knew from the moment he turned up, unexpected in the middle of the night, that he was only visiting, she could never have him for keeps.

He was such a reckless boy, but oh God she loved him so very much.

After she lost him for the first time, when he fell through the trapdoor into prison, she thought they might have a second chance when he came out. But he emerged so badly damaged that even Rowena had to get away from him, and for years the only person Edwina didn't blame was Charlie.

She indulged him, forgave everything, until the day he hurt Alicia. When finally it clicked: he was weak, he always had been.

But still she hoped for a miracle in Thailand. Surely if anyone could save him it was Rowena. But when it all went wrong she deprived herself of a daughter because she refused to see that, in the end, it was Charlie's decision, that he put that needle into his arm. No one else, just her beautiful boy.

She will never forgive Lucas for what he did in court, but at last she can see now how it happened, how from the moment she caught Dickie's eye there would be consequences. People react badly when they lose someone they love.

She should know. Her own behaviour when Charlie died was insane, blaming Rowena for her twin's death, punishing her daughter for years, ignoring her letters and refusing even to speak to her.

She has no reason to forgive me, thinks Edwina. The tea in the pot has gone cold and it seems unbelievable that Lucas was ever here in this room, but he must have been, because her jewellery box is on the table.

The box containing all the lost treasure that she can now take to Australia. Edwina picks up Rowena's latest letter from the tidied pile in front of her.

We live very near St Kilda beach. You can paint, Mum, you can paint and we will fire up the barbie. I wear your charm bracelet every day. We are here, and we are waiting.

She even has the tickets. She checks them every night: passport, tickets, and now she will add the photo, teeth, rings and the matchbox of hair to the checklist.

She will take the box too, old and battered though it might be. Funnily enough, as soon as she saw it she remembered: it's the only thing she's got left that belonged to her mother.

Blood, decides Edwina, is strong and it pulls like the tide.

SOPHIE

New Beginnings

A mile away, in a hospital overlooking the brown tide of the River Thames, an obstetrician smears a colourless gel over the neat swell of a young woman's belly.

'So this is Grandma, is it?' the doctor enquires, smiling at an older woman sitting anxiously by the bed.

Fern laughs. She is still a good-looking woman, although these days her flame-red hair needs a little 'enhancing' in a salon in Salisbury. She reaches for her daughter's hand, the familiar feel of her slim cool fingers. She has come up from the country for this; she wouldn't miss it for the world.

Sophie's partner can't be here because of work. Fern understands how hard it can be: after all, her husband was in the army too.

James is beside himself with excitement. He always wanted a bigger brood, but it didn't happen and they learnt to count their blessings. 'It's fate,' she told him all those years ago. 'Think how lucky we are to have Sophie. Some couples never get to have a baby and look how wonderful our baby is.'

She loved her from the moment she was born, but she watched her daughter closely as she grew, anxiously looking for signs that never came.

She was simply Sophie, soft-brown-haired, blue-eyed Sophie, a patient self-contained little girl who laughed quietly to herself at things only she found funny, a sociable little girl who occasionally liked to be alone, a dreamy little girl who nonetheless liked to keep her doll's house tidy, a clever little girl who drew with both her right and her left hand, a little girl who grew up to be kind and funny and patient and popular, and now she is a woman and she is expecting her first baby.

'Tell me,' says the obstetrician, 'is there a history of twins in the family?'

'No,' laughs Sophie, 'not that I know of, none whatsoever. Isn't that right, Mum?'

But there they are on the screen, two little heartbeats, separate, but together.